THE DUELIST

Holding his own gun slightly above belt height, Jean walked softly toward the Russian. The morning was very still, and he could feel the grass against his shoes. A bead of sweat was trickling down his cheek, and the stillness of the morning was slashed by a second shot. Only a split second had passed, yet he was moving, walking fast but counting his steps. When he had taken seven steps he was going to fire. He felt the shock of a bullet as it struck him and the air lash of two more as they missed, and then his foot came down on the seventh step and he fired.

He fired his shot from hip level, the gun thrust out, the trigger squeezed off gently. He felt the gun leap in his fist and thumbed back the hammer for the second shot.

The Russian wavered, then buckled at the knees. . . .

SITKA

LOUIS L'AMOUR

A SIGNET BOOK

SIGNET
Published by the Penguin Group
Penguin Putnam Inc., 375 Hudson Street,
New York, New York 10014, U.S.A.
Penguin Books Ltd, 27 Wrights Lane,
London W8 5TZ, England
Penguin Books Australia Ltd, Ringwood,
Victoria, Australia
Penguin Books Canada Ltd, 10 Alcorn Avenue,
Toronto, Ontario, Canada M4V 3B2
Penguin Books (N.Z.) Ltd, 182-190 Wairau Road,
Auckland 10, New Zealand

Penguin Books Ltd, Registered Offices:
Harmondsworth, Middlesex, England

Published by Signet, an imprint of Dutton Signet,
a member of Penguin Putnam Inc.
First published in a hardcover edition by Hawthorn Books, Inc.

First Signet Printing, December, 1997
10 9 8 7 6 5 4 3 2 1

To Kathy

1

Jean LaBarge stopped beside the trunk of a huge cypress, scanning the woods for Rob Walker. By this time Rob should have reached their meeting place by the Honey Tree, so after only a momentary pause, he started to go on his way. Then he stopped abruptly.

The woods were very still. Somewhere, far-off, a crow cawed into the stillness, but there was no other sound except the faint murmur of wind in the high leaves. The boy felt his heart begin to pound heavily.

In the leaf mold just beyond the cypress was a boot print, its toe pointing southward into the deeper woods.

At fourteen Jean LaBarge knew the track of every man in the small village closest to the swamp, of the farmers who worked the fields nearby, and even the occasional cattle drovers who traveled the road along the swamp's edge. But this was the track of a stranger.

Sunlight filtered through the leaves and dappled the forest with light and shadow. No breeze stirred more than the topmost boughs, for at this place, deep within the Great Swamp, all the wind was shut out, as were the sounds. In this place one found oneself walking with stealth, moving in these lonely, secret woods as one might have moved in the days of the earth's first awakening.

Under the feathered hemlock, beside the stagnant pools, upon the spongy, moss-green earth there was no movement but the flight of some small bird, or a butterfly on wraithlike wings suspended for an instant in a shaft of sunlight. Only the green golden twilight of the forest, only the rustling of a tiny animal among the leaves. This was a place lost, remote, unvisited, and this was home, the only home he had known since his father went to the far lands beyond the Mississippi, and his mother died.

No townsman came to the Great Swamp, nor used the trail through the deserted valley beyond, the trail known as the Shades of Death. Not many years before, during the War of 1812, soldiers had been ambushed here by Indians, and in both earlier and later years men had disappeared from that trail, leaving no evidence to explain their going. The old trail was grass-grown now, forgotten by outsiders, and the village people when passing either did not look at all, or darted hasty, half-frightened glances into the green, cavernlike silence. In the Pennsylvania villages along the nearby Susquehanna they believed the ghosts of dead soldiers marched endlessly here, mourning for homes to which they would never return.

The Great Swamp was a land untouched by plow, as lonely as upon the morning of the world's birth. Here was no columned corridor of mighty trees, no majestic avenue, but a dim, murky, silent place, dark even at noontime, shadowed except in the rare clearings or above the stagnant pools where lilies lay empty-eyed in the stillness, or forested themselves with cattails, or veiled themselves with green scum. A tossed stone into such a pool gave off few ripples, more the sodden gulp of something swallowed in darkness.

One of the soldiers who survived that long-ago march spoke of it as "a horrid, rough, gloomy country." Yet there was life in the swamp, life other than the birds and small animals. Throughout the swamp and in the rugged highlands that backed it there were squirrels, muskrat and mink, but there were deer, wolves, panthers and black bear, also.

Where Mill Creek Road divided the world of people and farms from the jungle of the swamp, it also divided the world of Jean LaBarge, divided the one he visited from the one in which he lived and where he was wholly himself. The swamp had been his first playground, and since then a school as well, and source of a precarious living.

Beside the cypress he waited, listening. The forest is a place of silence yet it has its own small sounds, the sounds a hunter knows. A wind stirring among the branches, the creak of boughs, the drop of an acorn or a pine cone, the movements of small animals . . . these sounds Jean knew and his brain accepted, catalogued and ignored, tuning itself for only the unfamiliar sound, the movement unnatural to the forest.

The man whose track he had seen was large, for the stride was long and the indentation left by his boot was deep, and he was a man not unaccustomed to woodland travel. This much became obvious as Jean followed along the trail the man had left, noting where he stepped and how he moved. Moreover, the man was neither hunting nor wandering at random, but moving directly toward some known objective, and his direction was generally south.

Nobody knew the swamp as Jean did. He had grown up on a small farm at its edge, and before his mother died he had come regularly to the swamp to help her collect the herbs she sold in the village. Now that she was gone he continued to gather herbs and take them to the village to sell to old man Dean.

Jean was a tall fourteen, a slender boy with large dark eyes and a shock of curly, almost black hair. Already his shoulders were broad, although his body was painfully thin. There was more than a hint of the man he would become in the size of his frame and the easy way he moved. Growing up in the forest he had early learned to move as silently as would a fox or panther.

After his mother died his Uncle George had come to work the small farm, but Uncle George was a good-natured, gregarious man who liked people and hated the loneliness of the cabin. Moreover, he disliked work as much as he enjoyed loafing and idle talk. The boy accepted his coming, and when one day Uncle George failed to return from one of his longer absences, he accepted his going.

Left alone in the cabin Jean carried on as always; there was nothing else to do. His uncle had gone but once to the village where Jean sold most of his furs and herbs, and his disappearance caused no comment: there were several villages within easy walking distance of the swamp, and he might be frequenting any one of them. Jean, a lonely, self-sufficient boy, had common sense enough to tell no one that his uncle had deserted him. The boy's coming and going had long since been taken for granted in the towns; and no one ever believed—or very much cared—that he was alone.

Of his father he remembered little except what his mother told him, that he had gone to the western mountains to trap and hunt, and that he would return eventually. To Jean he remained a vague, shadowy figure, bearded and in buckskins, who smoked a pipe and seemed always in a good humor. From time to time Jean heard mention of him in the villages, for he was that most fabulous of persons, a mountain man. And he was what Jean wanted to be.

Jean LaBarge had no friend but Rob Walker. To the village people he was the son of "that gypsy woman" and the way he lived was regarded with suspicion by the mothers of tamer sons who wanted them kept tame, and felt that his might be a dangerous influence.

The other children of the village despised him as a poor boy and the son of a gypsy, and admired him because he lived in the dreaded and fascinating Great Swamp. To the children of the village Mill Creek Road was a boundary they had been warned never to cross. Not even the village men ever hunted in the swamp: game was, after all, plentiful along the fences, and much easier to get than in the depths of the swamp—where a man might easily become lost or disappear in the treacherous sinkholes.

There was no reason for any stranger to be in the Great Swamp, so far from the road. But this was a stranger who seemed to know exactly where he was going. It had been four years since Jean had seen any man's track in the swamp . . . and then it was rumored that one of the Carters had returned to the country from which they had been driven.

To Rob Walker the swamp had been a dismal, frightening place, for he knew that even the older men, including his father, hurried along Mill Creek Road at the approach of darkness, and not without reason. Two years before a man had been severely mauled by a bear he had come upon in the night, and there was a story persistent in the neighborhood that a child had been carried off by a panther.

Rob was older than Jean, but shy due to his small size. As other boys of his age grew bigger and stronger he turned more and more to books for companionship, yet his alert mind and imagination were fascinated by a boy several years younger than himself who came and went in the Great Swamp without fear. From time to time he saw

Jean LaBarge come to town with his sacks of herbs and finally he began waiting at the store to watch Mister Dean sort them carefully into piles. From listening he learned the piles were of many kinds, but the largest were usually bloodroot, wild ginger, senega snakeroot and sassafras.

The friendship between the boys began with a question. One afternoon old Mister Dean was totaling the amount owed to Jean. Rob watched him as he bent over the figures, peering through his square-cut steel-rimmed glasses, his great shock of iron-gray hair making his head seem much too heavy for his scrawny neck. Catching Jean's eyes, Rob asked, "Where do you get all those?"

Naturally shy, Jean recognized the even greater shyness of the smaller boy. "Over in the swamp," he replied.

"Aren't you afraid?"

Jean considered the question with care. He was, he realized, afraid sometimes. But it was not when he was in the swamp. It was only at night, those nights when he awakened in the silent cabin and knew he was alone. Sometimes then he would lie awake straining his eyes into the darkness to see the fearsome creatures his imagination told him would be lurking there, in the corners of the room or just outside the walls. But he knew he must never speak of that fear because once the well-meaning people of the village knew he was a boy alone they would take him away from the cabin and the swamp and find a home for him, or send him to a workhouse, and he wanted no home but the one he now had.

At least until he had a rifle. Once he had a rifle he would go west and become a mountain man like his father, and perhaps in some trappers' rendezvous in the mountains he might meet him, a big, powerful man who knew Kit Carson and lived among the Indians. But was he afraid of the swamp? "Not very," he said.

"Folks say it's haunted."

"I never saw any haunts. It's wild, though, and a body better know where he's stepping or he can sink clean out of sight."

"How do you know which plants to pick?"

"My mother taught me." He knew what they said in the village about his mother being a gypsy. "She grew up in a house near a field where gypsies used to camp."

Dean counted out a few coins, peering at Jean over his glasses when he had completed the payment. "I can use more of that sassafras, son, and when berry time comes around I can use all the blackberries and huckleberries you can gather. Don't know where you find 'em. Biggest I ever did see."

Jean remembered those big, juicy berries. They grew in the thickest and most dangerous part of the swamp. Leaves fell there and rotted away in the dampness and upon their moldering remains grew the bushes with the fattest, sweetest berries. He had thought about that a good deal, and the place frightened him, but fascinated him also.

"Yes, sir."

"Ain't seen that uncle of yours," Dean commented, "the one who came here when your ma died."

"He goes to Selinsgrove," Jean told him. "Or to Sunbury."

The question had been more in the nature of a comment, merely making conversation, and Dean turned to greet another customer, adding, "Don't you forget that sassafras."

Jean stood where he was, his fingers on the edge of the counter, soaking up the rich smells of the old store. There was the fragrance of tobacco, licorice, and dry goods, mingled with the smell of new harness leather, and all the aromas of the old-fashioned shop. Rob Walker waited until Jean started for the door.

"That ol' swamp," he said, when they were outside, "I hear it's a mighty gloomy place."

"I like it."

"I'd think you'd be scared, out there alone."

"Nothin' to be scared of . . . not if you know where to walk." Jean dug into his pocket for the rattles clipped from a snake he had killed. "Got to watch for rattlers, though. There's big ones in there."

"They say there's a new rattle for every year a snake lives."

"Ain't so," Jean said. "There's a new rattle or button every time he sheds his skin, and they do it two, sometimes three times a year."

"Would you take me sometime?"

"You'd be scared."

"I would not. I've almost gone in alone—lots of times."

"All right. You can come now if you want."

That was how it had begun, nearly three years before their planned meeting at the Honey Tree. United in their loneliness, the boys had discovered they shared a dream, the dream to go west, far across the plains where the buffalo were, far away to the land of the Sioux and the Blackfoot, and there to be mountain men.

Around the village, wherever men gathered to talk, at the livery stable, the mill or the tavern or blacksmith shop, men talked of the mountains and dreamed aloud to each other, those men who often wish and never will, men who, bound to business, job, or family, dream great dreams of the far-off lands and the wonderful adventures they may someday have. And those other men and boys without ties, who will never take the lone trail because they want but they will not do. Perhaps because subconsciously they know that every dream has a price, and the price for the wandering life is hunger, loneliness and danger, the blistering thirst of deserts and the icy crash of waves, the tearing winds and driving sleet far from hearthside and the warm arms of loved ones.

Yet for Jean dreams would never be enough. The swamp became the training ground for that great day when he would be "big" and could go away. Yet in the secret places of his own mind Jean knew he would not wait for the remote time when he was big enough, a man grown. He would wait no longer than it required to save money for a good rifle, not the cumbersome old gun the cabin afforded . . . and the money was almost half saved.

It had been midafternoon when he found the track of the stranger, and Rob would have reached the Honey Tree. If so, he would be waiting there when the stranger arrived, as the man had chosen a route that could not miss the clearing around the tree. Rob would be there and he would see the stranger and be seen by him.

Jean's trap line was long and Rob had agreed to work half of it so they could hurry back to the village to listen to Captain Hutchins, who was in the village for a last visit before going across the Great Plains to the lands on the Pacific. He would be in the tavern that night talking of the fur trade and of his plans. Both boys knew about Captain Hutchins. He had made a fortune manufacturing shoes for the Army, as well as in the shipping business, and he was taking his capital west.

Jean had worked his trap line swiftly, finding little. It was time he moved his traps deeper into the swamp. Maybe he would move them over near the stone house; it had been long since he trapped that area.

Nobody else seemed to know about the house. It was very old, built of stones rolled down from the ridge behind it, and it stood hidden in a grove of hemlock, giant trees that kept the house invisible until one was almost at the door. Yet despite its seeming remoteness, Jean knew there was a place where Mill Creek Road bent within a mile of it. Of late he had not been so sure that he was the only one who knew of the house, although whoever did know of it was not anyone from the country around. Once he had found the ashes of a fire that he was sure had not been there when he visited the house before . . . that had been the morning after they found Aaron Colby's body on Mill Creek Road.

Jean descended into a hollow and crossed the creek on a fallen log, working his way up the slope through a thick stand of trees. When he reached a low hummock of firm ground he followed along its ridge, almost running, scrambling through the brush, hurrying to meet Rob. The Honey Tree was only a little farther on.

Quite suddenly he saw the footprints again. The man had taken the same route Jean had chosen, but when in sight of the Honey Tree he had veered sharply away and leaped back across the tiny stream: Jean could see where his feet had landed after the jump, and where he had slipped in climbing the wet bank.

Looking through the trees from where the stranger had suddenly turned, Jean saw Rob sitting on a deadfall waiting for him.

The tracks were very fresh; the stranger could be only minutes ahead of him. Obviously, the man had seen Rob and turned quickly away. Why should a man be afraid of being seen by a boy?

Jean walked into the clearing. "Hi," he said.

2

The Honey Tree stood at the edge of a small clearing, its long-dead limbs stripped and bare in the late afternoon sun. A gigantic cypress, lightning-blasted and hoary with years, it was all of nine feet through and hollow to at least sixty feet of its height. In that vast cavity generations of bees had been storing honey, and to Jean LaBarge it had been a source of excitement and anticipation since the first day of its discovery by him. Not a week passed that he did not attempt to devise a plan for robbing it.

Thousands of bees hummed about the tree, for not one but a dozen swarms used different levels of its hollow. Towering high above the clearing, it must once have been a splendid tree; now it was only a gigantic storehouse. When first Jean took Rob to the swamp, it was to the Honey Tree they had gone, and ever since it had been the focal point of their wanderings and explorations within the swamp.

Shortly after he arrived at the farm, Jean's Uncle George was shown the tree, and immediately plans were made to smoke out the bees and steal their honey. But that was before Uncle George realized that there was no way in which smoke could be made to affect all the bees simultaneously. Long before the smoke reached the bees near the top the wind would dissipate it, and to attempt the robbery would be to die under the stings of thousands of bees. Uncle George grumbled, threatened the bees and went away. He did not return to the Honey Tree and Jean did not mention his tree again, yet the thought of all that stored-up sweetness fascinated the boys.

"You going to smoke them today?" Rob was eager. "I'll bet there's bushels of honey!"

"Bushels?" Jean was scornful of such an estimate. "There's tons!"

He stared up at the tree, awed by the thought. Then he hitched up his too-large pants, remembering suddenly what he had meant to ask. "Did you see him?"

"See who?"

"The man . . . there was a man came this way, just ahead of me. When he saw you he turned off into the swamp."

"Who was it?"

"I'll bet he's gone to the stone house." It was strange he had not thought of it before. The trail the man was making would lead that way, and this might be the man who had left those ashes there. "I don't know who it was," he added.

Rob's eyes were big with excitement. Strangers were few along the Susquehanna in those years and most of them either passed by or occasionally stopped at the tavern for a meal or a drink. There was nothing to keep anyone in the village. And for anyone to leave the safety of Mill Creek Road for the dangers of the swamp was unheard of.

"Maybe he's one of the Carters."

Jean's heart began to pound heavily. The thought had not occurred to him before. The Carters were a band of outlaws known for their robberies, murders and brutality in all the regions near the Susquehanna in the early 1800's. The name was given them because the first of their number had worked as carters hauling goods along the high road. There had been some trouble at Sunbury and one of the cart drivers had killed a man in a most brutal fashion. Three of them had then looted the man's store and fled into the wild country along the West Branch of the Susquehanna. Later, they were believed to have shifted their operations to the Great Swamp.

In time their numbers had increased, although how many there were was never exactly known. A man caught stealing cattle had broken jail and joined them, and shortly after a farmer en route to the Mill had seen six of them gathered together at the bridge. A number of times in the months that followed travelers were beaten and robbed along Mill Creek Road, and two men were found murdered near Penn Creek shortly after they had been seen displaying money from a sale of cattle.

During succeeding years the Carters became notorious in all the country around. One was hanged, and another was shot and killed by an old soldier while attempting to steal a horse. By the time a concerted effort was made to deal with them they were already guilty of a score of murders. Two of them belonged to a family of evil character named Ring. It was said in the villages along the river that the Rings were all a little insane, but whatever else they were, they were also vindictive and dangerous men. It was believed the Carters had spies in the towns who warned them of impending trouble and let them know when prosperous travelers were on the road. The few attempts to capture them failed because the Carters knew the swamp and the villagers did not. Then after some fifteen years of terror the Carters suddenly vanished and for a long time travelers were safe again.

During those fifteen years the Carters had won a reputation as evil if not as widespread as those other murderers who haunted the Natchez Trace, far to the south. The stories of their crimes made exciting listening, and every lad along the river knew tales of the Carters and their bloody doings.

"What will do?" Rob asked anxiously.

"Let's go look."

Rob was frightened but he was even more curious, and moreover, was afraid to admit his fear. With Jean in the lead, the two boys started at once into the woods.

The afternoon was already late and in the forest it was noticeably darker. The direction taken by the stranger would take him nowhere but to the stone house or one of the several trails leading away from it. That stone house, Jean now realized, must have been one of the hide-outs of the Carters. If this stranger knew the swamp and knew of the house he could only be a Carter. There was no other alternative that made sense.

Rob was apprehensive. Not accustomed to shouldering responsibility for his actions, nor to being in the swamp this late, he was worried. He knew that if his parents ever learned what he was doing he would never hear the last of it, yet quite as much as Jean he wanted to know who the stranger was and where he was going.

"Maybe we should get somebody to come with us," Rob suggested.

"Nobody believes there's any Carters left hereabouts. They'd just laugh at us."

This, Rob knew, was exactly what would happen. Everybody was sure the Carters were gone for good, and it was unlikely that anybody would go into the swamp to investigate a rumor started by two boys.

The forest grew thicker and darker. Twice Rob fell, and once off to their right, something fell into a stagnant pool with a dull *plop* and both boys jumped. It was cooler now . . . the trees began to take on weird shapes and landmarks lost their identity as night made all things anonymous.

Some small creature sprang from the trail ahead of them and darted off through the woods. Probably a rabbit. They came down to a creek bank, the water gleaming a dull lead color in the vague remaining light. They crossed another log and entered a narrow opening in the forest wall. About them the darkness made tiny warning sounds, and they listened, aware of a strangeness they had not known before. It gave them an eerie feeling as if some great dark thing lurked in the shadows ahead, peering out at them, waiting for them to draw nearer, watching for the moment to spring. A loon called, far off beside some lost pool, and the lonely sound made their flesh crawl.

"Shouldn't we go back?" Rob whispered.

They should . . . Jean knew they should. He had no business spying on this stranger, and less business bringing Rob Walker into it, yet he could not turn back now. "You can if you want to; I want to see what he does."

It was not bravado that drove Jean on so much as an innate sense of self-preservation. The swamp provided him with a home and a livelihood. The presence of an intruder could only mean trouble for him.

If the Carters had returned he would no longer be able to move freely along his trap lines, and the source of his income would certainly be curtailed and might disappear. Young though he was, the idea frightened him, for the swamp was all the home he had ever known. He found nothing to attract him in the life of the village boys. Lonely though he was, often wistful with longing for the mother he had lost and the father he had scarcely known, he nonetheless loved the woods and would not have abandoned his free, easy life for anything.

The boys pushed on for some minutes; then Rob stopped again. "Jean. Please, I think we should go back," he insisted in a hushed tone. "We should tell somebody."

"We've nothing to tell. Anyway, Dan'l Boone wouldn't go back, nor even Simon Girty."

It was an argument for which Rob had no answer. But sometimes he doubted that he would make another Boone. It was one thing to play at such things, but when the swamp grew dark Rob was no longer positive he wanted a life of adventure. Jean, on the other hand, seemed as much at home here as any young wolf or deer. He belonged to the forest and the forest belonged to him.

Both boys had listened for hours to talk of Mohawk, Huron and Iroquois, of Simon Girty and Dan Boone, stories of hunting, Indian fighting and travel. They heard tales of the mountain men, and of the far lands of Mr. Jefferson's Louisiana Purchase, lands yet known to few. Many of the stories had originated with Jean's own father, who like most mountain men loved to yarn away the hours when he found himself among the wide-eyed citizens of settled communities.

The stone house huddled against the wall of the ridge that hemmed the swamp at that place, hiding itself in the deepest shadows under the ancient hemlocks. The boys crawled under a bush where no grown man could have gone and stopped just behind a huge hemlock, only a few yards away from the house.

Jean tried to remember what it was like close along the wall. He did not want to step on anything that would cause even a whisper of sound. Rob moved up beside him and they crouched there, wide-eyed, listening and tense. From within came a murmur of voices and they could see a thread of light from a crack in the boarded-up window. A few inches below, a shaft of light streamed from a knothole.

They moved forward from tree to tree until within a dozen yards of the house, then stopped again. Now they could distinguish the words of the men inside.

"You took long enough."

"Hutchins is there, and he's travelin' alone. Ridin' one horse, leadin' another. From the way he bulges at the waist he's wearin' a money belt."

"He's packin' two, three thousand in gold. Harry was there in the bank, seen him pick it up."

"Sam, I seen a kid out there. Settin' by the bee tree."

"He see you?"

"Nah . . . but what's a kid doin' in the swamp?"

"Well, what was he doin'?"

"Settin' . . . like he was waitin'."

"All right, then. He was waitin'. What more do you want? Maybe his pappy was huntin'."

"Nobody hunts in this swamp. Nobody."

"Probably LaBarge's kid. LaBarge built hisself a cabin over next the woods. I recall his woman used to collect bloodroot an' such to fetch down to the store. Made a livin' at it."

"You mean *Smoke* LaBarge?"

"You scared?" The tone was contemptuous.

"He never set much store by me. What you lettin' us in for, Sam?"

"Forget it . . . Smoke's dead and gone. Last I seen

of him was on the Yellowstone, but at Fort Union folks were tellin' it the Blackfeet killed him."

"Take some doin'."

"Well, they done it."

There was a sound of breaking sticks and then a fire crackled and a few sparks ascended from the squat chimney. The good smell of wood smoke came to the boys. Jean got carefully to his feet. If these men were mountain men as their conversation implied, they would be able to hear the slightest sound. But Jean had to look into that knothole; he had to see those men.

Signaling for Rob to stay where he was, Jean crept forward in the darkness. At the window he lifted his head slowly, holding it to one side of the knothole. He peered through, first from one side and then the other, and saw not two men, but three. The third man lay on a bunk asleep, his face in the shadows. The stranger whom they had followed Jean recognized by the boots he wore and the size of him. He was huge, awkwardly built, and dressed as a farmer would be dressed. His face wore an expression at once stupid and cunning. The man called Sam was hunched over the table, a shorter, broader, thicker man than the big one. His was a brutally strong face, but it possessed a hard, cynical cast that indicated a certain grim humor. Jean shuddered to see as he turned his head that there was an inch-wide scar through his eyebrow.

The stone house was as Jean remembered it, the old fireplace, a table, two benches and a barrel chair. The floor was of hard-packed earth. On the wall there now hung various articles of clothing. Several guns were within view.

The big man looked around the room. "This is a good place. Too bad we had to leave."

"It was time. We use some sense this time we can stay here for months before anybody gets wise. Hutchins, he's from out of state, an' he's headed west, so nobody will miss him."

"What about the body?"

"What d' you think? Right in the swamp where we should have put them all. The Rings was too careless."

Jean listened, his mouth dry with fear. Everybody in the village knew Captain Hutchins by sight. He had kin in the village and had visited there several times, but now he was going west to California and the lands on the Pacific, and he was carrying gold to buy furs along the way.

He remembered hearing them talk about it in the village. "Country's growing out there," Hutchins had said that very day, "and I want to grow with it."

"Ain't that Spanish land?"

"It is now," Hutchins agreed, "but unless I miss my guess it won't be very much longer. Someday the United States will span the continent. Might even cover all North America."

"Foolishness!" That was what old Mister Dean had said. "Pure foolishness! The country's big enough as it is. No sense taking in all that no-account land. Ain't worth nothin', never will be."

"There are folks who believe otherwise," Hutchins replied mildly. "And I know there's rich, black soil there, miles of fine grass, and a country that will grow anything. There's future in that country for men with the will to work and the imagination to see it."

These had seemed but the echo of words Jean had heard before. Had his father said them, long ago when he was too young to remember? Or had his mother repeated them to him? Whatever the reason or occasion, the words had struck fire within him and he listened avidly, knowing inside him that westward lay his destiny, westward with a land growing strong, westward with a new nation, a new people. And now these men within the house were planning to kill and rob Captain Hutchins.

Jean knew at once that he must get away to warn him, to tell him of these men and their plans. He got up, too quickly, and when he stepped back his foot slipped and he scrambled wildly for a foothold, then fell flat. Inside there was a grunt of surprise, and then a clamor of movement.

The door slammed open as Jean got to his feet and he was touched, just barely, by the shaft of light from its opening. He darted for the brush . . . once inside that brush, within its blackness . . . he tripped and fell flat, then crawled, scrabbling in the grass to reach the undergrowth only a few feet away. He was just about to make a final lunge when a large hand grasped his ankle. He kicked wildly, but the hand was strong. Inexorably he was drawn back and jerked to his feet.

The man with the scar grasped his arm. "Snoopin', were you? We'll be larnin' you better."

3

Sam gripped his arm and led the boy into the light from the open door. "This the one you saw?"

"Looks bigger," the big man said doubtfully. "I tell you, Sam, I ain't sure. He was settin' down. Could be, though."

Sam shoved Jean into the house and they followed him in, studying him thoughtfully. Jean stood very straight, his heart throbbing heavily. He was caught, and he had no idea what was to happen now; but he returned the man's stare boldly, although his mouth was dry and he felt empty.

"You're the LaBarge kid, ain't you?" Sam asked.

"I am Jean LaBarge." His voice was steady. For some absurd reason he was sorry his hair was not combed, that he was not wearing his other shirt. These men had known his father and he would not like them to think him unworthy.

"What you doin', sneakin' around here?"

"I was not sneaking," Jean lied. "I was coming to the door. I saw the light and wondered who was there. Nobody," he added truthfully, "ever comes here."

"What were you doin' in the woods?"

"I run a trap line." He tried to make his voice matter-of-fact. "And I collect herbs." From their attitude they apparently believed he had been alone, and therefore had no idea Rob Walker was outside. And they must not know.

"Pretty dark for that, ain't it?" Sam's voice was mild.

"I sold the herbs in the village. It is closer to the cabin if I come through the swamp."

"He's lyin', Sam." The big man had an ugly voice. "He lies in his teeth. When I seen him he was just a-settin'."

"What about that, boy?" Sam asked.

"I was studying the Honey Tree," he said. "I been aimin' to get me some of that honey."

Sam chuckled. "I studied some on that, too," he said. "It ain't easy." Sam ignored the bigger man, sizing Jean up with careful eyes, noting the shabby, often-patched homespun pants, the torn plaid shirt and the uncut hair. Sam found himself admiring the boy, for he put on a good show. He seemed wary all right, but if he was scared he managed to hide it. This was quite a boy. Old Smoke LaBarge would have been proud of him . . . but too thin, much too thin, and poor as a Digger Indian.

"Ain't you afraid of the swamp?"

"I grew up in it."

Sam had an idea but he was a slow man with his thinking. He took his time now, turning the idea slowly on the spit of his mind, studying it from all sides. They could kill the boy . . . that would be the easiest way, but it was a pity to kill a lad with his gumption. Also, if the boy failed to show up around the town folks would be sure to become curious and start looking for him. And Sam could stand for no snooping around. On the other hand, this boy was obviously very poor, probably making just enough to keep eating. A little extra money would look mighty big to him. If this lad was as smart as Sam was beginning to believe he would fit perfectly into their plans. Folks would become suspicious if an unemployed stranger hung about the tavern, but this youngster could go anywhere and nobody would think anything of it.

"Were you listenin' at the window, kid?"

"Not yet." Jean rightly guessed that frankness could hurt him none at all, and might win their friendship. "But I intended to. I'd have listened before I came around to the door."

Sam chuckled. "I'd have done the same, boy. I surely would."

The big man shifted his feet impatiently. "Sam, this boy means trouble. We've got to do something."

Sam gestured irritably. "Take it easy. I think this boy's on our side, Fud, and I've an idea."

Jean sat very still, waiting. Outside Rob would be creeping away, until he got far enough from the house to climb to the top of the ridge without being heard. Once atop the ridge he could follow it along to the road, but what if he took the wrong direction and became lost in the forest? For the ridge was but an offshoot of the higher land back of the swamp, and there was forest there, almost untouched, without track or trail of any kind.

Sam finished stoking his pipe and lighted it at the candle. The strings of his shirt were untied at the collar showing the thick black hair on his chest, and his big hands were thick and powerful. From time to time as he moved about he glanced at Jean. "Fud," Sam finally said, "you got to use your head. We can get rid of this boy a month from now as well as now, but on the other hand, he's not apt to run to the law, bein' he's dodgin' it himself.

"Oh, yes!" Sam grinned wisely at Jean. "You might fool those folks in town, but Fud an' me, we know you're livin' alone in that cabin. Your Uncle George ain't home, an' what's more, he ain't comin' home. Now if those folks in town knew that they'd have you in the workhouse. I know these here good folks, they can get themselves mighty busy about a poor little boy livin' all by himself. I know them, lad, an' you know them, too.

"Those folks, they'd never figure you liked it here in the swamp. They'd want to mess up your life makin' a home for you. Now I ain't sayin' a boy shouldn't have a home. Mighty good thing, homes are, but these fussy folks they get to watchin' over a boy, expectin' him to make mistakes, or tryin' to make him somethin' he ain't. You, f'r instance, you're a woodsman. Anybody can see that. Take after you pa, you do."

Jean waited, his attention on Sam. Instinctively he knew his only hope lay in Sam's suddenly aroused interest. Moreover he was fascinated by the obviously brutal strength of the man, by his big, hard-knuckled hands, so broken and scarred from fighting. Fud was the bigger of the two, but when it came to strength he was not in the same class with Sam. Suddenly Jean realized that Sam had said Uncle George was not coming back. How could they be sure of that unless . . . ?

"You get the idea, Fud." Sam was addressing his partner but he was talking to Jean also. "This here's quite a boy. He rustles his own living out of the woods, and as a body can see, he likes it. Of course, if folks knew he was alone they'd take him to a workhouse or 'prentice him to somebody. Either way they'd work the hair off him."

"Get to the point," Fud insisted irritably.

"Sure . . . this boy's on our side. We could tell on him, too. We could get him sent to the workhouse, and if he tattled on us we could say he was lyin' to save his own hide, usin' his imagination, the way kids do. We could even tell he'd been sneak-thievin' around, and maybe see something was found in his cabin to prove it. And who's to deny it?"

People would believe it, Jean knew. They would believe it because it would make them seem right for denying him the companionship of their children. Yes, they would believe it all right.

By now Rob would be climbing the ridge, and it would not be easy, in the dark like it was, when a body had no chance to choose a way. Soon he would be passing by the cabin along the ridge, and what if a rock rolled down?

"A boy like this," Sam continued, drawing deep on his pipe, "could do us some good. Got big ears, see? Good eyes, too. An' nobody suspects a kid. By now they're used to him comin' it around an' they would hardly notice he was there. He could find out who was carryin' money, how they traveled, and I'd bet he knows more hidin' places in this swamp than any catymount."

The climb up the ridge was steep, and Rob might slip back several times. He might fall headlong and get turned around in the dark when he got up. It had happened to Jean . . . but Rob had a good head and he had grit. He never took foolish chances. As soon as he got to Mill Creek Road, he would run. He would keep going, too: once Rob began on a thing he wouldn't let up.

"You got any real good friends in town, boy?"

"No, sir."

"How about the youngsters?"

"They say my mother was a gypsy."

"Right." Sam chuckled. He was pleased with himself. He had guessed that a boy living like this one would be at outs with the town. He had been a poor boy himself. He leaned forward. "Boy, is there anything you want real bad? I mean something for your very own?"

"A rifle," Jean replied promptly. "I'd like a rifle so I could go west."

Sam's laughter boomed and he slapped his heavy thigh. "That's it! There it is! By the Lord Harry, Fud! There's the LaBarge cropping out in the boy! A rifle so's he could go west, now doesn't that beat all?"

He sat back on his bench against the wall, puffing at his pipe. He held the pipe in one corner of his mouth and puffed from the other side. Fud looked bored and impatient, but the man on the bunk merely snored.

Rob should definitely be on the ridge by now. He would be frightened and breathing hard from the climb so he would stop to catch his breath. Up there on the ridge it would be bright moonlight, stark and clear. Below him on this side would be the swamp, and on the other, the forest. All he had to do was pick his way carefully along the top of that comblike ridge until it played out at Mill Creek Road.

How long would it take him to get to town? Two hours? Three? Rob was cautious, and on the ridge he would take his time. Up there among the jagged rocks and brush it would be rough going and to hurry might mean a sprained or broken ankle. Once out of the woods and on the road he could run. But how far could a boy run without stopping?

Rob would be frightened up there in the moonlight with a vast sea of darkness below him, a sea whose waves were the moving tops of trees and whose bottom was swamp and forest. It would be very still up there, except for the wind, and a sudden noise would stop a man, make the hair prickle on the back of his neck. The air would be cool, but there would be that strange odor of dampness and decay, the smell from stagnant pools, of rotting vegetation mingled with the fresh smell of pines and hemlock. Somewhere a night bird would call, an eerie sound that would make Rob stop, shivering. But then he would hurry on, perhaps falling, skinning his knees, rising again and going on . . .

"So you want a rifle? Now that's smart. A good rifle is a thing to come by, and mighty handy, but a good rifle costs money. Now you try selling herbs to buy a rifle and it would take quite a spell. You stick with us, do what I tell you and use that noggin of yours, then we'll get a rifle for you, and the best of the lot, too."

"What would I have to do?"

Sam chuckled again. "See there, Fud? No nonsense about this lad, comes right to the point. Business, he is, strictly business." Sam leaned his hairy forearms on the table. "Do? Nothing but what you've been doing, boy. You take your herbs to town to sell. On'y sometimes you go to Sunbury or Selinsgrove, too. And you sell 'em . . . what else? You listen. Just that. You listen. Sometimes folks passing through carry a sight of money, more'n is good for 'em. Well, we mean to he'p out, Fud, me, an' him.

"You see somebody with money, you just come to us. No townsfolk, mind you. Only travelers, folks goin' through on the pike or the river."

"Those folks who travel," Jean suggested tentatively. "Don't they have rifles sometimes?"

"Now." Sam slapped his leg again. "There's a lad! Eye right on the main issue!" Sam chuckled, winking at Jean. "Make a team, you an' me. We might even go west together, that's what."

"I can see that!" Fud sneered. "Sam, you're talkin' fool talk."

Sam lifted a thick, admonishing finger. "Don' take the boy lightly, Fud. Nobody in town is friendly to him, slurring his mother like they do, figuring his father no good, ready to clap the boy in the workhouse. No, sir! The boy's with us, aren't you, boy?"

"I hear things," Jean agreed, "an' folks don't pay me much mind."

Sam puffed on his pipe, his mind far away. The fire crackled on the hearth and the man in the bunk turned over, moving uneasily in his sleep, like a cat. Jean's ears strained into the darkness, striving to hear sounds he did not wish to hear. Was Rob safely out of earshot? How much time had passed?

"While you're doin' this plannin'," Fud's voice was sarcastic, "s'pose you figure what we'll do with him while we're gone. You goin' to leave him loose?"

Sam shook his head regretfully. "Not that I don't trust you, boy, but for safety's sake we'll lock the door."

Outside the wind was lifting. Sam got out a deck of worn playing cards and shuffled them. The man on the bunk fumbled at his face with a lax hand, and then his eyes opened and he lay for several minutes adjusting himself to the scene, his eyes continually returning to Jean. He was younger than the others, a lean, savage young man with dark hollows beneath his eyes and a yellowish cast to his face. He sat up finally, watching Sam handle the cards. Fud gestured Jean from the chair and sat down himself. The younger man, scratching his ribs and yawning, joined them.

"You slept long enough," Fud commented.

The young man turned his black eyes on Fud but made no comment. Sam began dealing the cards and Jean guessed that Sam was wary of this man. Fud he treated with casual contempt but there was something about this young man no one in his right mind would treat casually.

"Who's the boy?" he asked suddenly, without looking up from his cards. Sam explained, taking his time and attempting to make all the details clear. The young man did not look up nor did he interrupt, he just listened.

"We got to have information," Sam finished, "and we can't keep showing up in town. Certainly not you, nor me with this scar. There's men in town will remember how I come by this scar."

"They've never seen me."

"They know your family, Ring. They saw your father and brother, and you're like them as can be."

Jean's head nodded wearily, then jerked awake. The others still played cards. Sam glanced at him kindly, then nodded his head toward the corner. "Take a rest, boy, you'll need it."

There was nothing he could do. Wherever Rob Walker was, all was in his hands now, and Jean was terribly tired. His head no sooner touched the blanket than he was asleep.

A long time later he opened his eyes and the house was dark. He listened, but he heard no sound of snoring or breathing. Carefully, he sat up and looked around in the darkness. He was alone . . . the stone house was empty but for himself.

Rising quickly he went to the door. It was fastened on the outside. The earthen floor was packed hard, like cement, and he knew the stones of the house were sunk deep into the ground. Even if he had something with which to dig it would require hours to make a hole big enough for him to crawl out. The window was solidly boarded and too small, anyway. When he had exhausted all the possibilities of escape he sat down on the floor and stared at the small opening left by the knothole. Outside it was still night, but he must have slept a good long while. Soon it would be growing light.

4

When Rob Walker reached Mill Creek Road he was sobbing with fear and exhaustion. The ridge had proved to be a wild tangle of bramble, broken rock and wind-wracked pines. Under the white light of the moon it lay lonely and desolate and nowhere could he find the path which Jean had mentioned once, months ago.

Ghostly shadows of sentinel pines loomed about him, and he began scrambling over the jagged rocks and pushing through the brush toward the road. Branches tore at his clothing and twice he fell, skinning the side of his face on a rock. Briars snagged his clothing, yet he pushed on, knowing Jean was in danger, that he must bring help.

When at last he reached the road he was out of breath, his skin scratched and bruised, his clothing torn. The road lay wide and white in the moonlight with the black wall of the swamp on his right, on his left a rail fence bordering a pasture. Beyond the pasture was Mill Creek itself, and the air was damp and cool. He started to run, his short legs making hard work of it. Already breathless from his scramble over the ridge, pain stabbed at his side, but within him was a terrible fear that made a lie of his weariness.

He had no idea of the hour. It had been late afternoon when they started to follow the stranger, and dark when they lay outside the cabin. To circle around and climb the ridge must have taken at least an hour, for he had crept some distance before he trusted the noise not to reach the men in the cabin, and it had taken another hour to creep by the cabin. It must have taken him at least two hours to reach the road, maybe more: he had stopped many times to catch his breath and listen for sounds in the night.

It was the first time he had been away from home after dark and his folks would be frightened. They were not lenient, and it was understood he must either be in the house or his own yard before dark. Finally, unable to run farther, he began to walk. He wanted nothing so much as to stop, to sit down, to lie down. Never had he been so utterly exhausted. This morning his mother had put out a clean shirt for him and now it was soaked with sweat, bloodstained and torn by brambles.

Far up the road he glimpsed a light. That would be the old Chancel house, and not a quarter of a mile beyond was the tavern, and only a little farther, a few steps only, was his own home. At last he ran up the path and burst into the door.

His mother started to her feet, her face tearstained, and his father, who had been pacing the floor as he always did when worried, turned sharply, ready to scold. When he saw Rob's face and the condition of his clothing the words died unspoken.

"What is it, son? What's wrong?"

The story spilled out in sobbing gasps, and for the moment he forgot that he had been forbidden to go into the swamp or to associate with Jean LaBarge. His father listened, his eyes on Rob's face, seeing more than was being said. He knew his own son, and sometimes had wondered about the boy. Now he saw courage there, and if there was fear also, it was fear for Jean. Rob had always been frightened of his father, a quiet, stern man. Suddenly, for the first time, he felt they were on common ground. His father asked no foolish questions, wasted no time on angry complaints.

"You can take us back there? Do you know the way?"

"Yes, Father."

"Three men, you said? And Jean thought they were the Carters?"

"Yes."

"Come." Walker put his hand on his son's arm. "We'll go to the tavern."

"But can't you take care of it without him?" Rob's mother protested. "The child hasn't eaten, and look at his clothes! He . . ."

"He will have to come with me. Anyway," Rob's father added, "it is his story and I believe he had better tell it."

Side by side they walked to the tavern. Rob had rarely been inside, only when he and Jean had slipped in to listen to stories being told, when some traveler was there from the west, or going west. It was a large room, low-raftered and smoky. On the right was a huge fireplace and near it a dozen men sat about a worn black table with mugs of beer or rum, smoking their pipes. The place had a dark, rich smell that was always exciting, and the glint of light on burnished copper. As they entered, all eyes swung to them. Across the table Captain Hutchins lifted his level blue eyes and looked at Rob, then nodded to Rob's father.

"Hutchins," Walker said abruptly, "my son has something to tell you."

Rob began to speak, hesitantly at first, and then remembering Jean he spoke more boldly and swiftly, telling the story from the beginning. He repeated what conversation they had overheard from within the stone house, and Jean's whispered report that three men were inside. Captain Hutchins listened without speaking, his eyes never leaving Rob's. When Rob finished, Walker got to his feet and knocked out his pipe.

"I believe that is plain enough," he said. "How many of you are with me?"

There were nine in the group who rode out from the village. Four were from the local company of militia, and even old Mister Dean, armed with a tremendous double-barreled shotgun, had come along.

"Will there be time to reach the cabin?" Hutchins asked, turning in his saddle to look at Rob.

"No, sir. I don't think so. And with so many men there would be noise."

Walker spoke up angrily. "By the Lord, Captain, if they've killed that boy . . . !"

"Hsst!"

They drew up sharply at the signal, stopping in the black shadow of a roadside tree. They heard a murmur of voices and an oath as somebody stumbled. Men were coming through the brush.

Hutchins swung to the ground, very cool, very businesslike. Rob's father tossed his reins to Rob and dismounted. "Hold the horses, Rob," he said, "and don't be frightened."

Breathless with excitement, Rob watched his father. He carried a rifle, and from somewhere he had gotten a large pistol which was thrust into his waistband. Moreover, he seemed completely at home with both weapons. Rob had noticed with pride the businesslike way in which his father loaded them.

The four militiamen disappeared into the trees opposite the noise in the brush. Hutchins stood his ground, in the middle of the moonlit road. Some twenty feet farther along, standing partly in the shadow, was Walker. The other men had scattered themselves, two slipping into the brush, planning to come in behind the Carters and cut off any attempted escape.

Fud was the first Carter to reach the road. "Right across here there's a rock," he was saying. "We can wait there until Hutchins . . ."

His voice broke off sharply as he saw the slim,

erect figure standing in the light of the sinking moon.

The others emerged from the woods, Ring pausing on the edge of the brush, warned by the sudden breaking off of Fud's speech.

"Stand where you are, men," Hutchins spoke clearly. "You're well taken."

A rustle of movement in the brush behind him made Sam start, then relax slowly. Fud was weaving uncertainly as his slow brain attempted to cope with the situation, a situation already beyond him. The shock of the trap was too much for Fud.

"You'll drop your weapons!" Walker's voice was crisp. "If you do not comply at once, we shall shoot to kill!"

Fud found his voice. "What's this?" he blustered. "Can't a man travel the high road 'thout bein' held up?"

"Our point exactly," Hutchins replied cheerfully. "I'm Hutchins, if you'd like to know. I understand you planned to meet me later. Now tell us: where's the boy?"

"What boy?" Fud tried to seem surprised.

"Don't pretend, man." Hutchins walked up to him. "You have been found out so you'd best tell us. If that boy has been harmed I shall personally attend to your hanging."

Rob's attention had been riveted upon the tense scene in the road's center. All at once his eyes swung to the edge of the road. Sam was still there, a man behind him with a gun at his back, but the third man was gone.

"Father!" he called sharply. "The other man's gone!"

Before anyone could speak, Sam lifted his voice. "Hutchins, you'd better get to the cabin and save that boy. Ring's got away and he hates the lot of you. He'll kill that lad. I know Ring. He'll kill him certain sure."

Fud turned his heavy head to glare at Sam. "Why don't you keep shet?" he demanded.

Sam shrugged, smiling wryly. "You heard the man. If anything happens to that boy, we hang. Do you want to hang, Fud?"

"Did you say *Ring*?" Walker crossed the road to Sam. "I thought we'd killed the lot of them."

"This here's Bob Ring. You killed his father and brother. They were the first of the Carters."

Walker turned to his son. "Rob, can you take us to the cabin? I don't like to ask you. I know you're tired, but . . ."

"I want to go!" Rob slid from his horse. "I know the way."

Four men took Sam and Fud, their hands tied behind them, and started for the village. The others followed Captain Hutchins and Walker into the woods, and Rob led the way. Out there in the stone house Jean LaBarge waited for help, and he was bringing it.

The light outside the knothole slowly turned gray. Unless Rob had reached them in time Captain Hutchins would now be approaching the place where the Carters lay in wait for him on Mill Creek Road.

What if Rob was not believed? But he would be, for Rob was a serious boy, not given to pranks, and he had a way of making people listen to him. He knew how to talk, and had the words for it. That was because he read books. Jean made a mental resolution to read more . . . if he got out of this.

He got to his feet and went to the door. The cabin smelled of dirty clothes and stale tobacco smoke. He tried to get his fingers into the crack between the door and the jamb but there was no space for them, nor could he budge the heavy planks at the window.

Somewhere out in the woods there was a sound, and he went to the knothole, peering out. The grass of the clearing beyond the hemlocks was gray with morning dew; with the rising sun it would turn to silver. A bird came out of a tree and sat on a stump, preening his feathers. There was no sound, there was no other movement.

Yet there was . . . a stirring of leaves, a branch that moved, and a man peering furtively out. The bird, frightened, took off in a low swoop for the trees, and the man named Ring came from the forest and started toward the house.

Jean's throat tightened with fear. Ring was back and he was alone. He had been running: his breath came in ragged gasps and he walked with swift, jerky steps. That meant something had happened—

Ring hesitated, staring back at the forest and listening. His lank black hair hung around his ears, his eyes were wild and staring. There was a pistol tucked in his waistband. He ran on to the stone house and Jean heard him fumbling with the hasp on the door.

Frightened, his mouth dry, Jean hid where the opening door would conceal him until the last moment. They would be coming. Rob must have gotten help; Ring was being chased. If only he could . . .

The door slammed open and Ring stepped into the room, glaring about like a wild animal, looking for Jean. Gasping hoarsely from his run, the man was beyond reason, beyond thought, filled with murderous rage. He stepped on into the room, and instantly Jean ducked around the door and ran.

Wheeling with amazing swiftness, the black-haired man grabbed for him. Jean felt the fingers clutch at his arm, slide off. Then he was out of the door and around the corner of the house. The man was like a cat. He sprang after him, but Jean ducked behind a hemlock and froze in place, eyes wide, fear choking him.

Ring stood in the clearing before the house and looked around him slowly. When he spoke it was in an amazingly cool, almost conversational voice. "You surely needn't try to get away. I know these here woods better'n anybody. My name is Ring and I growed up here."

Jean looked toward the brush, judging the distance. The black-haired man would not want to use his gun and draw the pursuers to him. The brush was only fifteen feet away, yet for the time it took to cover that distance he would be in full view.

"I'm surely goin' to kill you, boy. They done kilt my daddy, an' I'm a-goin' to kill you."

Jean sprang out and leaped for the brush.

Ring swore, a shrill, whining scream, then lifted his pistol. Realization of what it might bring made him lower it again. He raced after the boy, but Jean LaBarge was already in the woods and once more in his own element. He ducked, dodged, then plunged out into an unexpected little clearing. Behind him Ring yelped a cry of triumph. And then out of the bushes ahead of them stepped Captain Hutchins. "It's all right boy," Hutchins said quietly. "Let him come."

5

The hardest part had been saying goodbye to Rob Walker, for they had always planned to go west together, and now he was going and Rob was staying behind. The next hardest part was to leave the swamp.

Before he left he walked alone to the Honey Tree, and he sat down there where he and Rob had sat so many times together, and where he had sat so many times alone. Around the towering tree millions of bees hummed unceasingly, and he watched them, a lump in his throat.

He told himself he would come back and take that old Honey Tree yet, but deep down inside he knew he never would, and suddenly he found himself hoping that nobody else would, either . . .

Neither Rob nor he had felt like talking. They just stood there, and he kicked a clod out of the grass on the Walker lawn.

"Guess you'll be seein' Indians, and everything," Rob said.

"I guess so."

"You going to write me? You going to tell me all that happens?"

"I'll write . . . maybe won't see any post carrier for a long time, but I'll write."

It was his first goodbye, and he did not like it. A long time later, sitting under the cottonwoods and watching the campfire on the little creek west of Independence, he thought of that. He missed Rob, and he missed the swamp, too, but he missed them only a little now because there was so much to see.

Not that there was no trouble, for trouble seemed to go with him wherever he went. He remembered what had been said when the others of the westward-bound company discovered he was a boy. The objections had been violent and profane. But Captain Hutchins faced them, his feet a little spread, cool as he had been that morning when he killed Bob Ring. "The boy goes or I do not. I've a notion he's worth the lot of you, and he'll walk as far or trap as much fur as any of you."

Captain Hutchins owned most of the horses, and Captain Hutchins had been free about providing powder and ball and the others knew they would be a while finding a man to replace him. It finally simmered down until only one man objected and Captain Hutchins faced him. "If it's a choice between you or the boy," he said coolly, "I'd rather have the boy beside me. If you don't like his going, I'd suggest, sir, that you find a party more suited to your temperament."

A man named Peter Hovey, leaning on his elbow against a wagon wheel, had said, "Was I you, Ryle

Beck, I'd back up an' set down. I've a notion you've overmatched yourself."

Beck glowered and grumbled, but after a little bluster he shut up and went back to the fireside.

Captain Hutchins turned to Hovey. "Thanks, man. It'd be a bad thing to begin a journey with trouble."

"Aye, an' trouble enough for us all will be seen before we've found our bait of fur." He glanced at Jean. "Are you a trapper, boy?"

"I caught my living at it, furs and herbs, more'n four years now," he said, "but it was swampland and not the mountains. I'd be obliged if you'd teach me."

"You'll do." Peter Hovey grinned. "I've a thought you'll do your share."

And so it began.

Days later, moving westward, Captain Hutchins swung a wide arm at the country about them. "One man, Jean, a man with a vision, gave us this. If Tom Jefferson hadn't gone ahead, overriding the little men without vision, all the frightened little men, we'd not have this. By signing the Purchase agreement he risked his political future, but he doubled the size of the nation. You might even say he created a nation. Before the Louisiana Purchase we were a cluster of colonies; after it we became a world power."

"Is that good, sir?"

"Who knows, Jean? But nations and men are alike: they go forward or they stagnate and die."

There was new respect for him when it was

learned he was the son of Smoke LaBarge. Peter Hovey had known him, had trapped with him on the Upper Wind River. Smoke had been killed by Blackfeet the following year, Hovey thought. But you could never be sure. He had a way of turning up.

They went to Pierre's Hole and traded there, and for the first time the others began to see that young Jean LaBarge knew fur. He had learned it by selling his own, and had learned trapping, too. Although only a boy, his take for the season was almost as good as the men's.

With Captain Hutchins and a party of twenty mountain men they went up through the country along the Wind River and the Teton Peaks, and then floated down the Missouri to St. Louis. It was the biggest town Jean LaBarge had seen, and it was there, from old Pierre Choteau, that he first heard the magic name . . . Alaska.

"Alaska," Choteau said, "you know . . . Russian America. Talked to a man who had been there to trade with Baranov. A rich land he said, the furs are thicker there because of the cold. Untrapped country. If I was younger . . ."

Alaska was an exotic name like Kashgar, Samarkand and Bagdad, but different, stronger, stranger. It was wild, untamed, lonely . . . or so it sounded to him.

That night he had written to Rob Walker about it, his first letter home, after so long a time. He told him, in pages of writing, what they had done, of the mountain men he had met—Jim Bridger, Milton

Sublett, Peter Hovey. But he wanted to go to Alaska. Rob must meet him in San Francisco and they would go together.

Was that when their love for Alaska began? Or had it begun in that other so-called wasteland, the Great Swamp? Others despised and feared it, yet Jean had lived there, made his way there, known its riches and its beauty. The experience made him wary of the term wasteland.

Now he was seeing great western lands that old Mister Dean had disparaged. He was seeing millions of geese, millions of buffalo, streams with beaver, forests of splendid trees, and the waters of the Missouri. He remembered a big, hairy-faced trapper who grinned at him and said, "Takes a man with hair on his chest to drink from the Missouri. Cowards cut it with whiskey!"

Rob had been away at school when Jean next heard from him, receiving the letter at Astoria, and a package containing a translation of Homer. Captain Hutchins had already given him a Bible. Later, a drunken trapper gave him a copy of Plato's *Dialogues*.

He read his books at night beside the campfire, and read them lying in his bunk at Astoria, and later in San Francisco. Several times after they arrived there he took trips with Captain Hutchins back into the Sierras or the Rockies, and each time he took a book with him.

At sixteen he had read just seven books, but had read them over and over, and at sixteen he was a veteran of nine battles with Indians, and victor in a man-to-man fight with a drunken trapper.

When his seventeenth birthday came around, he had read only one more book, but had read it, Plutarch's *Lives*, four times. He had a fight with Comanches under his belt by that time, carried the scar of his first wound, and had recuperated in Santa Fe.

By the time he was twenty he had covered the length of the Rockies and the Sierras, had nearly died of thirst, carried the scar of another wound and was over six feet tall, lean as any savage warrior, and stronger than any man he had so far met. That was the year he lost all his furs on the Green River when his canoe upset, and lived two months with Ute Indians while they made up their minds whether to kill him or not. By the time they decided he had chosen his horse and rifle, and the night before his captors came for him, an Indian who had befriended him loosed the rawhide bonds they had finally tied him with, and he slipped out of camp in the darkness and rode south until he struck the trail from Santa Fe to California. Two months later, broke, ragged and hungry, he had showed up at Captain Hutchins' office on the wharf at San Francisco.

The following year he bought furs for Captain Hutchins, read twelve more books and tried prospecting in the gold fields without luck. Twice he made strikes but both petered out.

Returning one night from the wharf he heard a woman cry for help from an alley in Sydney Town.

He rushed into the alley and something struck him a terrible blow across the back of his head. He came to, to find himself lying in a stinking bunk in the fo'c'sle of a windjammer bound for Amoy and Canton, China. The mate, a burly ruffian with tattooed arms and a heavy chest, came down the ladder with a marline-spike and jerked men from the bunks. Tentatively, Jean LaBarge swung his feet to the deck.

"Hurry it up, you!"

He looked up and started to speak and the mate hit him. His head still throbbed from the night before and this second blow did him no good. He painfully got to his feet, as tall as the mate when standing, lean and hard as a wolf, but he only choked back his anger and went on deck.

By the time they reached Canton he knew his way about a ship. He learned fast, paid attention to his job, and bided his time. Captain Swagert eyed him doubtfully, but the mate, Bully Gallow, shrugged it off. "Yellow. He's big, but he's yellow."

At trappers' rendezvous Jean LaBarge had won a dozen rough-and-tumble fights, and had lost one. He found that he liked to fight, there was something savage and wild in him that reveled in it. One of the trappers who worked for Captain Hutchins had once been a bare-knuckle bruiser in England, and he added his teaching to what Jean had learned the hard way. And now Jean's time came in Amoy.

It was a waterfront dive where sailors went, and it was filled with sailors the night Jean LaBarge went hunting. He knew all about the back room at the dive, the place reserved the officers, and it was there he found Captain Swagert, and beside him Gallow.

A big man, Gallow was, with two drinks under his belt and his meanness riding him like a devil on his shoulders. He saw LaBarge and LaBarge grinned at him. Gallow waved a hand. "Get *out!* This room is for your betters!"

"Get up," Jean LaBarge told him. "Get up. Stack your duds and grease your skis because I'm going to tear down your meat-house!"

Gallow left the chair with a lunge and learned for the first time the value of a straight left. It stabbed him in the mouth as though he had run into the butt end of a post, and it stopped him in his tracks. What followed was deliberate, artistic and enthusiastic. Jean LaBarge proceeded to whip Bully Gallow to a fare-thee-well, dragging him from the back room for the entertainment of the common sailors and when the job was finished he went into the back room again where Captain Swagert sat over a bottle and a glass.

"Captain Swagert, sir," he said, "you'll be needing a new mate. I'm applying for the job."

The older man's eyes glinted. "You'll not get it," he said abruptly. "You'll not get it at all. One more trip and you'd be after my job. You're through, lad, and you're on the beach in Amoy, and I envy you not one whit."

So that was the way of it. And Jean wrote to Rob from Amoy but he did not tell him he was on the beach there, only what the port was like, and that he was staying on awhile.

There was no love in Amoy for the white man since the Opium Wars, and for a month Jean LaBarge lived a hand-to-mouth existence, then signed on with a four-master sailing north to the Amur. It was a Russian ship, clumsy on deck and dirty below, but it was a ship, and when they had discharged cargo in the Amur they sailed for Fort Ross on the California coast. There, evading a guard who walked the decks by night, he slipped over the side into the dark water and floated ashore with an arm over a cask.

Once back in California, Jean had a long letter from Rob. His friend had gone far since the Great Swamp days. He had borrowed money and gone to college. He had graduated from the University of Pennsylvania at the age of eighteen and paid the money back by his own efforts. Then he had married the granddaughter of Benjamin Franklin and moved to Mississippi. A successful lawyer, he was now rapidly gaining eminence as a senator . . . Rob had always had a gift for words and a way with people.

Jean LaBarge settled down in the growing city of San Francisco, buying furs and selling supplies to the Alaska traders and other seagoers. On the foundations of their first efforts Captain Hutchins had begun a thriving business, ignoring the gold rush and building for the future when the boom would be a thing of the past. Not only did Jean know furs, but his sea experience had given him the knowledge to talk equipment and supplies with the best of them. And always in the back of his mind was the thought of Alaska.

It was waiting there, a great subcontinent, almost untouched, overflowing with riches, and all in the hands of a greedy, self-serving company under a charter from the Russian government, a company that kept out all interlopers despite regulations and international treaties. Yet soon Jean LaBarge discovered that nobody had any exact information about Alaska or the islands off the coast to the south. For the greater part they had never been explored and no proper charts existed. The smattering of Russian he had picked up was quickly improved by conversations with the few Russian shipmasters who came to Captain Hutchins' chandler's shop or to trade privately a few furs they had purchased on their own. From these casual conversations and further talks with seamen from the ships, he gleaned what information he could.

Later, on a ship of which Captain Hutchins and he were part owners, he sailed down the coast of Chile and to the Hawaiian Islands. There they picked up an old man, a survivor of Baranov's ill-fated attempt to capture those islands many years before. Relatives of the old man still lived near the abandoned Fort Ross, and on Jean's authority the old man was transported back to California. For hours each day and night Jean's interest kept the old man yarning about his own trading days in the vicinity of Sitka.

Not long after his return Jean learned that Rob Walker had led an attempt in the Senate to buy from the government of Mexico all of Baja California and fifty miles deep into Chihuahua and Sonora for a price of twenty-five million dollars. The Mexican government was prepared to sell, and Walker desperately urged the purchase, but an economy-minded Congress turned down the offer. Wasteland, they said.

The letters were not many but they continued. No longer was there talk of the two going to Alaska together, although Rob did plan to come to California where he had clients, and there was some talk of a trip to China, but neither trip materialized as the growing demands on Robert Walker's time increased, and his own importance to the nation he served.

From time to time Jean LaBarge heard of his father. He was dead . . . he was not dead . . . he had gone to Canada . . . had been seen in the Yukon country. The swamp on the Susquehanna seemed far away now, but Alaska was closer. What he needed was a ship.

6

When the lighter came alongside the dock with its load of furs, the man in the blue jacket sprang ashore, then turned to look back at the harbor. Crowded with shipping though it was, he had eyes but for one vessel, a low-hulled black schooner that lay some three hundred yards off the landing.

Jean LaBarge looked what he was, a man born to the wild place and the tall winds. The mountain years had shaped him for strength and molded him for trial, the desert had dried him out and the sea had made him thoughtful. His boyhood in the Great Swamp near the Susquehanna had given promise of the man he had become.

His eyes traced the lean, rakish lines of the schooner, making a picture of her as she would appear against the fjords and inlets of the northern coast. She would do well in that trade where the number of skins one took was less important than the number one successfully brought away. With that color, and with her low silhouette and slim masts, she could easily lose herself against the changing greens and browns of the iron coast. And with her shallow draft she could hug the shore so closely as to be almost invisible from seaward.

Jean knew that if he expected to trade in Russian America and avoid capture or sinking she was just the craft he required, and he intended to own her.

The man suited the ship as the ship the man, for Jean had about him the same lean look, big though he was. His were the hands and shoulders of one who had worked much against the sea and wind. His eyes measured the schooner, studying her lines and guessing at her speed and capacity. She had come into the harbor and dropped anchor while he was bartering for furs aboard the Boston ship, and his first glimpse of her had come as he started for shore. Obviously she was strongly as well as lightly built, fashioned for speed and durability by a knowing hand.

It was a raw morning with a cold gray sky above a slate-gray sea, and a wind blew in through the Golden Gate with a hint of rain. Nevertheless, he remained on the dock studying the schooner. She lay too far off for him to make out the port of registry, but he remembered no such schooner in these waters since he had first come to San Francisco.

With such a schooner, if a man steered clear of the Russian capital at Sitka and its immediately neighboring islands he might trade along the Alaskan coast and be gone before the Russians were aware of his presence in the area. With luck he might slip in and out of that network of channels like a dark ghost ship, for the Indians were not apt to talk to their Russian masters, preferring to deal with the "Boston men" as all Yankees were called by them. The Russians were all too willing to let the Indians have a touch of the knout.

Yet trading among the islands was not a simple thing, and within the past few years a dozen ships had vanished there, ships mastered by men who knew the waters, the bitter offshore winds and fogs. Furs were not coming out as they had been, and prices had risen. Now if ever was the time for a private venture.

There are men who give their hearts to a horse, a boat, or a gun, men who are possessed by all these things, absorbed by them to the exclusion of all else. Jean LaBarge was such a man, but he was absorbed by a land. To the north lay a country vast and unpeopled, without cities, a land of glacier and mountain, of icy inlet and rocky fjord, of long grassy valleys and canyons choked with snow, of endless tundra and mile upon mile of mighty timber. It was a land with broken shores where the icy tongues of an Arctic sea licked at gaping mouths of rock, while above it the sky was weirdly lit by the vast play of color that was the northern lights. Long before he had seen the land he had loved it, for he had felt its strength and beauty in the richness of its fur, in its timber and gold.

He knew of the gold. There had been a trapper who had come to him with furs, a man who had wintered with the Tlingit Indians north of Fifty-four. Jean had bought furs from him, wondering at their richness, and he asked the man when he was going back.

The trapper turned sharply around, his face flushed and angry. "Back? Are you crazy? Who'd go back to a country that freezes the eyeballs in your skull, the marrow in your bones, where the bears grow tall as horses and heavy as bulls? The Russkies can have it, and welcome. I wouldn't even go back for the gold."

"Gold?"

The trapper dug into his pocket and drew out a bit of tanned hide, unrolling it to reveal a nugget of walnut size. It gleamed there on his calloused palm, heavy as sin in the heart of a man. "If that isn't gold, what is it?"

Jean remembered the feel of it in his own palm, the weight of it and the brightness. This was gold, all right, raw gold, of which he had seen plenty here in California. Yet this was from Alaska.

"Found it in the shallows of a mountain stream when my canoe tipped over. I was picking my gear off the bottom when I saw it lying there, and could have picked up a dozen more. Only the country was freezing up and my grub was gone.

"Rough gold, see? Means it wasn't carried far from the lode or it would have been worn smooth by rocks and gravel. The Tlingits have gold but they value it less than iron." He made a brushing gesture before his face. "I'd set no value on it either, if I had to go to Alaska for it."

Yet a year later Jean LaBarge heard the trapper had been killed in Alaska in a fight over a Kolush squaw. They were all the same, these men who went to the north country, they claimed to hate it, but they went back. And Jean knew it was not the furs or gold nor was it the wild, free life. It was the land.

Thoughtfully, he considered the problem presented by the schooner, her probable cost and the additional expense of outfitting her. Beyond the trim, black-hulled schooner was a big square-rigger flying the Russian flag—it was almost a challenge. He grinned thoughtfully, thinking of the places that schooner could go where the square-rigger could not hope to follow.

Few Russian ships came to San Francisco since the closing of Fort Ross, yet occasionally they made their way down from Sitka to buy grain or other food even as they had done in the days of the Dons when they had bought much from the missions. The square-rigger had come into port only a short time ago.

Glancing around at an approaching footstep he saw a short, thickset man with a captain's peaked cap shoved back on the hard knot of his head. Despite the damp chill the man had his coat over his arm and his shirt open at the neck. In his mouth was a short-stemmed pipe. "That schooner, now. She's a pretty thing, isn't she?" He slanted a shrewd, measuring glance at Jean. "And the beauty of it is, she can be had. In a week I'd make no bets on it, but right now, for hard cash, she'd be a real bargain."

He made a thrusting gesture, his pointing figure held waist-high, like a pistol. "Right now her owner's got a touch of the yellow . . . he's discouraged."

"Discouraged?"

There was a hard competence about the man, and a scar on his cheekbone, scarcely healed. His eyes, however, held a quizzical humor that belied the toughness. "Bad luck in the Pribilofs. The Russkies got him."

"They didn't take the schooner?"

"He hadn't the schooner with him. That time he was sailing a barkentine. They didn't take her, either, just the cargo. Six thousand prime sealskins. Six *thousand* mind you." The man spat. "And lucky, at that. Had it been Baron Zinnovy he'd have been lucky to be alive, to say nothing of ship and crew."

"Zinnovy?"

"If you're in the trade it's a name you'll know soon enough. He's out from Siberia to command the Russian patrol ship, the *Kronstadt*. And none of your vodka-swilling scenery bums such as they've been sending out, but a tough man, one chosen to do a bloody job and put the fear of the Lord in such of us as sail north."

"He's already on the north coast?"

"He's right here . . . in Frisco." He indicated the square-rigger. "He came aboard of her, but as a passenger, mind you.

"If I'm to fight a man, give me a brute every time, but this one is cold and he's smart, and fresh from the Russian navy with a lot of ideas. I've heard them say his idea is to end the free trading with a rope, a knout for the Indians and a noose for the Boston men, and the deep six for their ships."

"That's a large order."

"Ay, but this one's man enough, don't you be doubting that. I say it as hate to, he's man enough."

The square-rigger had lowered a boat that was coming shoreward. Jean strained his eyes against the distance, making out but one passenger aside from the boat crew.

"You've been sizing up the schooner, and she's a likely craft, but you'll be needing a skipper, a man who knows the islands. You'll find none who know them better than myself, from Vancouver Island to the Circle."

He gestured at himself. "You see me now, name of Barney Kohl, standing in the middle of my property. But wealth, man? 'Tis not property that makes a man rich, but what's in his skull, and I've a pretty lot upstairs. You'll be needing a man with more in his head, Jean LaBarge, than mincy ways and nancy talk. You'll be seeking a man who knows the way of a ship and the sea, and the tricks of the Kolush prominent among them. You'll be needing me, LaBarge, if it's yonder schooner you'll be buying."

Kohl was a name well known to shipping: a tough rascal by all accounts, not above cutting a corner or two, but a good man with a ship, and a fighter. He had bargained with the Kolush and dealt with the Eskimo, and had a couple of running battles with Russian patrol ships.

"You know the kind of man Zinnovy is and you'd still go north?"

Kohl took the pipe from his teeth. "That's why I want to go. There was a ship lost up there, and I know what happened.

"You've heard of the mosquitoes on that coast? They'll cover every naked bit of a man and eat him alive. I've seen a man after being left naked by the Kolush, black with them, driven crazy by them.

"Well, there were six men left alive when their ship was taken, and Zinnovy had the six whipped with cat until the muscles were laid bare and then tied them, bloody as they were, to trees. Then he left them for the mosquitoes, and I was the one found those men—or what was left of them."

"You're hired," Jean said, "if I can buy the schooner."

"You'll get it. I'll see to that . . . you'll have her within the week."

7

The second lighter had now reached the dock, piled high with bales of furs. It bumped alongside and a heaving line was tossed shoreward. A dockside hand started for it, but LaBarge was nearer and snared the monkey's-fist on the end of the line with a one-handed catch. Barney Kohl grasped the line beside him and together they hauled it in, hand over hand, then the heavier line to which it was belayed. They drew three fast turns around the bollard and topped it off with a half-hitch to complete the tie. Stepping back, they grinned at each other.

"I've a thought where the owner may be," Kohl suggested, "so let me handle the deal. He knows I'm on my uppers and I can wrangle a better price than you."

A dozen husky longshoremen moved toward the lighter and began tumbling bales within reach of the crane. Jean LaBarge ran an appraising eye over what he could see of the skins. Without breaking a bale he knew they were prime stuff; he had broken enough bales while he was aboard the Yankee ship to assure him of his judgment.

A few spattering drops of rain fell, and he stood on the dock, liking the feel of them on his face. Beneath the wharf the waves slapped against the piles, a pleasant sound, a sea sound. He liked the damp, chill morning and the salt air, the ships lying out there on the waters of the bay, the black-hulled schooner he hoped might soon be his own.

"Go ahead," he said finally. "You'll be sailing as mate."

Kohl had started away, but the words brought him up short. "What?" Obviously he did not believe what he had heard. "Me? As mate? And who'll sail as master? What man is fitted to—"

"I'll be in command."

Their eyes met and held, measuring each other. Kohl was astonished, then angry. For fifteen years he had sailed as master of ships, and half that time aboard his own vessel. And now he was expected to take a back seat.

"You've commanded before?" he asked skeptically. The thought of sailing as second-in-command to a man who, so far as he knew, had never gone to sea was not to be borne.

"I have. And I can use a mate if you've a liking for the job. If you haven't, I'll get another man."

"Oh, I'll take it!" Kohl was exasperated. "What else can I do? I've no liking for the beach, that's certain, and a man must eat. You've got me over a barrel."

"I'll have no discontented man aboard my ship," LaBarge said flatly. "If you're shipping with me because you're broke, I'll stake you so you'll have no worries until you get another ship."

Kohl's irritation waned. "Well," he grumbled, "that's fair enough. It's more than fair. No, I don't want your stake, I'd rather have the job even if I am stepping down. I'll go to sea."

"Good . . . you're on the articles as of now. Come see me tonight and sign them—or as soon as you've lined up a deal for the schooner."

Kohl turned away, still a little angry, yet as he walked away, his irritation waned. He was going to sea again and in a schooner that was as sweet a bit of seagoing merchandise as he had ever seen. He was no dockside sailor who did his seafaring when talking to the girls, but a deep-water man who liked it out where the big ones rolled. Besides, around Frisco there was every chance he'd some night have a drink in the wrong place and wake up, shanghaied aboard the ship of some lubber who couldn't navigate a dory in a millpond. Anyway, he reflected with a grim pleasure, after a trip north LaBarge might lose his stomach for those waters and be only too happy to turn the ship over to him.

Jean LaBarge smiled as his eyes followed Kohl's broad shoulders down the dock, then he turned to watch the crane swing shoreward with several bales of hides. As it swung in to the dock he saw one of the bales slip, realized instantly it was improperly slung, knew the whole load was going to fall. At that moment a young woman stepped around a pile of lumber directly into the path of the sling. The crane jerked and the bales broke loose and there was a shout of warning from the lighter, but Jean was already moving.

Scooping the girl into his arms he lunged for safety. One of the bales struck him a glancing blow that sent them both rolling. The bales of furs tumbled to the dock, and Jean sat up, shaken by his fall.

The girl sat beside him, flushed and angry. The scarf that bound her hair had come loose and the wind blew a strand of dark hair across her face. Angrily, she brushed it away, glaring at him. She was younger than he had first thought, and uncommonly pretty. At that moment, her face flushed and her hair blowing, she looked . . . he leaned over and kissed her full on the lips.

For an instant, startled, she stared at him. Then her lips tightened and she drew back her hand to slap him, but he rolled swiftly away and got to his feet, grinning. He offered his hand.

She took his hand and he drew her to her feet, and when she was standing properly she slapped him. There was a whoop of laughter from one of the men on the dock and Jean LaBarge turned. His hat had been knocked off by the fall and his dark hair fell over his brow. "If the man who laughed will step out here," he invited, "I'll break his jaw."

Nobody moved, all the faces looked equally innocent, and carefully they avoided each other's eyes.

The girl was brushing a few slivers of the dock from her clothing, "Ma'am," he said apologetically, "you were in the way of being hit by those bales, and—"

She straightened to her full height, her chin lifted. Coolly, imperiously, she said, "I have asked for no explanation, and I expect no comment. You may go."

He was puzzled. "Sure," he agreed doubtfully, "but if you'll accept a suggestion you'll take a carriage. This is no place for a woman to walk without an escort."

Her eyes straight ahead, she said quietly, "You may call a carriage."

Gathering the folds of her skirt, her chin lifted, looking neither right nor left, she walked to the edge of the street. Jean glanced at her profile, so perfectly carved, and her hair, rumpled now, showing dark from beneath her scarf. When the carriage for which he signaled drew up before them she disdained his offered hand and got into the carriage and drove off without a backward glance.

He stood alone on the edge of the street, staring after her. She had spoken with an accent faintly foreign. He knew of no woman, even in this town of San Francisco, who dressed so well. There was some vague difference in her manner, some inner poise and awareness that puzzled him. He turned his back on the street and walked slowly back to the growing stack of bales.

There was no reason why he should think of the girl, yet he did. He knew many girls, for in San Francisco a rising young man as tall, ruggedly handsome, and as well off as he was, was naturally an object of attention. He had kissed her strictly on impulse, but the more he thought of it the more he was glad that he had done it.

The black-hulled schooner was stern-to now, and looking along the line of her hull he sharpened his eyes with genuine pleasure. What a craft she would be for the fur trade! How easily she would slide through the water in those narrow channels to the north!

From the beginning both Hutchins and Jean had looked to the furs from the north for their business. They had supplied the mines with equipment as they had supplied ships, but they knew the fur industry was the coming thing.

Now, if ever, was the time to go. Rumors had been affecting the market, and he had an idea prices on fur were going to rise drastically. Just such stories as Kohl had told him were sure to have their effect.

Theoretically there were no restrictions on the trade with Russian America. Actually, the Russian American Company exercised complete control over Alaska and the coast islands; the authority of the Company was subject only to the Czar himself, and as they said in Sitka, "God's in his heaven and the Czar is far away." The governor of Siberia was a stockholder in the Company, and like most stockholders concerned only with profits. The Boston traders had cut deeply into those profits, with better offers for furs, and with ways that were generally more considerate of the natives.

The claim of the Russian American Company to

exclusive trading privileges in Alaska and the neighboring islands was a claim not many Americans were prepared to admit. The Boston men had been encroaching on the area for years just as the *promyshleniki*, those free-roving hunters and traders from Siberia, had been moving into Canadian or American territory when opportunity offered. Under Baranov, trading in the Russian-American area had been distinctly dangerous unless that trade was carried on with Baranov himself, then the government of Russia had interceded and opened Russian America to free trade. The ruling was still in effect, but it meant no more to the Company than many another, and they waged open war on all who dared trade in their territories.

Restrictions of the Company, or even of a far-off Czar, had little effect on Americans, a people impatient of any restriction, and trade with the Pribilofs continued.

The seal islands did not interest Jean LaBarge. The risk was great for the profit involved, but the coastal islands were a veritable maze. Charts of the area were sketchy and inadequate and what knowledge of its waters existed was only in the memories of those shipmasters who had cruised the channels and traded in the islands, or among the Indians themselves.

With such a schooner as the one in the harbor a man might slip in and out of those channels with small chance of encountering a Russian patrol ship. The furs of the coast were excellent and Jean had made it his business to learn which villages were outlets for the furs of the interior. Tonight he would learn more. Tom Herndon's parties were a clearing-house for news. Whoever was somebody in San Francisco might be found there on Tuesday nights. Herndon's wife came from the Carolinas with southern ideas on entertaining, and with money enough to gratify her every whim, she entertained on the grand scale.

The face of the girl on the wharf kept forcing its way into Jean's thoughts. A connoisseur of accents, as everyone in San Francisco must eventually become, he could not place hers. There were many German and French settlers now, but her accent was not German or French. Suddenly, he remembered the square-rigger recently arrived in port. But what would a girl, and such a girl, be doing on a ship from Sitka? During the Russian occupation of Fort Ross there had been several girls of good family there, and others had visited with their husbands or fathers, but Fort Ross had been long abandoned.

Disturbingly, her face remained in his mind, and the feel of her body in his arms. There had been that brief instant when she rested, passive, in his arms, an instant when it seemed natural and right, as if she would always be there. When she had realized the situation she had straightened quickly away from him. Yet for that moment. . . .

The Herndon party was an hour old when Jean entered the crowded rooms. Hutchins was there, a tall, handsome man of soldierly bearing with a shock of pure white hair and a dignity few could match. Royle Weber was there, too, a small, fat man, very busy and very talkative, always gesturing and smiling. Weber was an agent for the Russian American Company, buying and selling for them locally. Perhaps, Jean suspected, a spy for them also. That might explain the disappearing ships.

As he was passing Sam Brannan, the latter stopped him. "We've been wanting to talk to you, LaBarge. We may need your help."

"Thanks, no. I appreciate the problem, but I'll skin my own cats."

"There is power in organization, LaBarge," Brannan said seriously. "Alone, a man is helpless."

"They've not bothered us so far."

Brannan nodded. "You've been fortunate. The hoodlums from Sydney Town are growing bolder every day."

From the beginning Sam Brannan had been one of the most intelligent and far-seeing citizens of the town, and one of the few willing to stand up to the Sydney Town thugs. He had been one of the original leaders of the first Vigilante organization, and it had been successful largely because of the men Brannan had selected, and because it had been no incoherent and hastily assembled mob. The men he had chosen were solid citizens as well as men of courage and integrity.

When LaBarge had passed them, Brannan turned to his companions and said, "If there's trouble again, I want him with us."

Charley Duane lifted his eyebrows. "Why? I've not seen any of his graveyards."

Brannan knew enough about Duane not to like him. "No? Next time try Nevada."

Royle Weber was emphatic with his nod of agreement. "I know the story, Charley. It was an attempted claim jumping, and two men lost out in a gun battle with LaBarge, but LaBarge didn't stop there. He went to town to see the man who sent them."

"And . . . ?"

"He sent *him* out of town—walking. He had only what he stood up in, and a broken arm."

Duane was thoughtful. His friends from Sydney Town had been wary of LaBarge, and this might be the reason.

"I hear he's growing wheat," Herndon commented.

"He bought property from you, didn't he, Sam?" Weber asked.

"I handled the sale. Yes, he's growing wheat, which more of us should be doing. He'll sell his crop this year for much more than many a miner will get from a claim. If you're doing business with them it isn't a good idea to underrate anything either Hutchins or LaBarge are doing."

Weber turned a cigar in his fingers, then bit off the end, his manner thoughtful. "What," he asked then, "is all this interest in Alaska? I hear he's forever asking questions about it."

"You'll have to ask him," Brannan replied shortly.

* * *

Jean LaBarge moved from group to group, pausing only briefly here and there. More than one pair of feminine eyes lingered on his broad shoulders and his dark, lean face with its high cheekbones and scar. His manner and dress was that of a gentleman, but his face was that of a pirate. He was carefully dressed: well-tailored suit, ruffled shirt and a black tie; but no matter how carefully he combed his hair it soon resumed its natural tumbled curliness. His boots were of Spanish leather, handmade. Turning away from the group where Hutchins stood, he came to an abrupt stop, audibly catching his breath.

Before him, wearing a satin evening gown surely from Paris, was the girl from the wharf . . . and as his eyes found her she turned slightly and saw him.

For an instant their eyes held, then moved away as if by agreement. Jean felt a queer excitement. His mouth was dry. He turned to answer some comment from Hutchins, and replied to the question without really knowing what he said. The man who stood beside the girl was tall, much older, with iron-gray hair and the thoughtful face of a scholar. There was something about his poise, his dignity that commanded attention. But it was the other man who immediately drew Jean's attention so that he scarcely noticed Royle Weber, who stood between them.

He was an inch taller than Jean's six feet two inches, as broad of shoulder as Jean himself and somewhat heavier in the body. His hair was blond clipped high on the sides and close-cropped on top. His eyes were gray-white and closely set. He carried himself with a military bearing; his white uniform coat was ablaze with decorations. His trousers were black with a thin white stripe down each leg and he wore black boots. Yet the insignia he wore, despite the uniform, was of the Navy. This could only be Baron Paul Zinnovy.

"Mr. LaBarge?" Weber spoke loudly. "May I present Count Alexander Rotcheff? You were asking about wheat, sir. Jean LaBarge is one of the few, these days, who think of planting. If anyone will have wheat to sell, it will be Mr. LaBarge."

The older man bowed slightly. "It is good to know, Mr. LaBarge. It is the reason for our visit. We must have wheat at Sitka."

"Well, we have the wheat," Jean answered. At once his mind seized upon the idea. Wheat for Sitka? Free, unquestioned access to the islands? It was just what he had been hoping for, planning for. "I am sure we can reach an agreement."

Rotcheff turned to include the girl and the tall blond officer. "Mr. LaBarge? May I present my wife? And Baron Zinnovy, of the Imperial Russian Navy."

Some of his dismay must have been evident, for there was something in her eyes that responded to his . . . was it regret?

"Baron Zinnovy," Rotcheff continued, "is in command of the patrol ships at Sitka."

"To a dealer in wheat that will not be important.

If Mr. LaBarge dealt in fur it might be very important indeed."

Jean smiled, but his eyes held a challenge. "But I am a dealer in furs, Baron Zinnovy! Wheat is just a sideline with me. My real business is in fur. In fact, Captain Hutchins and myself are among the largest buyers of fur on the coast."

"No doubt," Zinnovy said, his voice arrogant, "you have bought many Russian skins. For the future, if I were you, I would put no trust in that source."

"Russian skins?" Jean furrowed his brow with exaggerated perplexity. "You have the advantage of me, Baron. I have taken the skins of fox, marten and mink, but so far I've never had to skin a Russian."

The girl laughed outright and Count Rotcheff smiled. "Let's hope you never do," he said agreeably. "There are furs enough for us all without our skinning each other. Don't you agree, Baron?"

"I think," Baron Zinnovy replied distinctly, "this merchant is insolent."

Count Rotcheff started to interrupt, obviously uncomfortable and hoping to turn the conversation. Jean spoke quickly.

"You use the term 'merchant,' " Jean said, "as if you considered it an insult. I think of it only as a compliment, for it was the merchant adventurers of the world who opened the roads and discovered continents and developed the riches of the earth while, if Count Rotcheff will forgive me, the titled lords were mainly concerned with waging petty wars or robbing priests and women."

Zinnovy's face was pale. Never had he been spoken to in this manner, and although he despised Count Rotcheff for his diplomacy and political views, to be openly insulted before him was insufferable.

"If we were not guests—"

"But we are!" Rotcheff interrupted sharply. "We are guests, Baron Zinnovy, and this visit is of great importance to our colony at Sitka. We can have no quarrels here."

Zinnovy bowed slightly, his eyes coldly furious. "I regret my haste, Count Rotcheff. As for Mr. LaBarge, I hope he makes no further attempts to open his merchant roads to Russian America."

Jean feigned surprise. "But Baron, you forget! Count Rotcheff has just been discussing a purchase of wheat. If he buys my wheat I'll have to deliver it."

"It will be a delivery I shall watch with interest." His cold gray-white eyes met Jean's. "Who knows but that we shall meet when neither is a guest of the other?"

"I'll look forward to it." Jean turned. "Countess . . ."

"The name," Rotcheff interposed, "is Princess. My wife is the Princess Helena de Gagarin, niece of His Majesty, the Czar of Russia."

"Oh . . . of the Czar?"

"And the niece of the Grand Duke Constantin also—you may have heard of him."

"A lot of us Americans admire the Grand Duke for his liberal views . . . naturally, they would be popular here."

"If you approve of the Grand Duke," Zinnovy suggested, "then you must approve the policies of Muraviev?"

"If he were an American I might approve. As he is a Russian, I do not."

"You approve his territorial claims against China? As you might approve of your own government if they laid claim to Russian America?"

Jean shrugged. "I don't know anything about statecraft, Baron, but I have heard of no claims made by the United States on Alaska. As to purchase, that is another thing. We might be interested in that question."

Count Rotcheff studied Jean more carefully. This young American was no fool . . . or did he speak with information of some sort? There had been talk in St. Petersburg of a bargain with the United States. It was most interesting that it should be mentioned here.

Rotcheff had been listening to the discussion with irritation. The Russian colony at Sitka was dependent on foodstuffs from California and Hawaii for its very existence. Russian ships were received without undue warmth and any dispute might bring an end to trading; the success of his own mission depended on friendship with the business interests of San Francisco. He seized the moment to change the subject. "My wife is very interested in your country, Mr. LaBarge, and I would be honored if you could show her something of the state outside the city."

Rotcheff led Zinnovy aside, anxious to break up the circle and avoid a discussion that could lead to trouble. The music started and Jean led Helena de Gagarin out on the floor. For a time they danced without speaking, each content with their own thoughts. She danced lightly, gracefully, moving easily to the waltz. And he could only think that being a princess as well as a wife she was doubly lost to him.

The thought brought irritated amusement to his eyes: he had never before thought of a woman in terms of marriage, and now he had chosen someone as remote as a star. Yet he had never seen a woman so beautiful and desirable.

She looked up at him. "You've not said you were sorry."

"That you're married? Of course I'm sorry."

"I did not mean that. I meant for what happened on the wharf."

He grinned cheerfully. "Sorry? I'm not a bit sorry. I liked it!"

Late that night, Jean LaBarge climbed the stairs to his rooms and opened the door. He felt gay and more excited than he could remember, and although it was two o'clock in the morning he was not in the least sleepy. All the way home through the poorly lighted streets he had thought of nothing but Helena. Throwing off his coat he sailed his hat to the settee against the wall and as he lighted the lamp he glanced at the map that covered the wall.

Not even Captain Hutchins knew of his map. It was on canvas and was six feet wide by nine feet long, and it had been pieced together, bit by bit, fragment by fragment, for six years. It embodied information acquired from ship's masters, common seamen, hunters, trappers, traders and occasional Indians. Each day or so Jean added another bit of information to the map or checked something already there.

In his business of buying he had occasion to do much listening and to ask many questions, and most of the traders or mariners were eager enough to talk of their successes or discoveries. Yesterday he had added an inlet to the map, two days before it had been a rocky ridge with pine trees at the tip. Beside the map, on a small desk, was an open book. It was one of a number of such books, and each item of information on the map was also entered in the books, along with much more. Descriptions of landmarks, tides, currents, timber, people, customs, weapons and living conditions. Without doubt his knowledge of Russian America was greater than the knowledge of men who had lived there for years. Each of those who lived in Alaska knew their own area and perhaps a little more, but Jean LaBarge's books contained knowledge gleaned from thousands of men, and it was gathered by himself, who knew how to ask questions, how to make leading remarks, and who could ask those questions from a broad base of already acquired knowledge.

He knew the depth of water and best anchorage

in Yakutat Bay, the best place to anchor and trade on Kassan Island. He knew by name the Indian in each village who was the best trapper and therefore most likely to have furs. He knew each chief by name and reputation, and knew his relations with other tribes. He knew of a fine salmon stream that flowed into Humpbacked Bay, and of the waterfall about a half mile back from the beach. He knew the channels where tidal currents were most dangerous and where lay hidden rocks likely to rip the bottom from a ship.

Most of all he had made discreet inquiries about landlocked harbors, hidden channels, portages, and places likely to offer concealment from a patrol ship. Not one of the men to whom he talked knew very much, but in the aggregate they could tell him a great deal. No hunting story was too long to listen to, and any drunken trader or trapper found LaBarge a willing audience.

The few charts of the Sitka area were woefully inadequate, but he secured copies and studied them. No day passed that he did not review the information he had gathered, for it was not enough that he had it in books; all he had gathered must be in his own head. Only one other man knew of that map, and that man was Robert J. Walker.

After all these years, the two friends still occasionally corresponded, keeping track of each other's progress. Rob Walker's success continued to be striking. After his term in the Senate he had returned to his law practice, but always with a strong interest and influence in political circles.

Jean LaBarge knew that Walker's interest in Russian America was different from his own, which was strictly commercial. To Jean, the Alaska fur trade offered a great chance for wealth, and once the country was opened to American interests, there might be much more that could be done. He already knew of the gold; there was no way of guessing what else the cold land might ultimately yield.

Rob Walker thought of Alaska in terms of their childhood dreams, as another potential Louisiana Purchase. Jean LaBarge's view was simpler and more immediate: Alaska meant money and adventure. That was enough for him.

Now, after all his planning, it looked as if he would at last gain access to that northern land. If Rotcheff bought wheat from him he would himself transport it to Sitka or it would never leave the farm. It was for just this sort of opportunity that his wheat had been planted. True, he was always sure of a local market, but north was where his interest lay, and a cargo of wheat was a sure passage to Sitka.

This was his chance, and there must be no mistakes. A cargo of furs in San Francisco three months or even two months from now would bring premium prices, but he must be wary . . . Baron Zinnovy would be sure to keep him under his eyes. Yet much might happen in those northern fogs and that maze of channels. He must select the most likely places for a quick cargo of furs, slip in and out and then run for it, a fast voyage south, and—

He got up and paced the floor, considering tonnage, arms, trade goods.

His thoughts turned to Helena. He remembered the gray eyes, the dark hair drawn back, the quiet poise and beauty of her . . . he was a fool to waste thought on her, even for a moment. She belonged to another man. She was a niece of the Czar! Yet he did think of her, and he was not likely to stop thinking, for he was, he realized it suddenly, he was in love.

There was a light step on the stair outside his door. Jean dropped his hand to the pistol he always carried, and waited. The Sydney Town toughs had broken into more than one home, robbing and murdering as they would. Outside the door there was a creak, then a light tap. With his left hand, he opened the door. It was Barney Kohl.

He was grinning widely. "I think we've got it! I've bought us a schooner!"

8

———◦◦◦◦———

Count Alexander Rotcheff folded his *Alta Californian* and placed it neatly beside his plate. He was a tall old man, finely featured, with graying hair and a pointed beard. He glanced thoughtfully at his wife. Helena, he observed, was unusually quiet this morning.

Moreover, she was up earlier than usual. She seemed younger, somehow, and fresher. The ribbon around her hair was attractive, and he wondered absently how she would look with her hair disarranged, and decided the effect would be even more charming. If only he were a few years younger....

He sighed. Unfortunately some things did not comport with the dignity of an aging diplomat, courtier, and emissary of the Czar. It was a pity.

He smiled, remembering that some philosopher, he could not recall the name, had said that no wise man ever wished to be younger. Obviously the man who made such a remark had not seen Helena in the morning, fresh from the bath. And this morning there was a glow in her eyes as well as on her cheeks. A pensive glow.

Whatever else the years had taken from Count Rotcheff they had not taken his knowledge of women. His marriage had come late in life, and had been largely a matter of expediency, joining two powerful families in an even more powerful alliance. The marriage had served him well and had been successful in itself, beyond expectation, and that success had been due quite as much to Helena as to himself.

She had given him companionship, tenderness, and a well-managed home, she had given him intelligent understanding of his problems, approaching their life together with a maturity of judgment that would have been surprising in one of her years to any other person than Rotcheff. The Count, although this had been his first marriage, had successfully survived numerous less formal attachments, and had learned thereby. He was aware that it did not necessarily take years to make a woman practical, or experience to make her wise. To a fool time brings only age, not wisdom.

Helena's understanding of diplomacy and statecraft was scarcely less than his own, and it is a business in which a beautiful and intelligent wife is the greatest of assets. She had used her talents, her knowledge and connections to a superlative degree. She listened well. Men talk easily of their plans to a beautiful girl, and Helena had the faculty of making the most horrendous bore feel brilliant. What was even more important, she could remember what she heard, and no one could guide a conversation more skillfully without seeming to do so.

She was warm, lovely and exciting, yet beneath it there was steel. It was one thing, he reflected, to love a woman. It was quite another to admire her and respect her judgment. Yet he admired her most of all because she was successful at being a woman, she was always and forever feminine.

He tasted his coffee and found it too hot. Putting down his cup, he got out his pipe. That young man . . . what was his name again? LaBarge . . . Jean LaBarge. For an American he seemed uncommonly well informed. The other Americans he had met were absorbed in their own affairs, their own country to the exclusion of all else, knowing little of the problems of other countries and peoples. That was one of the benefits of being a secondary power, for it is only when a nation becomes a world power that it becomes imperative to understand other peoples or fail in its objectives. One rules by knowing. Russia had never learned and that was why Russia had always remained on the outer fringe of world affairs. England, France, Germany, and Spain, even Austria-Hungary and the Netherlands, all helped to shape the destiny of the world while Russia sat astride a great and integrated empire and was rarely consulted.

LaBarge had been correct, of course, in his comment on titles of nobility. Too often such a title was won by a man of energy and used thereafter to mask the indolence and complete uselessness of his descendants. In the United States a man could not rely on a family name to carry him through, although that unhappy time might come as it did to all aging countries. In his own Russia too many of the old families were producing effeminate, idle, and extravagant young men more preoccupied with fashion and gaming than with the destiny of their nation. He smiled ironically, realizing that none of this was true of his political opponent, Baron Zinnovy, nor of Muraviev of Siberia. Say what one might of them, they were able and dangerous men. And Zinnovy was basically more dangerous because he was a man without honor or conception of it. He lived to win, and cared not one whit how it was done nor who suffered from his actions.

It was a credit to LaBarge that he had faced Zinnovy so calmly. Not many either could or would dare to do so.

"I believe," he commented aloud, "the Baron would have challenged LaBarge in another minute. I have never known him to anger so quickly."

"What do you think of him?"

Rotcheff put down his pipe, smiling to realize that they both understood of whom she was asking. "LaBarge? A damnably handsome man, and an able one, I'd say."

There was something about that lean, dark face with its scar that sent a thrill of excitement through her. The way he had looked at her!—she flushed at the thought. But she had been most impressed by the confidence with which he replied to Zinnovy. "He is a dangerous man," she said thoughtfully, "and a man who knows where he is going."

Something prompted Rotcheff to say, "Dangerous to Zinnovy, you mean? Or to me?"

"You?" She looked up quickly, then gathering his intent, she blushed again. "No one is dangerous to you, my love."

He was embarrassed. "I am sorry." He waved a hand, dismissing the comment. "I had no reason to say that. Only, he is very handsome, such a man as any woman would notice."

"I did not believe you saw such things."

Rotcheff laughed lightly. "When a man has a beautiful wife he had damned well better!" Dropping the bantering tone he added, "He can help us. Weber informed me that the wheat LaBarge has to sell is the only wheat available."

"He will bring it to Sitka?"

"I doubt if other ships will be available. We have no real right to trade here, you know."

Rotcheff drank his coffee and smoked, the paper at one side. There was more to his trip than even Baron Zinnovy guessed. Reports had reached St. Petersburg that the Company was victimizing the natives, inflicting many cruelties upon them and hesitating at nothing in their grab for profits. If these rumors were proved true then the charter of the Company would not be renewed, nor would another charter be granted.

Alaska had long represented a problem to Russia, lying outside the continental limits as it did. Russia was a land rather than a sea power. War would leave Alaska exposed to seizure, and it was well known that Great Britain looked upon Russian

America with acquisitive eyes. If war with Britain and France should again develop Alaska would be vulnerable and its loss a serious blow to Russian prestige in the Far East.

Rotcheff believed as did the Grand Duke that it was better to sell Alaska than risk its loss with the accompanying loss of face. And he knew California might be just the place to lay the groundwork for such a sale. There were men here accustomed to thinking on the grand scale; to men who have crossed a continent, won a state, and ripped open the earth for gold, the buying of Alaska would present no great problem.

LaBarge . . . the man might actually be a government agent. No, he was thinking like a Russian again. The Americans were naïve, something only time would cure, time and some great hurt. As yet they were unaccustomed to intrigue on the great scale. All but that man Franklin; too bad he was dead. The old Quaker had been a master in the field, perhaps the equal of Metternich. But in general American diplomatic success had so far been largely due to their bluntness of manner and the obviousness of their motives. It was a method calculated to cause the more subtle Europeans to suspect them of hidden objectives.

It would be wise to talk to that young man again, even at the risk—he glanced at Helena—but it was no risk. The cynics said a man was a fool to trust a woman. Perhaps. Yet he trusted her.

"My husband?"

"Yes?"

"Be careful of the Baron. I have a feeling he knows why you are here, and that he has been sent here for the express purpose of defeating you."

"You could be right." He pushed his empty cup away. "Helena, I wish you would arrange for me to talk to that young man . . . in private."

She was thoughtful. "Alexander, does it strike you at all that it might be significant that he owns wheat? The only wheat available?"

He glanced at her curiously. "What do you mean?"

"I am foolish, of course. But in a place where all seem to think of seeking gold or raising cattle it is surprising to find a man growing wheat on such a scale. And such a man. Suppose he wished to make a trip to Alaska? He must know that we buy supplies both here and in Hawaii, and what better way to come to Alaska unsuspected?"

Rotcheff rubbed his chin. Helena was thinking in European terms herself. On the other hand, in the case of LaBarge it might be the right way. "Are you merely surmising?" he suggested. "Or have you something on which to base this feeling?"

"Mrs. Herndon told me her husband tried to buy wheat from Mr. LaBarge, and he would not sell. And the offered price was good."

"I see . . . of course, as he himself said, he is in the fur trade."

"To let his wheat be wasted? No, I think he had other reasons. He might be saving his wheat for a wedge."

It was easy to understand a man who wanted something. Those were the obvious ones with whom it was simplest to deal. It was the idealists who worried him. He said as much.

"What of the idealists who pursue profits along with their ideals?"

"They are worst of all," Rotcheff said. "The worst to deal with, I mean. They drive a hard bargain."

LaBarge might be just such a man, but the only fact they possessed was that he was a fur trader, and without doubt there was fur in Russian America. That was motivation enough.

"Mrs. Herndon was telling me that Jean LaBarge has an obsession: he asks questions about Alaska."

"She told you that?"

"It's common knowledge. And there is something else. Mr. LaBarge has a very old friend with whom he corresponds, a former senator named Robert J. Walker."

The Count was pleased—pleased to have the information, pleased with his wife for discovering it, and pleased at finding here in America what seemed to be some genuine European duplicity. This innocent young man, who looked like a professional duelist and who bought furs, this young man was an associate of one of America's ablest politicians.

"You know the name?"

"Robert Walker," Rotcheff said quietly, "is one of the least appreciated of American statesmen, but one of the most able and tireless."

"Mrs. Herndon said he was no longer in office."

"My dear"—Rotcheff filled his coffee cup again—"such a man is never out of office. Once tarred with that brush they are never free of it. I've no doubt that politics is Mr. Walker's lifeblood, and his country is his life." He chuckled. "It pleases me that our young friend is not so naïve as one might suspect."

"It may be a coincidence."

"He has wheat which he will not sell to a friend, but will sell to Alaska. He has a political friend to whom he writes. He asks questions about Alaska, and he has a friend who would gladly see the Yankee flag flying over the whole continent. I think, Helena, this young man may help us. He may help us very much indeed."

9

Jackson and Kearney Streets met at an intersection known locally as Murderers' Corner. The Opera Comique faced Denny O'Brien's Saloon across this corner and there was but little to choose between them. The saloon was the hangout for Sydney Town hoodlums and later for those toughs known as the Barbary Coast Rangers. It was burned and rebuilt with few added features and no change in clientele. In the cellar beneath the saloon were other forms of entertainment than the usual drinking and gambling. In a pit situated in its center dogs were fought against each other or a variety of other animals. A man who had a job to be done by tough men could be sure of finding them at O'Brien's.

On the Tuesday following the meeting between LaBarge and Zinnovy, three men sat at an inconspicuous table in O'Brien's. Charley Duane, Royle Weber and the Baron Zinnovy had scarcely seated themselves when O'Brien himself appeared. Weber and Duane he knew very well, especially Duane who was a fixer, a politician, and a man with a hand in a number of illegal pies. These two were enough of a magnet; but the elegantly cut clothing of the Baron smelled of money, an odor calculated to draw immediate attention from Denny O'Brien. He went to the table rubbing his fat hands on his vest front. "Somethin' for you, gents?"

"A bottle of Madeira," Zinnovy said. He measured O'Brien with his cold eyes.

O'Brien smiled. "Yes, *sir!* We have just what you want. We cater to all tastes an' kinds, don't we, Mr. Duane?"

He brought the wine and the glasses himself and lingered over the decanting, for Denny O'Brien was a knowing man and these three had not come here without a reason. O'Brien had had his dealings with Duane and Weber. He was, after all, known to them both as a man who could be counted on to deliver five hundred votes at election time, provided several of the boys repeated their voting. He could also be counted upon to deliver almost anything else.

O'Brien leaned his fat hands on the table. "Girls, maybe? Got any kind you want. You just name it, and—"

"No," Duane came to the point. "We want to talk to Woolley Kearney."

O'Brien did some fast thinking. Kearney was a former Australian convict who made his boast that he could whip any man alive in a brawl. He had killed a fellow prisoner, then killed a guard in escaping, and in San Francisco he had killed at least one man publicly, with his fists. If it was Kearney they wanted it was a beating somebody was to get.

Kearney would hog all the money and O'Brien would never see a red cent of it. "Kearney?" he said doubtfully. "The man's not been seen around, last few days." He lowered his voice. "Who be the gent you want called upon? I know just the lads for it."

Weber shifted in his seat. He was sweating a little. Duane glanced at Zinnovy and the Baron shrugged. "It will be Jean LaBarge."

Zinnovy was surprised at O'Brien's sudden change of expression. The saloonkeeper drew back a little and touched a tongue to his lips. "LaBarge, is it? You'd want Wool Kearney, all right. Or maybe three of my boys."

"Three?" Zinnovy lifted an eyebrow.

"He's a skookum man, that LaBarge. Most of those about town will have no part of him, but I know three lads who'll do just the job for you, and no kickback."

Zinnovy's eyes were chilled. "If there *is* a kickback, as you phrase it," he said quietly, "I'll have you shot."

Startled, O'Brien looked at Zinnovy again. The man was not joking. "Is it a beating you'll be wanting?" he asked.

"I want him out of business for a while." Zinnovy did his own talking now. "A beating, but a broken arm or leg included. Also, I want the warehouse that holds his wheat burned to the ground."

O'Brien hesitated. "It will cost you one thousand dollars," he said at last.

Baron Zinnovy looked up, his gray eyes showing no interest. "You will be paid five hundred. If

LaBarge gets a very severe beating, five hundred more. If the warehouse is destroyed, another five hundred."

O'Brien took a long breath. "It'll be done tomorrow night."

Zinnovy pushed a small sack across the table. It tinkled slightly as O'Brien's fat hand closed over it. "See to it," Zinnovy ordered.

Duane lingered as they started for the door, and whispered, "Don't slip up. He isn't playing games."

"When did I fail, Charley? Ask yourself that—when did I fail?"

10

Captain Hutchins stood at the window of the small office above the warehouse. It was late afternoon and a dismal, rainy day. Now, for a few minutes, the rain had ceased and the waterfront lay wet and silent. The sea in the harbor was a dull gray and the hulls of the vessels had turned black. Here and there a few anchor lights had appeared. There were two windows in the office, and the one at which Hutchins stood, hands clasped behind his back, looked out over the edge of the dock and the bay. The other window looked across the street and up the length of the dock to where the shore curved away into distance. The office held little furniture. A roll-top desk, a swivel chair, a bank of pigeon-holes on the wall, each stuffed with invoices or receipts, a black leather settee and two captain's chairs, very worn.

From the window there was nobody in sight but a tall man who stood looking out over the water, yet several times he turned and glanced back at the warehouse. Hutchins frowned. In a city practically ruled by hoodlums such a fact was not to be overlooked. Behind him, Jean was outlining his plan for the trip north.

The man at the dock edge turned again and for the first time Hutchins got a brief glimpse of his face. "Jean, do you know Freel? The fellow who hangs out with Yankee Sullivan?"

"I know him."

"What would he be doing on the dock at this hour?"

LaBarge got up and walked toward the window. Freel, one of the Sydney Ducks, was known to him as a thoroughly vicious character, figuring in a number of knifings and assaults. He stepped closer to the window and noticed a flicker of movement farther up the waterfront. After a moment he saw that two men stood in the shadows near a darkened warehouse about a block away. "He's not wasting his time looking at sunsets. He's got something else on his mind."

"They've left us alone so far."

Jean walked back to the center of the room and drew his pistol, checking the loads. "If they start trouble, Cap, I'm taking it to them. We've been lucky so far, but if they start it—"

"That's quite an order, son."

"Coyotes run yellow in the pack. I've hunted them before."

He turned to his lists. Spare sails, heavy cable, lines. He had never done this for a ship of his own, and it was a wonderful feeling. Item by item he went down the list. The heavy gear was his own idea. Kohl had questioned the usefulness of the heavy blocks and wire rope, but Jean had been adamant. What lay before them they could guess, but there was always the unexpected, and they might need to make repairs somewhere in those strange channels to the north. He wanted to be prepared for any emergency. And if a man had enough blocks and tackle he could move the world.

The men on the dock came briefly to mind. Ben Turk and Larsen would be staying in the warehouse, and neither was a man to back up from trouble.

"It's late, Jean, and that work will keep."

"Are they still out there?"

"Yes."

The door opened and Larsen came in, followed by Ben Turk. Larsen was a rawboned Swede with thick blond hair that fell over his brow and curled over his collar at the back of his neck. His shoulders and arms were massive and blue anchors were tattooed at the base of thumb and forefinger of each hand. Ben Turk was a man of slight build, a compact and swarthy man with a black, handle-bar mustache. He was lean, alert, and dangerous. He had served on whaling ships and had made three voyages to the sealing grounds of the Pribilofs. He had trapped in Canada and Oregon.

"Where's Noble?"

"He's strutting it around Bartlett Freel, trying to egg him into a fight."

"Get him in here."

Briefly, he gave them their instructions. One was to keep awake at all times. Hutchins' carriage came and Jean walked to the door with him. Hutchins hesitated with a foot on the step. "Sure you won't come with me?"

"Later." LaBarge glance at Freel who was looking unconcernedly across the bay. "I'll walk up." He deliberately spoke loud enough for Freel to hear. If Freel wanted him he wanted him to know exactly where he could be found, but if Freel followed Hutchins, LaBarge could be right behind.

There was nothing reckless about Jean LaBarge. He avoided trouble when he could, never sought out a fight until the proper moment for it. He considered the situation tactically. The men up the street, and there seemed to be two of them, were at least sixty yards away. Freel was close.

There are times when trouble cannot be avoided, and he knew that if they wanted him, they could get him. The thing to do was to choose his own ground, and he was ready now. The way to be left alone was to let them know what the alternative was.

He knew that Larsen, Turk and Noble would relish a fight. None of them had any love for Freel and his crowd, who frequently shanghaied and robbed seafaring men, but Jean did not want help. This was a situation he wanted to handle himself. He wanted it understood that he did not need help, even when it was ready to hand.

"You fellows sit tight," he told them when he was back inside. "Watch if you want to, but don't interfere. And stay inside."

"There's at least three of them out there." Turk looked at him curiously. "That Freel is bad with a knife."

LaBarge dropped his hand to the latch. Suddenly he felt very good. He felt better than he had for a long time. There was too much fear in San Francisco, too many people were afraid of the hoodlums, of their beatings, their murders, of their looting. "Just stay out of it, boys. This one's my show." He pulled the door shut after him, and stood on the dock.

The edge of the wharf was perhaps fifteen steps from the door of Hutchins & Company. And Bartlett Freel was standing over there under a dock light. A light rain was falling, a fine mistlike rain. The hour was not late but due to the clouds it was already dark. There was a faint light showing from the front window of the warehouse, and besides the light under which Freel stood, there was another light on the street corner a dozen yards away, and there was light up the dock, perhaps a hundred yards off.

Obviously they would not attack near the warehouse where help waited, but would follow him up the street into the darkness. They would have no reason to doubt their success and little reason to expect retaliation, and certainly there was nothing to fear from the law or the corrupt political machine behind it. Since the Vigilante movement the town had shown little disposition to fight back.

Without too much reason Jean decided the attack had been instigated by Baron Zinnovy. Freel moved to the dictates of Yankee Sullivan who was a henchman and friend of Denny O'Brien, and O'Brien was a man who would arrange beatings, murders, disappearances for a price. Neither LaBarge nor Hutchins had had trouble with the hoodlums, neither had antagonized any of them, and neither had any local enemies. The attack that he could see shaping up came immediately following his trouble with Baron Zinnovy. True, there had been only a few words passed between them, but Jean's hunch was that Zinnovy had other motives. Suppose Zinnovy, for reasons of his own, did not want wheat shipped to Alaska? Or did not want Jean LaBarge taking it there.

As Jean LaBarge moved away from the building Freel turned. Up the street the two men started to move; Jean heard a foot scrape up there in the darkness.

The reading of Greek history might seem a dull occupation, but there is an axiom to be found there that suggests the military principle of "divide and conquer." It was a good thought . . . Jean started for the corner and when Freel moved to follow Jean turned quickly and faced him, his hand gripping his left lapel.

"Looking for me, Freel? The name is LaBarge. Jean LaBarge."

Freel hesitated. Why didn't those fools *hurry*? "And if I am?"

"Who sent you, Freel?"

Bartlett Freel was a lean, savage man, surly even among those who knew him best, but more intelligent than most of his kind. He had a flaring temper and he both envied and resented LaBarge. "You won't know," Freel said, "you'll never know. You been comin' it mighty big, and now—"

There was a time for words, but the other two men were coming swiftly now. LaBarge's left hand gripped his lapel lightly and when he struck he struck from that position and he stepped in with the punch. He felt Freel's nose crumple under the blow but before the man could even stagger, Jean hit him hard with his right fist.

The other men ran up. Grabbing Freel, who was badly hurt, Jean turned swiftly and threw him into their path. The nearest of the oncoming men tripped and fell and Jean kicked him in the head, and the second man, holding a knife low down in his right hand, took the moment to move in.

Jean struck swiftly with the barrel of his pistol, hastily drawn. The descending weapon caught the knife-wrist and the knife clattered on the dock, the man dropping to his knees clutching a broken wrist.

The man he kicked was on his feet now but Jean had him stopped with the gun muzzle. "Can you swim?" Jean asked pleasantly.

"Huh?"

"I hope you can," LaBarge continued, "because you're jumping in."

"I'll be damned if—!"

"Jump." LaBarge spoke conversationally. "If you can't swim, you can drown, but don't try climbing back on this dock or I'll part your hair with a bullet."

"You won't get away with this!" The man was impotent with fury. "Yankee will—!"

"Jump . . . I'll talk to Yankee."

"He'll smash yer!" The man shouted from the dock edge. "He'll blind yer! He'll bash yer bloody fyce! He'll—"

The pistol lifted and drew a line on the man's head. The water would be cold but a grave was colder still. As Jean's arm straightened the fellow jumped.

There was a splash and then the floundering of a poor swimmer. Jean LaBarge turned and walked to the others. Freel was sitting up, trying to staunch the flow of blood from his nose. The knifeman clutched his broken wrist, moaning.

"Yankee shouldn't send boys to do a man's job," he said, and catching Freel by the coat he jerked him to his feet. Twisting him around, Jean began to go through the hoodlum's pockets.

Freel tried to pull away but Jean threatened him with the gun barrel. "You can take it standing still or lying on the dock with a split skull. Make up your mind."

"I'll stand," Freel said hoarsely.

There were several gold coins in his pockets, and the coins were Russian. Jean pocketed the lot, then went to the man with the broken wrist. "Yours, too."

"I ain't got a thing!" he protested. "They wasn't to pay me—"

"Stand up!"

Shakily, the man got to his feet. There were three gold coins in his pocket. The man began to curse bitterly.

"You didn't do the job," LaBarge told them. "I'll return these to Yankee."

"I wish you would!" Freel's voice was bitter. "I just wish you had the guts."

That area of San Francisco of the 1850's and 60's that lay back of Clark's Point was a hellhole of dives and brothels. Robbery was too frequent to warrant mention, and murder a nightly occurrence. To walk that area in safety one must be a pimp, a prostitute, or a thug, and along such streets as Pacific, Jackson, Washington, Davis, Drum, Front, Battery and East (the Embarcadero) moved some of the choicest rascals unhung. The shanghaiing of sailors was a major industry, engaged in by at least twenty gangs who worked in close association with keepers of brothels and cheap saloons.

Another closely allied gang was that which specialized in claim jumping within the city. The absent owner of a lot might return to find a thug in possession who enforced his point of possession with a pistol. Litigation was a long-drawn-out affair and more often than not decided in favor of the claim jumper. All of this Jean LaBarge knew and like most residents accepted it as part and parcel of a booming seaport with gold in the back country. Trouble had so far avoided him and he had avoided trouble.

Freel and his men had acted, without doubt, as directed by Yankee Sullivan. Now the lads of Sydney Town must be taught, once and for all, that action against Hutchins or himself would meet with immediate reprisal. One sign of weakness and they would be stripped of all they possessed. He could move against Denny O'Brien, but such a move would not be nearly so effective as against Sullivan himself.

Yankee Sullivan, born James Ambrose, in County Cork, Ireland, had grown up in the slums of East London. As a hard-fisted young Irishman in Whitechapel he won a reputation by defeating Jim Sykes, Tom Brady and a man named Sharpless in brutal bare-knuckle prize-ring battles. On a brief trip to the United States he defeated Pat Connor, then returned to England to whip the great Hammer Lane in nineteen grueling rounds. After a term in Australia as a convicted criminal he escaped and appeared in New York where he whipped Vic Hammond in fifteen minutes, fought his great fight with Bill Secor and beat him in sixty-seven rounds at Staten Island. He won four other fights and then was soundly beaten in his own saloon by Tom Hyer, son of a former heavyweight champion. However, this was a rough-and-tumble brawl, no more, and the unsatisfied Sullivan met Tom Hyer in a ring at Rock Point, Maryland, for ten thousand dollars as a side bet, and lost again. Later, a losing fight with John Morrissey, soon to be heavyweight champion, broke up in a riot after thirty-seven rounds.

Throughout this period Sullivan had been a criminal and an associate of criminals. In Sydney Town he carried an authority backed by his own malletlike fists and his former Limehouse and

Whitechapel associates. Whatever else he was, Yankee Sullivan was a first-class fighting man. Powerful, brutal, and without either scruples or mercy, there was no man in Sydney Town more influential than he. He was a known center of criminal activity.

Jean LaBarge had no doubts that the job he had set for himself would involve him in the most brutal fight he had known, yet the fighting of fur traders' rendezvous had been the dirtiest kind of rough-and-tumble fighting.

Opening the door of the warehouse, he stuck his head inside. "Slip a couple of pistols under your jacket and come along, Ben. We've a job to do."

Turk glanced at the men on the dock. "I'd say a job had been done. Will it take more?"

Denny O'Brien's was in full swing. At the bar were a dozen of the Sydney Town toughs, and among them Jean could see the massive shoulders and bull neck of Yankee Sullivan. He looked as invulnerable as a battleship. Also at the bar, talking to a sour-faced man in a stained canvas jacket, was Barney Kohl.

Ben Turk stopped beside the door and leaned against the jamb, a cigarette between his lips. A music box was jangling and somebody in a corner was singing an old sea chantey in a loud, off-key voice.

Jean LaBarge walked across the room and took Yankee Sullivan by the shoulder and spun him around. Yankee threw up a hand an instant too late. Jean hit him.

The blow was unexpected, and it had been years since anyone had tried to hit him outside a prize ring. He was stunned by that quite as much as by the punch. The man facing him was big, lean and tough-looking, his black eyes blazing. The blow slammed Sullivan against the bar and before he could get his hands up, LaBarge knocked him down.

In an instant they were surrounded by a milling, shouting mob. Jean drew back and gave Sullivan a chance to get up. It was foolish to give the man any break at all, and he would get none. At that instant there was a pistol shot.

Ben Turk had a gun in either hand and he was smiling. A thin thread of the smoke lifted from the left-hand gun. "Let 'em fight," he said. "If anybody interferes or gets between the fighters an' me, I'll kill him."

Sullivan got up slowly. He had been hit, and hit hard, harder than John Morrissey had hit him, harder than Tom Hyer. The man before him looked like a rough evening. Yet Yankee had whipped some tough men. He came up fast and went in, punching with both hands. Shorter than Jean, he was wider and thicker, and aside from his prize-ring skill he was a brutal barroom fighter.

As Sullivan attacked, Jean met him with a left to the mouth, and then struck again as Sullivan went under his left and hooked viciously to his ribs. They clinched and Sullivan back-heeled him to the floor, trying to fall on him and drive his knees into his belly. Jean rolled away and got swiftly to his feet and met Sullivan as he came in. The blow landed hard and Jean saw Sullivan go white around the eyes. Sullivan lunged, landed a glancing blow and Jean went under him, throwing Sullivan over his head to the floor.

This had won many a fight at Pierre's Hole but the Irishman had the agility of a boy. He had tucked his head under and taken the fall on his shoulder.

With blood streaking Sullivan's face they fought for several minutes, smashing, kneeing, gouging. Both men went down but neither could be kept down. Yankee's lips were puffy from stabs to the mouth and Jean had a swelling on his cheekbone half as large as an egg. He felt better. He could never really fight until he had been hit hard, and now he walked in, finding he could punch a little faster than Yankee. He feinted a side step and smashed the Irishman in the mouth with a right.

There was little sound but the heavy breathing of the fighting men, the dull smack of blows and an occasional grunt. For the first time the Sydney toughs were seeing their hero in a fight he might not win. There was something grim and terrible about LaBarge. Yet it was grueling and bitter. LaBarge's years of living in the forest and on ships stood him well now. He absorbed the punishment that came his way, hooked and smashed and heeled. Sullivan, boring in, thought he saw a good chance at Jean's chin and put all he had into a right-hand.

Something exploded in his mid-section and he grunted with pain as his knees buckled. Setting himself, LaBarge swung both hands at Sullivan's unprotected face. Sullivan swung a hand to wipe the blood from his face and Jean caught the wrist and with his other hand, grabbed Sullivan's wide leather belt. He bent one knee, turning slightly, then threw Sullivan bodily into the crowd. The fighter lit on his face and skidded with a jolt against the wall.

LaBarge's shirt was torn, revealing the powerful muscles of his arms and chest. He wiped a smear of sweat and blood from his face.

"I wanted no trouble," he said, "and he sent trouble to me." Jean LaBarge lifted a hand. "Ben!"

Turk slid a pistol behind his belt and tossed a bowie knife. Jean caught it in mid-air and faced the crowd. "Anybody else? I'll open any of you lads to the brisket if you want to back the Yankee's fight."

Nobody spoke. Jean held the knife low, cutting edge up. Somebody sighed and shifted his feet and LaBarge turned to Denny O'Brien. The saloon-keeper had never seen steel that looked so sharp, and he was a man who had seen many knives, and seen them used.

"I've a thought, Denny O'Brien, that you've taken some Russian money. Don't ever spend it, Denny, for I'll hear of it and have your heart out and lying on your own bar. You hear me, Denny?"

O'Brien swallowed, muttering something inaudible. Jean flipped the point of his knife . . . once, twice. Each move slashed a suspender and

O'Brien's trousers fell around his boots, yet he did not move, breathing hoarsely, knees trembling, his face yellow-sick. Sweat stood on his brow and cheeks, it dripped from his fat chin.

Jean continued to smile, a wolfish smile that turned O'Brien's insides to jelly. With flick after flick of the knife he took the buttons from O'Brien's waistcoat. It was a moment long-treasured on the coast, a story told many times in Sydney Town, and in the fo'c'sles of many a ship outward bound. It was a story men loved to hear, of the click of falling buttons and the sweat dripping from O'Brien's fat jowls.

"And Denny," LaBarge warned, "tell Charley Duane to be careful. Tell him if he crosses me again he'll be getting his tail in a crack. You hear me, Denny? You tell him that."

11

By noon of the following day the story of the battle at O'Brien's was being repeated in excited whispers in every boudoir on Rincon Hill, where the name of Jean LaBarge was well known in other fields of endeavor. At the Merchant's Exchange they could talk of nothing else, and the click of those falling vest buttons was heard wherever even two people happened to meet.

Count Rotcheff even found a brief reference to the fight in his *Alta Californian*. "Your friend LaBarge seems to possess a variety of talents," he suggested.

Helena looked up quickly. "The maid told me while I was having my bath." She paused. "She also told me something else. There is a rumor the original attack was paid for by a Russian."

Rotcheff rustled his paper angrily. "The man's a fool! Why would he get involved at a time like this?"

Helena put down her cup. "Do you actually believe he would do something of that kind merely because he was angry?"

"You think it was done because LaBarge was to

sell us wheat? But why would he do that? The wheat was for the Company."

"And we both know he is interested in a new charter, for another company."

He was too trusting—though not of foreign diplomats, only of his own countrymen. It was a fault from which all the Russian liberals suffered. Alexander knew how to cope with duplicity, but the Renaissance type of violence used by Paul Zinnovy was beyond the realm of his consideration; this Helena told herself. Her husband was a gentle man, and Paul Zinnovy was cold, efficient, deadly.

"Another thing," she warned, "you must yourself be careful. Paul wants two things: to get a charter for the new company and to return to St. Petersburg with a brilliant coup behind him. You stand in the way of both goals." She put her hand on his. "Alexander, you must be very careful! Your report can ruin him, and he knows it!"

Rotcheff shook his head. "You exaggerate, my dear. He would not dare use violence against anyone as close to the Czar as I am."

"You are a thousand miles or more from any Czarist official, you are many thousands of miles from St. Petersburg. Who is to know what happens out here?"

Somehow the idea had not occurred to him, yet instantly he saw that she was correct. He was far from the capital and no longer young, and accidents could be arranged. If he were murdered out here it would be months before the Czar even heard of it, and years before any investigation could be conducted to a conclusion. For the first time he was uneasy, less for himself than for Helena.

"Why, Alexander, was Paul Zinnovy sent here? Stop for a moment and think of that."

"He was in trouble"—Rotcheff was worried now—"and of course, he is a capable officer."

"Do you remember Paul's last duel? Rodion announced he was going to demand an investigation into some of the Company affairs, and three days before he was to appear before the Czar he was challenged to a duel by Zinnovy over some fancied slight. And Rodion was killed."

Rotcheff was silent. There was much to be said for Helena's interpretation of the situation although he was hesitant to admit that Paul Zinnovy might have been sent out for the express purpose of removing him. Three groups were involved in the affairs of Russian America. The Grand Duke's party, of which he was one, wanted to sell the territory of Alaska to the United States, if they could be induced to buy. The Russian American Company were bleeding the Indians white to pay dividends, but they were also bleeding their own stockholders and the government as well. The third group, of whom some were stockholders in the present company, wished to secure the lucrative charter for their own group who were establishing a new company with even greater dividends in prospect.

Suppose he were murdered by a drunken native? Or fell overboard in a storm? Or was suddenly taken ill? Who but Zinnovy would prepare the report? Even at Sitka, it would be Rudakof, who would do what Paul Zinnovy told him.

Count Rotcheff knew that if the investigation he was conducting brought out the evidence the liberal party believed it would, if it substantiated the complaints the government had received from parties in or visiting Russian America, then the Company's charter would not be renewed nor would another be granted.

"Helena," he said abruptly, "I believe you should return to St. Petersburg. If the situation is as serious as you believe, this is no place for you."

"On the contrary, it is all the more reason I should be with you." She glanced over her teacup. "Have you thought of Jean LaBarge? He might help us."

In his rooms, Jean sat over the books spread out on the table before him. He ran a finger over a small map, searching for Kootznahoo Inlet. He had checked all the reports of furs bought in San Francisco in the last four months and nothing had come from Kootznahoo. He listed it as a likely call, then added four more names to the list.

This first trip must be fast. The places he visited must be near the accepted route but where he could lie at anchor in concealment, and every stopping place must have more than one opening so that if discovered he could get out fast.

The deal for the schooner had been consummated, the rifles, ammunition and trade goods had been loaded. Kohl wasted no time, and the schooner was a tight, shipshape craft, easily handled and loaded. She would carry but one gun, and despite her strength and capacity she was a "light" ship with none of the bulky, overweight gear that characterized so many ships.

The sour-faced man who had been in the saloon at the time of the Sullivan fight appeared and was signed on as second mate, and the last two members of the crew were signed. Gant was a broad-built man, and Boyar was tall, stooped in the shoulders, and spoke fluent Russian.

Kohl looked at him without favor. "You a Russky?"

"I'm a Pole. But I worked for the Company."

Kohl turned to Jean. "Cap'n, you sure you want this man?"

LaBarge turned. "Take off your shirt, Shin."

Shin Boyar shucked off his shirt and turned his back for Kohl and Captain Hutchins to see. Scars lay like livid bands across his back, scars like twisted cords of white. Kohl glanced at them, then at Boyar's face.

"I served in the Navy under Zinnovy. That was ten years ago." The tall man pulled on his shirt. "I have a good memory, sir, a very good memory."

"We can use you," Kohl said.

"After that I was *promyshleniki* for the Company, and I smuggled gold out of Siberia to China for a while. I was thrown into prison, but escaped."

"No argument," Kohl said. "You'll do."

"After Monday," LaBarge told Kohl, "I want the crew kept aboard. No more than two men ashore at any time, and ready to sail at a moment's notice.

When a man goes ashore, you know where he'll be, just which place. No last-minute delays."

When all were gone he concealed his invoices under a board behind a bookshelf. Then, finally, he wrote one of his rare letters to Rob Walker. He was, he told Rob, going to Alaska himself. When he came back—

Behind him there was a slight rustle. An envelope had been slipped beneath his door.

He ripped it open. From the feminine handwriting and perfume he knew at once who it must be.

Can you come to see us? It is important.
Helena

"Us" she wrote. She wanted him to come and see them both, but nonetheless, it was signed Helena.

He got up and walked to the window. Outside the street was empty and still. It was now Friday, and by Monday he wanted to be at sea, sailing north, and the master of his own ship. To Alaska . . . to Sitka.

They would be leaving soon, and he might even see them there.

He remembered how Helena had looked that first day, flustered, mussed, and angry. He grinned at the thought. And then how prim, with her lifted chin, her too precise English.

She was charming, and so lovely, and he was in love with her and it would do him no good at all. She was married, and to a good man, a man of her own kind, her own rank.

He was a fool. . . .

But on Monday there would be the sea, the wind and spray in his face, and beyond there the places where nobody would mind, and where at night in the lonely hours, watching the seas roll aft, he could remember or forget.

12

———◆———

The tawny slope of the hill lay before them, dull gold in the afternoon sun, and beyond the hill the blue Pacific waters rolled to the horizon. When the two riders reached the trail's end high above the waters, Jean drew rein and relaxed in the saddle.

It was their second ride in two days, and might be their last. When riding Jean wore a tight-fitting Spanish-style jacket of buckskin, fringed in the Indian manner. It molded itself against his wide shoulders and was, Helena decided, most becoming.

"You ride like a vaquero," she said.

He pushed his flat-crowned Spanish sombrero back on his head and hooked a knee around the saddle horn. Filling his pipe, he watched her profile against the sky. "What about the plans for Alaska?"

"It is really the Baron who interests you, isn't it?"

"Of course. But when Count Rotcheff leaves, you will leave."

"We have more reason to fear the Baron than you, Jean. He is our enemy also."

"But you are the niece of the Czar!"

"You know what they say? 'God's in His heaven and the Czar is far away.' "

Far out at sea a windjammer was beating in toward the Golden Gate, and they watched it for several minutes without speaking. There was intimacy in the silence, and it was such moments they had come to treasure above all else. There was no need to use words to build a fence about their emotions; during those long silences the barriers were down and something within each of them reached out to the other.

"You see, Jean, any investigation of what happens in Russian America would require a great deal of time. And any investigator they might send from Siberia would be corrupt, and whoever came from St. Petersburg would have to ask questions of the very people who have most to conceal. Paul has power even in St. Petersburg, Jean. Actually, he was sent out here because he was in trouble, but it is temporary only, a mild punishment, a means of keeping him out of the way for the time being. I believe he was sent here for other reasons as well. I believe his friends decided to accomplish two objectives with the one move. Get Paul Zinnovy out of the way of more severe punishment, but also place him where he could be of use to them."

She paused. "You know, in Russia he is considered very dangerous. He has killed several men in duels. And sometimes these duels are not exactly what they seem. Often it is not a case of offended honor but simply that some powerful person wishes to be rid of a man."

"Suppose," Jean suggested tentatively, "the charter is not renewed, nor another granted. What will become of Alaska then?"

"Who knows? It might be sold, but certainly not to England. Perhaps to the United States."

Jean lit his pipe, which had gone out. "I suppose it could be done if the negotiations were handled carefully. But it wouldn't be easy. There are a lot of Americans who think that Alaska's only a wasteland, not worth a penny."

The sailing ship was closer now, making slow time of it against the strong current and a wind that helped little. They watched the ship while the afternoon trailed away like distant smoke, fading slowly. Soon it would be dusk.

"You've never married, Jean? I wonder why?"

He swung his horse a little. "For a long time I couldn't find a girl I wanted, and when I did find her she was married to another man."

"But there must be others, Jean. You're very attractive, you know."

"Oh, I've known girls . . . here and there."

"You would lose your freedom, and a man like you should be free, free to fly far and high, like an eagle. A wife would tie you down, she would hold you."

"Maybe. It might not even be so bad. I've been alone all my life, never known a real home. If you want to find a man who will love his home, find a man who never had one."

"I should think a man would always long for freedom. It is hard, I'd think, for a man who has known freedom to give it up."

He watched the ship. "Hard? With the right woman most men will settle down easy enough. Oh, sure! They look at the geese flying south, or maybe some night their eyes will open into the darkness as they lie in bed beside their wives, and they'll lie awake in the darkness and remember how native drums sounded, or the surf along a rocky shore, or how the bells ring from the temples . . . but they stay where they are."

"Why?"

The ship was taking in sail now, approaching the passage gingerly, for many a fine ship had been wrecked in the Golden Gate.

"Because they've . . . accepted their destiny, I suppose. They might think about the great world outside, but they wouldn't trade it for home."

"Not you . . . I believe you would go."

"I'd be the easiest of all, Helena. I've never known a home, so even the faults would seem virtues to me. As for love, who doesn't want it? To love and be loved in return?"

"I think, Jean, you will find what you want."

"Will I, Helena?"

The sea was darker now. The last of the color was deepening reluctantly into darkness.

"We'd best be going back."

Swinging their horses they put the sea behind them. Jean's gelding tugged at the bit, eager to be running. Helena's mare started and then both horses were running. Over the tawny hillside, still faintly tinged by rose from the sun that had set, a hill that changed as their horses ran to an inverted bowl of burnished copper against which drummed the racing hoofs. Laughing together, they cantered down the long hill and something trailed off behind them like whispered laughter. Abruptly, as they rounded a bend, the city lay below them and a column of smoke lifted from the waterfront. Jean drew up sharply, standing in the stirrups.

"It's my wheat, Helena," he said. "They're burning my wheat. The warehouse is going and everything in it."

He touched the spurs to his horse. The gelding left the ground in a tremendous leap, and with Helena beside him they raced neck and neck down into the city and through the empty streets. Their hoofbeats echoed from the false-fronted buildings and thundered in the empty channels of the town, stripped of people by the demands of the fire.

Helena rode magnificently. Rounding a corner he caught the glow of reflected flames on her flushed cheeks and parted lips, and then they were running their horses down another chasm between buildings. As they thundered out upon the dock he knew this must have been a planned effort to destroy the wheat.

Squads of men with buckets were wetting down the buildings around, and two long bucket brigades were passing water from the bay to the fire. One engine was working its pump near the wharf, another in the street behind the warehouse, yet he saw at once the building was doomed.

Swinging down from the foam-flecked horse, he pushed through the crowd and saw Captain Hutchins shouting to Ben Turk above the crackle of flames. Close by, Larsen and Noble were busy with a bucket brigade.

"Anybody in there?"

"No . . . thank God!"

The roar of flames all but drowned the reply, and Jean watched his wheat go up in flames, the black smoke shutting out the stars and sending the dark banners of its anger streaking across the bay, shrouding the silent ship in sudden clouds, then whisking away to leave the ship standing, amazed at the sight before it.

There was no wind. Had there been wind the whole of the waterfront would have gone, and nothing could have saved Sydney Town or any part of the city back of Clark's Point. Yet no wind blew, and there was only the crackling flames beating their great red palms together above the bay's black water.

His first impulse was to find Zinnovy for a showdown, but this would lead to nothing and might close all doors to Russian America. Wheat was the answer. The importation of wheat into Sitka was obviously something Zinnovy wished to prevent, but it was also his own open sesame to the northern fur trade. Staring at the fire, he began to think.

Sutter had grown wheat but had none now. How about Oregon? Many farmers had settled in those fertile valleys and they would need bread. Despite its proximity less news reached California from Oregon than from Hawaii; still there was a chance. The settlers of Oregon were a more substantial lot than most Californians. There would be wheat there, there had to be wheat.

Swiftly, he pushed through the crowd, searching for Barney Kohl. When he found him Kohl was standing with the new second mate. "Tomorrow night," Jean said. "You sail tomorrow night."

"Without a cargo?"

"Fitzpatrick has some goods for Portland and has been looking for a vessel for a month. I don't care how you do it, but be loaded and under way by five tomorrow afternoon."

"If you say so," Kohl said. "Damn it, man. I was ready for Alaska. I was all ready."

"You'll go . . . but meet me in Portland first."

Oregon . . . Jean watched the wall of the warehouse fall in, saw the flames and the smoke puff up, saw the great smoldering ball of his wheat. Sparks showered upward. No need to think of that. What was done was done.

He went swiftly to his horse and swung into the saddle. "Helena"—he turned the gelding—"I'm taking you home. Tell Count Rotcheff he'll have his wheat in Sitka as promised. Tell him not to worry."

"But *how*?"

"Leave that to me." They were walking their horses away from the fire. "I wish I knew I'd see you again. I wish—"

"So do I," she said simply. "Oh, Jean! I do, I do!"

* * *

At the door of the house on Rincon Hill he helped her from the saddle and watched the boy lead the horse away. For a moment they stood together before the empty eyes of the dark building. He could hear her breathing, smell of the faint perfume she wore and which he would never forget. Together they looked back at the red glow of the dying fire. "It's been a good day," he said at last, "a good, good day."

"Even with that?" she gestured.

"Even with that."

He gathered the reins. If he looked into her eyes he knew he would take her into his arms, so hastily he stepped into the saddle. She took his hand briefly. "What is it they say here, Jean? *Vaya con dios?*" He felt the quick pressure of her fingers before she released them. "I say it now, Jean. Go with God. Go with God, Jean."

At his rooms he paused only a moment, throwing things into his saddlebags, packing some small bags of gold, filling a money belt. He took his rifle and his spare pistol, then for a long moment he stared at the map. He would not see that map for a long time.

There was a rush of feet on the stairs. Hand on his gun, he swung wide the door. It was Ben Turk.

"I knew it!" Ben was ready for the trail. "You're riding! I'm comin' along."

"I'll travel faster alone. You go to the schooner." He stuffed extra ammunition into the saddlebags.

"Nothing doing. I ride along or I quit. There's nowhere you can go that I can't."

Turk was a good man, a very good man, but . . . "All right. We leave our horses at the river landing. We're taking the first boat for Sacramento, and if you can't ride a thousand miles you'd best head for the schooner."

Ben Turk stared at him. "Mister LaBarge . . . Cap'n, you . . . you ain't goin' to ride to *Portland*?"

"It worries you?"

"There ain't no trail, Cap'n! The Modocs will kill a man as fast as look at him! That's outlaw country. Why, man—I'm comin' with you!"

"You're inviting yourself. You're a damn fool."

"Why, now." Ben chuckled. "I just figure we're a couple of damn fools."

The riverboat was already moving when they raced their horses onto the dock. Jean swung his horse alongside and tossed his saddlebags. Then, rifle in hand, he sprang for the boat's deck and lit, sprawling.

It was a bare four feet of jump, but both horse and boat were moving. Ben Turk hit the bulwark, caught it with his hands and swung himself over to the deck. Together they looked back. The fire was only a sullen red glow now.

McCellan yelled at them from the pilothouse. "Law after you, is it? I been expectin' it for years!"

"Shut up!" Jean yelled genially. "Get a move on this crate! I've business in Knight's Landing!"

"Turn in," he yelled. "I'll call you!"

The last thing Jean LaBarge recalled as sleep took possession was the pressure of Helena's hand, the expression on her face. He remembered how she had ridden beside him through the dark streets, how she had waited to be with him after he realized his wheat was destroyed, his hopes ruined. She had waited for him as a man's woman would, only she was another man's woman.

He opened his eyes. "Don't forget, Mac. Knight's Landing."

13

━━━◆━━━

A rough hand on his shoulder awakened him. Mac's florid face and blond handle-bar mustache bent over him. "Rise an' shine, boy. We're comin' up to the Landing now."

Ben was already on his feet rubbing the sleep from his eyes. Through the murky light the landing was visible, right ahead.

Jean LaBarge got to his feet and hitched his gun belt into position on his lean hips, then threw the saddlebags over his shoulder and took up his rifle. McClellan peered over his shoulder at him. "I hope you don't need those guns, boy."

"We'll have to be lucky."

If anyone had ridden the route they were to follow LaBarge was unaware of it. There would be settlers here and there and a trail of sorts, but it would be sheer luck if they got through without fighting.

Thirty minutes later they rode out of Knight's Landing headed north. The day was bright and clear, the horses eager. A few hours from now they would be less eager, Jean reflected, yet the horses proved gamer than he expected and it was almost midnight when they sighted a fire ahead of them. As was the custom of the country they drew up and hailed before approaching.

A shadow moved but for an instant there was silence, then a cautious voice called, "What do you want?"

"Name's LaBarge. We're hunting a couple of fast horses. Can you help us?"

Walking their horses into the firelight they waited. There was a wagon here, and a small camp, such a camp and wagon no outlaw would be expected to have. Six head of mules were in sight and some good-looking saddle stock.

Two men, both armed and spread wide apart, emerged from the shadows. At the edge of the brush LaBarge could see two women who no doubt believed themselves concealed in shadows.

"You ridin' from the law?"

"No." LaBarge got down on the far side of his horse. A man could shoot better from the ground and there was no telling what might happen. "But we need horses mighty bad."

The bearded man was a thin, high-shouldered fellow in torn shirt and homespun jeans, but he looked like a man who could use the rifle he carried. He sized up their horses with shrewd, appraising eyes. "Reckon I'll swap. You got boot to offer?"

"Look, friend," Jean smiled, "we want horses, but not that bad. I'll trade our horses for that Roman-nosed buckskin and the gray. You can throw in a couple of sandwiches and some coffee."

The man glanced at the horses, both fine animals. "I reckon it's a trade. Sal"—he looked toward the woods—"fetch these men some supper."

While Ben switched saddles, Jean faced the fire and the two men. The bearded man had been studying Jean's expensive boots and drawing conclusions. The boy could be no more than half-witted and the women were hard-faced.

The coffee was black as midnight and scalding hot, and the sandwiches were slabs of bread inclosing hunks of beef.

"Anybody comes along," the man suggested slyly, "what should I say?"

Jean grinned at him. "Tell 'em you saw two men nine feet tall riding north with fire in their eyes. Or tell 'em whatever you want. If anybody was chasin' us, we'd stop an' wait for the fun, wouldn't we, Ben?"

"Those who know us well enough to come after us," Ben agreed, "are too smart to try."

Ten hours out of Sacramento, they rode into Red Bluff, and ten minutes later rode out again, their extra saddlebags stuffed with food. Twenty-five miles farther they stopped at a lonely cabin for coffee and when they rode out they were astride two paint Indian ponies.

The air was cool and damp. Twice they glimpsed campfires but their horses seemed no more tired than at the start and they pushed on farther into the night. Once a dog rushed out to bark, amazed and angry that anybody should be moving at all. The night air, cool as a freshwater lake, washed them as they dipped into a hollow of the hills, and then for twenty miles they saw no one, nor any human sound save their own.

At daylight, for forty dollars, Jean swapped for a black stallion with three white stockings and a trim bay gelding. The stallion had an edge on his temper but distance robbed him of his urge for trouble.

They were climbing steadily through country where they saw few houses and no settlements. Before them and on their right was Mount Shasta, sending chill winds down across the low country, winds that blew off the white, white snows of her peak.

This was Modoc country and they rode with rifles across their saddlebows. The Modocs had been slave traders among the Indians long before the coming of the white man. At nightfall they reached Tower House, beyond which point there was no road and little trail. At daybreak, on fresh horses, they were moving again. Glancing back, when farther along the trail, Jean saw a rider at the edge of the trees, and later after they had crossed a clearing, he watched long enough to see three riders come out of the trees, then swing back under cover.

"Look alive, Ben. Trouble coming up behind."

A dim trail suddenly turned into the trees, a trail that by its direction might intersect with their own somewhere beyond the valley. They turned off, then obliterated their tracks as best they could in the few minutes they could afford and rode down through the forest. When their path turned off in a wrong direction they cut through the trees until they reached the main north-south trail once more.

At Callahan's they switched horses again, and Jean found himself with a tough line-back dun. Taking the old Applegate wagon road, they reached the mining village of Yreka just seventy hours of Knight's Landing.

Putting their horses up at the livery stable, Ben nudged Jean. "Look," he said, low-voiced.

Two men were riding into town on blown horses, one wearing a short buffalo coat they remembered as worn by one of the men seen behind them on the trail. As they watched the third man rode into town and the three went along the street, examining all the horses.

Jean led the way into the saloon and they stood at the bar, cutting the dust from their throats and some of the chill from their bodies for the first time on the trip. At a casual question from the bartender, Jean explained, "Riding north, buying wheat for a ship that will meet us at Portland, and there are three men following us, hunting trouble."

A man in a dark suit standing near them, backed off. "Not my fight," he said.

Taking his drink, Jean motioned to Turk and they crossed to a table and sat down, facing the door. The bartender brought steaming white cups filled with coffee and, of all things, napkins. Jean slid his Navy pistol from his belt and laid it under his napkin. The other gun was in plain sight in his holster.

When the three men pushed through the door they glanced sharply at LaBarge and Turk, then walked to the bar. The three were obviously thieves, trailing them to rob and murder. No honest man ducked off a trail as they had. After a quick drink they turned and started out.

"You in the buffalo coat!"

The three stopped abruptly at Jean's call and turned slowly, spreading out a little as they turned. They could see the gun in LaBarge's holster. Ben's gun was belted high and out of view.

The last man in wore a fur cap, the one in the buffalo coat had a thin, scarred face. The third was short with a wide, expressionless face. "You talkin' to us?" he asked.

"You followed us out of Scott Valley, and you followed us into town. Now get this. If we see you anywhere close to us again, we'll kill you."

"G'wan!" he said irritably. "You ain't seen nobody! We ain't even goin' your way."

"How come you know which way we're going? Look, when I see men dodging in and out of the brush on my back trail I get suspicious, and when I get suspicious, I get irritable, and when I get irritable I'm liable to start shooting, so just to avoid trouble, stick around town a few days."

"We'll go where we like!" The man in the fur cap was growing red in the face. "We wasn't dodgin' in no bush, either!"

Jean smiled pleasantly. "And I say you're a liar!"

The man's face seemed to swell. "By God!" he shouted. "You can't call me a liar!"

"I just did," Jean replied coolly. He was determined to bring the matter to an issue now, on ground of his own choosing. "Furthermore, you're a couple of thieves." He took a wild gamble. "As for you," he looked right at the man in the fur cap, "you stole that red horse you're riding at Callahan's."

The man in the fur cap was a coward, but he could see Jean with a cup of coffee in his right hand, and Jean knew the instant he started to reach for his gun.

"You called me a liar!" he shouted. "And by the Lord—!"

The gun cleared leather as Jean shot. He fired with his left hand, from under the table. The man jerked sharply with the impact of the bullet and dropped his gun. He fell, rolling over on his side with his knees drawn up.

Ben Turk was on his feet, watching the man in the buffalo coat.

Jean gestured at the third man. "Take your hand off that gun. I never like to kill more than one man while I'm eating."

The fat man seemed about to speak but Jean interrupted. "Bad company for you, mister. They'll get you into trouble."

"I guess you're right."

The wounded man was cursing now, in a low, monotonous voice. Gingerly, the others picked him up and helped him from the room.

At the bar the man in the dark suit turned to face them. "That was mighty cool," he said to Jean. "I don't know whether I like it or not."

"I don't like dry-gulchers trailing me."

"We don't know they were dry-gulchers."

"You'll have to take my word for it, and if you have any thinking to do, do it quietly. I'm hungry."

At the bar there was subdued muttering and glances cast in their direction. More men drifted into the bar, but a difference of opinion was obvious. Jean knew there would be no chance to sleep here now. They must ride, and at once.

The man in the dark suit turned on them. "You two stay in town until we decide what to do about this, you hear?"

LaBarge got to his feet. "Listen to me, mister. You said before this wasn't your fight, so don't make it yours. Those men were trailing us to rob us, and if any of you want to keep us here, you just stand out in the street. In ten minutes we'll be riding out with our rifles across our saddlebows."

He paused, letting it sink in. "And, mister, if you feel lucky, you just try stopping us."

Ten minutes later, mounted on a horse loaned him by Charley Brastow of the stage company, Jean LaBarge rode out of town with Ben Turk beside him. The man in the dark suit stood on the steps of the saloon chewing on a cigar, several men around him, but he made no move.

"I seen them come in," Brastow had said, "an' I can smell a bad one further'n most. They sized up your horses and asked where you went."

He looked over their horses. "I'll credit you with fifty apiece for the horses and you can leave mine at Johnson's Camp on Hungry Creek. Tell him you're to have the two grays."

Johnson met them at the corral as they rode up. He was a tall man with no chin and he came from his clumsily built log cabin on the run.

"Get the grays for us, will you? Brastow said we were to have them. We're riding on to Portland."

Johnson's Adam's apple bobbed against his frayed collar. "That's crazy, stranger! Pure dee crazy! Them Modocs killed a trapper up the crick yestiddy, and burned a couple of farms! Mister, you two wouldn't have a chance against 'em!"

Jean took a rope from the corral post and shook out a loop. One of the grays shied but he swung his loop and made an easy catch. Both were magnificent horses, and as he roped them, Ben stripped their gear from the others. Still protesting, Johnson watched them mount up and ride off.

Both men were dead tired. Their plan to sleep in Yreka had been blasted by impending trouble. Jean's eyelids felt thick and heavy, and he rode as did Ben, in a sort of stupor.

Hours later they were walking their horses along Bear Creek bottom when a bullet struck water ahead of them and whined away into the brush. Glancing around they saw five Modocs come out of the trees on their right rear, and fan out as they came down the meadow at a dead run, whooping shrilly.

"Make the first one count, Ben." Jean lifted his rifle and looked down the barrel. He was wide awake now. He took a long breath, let it out easy and tightened his finger on the trigger. The rifle jumped in his hands and the foremost Modoc fell face forward from his running horse. The report of Ben's rifle was only an instant behind his own, and a horse fell, spilling its rider.

Both men were using the Porter Percussion Turret rifle, .44 caliber, firing nine shots. Steadying himself, Jean fired twice more and saw Ben's second man swing away, clinging to his horse with only a mane-hold, his body slumped far forward. The Modocs drew off, two men gone, another wounded, and shaded their eyes after Jean and Ben Turk. Accustomed as they were only to single-shot rifles, the burst of firing was too much for them.

At Jacksonville they stopped for coffee and sandwiches, and an hour farther along they mounted a tree-covered knoll and caught an hour's sleep, trusting the horses to awaken them if Indians approached. Twice more they exchanged horses, giving up the grays with reluctance, knowing such horses were rare. They passed the place called Jump-Off Joe, and later, crossing Cow Creek, they saw more Indian signs. At Joe Knott's Tavern they exchanged horses again. After a meal and a short rest they pushed on.

An hour out of Knott's it began to rain and with less than two hundred miles to go they spotted a cabin, barn, and corrals. Beyond was some forty acres of stubble. They rode toward the cabin, hallooing their presence.

A man with yellow side-whiskers stood in the

door, rifle in hand. "Light an' set, strangers," he invited, "you're the first folks we seen in two weeks."

"Modocs are raiding," Jean explained, then jerked his head to indicate the stubble. "What was that . . . wheat?"

"Uh-huh."

"I'll buy it. How much have you?"

"Done sold it, mister. Feller name of Bonwit from Oregon City bought wheat all through here. Why, he must have upward of two thousand bushels headed for the Willamette."

A meal and thirty minutes later they stepped into the saddle. Bonwit of Oregon City was the man to see.

He was a stocky man in a store-bought suit and a cigar clamped in his hard mouth. His face was wide, his hair sparse and rumpled. He rolled his dead cigar in his jaws and spat into a brass spittoon. "I'll sell," he said flatly, "for cash!"

"I'll take two thousand bushels, delivered in Portland," LaBarge said, and began counting out the gold.

Bonwit rolled his cigar again and shot a glance at LaBarge from astonished eyes. "You carried that over the trail . . . just you two?"

"Part of the way we had Modocs with us."

They sold their horses in Portland and pocketed the money. They had ridden six hundred and sixty-five miles in one hundred and forty-four hours.

14

Baron Paul Zinnovy sat at his desk in a San Francisco hotel. The wheat had been destroyed but LaBarge had vanished, and it worried him. A close watch had been kept on the schooner until it sailed; LaBarge was not aboard.

He paced the floor, scowling. Rotcheff seemed willing to remain right here in San Francisco, and as long as he did so, he would be safe. He had his instructions as to Rotcheff but nothing could be done here. If Rotcheff was lost at sea farther north there would be no investigation but his own. Or at a landing on one of the lesser islands they might be attacked by the Kolush . . .

Officially, the Russian American Company was losing money, but actually a few key men were doing very well indeed between paying low prices to the *promyshleniki* and padding expenses in stockholders' reports. If Rotcheff succeeded in getting wheat to Sitka conditions would be alleviated and prices could no longer be held down.

It was dangerous to leave Rotcheff unwatched. There were Boston men here in San Francisco who could offer evidence on the cruelties of the Company, and Rotcheff could choose his own time to come north—perhaps one inopportune for Zinnovy.

None of his agents had learned anything of LaBarge. On the evening of the fire he had been seen riding with Helena de Gagarin, but had dropped off the world right after that, and whatever she knew she was keeping to herself. Without wheat, LaBarge could not really cause any serious trouble, and yet it was strange that he should have disappeared. Still, the thing to do was to take one thing at a time and the first was Rotcheff.

The *Susquehanna*, as Jean LaBarge had renamed the schooner, arrived in Portland only a few hours after he did. Knowing that if he reached Sitka before the Baron Zinnovy his chances would be greater to get the cargo of fur he wanted, he laid his course for Queen Charlotte Sound as soon as the last of the wheat was aboard.

Clearing the mouth of the Columbia with a cold wind kicking up whitecaps around them, the *Susquehanna* lay over on her side and took the bone in her teeth, pointing her bows into the cold northern seas as if anxious for the green water that lay ahead.

LaBarge, his wind-blown face wet with flying scud and spray, stood beside Larsen at the wheel, watching her move along under a full head of sail. His sea boots and oilskins were shining wet, the sky was gray and lowering with clouds, but the wind was good.

"How was the trip up the coast?"

"Flying fish sailing . . . it was good time."

"How about the Russian ship?"

"I think she go to sea soon. We see her loading stores."

He went below to study the charts again, glancing at Kohl asleep in his bunk, his body moving slightly to the roll of the schooner. If the wind held. . . .

Hours later when he came down to shake Kohl awake, the mate opened his eyes at once. "How is she?"

"Holding steady, and we're making knots." He took off his sou'wester. "She's raining a little, and we're catching some spray, but the wind is right. Just what the doctor ordered."

Kohl shrugged into a thick sweater. "You figuring on trouble in Sitka?"

"Not if we can get out before Zinnovy gets there. Sitka should be glad to see the wheat."

"What then?"

"We discharge as quickly as possible, stock with whatever we can get of food and water, then lay a course for Cross Sound. With luck we'll have our furs and be on our way south before Zinnovy can get his patrol boat to watching us."

"We'll be lucky to find furs that fast. There'll be ships ahead of us."

Jean grinned. "Don't worry about it. I know where there's furs to be had . . . plenty of them."

Kohl cocked an eye at him. "Seems to me you know a lot."

LaBarge shrugged. "I know enough. Listen, Barney, I hired you because you're one of the best men with a ship on the west coast. I hired your ability, all your knowledge, but this much I know. You may know things I don't about particular bits of this northwest coast, but I know more about the *whole* coast than any man alive. I've made it my business to know."

"That won't help if Zinnovy gets you."

"One thing at a time."

LaBarge rolled in his bunk. Outside the hull, just beyond his ear, he could hear the whispering wash of the sea, rustling by with its strange secrets, its untold tales. On deck the sky would be gray with the last of the day's light, and there would be phosphorous in the water. There would be no stars tonight, or if any, a mere glimpse between rifted clouds. Yet he was strangely content.

This was the world he wanted, this was the way. Sailing north in command of his own ship to trade along that coast that had so long held his thoughts.

Rising some hours later, Jean shrugged into a sweater and his oilskins and went topside. A pale-hearted moon hung above the fo'm'st and the sea rushed past in the half darkness. Spray blew against his face and he put out his tongue, tasting the salt.

Walking forward along the deck he watched the black, glistening water as the great waves rose and then slid away beneath the hull. Aft there was no sign of anything else upon the sea; they were a tiny microcosm, a little lost world of their own, moving upon the sea with their own heart beating in tune to the sea's great rhythm and the talking of the wind in the shrouds.

Far behind him there was a girl with green eyes and dark hair, a tall and regal girl who had walked beside him briefly, a girl who was not his and could never be his, yet a girl who held his heart now and would hold it always.

He walked aft and found Kohl, wide as a door in his bulky clothes, standing by the port rail.

"How does she go?"

"She's a dream ship, this one. If the Russkies get her, I'll shoot myself."

"See anything back there?"

"Once I thought I saw a light . . . probably a star."

For a long time Jean LaBarge watched the sea behind them, and saw nothing; if there was a ship back there it was almost certainly the square-rigger.

If Zinnovy was following him, would he have Helena aboard? Could that light Barney thought he had seen be hers?

Helena. He wished he could drive her out of his mind. Wanting her did no good. She belonged to somebody else, and that was that. He had never thought of himself as a lonely man before, but Helena had made him realize just how alone he was.

No man should have to walk the earth alone. A man should have a mate, to share his luck and his strength, but his sorrows as well. He had seen a Blackfoot squaw fight to her death beside the wounded body of her mate, and he had come upon a Chinese woman alone in the hills, giving birth to her child while her man worked five hundred feet underground to earn money to support them. Life had flavor when people had such courage. Strange how it was always the spoiled who weakened and cried first, and it was the injured, the maimed, the blind, and the poor who fought on alone.

Perhaps there was a life hereafter, a man thought of those things at sea, but he had never worried much about it because if he was not himself—this same collection of good, evil, bone, muscle, and blood—it wouldn't matter anyway. This was what he was, the bad with the good, and if he was anything less than this he wouldn't be himself, not Jean LaBarge.

He knew his faults, or most of them. Knew the kind of sinning he liked and where to put his salt and he did not want to get acquainted with new likes and dislikes. As for sinning, most of the things he enjoyed were sins in the eyes of somebody. Except for reading . . . and most of his books were written by pagan authors.

He was what he wanted to be, a free man. With luck he would not only keep his liberty but sail south with a cargo of furs, all the more precious because he'd taken them from under the nose of Zinnovy. He shrugged . . . here he was wasting his watch below. That was the trouble with the sea and the mountains, they made a man think. It was always the little men who huddled together in cities who believed themselves important, and they had a conspiracy among them to keep up the illusion.

They huddled in cities because a man at sea, in the desert or mountains had time to know himself, to examine what he was . . . so they stayed in their cities, knowing they could not stand to ever really look at themselves.

Spray blew over the rain and against his face. It had a fine, briny taste to it. No wonder the great countries were seagoing countries.

It was late, and it was his watch below. . . .

15

On the morning of the eleventh day the *Susque-hanna* was skimming along through a bright blue sea with the sun just above the horizon when Jean came on deck. Barney Kohl came down the port side to meet him. "Cape Burunof is just astern, and that's Long Island over there."

Jean took the glass and studied the horizon astern, but there were no sails in sight. Evidently they were arriving well ahead of the Russian ship.

"Barney, we'll have to work fast and smart. I'll go ashore and see Governor Rudakof and try to get things moving." He studied the islands ahead. "As soon as I'm in the boat, start getting that wheat up. I'll try to have a lighter alongside before noon."

"They won't move that fast," Kohl advised. "We'll be lucky if we start discharging cargo before tomorrow afternoon." A glance at LaBarge's jaw line made him qualify the remark. "Unless you think of a way to start them moving."

"I will . . . I've got to. But in the meantime I want a man on deck with a rifle at all times. Nobody is to come aboard without written authorization from me, and I mean nobody. The crew is to stand by at all times—we may have to get out of here at a moment's notice."

"Suppose they try to keep you here?"

"They couldn't unless they arrested me on some charge, and we haven't done anything wrong yet."

"Suppose they arrest you anyway?"

"It could happen . . . then you head for Kootzna-hoo Inlet and I'll join you there."

"If not . . . what?"

Jean chuckled. "If I'm not there in two weeks, come back and break me out. I'll be ready to leave."

For a man who had never sailed these waters LaBarge knew a lot about them. Kootznahoo was a likely spot. A ship could lie there for weeks and never be observed. Of course, LaBarge had said he did know this coast better than anyone; it might not be just a boast.

Ordinarily American ships had no trouble in Sitka. The government's friendship varied according to its needs, for the diet in Sitka, even on Baranof Hill, was often restricted, and famine a risk. Rudakof had been friendly on the surface, and now, with grain purchased by Rotcheff, they should be welcome.

The *Susquehanna* dropped her hook in nine fathoms off Channel Rock. At this distance from the port LaBarge knew he would at least have a running start for open water.

The sunlight was bright on the snow-covered beauty of Mount Edgecumbe, and it shimmered over The Sisters, and to the east, over Mount Verstovia. Moving down the channel, LaBarge could see the roof of Baranof Castle, built in 1837, and the third structure on the site. The Baranov era had been a fantastic one, for the little man with the tied-on wig had ruled some of the world's toughest men with a rod of iron, and had just barely failed to capture the Hawaiian Islands.

Jean wore a smoke-gray suit with a black, Spanish-style hat. His boots were hand-cobbled from the best leather, and he looked far more the California rancher and businessman than a ship's master and fur trader. And he chose to look so.

With him in the boat were Ben Turk and Shin Boyar, aside from the boat crew. "You're to get around," he said to the Pole, "listen, and if it seems advisable, ask questions. I want to know the gossip around town, patrol ship activity, what ships have called here, conditions in town. Then return to the boat."

Boyar nodded solemnly. "It is a beautiful place. I who have suffered here, I say it." He gestured toward Mount Edgecumbe. "It is as lovely as Fujiyama."

A dozen loafers watched the boat come to the landing, their manner neither friendly nor hostile. Boyar disappeared into the crowd, and with Turk at his side, LaBarge started for the Castle. Leaving the old hulk that served for a landing, they walked down the dim passage through the center of the log warehouse and emerged on the street leading to the Hill. Along the way were booths where Tlingit Indians gathered to sell their wares, baskets of spruce roots, hand-carved whistles of rock crystal, beaded moccasins and a few articles of clothing. Jean stopped at one stand to buy a walrus-tusk knife for a letter opener. He would send it to Rob Walker when he had a chance: a souvenir of Sitka.

As they walked, people turned to stare. Jean's hat was unusual, and his dress elaborate for the place and time, although many illustrious visitors had come to the Castle.

On the terrace before the Castle, Jean paused to look back. The town itself was little and shabby, but the setting was superb! Tree-clad islands dotted the channels that approached the town, their fine shores rising picturesquely from the sea. All this . . . and behind them Alaska, the Great Land.

A stalwart Russian with close-cropped blond hair admitted them and they waited in an inner room while the servant took their names to the governor. The waiting room was, for this place at the world's end, fantastic. Here were statues and paintings worthy of the finest museum.

The Russian appeared in the door, holding it open. "If you please," he said in a husky voice, "this way."

Rudakof was a stocky, corpulent man with a round face and sideburns. He got up, thrusting out a hand, but his smile was somewhat nervous. "Captain LaBarge? I am mos' happy to see you." He paused, obviously anything but happy. "What can I do for you?"

Jean placed his papers on his desk. "I am delivering, as of this moment, a cargo of wheat, ordered for delivery here by His Excellency, Count Alexander Rotcheff, emissary of His Imperial Majesty, the Czar."

Rudakof's eyes bulged a little. The roll of titles had their effect but he was afraid of Baron Zinnovy, who had told him definitely that intercourse of any sort with foreign ships or merchants was to cease. yet the wheat had been ordered by Count Rotcheff, and Rudakof was also afraid of him. Still, of the two he was most afraid of Zinnovy.

Jean guessed the sort of man he confronted. "There was a crop failure in Canada where wheat was previously purchased, and so the Count acted without delay."

A crop failure in Canada? Rudakof had heard nothing of this, but then what did he ever hear? Nobody told him anything. If there was a crop failure it could mean a serious food shortage in Sitka . . . perhaps famine.

He mopped his brow. "Well, uh, there has been no message, Captain, no authorization. You will have to wait until—"

"I can't wait. The money is on deposit in a San Francisco bank, but if you aren't prepared to receive this cargo I'll have to dispose of it elsewhere. I imagine there are businessmen in the town who would jump at a chance to buy."

Rudakof's face grew crimson. "Oh, come now!" he protested. "It is not so serious, no?" He struggled to find any excuse to delay the decision. "You will have dinner with me? There is much to do. I must think . . . plan."

"I'd be honored to stay for dinner. But in the meantime you will order the lighters for us?"

"Wait, wait!" Rudakof brushed a hand as if to drive away an annoying fly. "You Americans are so impetuous. The lighters are busy, and must be requisitioned. They must—"

"Of course." LaBarge was firm. "But you are the director; the authority is yours. You can order them out."

Rudakof became stubborn. "Dinner first, then we will talk."

Realizing further argument at this point would be useless, Jean shrugged. "As you like . . . but we plan to be out of the harbor by tomorrow."

"Tomorrow?" Rudakof was immediately suspicious. "You are in a hurry." He rustled some papers on his desk. "You talked to Count Rotcheff in San Francisco. Did you also see Baron Zinnovy?"

LaBarge frowned as if making an effort to recall. "Do you mean that peculiar young officer? The one in the pretty little white suit?"

Rudakof blanched with horror at the description. "The man you speak of"—he struggled with emotion—"is Baron Paul Zinnovy, of the Imperial Navy!"

"I believe he did say something of the sort. But wasn't he the one who was in some kind of trouble in St. Petersburg? Such a young man, too!"

Rudakof refused to meet his eyes. He was more worried than ever. This infernal American knew too much. He, Rudakof, had heard whispers about Zinnovy, but he did not like to think of them. Even a disgraced nobleman could have friends in high places, and if there was any shake-up here, trust the Baron to emerge on top, with those who served him.

Yet Rudakof did not wish to be held accountable for refusing a cargo of wheat that might save Sitka from famine. The colony was too dependent, and some of the citizens, like that merchant Busch, had friends who were influential also.

Promising to return for dinner, LaBarge left the Castle. "Stalled," he told Turk, who had waited for him, "but I think we can get it done by tomorrow night."

"You might even have a week," Turk suggested, without much hope. "A lot could happen in Frisco."

LaBarge wasn't so sure. Without doubt Zinnovy would have left for Sitka soon after the *Susquehanna* cleared, and some time had been lost on the Columbia River, picking up the wheat.

Count Rotcheff might delay because he did not relish putting himself in the hands of his enemies, yet he was not a man to shirk his duty, and sooner or later they must come to Sitka.

Sending Turk to the dock with a message for Kohl, he strolled through the few streets of the town. The dark-skinned Tlingit women, picturesque in their native costumes, gathered along the street, each with some trifle to sell, and each walking with a pride of bearing that belied the menial position into which they were placed by the Russians. The Tlingits had been a warlike people, an intelligent people, physically of great strength, who were in no way awe-struck or frightened by Russian weapons. They had wiped out the first colony at Sitka in 1802, and given the right opportunity, believed they could do it again.

Pausing before the clubhouse built by Etolin as a home for employees of the company, Jean watched two husky *promyshleniki* stagger by, drunk and hunting trouble. Shin Boyar was across the street, but he waited until the *promyshleniki* were gone before he crossed.

He stopped near LaBarge and without looking at him, said quietly, "You kicked up a fuss, Cap'n. Feller from the Castle hustled to the waterfront, jumped into a boat and took off for that new patrol ship, the *Lena*."

Rudakof was acting with more intelligence than he had given him credit for possessing. He must have come upon a plan that would place him in a better bargaining position before they met at dinner.

"Found a man I know," Boyar continued, "told me Zinnovy threw a scare into Rudakof. Officially, the director outranks him, but Zinnovy has frightened Rudakof with his influence in St. Petersburg."

"Go back to the boat and tell the boys I want a close watch. At the first sign of that Russian square-rigger I want to be notified, no matter where I am or what I'm doing."

They could leave now, but payment depended on delivery of the wheat, and moreover, he needed the cargo space. The schooner was small and lightly built, and without that space he could do nothing.

He walked to the knoll and seated himself at a table in one of the tearooms. A girl came to his table, smiling in a friendly way, and he ordered honey cakes and tea. Sitting over the tea he tried to surmise what Rudakof was planning. Obviously, he wanted neither to lose the wheat nor see the schooner leave before Zinnovy returned.

The waitress was a pretty blonde with braids wrapped around her head and dark blue eyes that laughed when her lips smiled. Her mouth was wide and friendly, and as she refilled his cup, her eyes caught his. "You are Boston man?"

"Yes."

"You have beautiful ship." She spoke carefully and chose her words hesitantly. "When I was small girl a Boston man gave me a doll from China. He said he had a little girl like me."

"I'll bet," Jean smiled at her, "he'd like a big girl like you."

"Maybe. I think so." Her eyes danced. "Most Boston men like to have girl." She wrinkled her nose at him. "Even Eskimo girl."

An idea came to him suddenly. How much pressure could Rudakof stand? Suppose a little pressure could be generated?

He spoke casually. "Count Rotcheff ordered a cargo of wheat for delivery here on my ship, and now Rudakof won't accept it."

"He is a fool!" She spoke sharply. Then what he had said registered. "You have *wheat*? Oh, but we need it! You must not take it away!"

"I'd like to unload tonight or tomorrow," he said, "but I doubt if I can get a permit."

"You wait!" She turned quickly and went into the kitchen, and listening, he heard excited talk. A few minutes later a stocky, hard-faced Russian emerged from the kitchen and stalked angrily out the door.

LaBarge sat back in the chair. The tea was good and the honey cakes like nothing aboard ship. He had a feeling something had been started that not even Rudakof could stop. Sitka was a small town. In the several hours before he was to meet Rudakof at dinner everyone in town would know he had a cargo of wheat, and if a wheat shortage existed, the director should begin to feel the protests.

When he had finished his tea he placed a gold coin on the table. When she handed him his change, he brushed it aside. "You did not tell me your name?"

"Dounia." She blushed. "And you?"

"Jean LaBarge."

"It is too much. I cannot take the money."

He accepted the change, then returned half of it. With a quick glance to see if anyone saw, she pocketed it. "You might," he suggested, "whisper something to the man who just left."

"My father."

"You might whisper that if Rudakof does not unload the cargo promptly, I shall be forced to leave. Unless . . . and this you must whisper very softly, unless someone came at night to unload it, someone who could sign for it, someone reliable, whose name Count Rotcheff would accept."

16

Rudakof's round face was beaming when Jean came into the room; he seemed a little drunk and very pleased with himself. It appeared that the problem the arrival of the *Susquehanna* presented was deemed to be over. He grasped Jean's hand eagerly. "Come, my friend! Sit down! Whatever else our Castle holds nobody ever complains of the cellar! What will you have? A bottle of Madeira?"

Jean was pleasant but wary. Rudakof was too sure of himself. "Thank you," he said, glancing swiftly around the room.

At Rudakof's signal the servant came with two glasses. "Dinner will be served at once," Rudakof explained, "and we have a few guests."

Jean tasted the wine. "You have a very interesting city," he said, deciding to strike a blow at Rudakof's new confidence. "I walked about a good deal, and talked with some of your people."

The smile left the Russian's face. Obviously this did not please him, but his spirits were too high to be undermined so easily. They toasted their respective governments and the glasses were refilled. "To the Grand Duke Constantin!" Jean proposed.

Rudakof hesitated, obviously startled, then repeated in a dull voice, "To the Grand Duke." He drank, but some of the bounce was gone out of him. Jean guessed that when one worked for the Russian American Company there were some to whom it was not good politics to drink.

The other guests were arriving. A French botanist and a German geologist who traveled in company, and a young Russian naval lieutenant named Yonovski, a handsome youngster with blond curly hair. "You have a fine schooner, Captain," Yonovski told him. "Have you had a chance to visit any of the islands?"

"We came by open sea. Count Rotcheff wished us to arrive as quickly as possible."

"Oh?" Yonovski was surprised. "You know the Count?"

"He is in San Francisco, but he'll soon return to Sitka."

Several of those at the table exchanged glances, obviously surprised. Rudakof, his face growing redder, filled Jean's glass. "Come, come!" he protested. "No business! The Captain is our guest!"

The conversation turned to California, the sudden westward advance of the United States due to the gold rush, and the somewhat similar movement in Siberia. Yet several of those at the table seemed preoccupied, and one of these was a tall man, stooped in the shoulders. He was a lean, hard, capable-looking man who was later introduced as Busch, a merchant-trader.

All were much interested in the American attitude toward Russia. Obviously with the situation in Europe growing serious this was becoming a major factor at Sitka.

When they moved into the next room for brandy and cigars Rudakof was beaming and jovial; the numerous drinks were having their effect. He opened his collar to give his thick neck more freedom and became involved in a lively discussion with the geologist.

Almost accidentally, LaBarge found Busch at his side. The tall man studied him out of cool, intelligent eyes. "Is it true, Captain, that you have wheat aboard? And you have not received permission to discharge the cargo?"

"That's right." Rudakof's broad beam was turned to them; he did not notice their conversation. "In fact, the director seemed upset instead of pleased, and when I asked to have lighters at once, he created delays."

"This wheat . . . how much is it worth?"

"That's just it. The wheat was ordered by Count Rotcheff and the money for payment is on deposit in a San Francisco bank. I can collect payment by showing a receipt signed by the governor, or"—he paused—"by other responsible parties who will see the wheat used for the benefit of the colony."

"Paid for?" Busch was astonished.

"Evidently," Jean suggested tentatively, "everyone is not anxious to see the wheat delivered."

For a few minutes Busch said nothing, then, "You will understand, Captain, that in our country as well as yours there are factions, and there are those who would make money even at the expense of their country. I realize this is hard to believe, but there are men who regard nothing as disloyal as long as the profits are large. Loyalty to their pocket- book or to their business firm is above loyalty to their country."

"It's the same in my country."

"I think men vary little the world over, but there are always a few who serve and ask nothing but to serve. The survival of the Sitka colony is of interest to me, and at this moment your wheat is almost the price of that survival."

Yonovski interrupted and Busch moved away. The conversation grew more desultory and more ribald. Finally, the party broke up and Jean started down the steps. His eyes swept the dark harbor, searching out the schooner. Another ship was showing her lights, anchored only a short distance from the *Susquehanna*! From her size she could only be the patrol ship.

He never recalled how he reached the boat. Boyar and Turk were sitting on the edge of the landing, smoking. Turk got up quickly. "No chance to do anything, sir. She just moved up and lay broadside to us."

Behind them in the dark passageway a boot scuffed. LaBarge stepped quickly out of the light and Boyar got to his feet. Light gleamed on a gun barrel in Turk's hand.

Two men stepped from the passage and walked to them. The first was Busch, the other the father of Dounia. "If we give you a receipt, Captain," Busch asked, "will you deliver to us the wheat?"

"The wheat was bought for Sitka. If you'll accept delivery, I'm agreeable. But you will have a problem." He indicated the patrol ship. "Have you an answer to that?"

"You underrate us, Captain." Busch spoke softly. "We saw the patrol ship while you were still at the Castle, and the men who stand the night watch aboard her were still in town. They were at the tearoom, of course, for all men come to the tearoom to look at Dounia, who is the prettiest girl in Sitka.

"Dounia is a clever girl and when she told them it was her birthday they drank to her health in vodka. They drank many toasts, Captain, and naturally they were supplied with bottles by my friend here, Arseniev, the father of Dounia. They celebrated very well, Captain, and we gave them a dozen bottles to take back to the ship."

"Good . . . the cargo will be on deck, waiting."

Hours later, in silence and darkness, he watched the last sack go over the side into the big, flat-bottomed scow. The scow had made several trips, always careful to show no lights and to moor herself on the off side of the schooner. Busch came aboard and signed the receipt, then gripped Jean's hand. "Thank you, my friend! Thank you!" he whispered.

The scow slipped away into the darkness. A few lights sparkled from the Castle on the Hill, and the snows of Mount Edgecumbe glimmered faintly through the night. Barney Kohl came down the deck. "If it wasn't for her," he said, "we—"

"Get everybody on deck. No lights, no noise. Then haul us up to the anchor."

"You going to slip the anchor?"

"And lose it? Not unless I have to."

A soft wind was blowing over the bay as the *Susquehanna* came swiftly and silently to life. Clothes rustled, a knot struck the deck, a board creaked, ghostly hands moved on a line.

Kohl spoke. "Over the anchor, Captain."

Several of the crew were beside Jean, busy with a queer contrivance. He looked around at Kohl. "All right, take her in. Gently now."

Their only worry was the patrol ship; the watchers there might be drunk or might not. There was no sound now from the *Lena*. Earlier there had been loud laughter and occasional singing.

"Ben?"

"Yes, Cap'n?"

"Ready?"

"Sure as you're alive."

Several of the crew moved up beside him and together they lowered the contrivance over the side and anchored it in place. It was a long, narrow raft that supported two thin masts and a boom. On the end of one mast and on the boom, lights were mounted. From a distance, if the observer was drunk enough, it would look as if the schooner were still there.

"Douse your lights, Kohl. Then light these."

The tide was setting northward toward Channel

Rock. Jean let the schooner drift, and there was no sound above the ripple of water past her hull.

"When she comes abeam of the Rock," Jean said, "shake out a jib. I want no noise. Sound carries too well over the water at night."

There was, for several minutes, no other sound. Then across the water on the patrol ship somebody moved and spoke. Kohl swore softly and Jean held his breath. The schooner seemed to lie still on the dark water, and ashore on Japonski Island, an Indian chanted. Behind him, higher in the forest, a lone wolf howled inquiringly into the night. The night gave back its echoes to his repeated question.

"We're movin'!" Pete Noble whispered hoarsely. "Look at them lights!" Astern of them, almost fifty yards off, were the lights that simulated the schooner.

They were moving but the movement was desperately slow and at any moment some drunken sailor aboard the *Lena* might realize something was wrong. The crew stood in silence, almost afraid to breathe, wondering what a Russian prison would be like.

"Channel Rock ahead, Cap'n. Shall I shake out the jib?"

"Hold it."

The minutes walked by on cat feet. A star appeared through a veil of cloud, then was quickly banished behind a dark mass of rolled black-cotton cloud. The patrol ship was well astern now. Somewhere ashore and far off, a dog barked.

Channel Rock was abeam. "All right, Barney," Jean said, and watched the white flag of the jib shake out and fill itself with the light breeze.

"Stand by the mizzen," he said, after a minute. Channel Rock fell astern and the dark bulk of Battery Island loomed on the port side, yet they were still far from free. There was no more time. "All right, Barney. Get some sail on her!"

Smartly the mizzen was hauled aloft, then the mains'l. The *Susquehanna* gathered speed. Out from behind Japonski Island the wind filled her sails and she heeled over and began to dip her bows deeper. With luck they would soon have a full cargo and a ticket home.

"Sail, ho!" The call, from the lookout in the bow, was low and desperate.

Jumping to the bulwark, Jean strained his eyes into the darkness. A big square-rigger was coming up the Western Channel, headed into port under a full head of sail, although even as they sighted her she began to take in canvas.

Barney swore. "Look at that, would you?"

"I'm looking."

She was bearing down upon them and coming fast. The man at the wheel turned and glanced at Jean but LaBarge shook his head. To change course now would be to lose distance they could not afford, yet the big windjammer was headed as if to run them down.

"Cap'n." The man at the wheel had a pleading note in his voice.

"Hold your course!"

Kohl drew a sharp breath and looked up at the towering heights of canvas. Before he could speak he was interrupted by a shout from the square-rigger and a command to put the wheel over. The big ship sheered off and a man ran shouting to the rail. A dozen faces joined him, peering over the side of the schooner.

A rough voice hailed them. "What ship is that? Who are you?"

The hail was in Russian, then in English. LaBarge ignored the shouts and then suddenly, in the white light from a scuttle, he saw a face, and it was the face he could never forget, that would always be with him. There it was, not more than heaving-line distance away, and for a moment as the two ships passed their eyes met across the space, and then as they drew apart, he lifted a hand.

She hesitated, then waved back, a vague, sad gesture in the night, and then the square-rigger fell astern and there was no sound, no light, and only a memory of a white face lonely in the light from an open scuttle, and the memory of a girl who had ridden beside him over the tawny, sunlit hills.

The schooner dipped her bow and spray swept the deck. On the wind there was a smell of open sea and of the far-off pine-clad islands to the north, those far green islands where the schooner was bound.

17

Within a very short time Baron Zinnovy would realize that despite all his efforts the wheat had been delivered, and he would know that LaBarge and the *Susquehanna* were at large in the Alexander Archipelago.

The immediate problem was obvious. They must be where the patrol ship was not, they must pick up the cargo of furs as planned, and slip away to the south at the first opportunity thereafter.

The schooner carried eighteen men and three officers, all carefully selected men. A third of the number could have handled her, but the others were needed for trading, fighting, or any move LaBarge might make ashore.

"We're pointing for Cross Sound. Do you know it, Kohl?"

"As well as any man, which means nothing. I know there's glaciers north of it that keep feeding ice into the Sound, and there are bad fogs."

"Do you know a small cove with an island in its mouth? It's on the north coast of Chichagof?"

"That's old Skayeut's village."

"All right. Take us there."

Jean walked forward to the waist. There were no sails in sight and they could expect a few hours' grace. With the following wind they could make good time and farther north they could hug the coast. The wind was cold now, the sea choppy. From now on they would need luck, ingenuity, and every bit of their combined knowledge. Fortunately, the schooner was new, she could sail close to the wind and could carry canvas.

The shores of the island, when they reached it, were heavily wooded right to the water's edge. Here and there a small indentation, each with a minute section of beach, broke the monotony of the forest-clad shore. The morning was bright and the day cold. Taking the schooner in past the George Islands they reached toward the cove, seeing no sign of life except a lone tern floating comfortably on the gray sea.

"The entrance is narrow," Kohl advised, "right abeam of the island."

It opened before them as he spoke and he conned the schooner into the opening between island and shore. Trees came down to the water and there was a fringe of ice along the shore. Inland, over the trees, they detected a column of smoke.

"This Skayeut," Kohl said, "he's a mean old blister."

"Can we go on in?"

"The passage is narrow, and there's only three feet of water over the rocks at low tide, but you could make it at high tide, and inside it's deep enough."

"We'll stay here."

Two canoes put out from shore and circled the *Susquehanna* just within hailing distance. There were four men in one canoe, two in the other, but no movement showed on the shore, although all knew Indians were there, studying the schooner. These Indians had suffered too much from the greed and rapacity of the Russians.

The dark green walls of the forest closed them in, and the schooner lay like a ship in a dream on the still, cold water. There was a faint slap of paddles on water as the canoes circled closer. The Indians stopped rowing.

"Where's Skayeut?" Kohl shouted.

The Tlingits said nothing. The schooner was new in these waters. One Indian shaded his eyes to stare at Kohl. "You Boston men?"

"Sure! Come aboard!"

They hung off, reluctant to risk it. One of the Tlingits indicated LaBarge. "Who that?" he called.

"LaBarge!" Jean called back. "You tell Skayeut that Jean LaBarge has come to see him!"

The paddles dipped deep and the canoe shot shoreward. Two of the men in the larger canoe turned to stare at LaBarge and Kohl turned to his captain. "They acted like they knew your name."

"They know it," Jean replied blandly, enjoying Kohl's mystified expression. "He knew me, Barney."

Just before noon a half dozen *bidarkas* shot out

from shore, each packed with Indians. In the first was Skayeut, a tall man with a wide, deep chest and massive bones. He thrust out his hand to Jean and they looked into each other's eyes, and then they both smiled.

Trade was brisk. The Tlingit Indians were born traders. Even before the arrival of Captain Cook they knew the value of the land trade routes and their economic value to the tribe. At one time the tribe had traveled three hundred miles to stop the establishment of a Hudson Bay post where it would interfere with their own trade with tribes from the interior.

Of this Jean knew, and that old Skayeut could give him information about the interior. The old chieftain was about to learn that information itself could be a valuable item of trade.

For three nights they remained at Elfin Cove, and each night LaBarge noted down the results of his talks with the old chief and the procession of Tlingits and Salish the chief brought to talk of Alaska. Later, alone in his cabin, Jean noted down what he had heard for future reference.

. . . the gold is known to the Russians. An effort was made to mine it without success and for some reason further attempts were discouraged, probably they did not wish to attract attention to territory so insecure in a military sense.

Old Skayeut knows where more gold can be had and will trade for iron. The iron here is in small deposits and difficult for the Tlingits to work. They are a superior people and the blankets they weave of dog hair or cedar bark are equal to the best, anywhere.

For a month the *Susquehanna* worked her way south, down Saginaw Channel into Stephens Passage, pausing at this island or that village. As planned, they touched a dozen villages where no traders had been in some time and soon the hold of the schooner was filled with prime fur.

Occasionally they sighted some native canoe, but heard of no other vessels in the area. Yet Jean was nervous, for the channels were narrow, allowing no chance to maneuver, and steep mountains rose on either side to about fifteen hundred feet in solid banks of forest before giving way to bare rock or snow. The presents he had sent north were paying off, for everywhere he was welcomed as an old friend.

The seventh week of trading was ending when Kohl came to the cabin where LaBarge was busy adding more information to his books. "Cap," Kohl said abruptly, "I've mastered my own ships and I'm not one to butt in, but the crew are getting nervous. We've been lucky this far; now let's head for home."

"You know Kasaan Bay?"

"Sure."

"That's our last stop."

Kohl dropped into a chair and shoved his hat back on his head. "I'm not one to show the feather, Cap, but this trip worries me. Maybe it's the fool luck we've had, cutting that square-rigger so close aboard you must have scared them out of a year's growth. I know you scared me. You done it deliberate, too . . . and she couldn't have come around in a half hour, not to chase us, she couldn't. But it's fool luck we've had, every village loaded with prime fur, and no patrol ship in sight. You know what I think?"

"Let's have it." Jean tipped back in his chair.

"They're waitin' for us, Cap. Zinnovy will be to the south, knowing we've got to go that way, and he'll be lyin' where he can cover the best routes. He'll have both the *Lena* and the *Kronstadt*, and men staked out to cover every passage."

"I think you're right."

"Look." Kohl bent over the crude chart on the table before them. "We're heading down Clarence Strait. Once we cross the bay down here we'll be in Canadian waters, but that won't stop Zinnovy. Only right there some ships would head for open sea and a straight run to Frisco. So what does he do? He waits for us in the mouth of the Strait."

"Just where do you think he'll wait?"

"My guess is right off Duke Island, but maybe a little south so he can check both channels."

Kohl had made a point that disturbed him. LaBarge was not sure that Zinnovy had even bothered to make a search, for such news travels from island to island and village to village by swift traveling canoes. It was likely Zinnovy was doing just what Kohl suggested, patrolling the outlets to the south.

He did not tell Kohl that he had been, for days, worrying the problem as a dog worries a bone. "Barney, if you've got it figured straight, we'd better stand ready for action."

"You'll fight?"

"I won't be taken. We'll run if we can, but when we can't run any more, we'll fight."

Kohl went aft with a small grin on his lips. He had begun the voyage in a surly mood, hoping LaBarge would get his belly full and decide that San Francisco life was better. But as the voyage progressed he grew to like the man more and more. He had nerve, and he had brains. He still did not understand LaBarge's vast knowledge of the islands.

Later, they discussed the question again. "There are channels," Kohl said, "but too many dead ends and some of the channels are filled with ice. A man needs local knowledge."

The lantern above their heads swayed with the gentle roll of the schooner. Her timbers creaked and they studied the chart. It offered few alternatives.

"This island?" LaBarge put his finger on a large mass of land ahead and to the east. "That's Revillagigedo, isn't it?"

"Uh-huh. You can call it an island, Cap'n, but nobody knows whether it is or not."

"Ever see a Russian chart?"

"A dozen. On their charts it's part of the mainland."

"Good." He got to his feet. "That was what I'd hoped. Understand now, Barney, no fighting unless we have to. Until then we play hide-and-seek around the islands."

Suddenly, there was a shout from aloft, and running feet on deck. Then the cry, "Sail, ho!"

"Where away?"

"Dead ahead, an' comin' up fast!"'

"Well." Kohl grinned at LaBarge and rolled his quid in his jaws. "Here's where we start to run."

Together they went up the companion to the deck and studied the oncoming ship through the glass. A flag was climbing the halyard and when it was caught by the wind it was easily seen. It was the flag of Imperial Russia.

18

The *Susquehanna* fell off before the wind. Standing in the waist, Jean LaBarge watched the oncoming ship. It was the *Lena*. Although a patrol ship she was only a middling fast sailer, quite fast enough for the average ship in these waters but not in the same class with the schooner.

He wanted to draw her deeply into Clarence Strait, for from her present position she could cover both the Strait and Revillagigedo Channel, a position fatal to his plans.

On the east side of the Strait, only a short distance off, there was the mouth of a channel opening between Gravina and Annette Islands, which in turn opened on Revillagigedo Channel. From there several openings offered themselves, but of five possible openings three were dead ends. If he could win to the head of Nicholas Passage and disappear, the *Lena* would have small chance of finding him unless Zinnovy was shrewd and patient enough to return to the former position and wait. And once the quarry was sighted, Jean did not believe Paul Zinnovy would be patient.

The sky was overcast, the sea gray. Lying close off-shore he waited, hoping to draw the Russian ship deeper and deeper into the Strait. The shores were thick with forest except where cliffs of gray rock jutted out. White water broke over Hidden Reef. The wind was good and he allowed the schooner to loaf under reefed sails while the Russian ship came on. Jean waited, judging the distance.

"All right," he said suddenly, "let's go!"

In an instant Kohl was shouting orders and the crew exploded into action. Eagerly, as if welcoming the chase and knowing what was demanded of her, the schooner answered to the wind. There was a low cheer from the crew as her sails filled and she stared to run for it. From the Russian ship there was the dull boom of a gun, a warning signal, an order to heave to. She was much too far away for a cannon shot.

Jean took the wheel from Larsen and when the schooner was rolling along he put the wheel over and headed into the passage that led to Smugglers' Cove. From behind them the gun boomed again, impatiently. Standing at the wheel Jean watched the shore line, and suddenly glimpsed the lightning-blasted pine of which he had been told. Three minutes later by careful count he put the wheel over and slid between Hidden Reef and another rock patch, unnamed as yet. Then he was in full channel and reeling off a good eight knots.

"If we can make the head of the Passage before he rounds the point," he told Kohl, "we'll be all right."

"I hope you know what you're doin'." Kohl was worried. "This is dangerous ground."

"I know."

He hoped he did. There was a chance despite his endless checking that the information in the little black book was wrong. Beside the channel the somber walls of timber closed them in, virgin timber, untouched by man or fire. Ahead of them the outlet was filled with dangers, and there would be little margin of safety, yet if he could make the turn. . . .

He glanced back . . . nothing in sight. Sweat broke out on his brow despite the wind. If they were trapped in a cul-de-sac they would have no chance, for Zinnovy could stand off and shell them to pieces, and with the greatest enjoyment.

He stood with his legs spread to the roll of the ship, taking his time. Whitecaps dotted the sea, and a cold wind came down off the mountains. Nobody said anything until Larsen, glancing over his shoulder, said, "I think we make it."

Momentarily, Jean resigned the wheel to him. He walked forward, scanning the sea and the marks on the cliffs. The distance was slight, but if the *Lena* had continued her pursuit she should be rounding into the Passage by now.

"Head her toward the island." He pointed. "We'll get behind it and out of sight."

Kohl was in the stern with a glass to his eye, anxiously watching the point on Annette Island beyond Hidden Reef, but there was no sign of the patrol ship. The dark green shores of the island were close aboard now, and he could make out details of the trees. There was a white streak of quartz in the rock at the island's end and a cluster of bedraggled pines.

Kohl called out suddenly. "She's on our tail, Cap! She's comin'!"

"Think they saw us?"

"I doubt it. If they didn't they'll have to look in those other inlets before they come up the Passage."

"Zinnovy knows I'm not the waiting type. He'll come on."

Out of sight of the pursuing ship, Jean conned the schooner around the kelp. Ahead of him was a strip of dark water and he pointed into it, muttering a wordless prayer that it was deep as it looked. The schooner slid through with yards to spare on either side, and then swung into the Tongass Narrows that divided Pennock Island from Gravina. Before them lay thirteen miles of clear water and Pennock was more than three hundred feet high and good cover for him. Even if Zinnovy had guessed right there was still a chance they could reach Behm Cannal before they were seen.

The black battalions of clouds lowered above storm-gored ridges, and the gray-furrowed sea licked at narrow beaches of sand and bare, black rocks. It was a strong land, a good land, unchanged through thousands of years. Off to the right the black, glistening arch of a rock showed momentarily above the water like the back of a porpoise and brown streamers of kelp trailed their mute warning into the gray of the sea.

The Narrows opened and the great bulk of Pennock fell behind. Kohl paused at the companionway rubbing the back of his neck. He hated to leave the deck, yet he knew fresh men would be sorely needed later. He stumbled down the ladder and fell into his bunk and was asleep as soon as he hit the mattress.

Duncan Pope, the sour-faced second mate, was on watch. He was a slovenly-appearing man with a cast to one eye, yet long since Jean had learned he was a capable officer whose lean, almost scrawny body possessed an amazing resistance to hunger, cold, and long weary hours on watch. Pope was a man who kept his own counsel. He did not like Russians. He did not like the thugs of Sydney Town. He disliked most ship's masters on general principles, and he cared for few things aside from standing watch, reading his Bible, and fighting.

LaBarge was scarcely aware Pope had taken over. He was watching the Narrows open out before him, and soon he would make the turn around Revillagigedo where his information told him there was a passage. He was gambling everything on that, and hoping Zinnovy would continue the pursuit. If his luck held he would pass by within a short distance of where the patrol ship had originally waited and the *Lena* would be lost in the maze of islands, channels and inlets that lay behind.

An hour and a half later, with no evidence of pursuit, he rounded the corner and started north. Ahead of him was a wooded island with a yellow cliff, which would be Tatoosh. He kept close in so the ship would be invisible against the island if anyone was within sight.

He thought all at once of the Swamp, where as a child he had used the cover to hide from hostile eyes. And then he remembered Rob, and their dreams of adventure. "Rob," he said, half-aloud, "you should have been with me today. You would have liked this, I know you would."

19

Helena stood on the terrace outside the Castle. It was late evening. For two days there had been no news from the *Lena*, and a message from her meant news of the *Susquehanna*. Each day until then there had been a *bidarka* to bring news or lack of it. The last canoe had brought word the *Susquehanna* had been sighted and capture was imminent.

Reception of the news in Sitka had been mixed. Despite the fact that the Americans were foreigners they had brought wheat to Sitka, and their plight found sympathy among the people of the town. Baron Zinnovy was already unpopular, and the fact that he had impounded the wheat had won him no friends.

The wheat would have been lost to them but for an unexpected show of firmness by Count Rotcheff, who refused to permit the impounding and took the matter out of Zinnovy's hands. Rudakof, straddling the fence on most issues, met this one head on from necessity. Reluctantly, he backed up the Count, who was, after all, in authority.

Rotcheff's words were repeated all over the settlement. "I am afraid, Baron Zinnovy," he had said sternly, "you have exceeded your authority. Your mission is to protect Russian trade and traders, not to enforce your arbitrary decisions in matters of no concern to you. I must remind you, sir, to restrict yourself to your duties and cease interfering with the civilian authorities."

Helena, who had been present, was suddenly bursting with pride for her husband. The Baron had stood at attention, ramrod stiff, his eyes straight forward, his body fairly trembling with repressed fury. He saluted, made an abrupt about-face, and strode from the room, heels clicking on the hard floor. Yet all knew it was but one battle in a campaign and the decision was not yet.

Helena realized that there was more to the search for the American ship than the personal animosity Zinnovy bore for Jean LaBarge. If the *Susquehanna* could be captured with a cargo of furs—Zinnovy could claim she had been trading with the secret connivance of Rotcheff, and trading illegally. More than ever she appreciated the danger of their position, for had Rudakof failed to back up her husband, Zinnovy might have taken drastic action to free himself from interference, and orders were of no importance if they could not be enforced.

Scarcely more than a child when she had married Count Rotcheff, she had not been unhappy. He was thirty years older than she, but an intelligent, attractive man, respected for his genuine ability and his sometimes biting wit. She had grown up listening to talk of politics and intrigue, a game at which her husband was a master.

A door closed behind her and she turned to greet her husband. "I am glad you are out of that stuffy office."

"It is nice here." He inhaled deeply, then glanced at her. "Do you believe they will catch him?"

"No . . . no, I don't."

"Nor I." They walked a few steps together. "He is clever, this American of yours. Busch tells me he has friends all through the islands, and what Busch has learned of LaBarge's dealings convince him that LaBarge is extremely astute."

Somewhere out among those dark, mysterious islands he might even now be fighting, dying. The air was growing colder but she felt no desire to go in . . . this was the same air that he was breathing; even now he might be standing on his deck, watching the dark water slip past.

"I like it here," she said suddenly.

"Sitka?" He was surprised.

"I mean all of this, as it is now, young and free."

"And barbaric."

"Of course . . . and I like even that."

"There is something primitive in all women, I suspect. Women think in terms of the basic. Love, marriage, children."

"What better things to think of?"

"Of course. It is as it should be and lucky for us males, God knows. You are coming in?"

"Soon."

He paused near the door, watching the dark serrated edge of the pine forest against the night sky. Somewhere down in the town someone dropped a piece of iron and it rang loudly on the pavement. He glanced at Helena, feeling his age now in the growing chill of the evening. This bout with Zinnovy might be his last. He must move shrewdly . . . the man had influence, damn him! And he was vindictive, which Rotcheff was not. It was a pity, he reflected, that the men of good will are so poorly armed, for at times it was a handicap not to hate. It took a fanatic to win, a fanatic believer or one utterly ruthless. He, Rotcheff, thought too much of the other man's point of view, he could always see both sides of an argument. That would not do in a world where there were Zinnovys.

Yet Zinnovy was a Russian and they talked loudest when they faced weakness. We are basically, he thought, a race of tyrants and poets, and his own fault was in being too much the poet, too little the tyrant.

He looked again at Helena, standing by the stone parapet. In the world from which they had come it would be considered an absurd thing, but he loved his wife. He had not married for love. Helena was beautiful, she was wealthy, and her family was powerful in his world of intrigue and politics. Theirs had been a marriage of purpose. Yet he had been a lover once, and a successful one, with many conquests behind him. He knew all the little things that please a woman. He smiled thoughtfully. The best lovers were those who did not really love, for if one became too emotional there was in the place of eloquence a stumbling tongue, in the place of charm, awkwardness.

The surprise had been his. He found Helena, even though he was sure she did not love him, a thoughtful, attentive, and considerate wife. Had he met her twenty-five years before she might have loved him . . . but then he could not have afforded her!

Their life had been singularly happy, and if she did not love him she did respect and admire him. These last years had been his happiest. He was not sure when he fell in love with his wife; nonetheless, it had happened, and now for the first time he sensed her unrest, and he knew the cause.

Jean LaBarge was a handsome man, not in a pretty way as were some of the Czar's officers who had paid court to her, but in a tough, dangerous way. The Count, considered in his day a superb swordsman, and victor in four duels to the death, admitted to himself he would dislike to face LaBarge with rapier in his hand.

The man had it in him to kill . . . not from malice, for there did not seem to be cruelty in him, but simply because he was, more than anyone in the Count's experience, a fighter.

"Helena"—he turned back to her—"have you ever been sorry you married me?"

Scarcely had he uttered the words than he was wishing they had not been said. Was he a boy to expect such a question to receive more than the obvious answer?

She turned to face him. "No, Alexander, I have not been sorry, and I shall never be sorry."

He welcomed the sincerity in her voice. "I'm afraid I have been a bad husband . . . too preoccupied." He waved an irritated hand. "Marriage in our lot is so much a matter of state. We scarcely know each other until it is too late."

"It has never been so with us," she protested. "You know it hasn't."

She was right, of course. There had always been a warm, friendly understanding between them, and in the past few years it had become even better. They had, really, been two of the lucky ones.

He remembered the first time he had seen her, when he was a young officer in the Imperial Army, and had come to her home to visit, accompanying her uncle. She had been a little girl with large, serious eyes who was always in a corner, reading. She had come running from the door to greet her uncle, followed by a huge wolfhound she called Tovarich. Suddenly seeing the strange young man, she had stopped, torn between eagerness and embarrassment.

He had seen her fear and had walked to her, bowing deeply. "Princess, I am your servant. And when was a mistress afraid of her servants?"

She laughed then. "You! You couldn't be a servant! With that nose?"

They had laughed together, and from that day on, they had been friends. . . .

The wind puffed through the pines and flurried her skirt. "It is cold," he said. "I shall go in."

"I'll follow . . . I want to be alone for a minute."

When the door closed behind him he went to the sideboard and poured a glass of brandy. He tasted it and the warmth went through his veins.

Zinnovy now: the man had friends in the high places but more than one road led to St. Petersburg. There was that boy, for instance, the boy Zinnovy had ordered flogged . . . did he not have an uncle who was a power in the iron industry? The uncle would be a man to be listened to. Yes, that was it, and they had met once in Kiev, a hardheaded man named Zarasky who had fiercely resented his nephew's flogging. It had nearly killed the boy.

That way it would not involve the Grand Duke or the Czar. There was no way of making someone tired of you faster than endless requests or complaints. It was the value of being a politician, that one knew other ways.

It occurred to him abruptly that being the kind of man Zinnovy was, and wanting what he wanted, Zinnovy dared not let him, Rotcheff, return to St. Petersburg.

Coolly, he considered the situation. There were ways of escape, of course, but he was no longer a young man, and all shipping out of the harbor could be controlled by Baron Zinnovy. Escape by the usual means would be barred to him, and any other means was closed by the danger to his health. That meant he must prepare a report now, with several copies, and see that at least two copies were smuggled out, for certainly Zinnovy would be checking all communications.

Busch . . . that was the man. Busch detested Zinnovy and was a patriot as well, shrewd enough to realize the danger Zinnovy meant to all legitimate business in Sitka. Moreover, and this was important, Busch had his own corps of tough and loyal *promyshleniki*. He was not a man to attack with impunity.

A long time later, while his pen still scratched, the clock chimed.

Eleven o'clock. It was very late. . . .

20

Shortly after noon the wind fell away to nothing, and the *Susquehanna*, now barely making steerageway, held in toward the rocky shore. Jean was hoping to pick up vagrant breezes out of the numerous ravines that slashed the mountains. Twice during the afternoon there were brief squalls accompanied by heavy rain, and each time the schooner gained ground.

All hands that could be spared were catching sleep against the long watches ahead, and when they turned to, every one of them was given a jolt of hot rum. It was almost dusk when the wind picked up. Moving at a bare four knots they rounded into Gedney Pass.

Both shores sloped steeply back to three thousand feet, with the shore steep-to. Creeping along, the schooner made Shrimp Bay and dropped anchor until morning.

During the night it rained hard. The man on watch was relieved every hour; Jean wanted to take no chance because of a sleepy watch. All hands slept in their clothing, ready to turn to at a moment's notice, and LaBarge bedded down under the bottom-up whaleboat.

Tired as he was, he could not sleep. The cold wind made him grateful for his heavy blankets. Once while lying awake he heard something crash far up the mountainside and then a sliding of rocks and timber. There was a faint following rattle of stones, then silence. The schooner was ghostly in the night, but toward morning the air warmed a little and the fog lifted, shrouding her rigging in cobwebs of mist. His cargo was worth at least eighty thousand dollars and depending on how the market stood at the moment, might be worth at least half again that much.

Sometime after that he must have fallen asleep for he was awakened to find the sky turning pale yellow and the watch standing beside him with a steaming cup of black coffee. By the time the sun was halfway up the sky they had rounded Curlew Point and entered the Narrows along Bell Island. Here, for approximately eight miles, the channel varied from three-tenths of a mile in width to more than a mile. By report the water was deep and the shores steep-to, but as the fog held they had no idea if they were pursued or not.

Like a ghost ship on a ghost sea they slid along through the fog. He was coming up from below when Kohl called him. The schooner faced a continuing channel ahead, but to their right lay another opening, a little wider.

"What d' you think, Barney?"

Kohl rubbed his neck. "A man can only guess."

Together they walked to the bow and looked at the water. Just beyond the entrances both passages were blocked off by fog. One might be an escape, the other a trap, but which was which? A decision had to be made, yet Jean delayed, hoping for some indication, some evidence on which to base a choice.

"What's the book say?" Kohl had noticed the black book LaBarge occasionally referred to.

"It doesn't say. The man who told me about this channel hadn't navigated it, he'd only crossed it at the Narrows with some Tlingits after him. He did get a taste of the water and it was salt."

He stiffened suddenly, lifting a hand. "Listen! I heard something then! Something dropped on a deck!"

All ears strained into the silence and fog. Kohl grabbed his arm. "Cap'n . . . look!"

It was a piece of shelf ice such as forms along a shore, and it had drifted from the opening that lay ahead. It was moving upon some strong, unseen current.

"Put the helm over, Noble," Jean said. "We take the other opening."

Suddenly from out of the fog there was a cry, "Sail, ho! Dead ahead!" And the words were in Russian.

As one man the crew sprang into action, getting sail on the schooner. Putting the helm over sent them into thick, blanketing fog, and like a gray ghost the *Susquehanna* gathered speed, while behind them they heard excited talk in Russian.

"Gant, Boyar, Turk!" LaBarge grabbed the three men. "Lay aft with your rifles. Stand by to fire but not a shot until I give the word, understand?"

He turned on Kohl. "How did they see us before we saw them?"

"They must've had a man at the masthead."

Behind them a cannon boomed suddenly, and they heard the shell crash into the forest, some distance off.

"Shootin' up the other channel," Gant said. "They didn't see us duck out."

A half hour later, sliding more swiftly through thinning fog, they heard another shot, far behind them. The patrol ship had obviously taken the other, more obvious channel. Yet they themselves were sailing into the unknown and from brief glimpses of the shore nobody could guess the position.

Abruptly, they emerged from the fog and saw dead ahead of them a mighty shaft of rock towering over two hundred feet into the air!

Kohl whooped. "Cap'n!" He grabbed Jean's arm. "We're okay! That's Eddystone Rock an' we're not more than twenty miles above Revillagigedo Channel! I've been this far a dozen times!"

Far behind them the patrol ship *Lena* captained by Alexi Boncharof, with Baron Zinnovy aboard, felt its way slowly up the unknown channel. Boncharof, knowing the temper of his passenger and superior, was growing more and more worried.

There was a current flowing against them and he was positive it was no tidal current.

"I think," he began hesitantly, "there is a river at the end of this inlet. I do not believe they went this way."

"I heard them, I tell you!" Zinnovy's voice was coldly furious.

They proceeded another mile, two miles. Boncharof was thoroughly unhappy. Experience had taught him it was foolhardy to pursue poachers; one had to wait until opportunity offered rather than venture into narrow channels filled with dangers of all sorts. But who was he to advise his superior, an officer of the Imperial Navy?

Yet when the fog broke they saw two rivers flowing into a dead-end inlet, and no sign of the *Susquehanna*.

Baron Paul Zinnovy stared wide-eyed with anger at the shore and the rivers, then he turned abruptly and went below, nor would he appear on deck again until they reached Sitka.

Below deck he poured a glass of cognac. The American had escaped him again, yet he dismissed his failure as he dismissed all failure. One thing he had decided. He dare not let Rotcheff return to St. Petersburg, nor his wife, either, for that matter. He turned the glass in his hand, knowing he must move soon and swiftly. He wished to return to St. Petersburg a wealthy man, to establish himself in the capital. There was no better place for a man to be who had wealth, but without it, one was nothing.

LaBarge now: the man must have taken a small fortune in furs! That schooner was well down in the water; it would take a lot of fur to bring her down so far. If he could have captured the schooner with that fur . . . !

Paul Zinnovy had come into the world as an only child in a country mansion remote from all others of his class, and on an estate where he ruled almost as a prince. His father's overseers had gotten work out of the peasants with the knout, and Paul had been taught to do likewise.

Zinnovy recalled his mother as an inconsequential woman in black who had lived for twenty years in fear of her husband, and as he grew up she came to live in equal fear of her son. At school he was the only child from the gentry and tyrannized over the others, yet he was intelligent and his grades were good. Later, at the university his grades were even better, yet there for the first time he felt discontent. He was no longer first. He found many who were richer, stronger, students who lived on vaster estates, and knew more important people.

A tall, handsome and somewhat cold young man, he repelled people rather than attracted them, and soon learned that his father, a tyrant on his estates, was only a provincial member of the petty nobility and of no consequence in St. Petersburg.

A fine navigator and an excellent officer, Zinnovy soon won promotion on his own merit. Several friends sponsored him in various ways, only to be promptly discarded when their usefulness was at an end. Paul Zinnovy had never heard of Machiavelli, but the Italian could have taught him nothing.

His reading had been limited to gunnery tables, charts, books and papers essential to his career. He was fiercely proud, without scruple or loyalty, and if it is given to any man to be so, he was without fear. His first duel at the university, where duels were usually concluded with the drawing of blood, ended in death. He easily ran his man through, and from that day he was feared. His second duel, with pistols, was with a drunken artillery officer and again he killed his man. Then had come the first of those "duels by request." A young journalist had written articles critical of the Navy, and a superior officer of Zinnovy's casually suggested that if Zinnovy were a loyal officer of the Navy he would resent the articles. He resented them, and killed a man who had known no weapon but the pen, until given a pistol for the duel.

There are always those who admire skill with weapons as there are women who are attracted by a reputation with no thought of what the reputation implies. Paul Zinnovy was valuable to the right people so he obtained promotion. He dressed with care and danced well.

There had been a riot at Kronstadt when Zinnovy was Officer of the Day. Although a mere outburst of rebellious fury on the part of seamen who had endured too much, Zinnovy treated it as the beginning of revolution. Acting with ruthless speed, efficiency and cruelty, he personally killed the ringleader with a pistol and summarily executed three others. He was commended publicly by his commanding officer, who commented in private, "Efficient, but too bloody."

During this period in Russia all books on logic and philosophy were forbidden, and although there was reform later it was so slight as to warrant no discussion. Censorship subjected all printed matter to rigid scrutiny. It was a period of stifling tyranny and obedience without discussion, an atmosphere suited to the development and rise of Paul Zinnovy.

Yet the new Czar, Alexander II, did not approve of undue violence, and his policy was somewhat more liberal than Russia was expecting. Baron Zinnovy had ordered the knout for a cadet, and he was about to be broken in rank for this offense when influence was brought to bear and he was sent to Sitka, instead. If he made good there he would be returned with honors. He was given other, strictly confidential orders.

Those orders concerned the mission of Count Rotcheff and future plans for a new company charter. The Count was to be rendered ineffectual at Sitka, and if this could not be done, he was to be destroyed, and in such a way that the Baron's hand would not be visible.

As for Jean LaBarge, Zinnovy thought, his time would come too. He was not important except that he was aiding and abetting Rotcheff, but Paul Zinnovy hated him.

He finished his cognac. LaBarge had gotten away, and nothing could be done about that, but there was much to be done in Sitka. He must make careful moves that would cut the ground from under Count Rotcheff's feet and leave him without authority.

Authority, to matter, must be enforced. If the means of enforcing it be taken away nothing but prestige is left, and little enough of that. Paul Zinnovy thought he knew a way. . . .

21

Three times in the following year Jean LaBarge took the *Susquehanna* to the northwest coast, and not until the third of these voyages did he encounter the patrol ship. Each voyage was carefully planned beforehand, and the route mapped out only after considerable study and an analysis of all reports from Alaska. On two of the voyages they held to the inside passage; on the third they remained far out to sea until in the latitude of the first trading point.

Contrary to usual practice among traders, they moved the ship only by night, in the first hours of the day or the very last before dark, and during the day they anchored in tiny, out-of-the-way inlets. Despite his precautions LaBarge was sure there had been spies in some of the villages and that Zinnovy was aware of his presence.

When each trip ended he paid his crew and gave each man a bonus depending on the size of the cargo and what the furs brought on the market. There was no news of either Rotcheff or Helena, though his crew circulated in port, listening to pick up information, and were given additional bonuses for this.

There was a rumor they were still in Sitka but he placed no faith in the story. Nor could he forget Helena.

His voyages had been highly successful, the profits enormous. On the last voyage he had bought gold from Skayeut.

He had written Rob Walker a long letter after returning from his first trip to Sitka, and had received some months later a very serious reply, which said in part:

> Your letter is here beside me, and if you were to see it you would find those passages concerning Russian America, which you call Alaska, underlined in red ink. You would be even more surprised to find that you are very much quoted in the cloakrooms of both House and Senate. You have told me much of the wealth and size of Alaska, and of its proximity to Siberia. Nowhere else is the United States so close to the troubles of the old world as there, and, as long as Russia is on the continent of America, there is danger. I know . . . our two governments are now friendly, and I trust this may be ever so, but, should Russia and the United States ever have a falling out, it would be well that they have no foothold upon this continent. Jean, we must buy Alaska!

March of another year was drawing to a close when Jean, wearing a carefully tailored suit of dark gray, stopped by Winn's Branch for dinner. Part of the afternoon and most of the evening he had spent in the office of the rebuilt warehouse, planning a new trip to the northwest. The Branch was a large salon furnished in a manner both tasteful and elegant, standing at the corner of Washington and Montgomery Streets. It had become almost immediately after its opening a gathering place for the wealthy and successful of San Francisco. Seating four hundred and fifty, it was crowded most of the time.

Pausing in the entrance, Jean let his eyes move over the crowd, seeking familiar faces. His own table, reserved each evening at this hour, was empty. Captain Hutchins had not yet arrived.

At a table not far from his, Royal Weber sat with Charley Duane. Jean was quite sure Duane had at least protected the arsonists after the burning of the warehouse, and possibly had instigated the burning or served as a go-between.

He started for his table, but Royal Weber called out to him and motioned for him to join them. Hesitating, LaBarge remembered suddenly that Weber was agent for the Sitka people, and walked to the table. "You want something?"

Weber's face flushed at the tone. "Look, LaBarge, I have news for you."

"What news?"

"Sit down. We'll talk."

"I can stand, or you can come to my office. I won't sit down because I don't like the company you keep."

Duane's face went white and he started to rise but Weber put a hand on his arm. "Forget it, Charley. LaBarge is joking."

Duane stared up at LaBarge, his hatred evident. "He's not joking," he said, "and I like neither the words nor the tone."

"With your associations, Duane, I shouldn't think you'd mind."

Duane wanted desperately to rise and smash LaBarge's face, but his memory of what had happened to Bart Freel and Yankee Sullivan was still ripe. He had himself seen the finish of the Sullivan fight, and knew he was in no such class.

He shrugged. "Have your fun."

LaBarge turned to Weber. "Whatever it is, I'll listen, but make it quick."

"You'll be interested to hear that Count Rotcheff has been ordered back to St. Petersburg immediately, and he has suggested a desire to be taken to Siberia in the *Susquehanna*, and by you."

"The order is signed by Rotcheff?"

"Yes. He wishes you to bring another cargo of wheat to Sitka, and you will be permitted to take a cargo of furs from there."

"I'll think about it."

"You don't understand. You must go at once."

Jean LaBarge crossed to his table and dropped into his chair facing the room. This could very well be a trap, a means of drawing him into Alaskan waters where he might be taken at will. On the other hand, the last thing Russia would want would be trouble in the Far East or Alaska. If the signature on the request from Count Rotcheff was genuine, he would go. Obviously, the Count did not trust himself on any ship under the command of Baron Zinnovy or subject to his supervision. . . . A cargo of wheat would bring a good price in Sitka, and with the furs he could make a substantial profit . . . and he would see Helena again.

Or would he? Weber had said nothing about the Princess. She might have already preceded Rotcheff to St. Petersburg. Jean chewed his lower lip, considering the situation . . . but there was no reason to consider . . . he was going.

Sitka lay warm in the morning sunshine when Jean LaBarge walked along the passage through the log warehouse. Much had changed. The equipment was worn, the clothing shabby, and it was apparent that few ships were arriving from the homeland.

Duncan Pope was in command of the schooner, and Kohl had accompanied Jean ashore. There were many men standing idle about the streets, most of them the hard-bitten *promyshleniki*, the same crowd who had brutalized the natives and fought the Tlingits. Many were former convicts, criminals shipped over from Siberia; others were renegades from various countries.

Leaving Kohl in the town, Jean started up the street alone. The booths of the merchants lined the way and the Tlingit women looked at him with interest. Two Tlingit men watched him approach, and one inclined his head as if to nod. LaBarge acknowledged the greeting, if greeting it was.

Baranof Castle was just before him. At the thought of seeing Helena his heart began to race. He was a fool to think of her, yet the fact remained that he could think of no one else. And as long as Rotcheff lived she would make no move nor allow him to make one.

The door opened as he crossed the porch and a servant bowed. "Captain LaBarge? Count Rotcheff is expecting you!"

Crossing the foyer, his heart pounding, he went through the door and saw Rotcheff rise from behind his desk, hand outstretched. He looked older, more tired.

"My friend! My very good friend!" His sincerity was obvious. "Captain, there have been times when I did not expect to see you again, but it is good! Believe me, it is good!"

The warmth of the greeting found him responding in kind, and he realized anew how much he liked this fine old man with his scholar's face and ready smile. "It is good to be here," he said simply.

"You brought the wheat?"

"Yes, and other things as well." He hesitated. "The Princess? She is well?"

"Waiting to see you. You will join us now?"

Helena turned quickly from the table where she was arranging tea, and he saw the sudden way her breath caught, the quick lift of her breasts, then a glad, lovely smile.

"Jean! At last you've come to us!"

Over tea Rotcheff explained. Zinnovy was in charge, the director no more than a figurehead. Rotcheff's messages were intercepted, and although they were treated with bland respect, it was obvious they were prisoners. His demands for a passage to Russia were shunted aside with the excuse that there were no ships.

"I am sure the only reason we are alive is a fear of repercussions. But," he smiled, "please believe me, our greeting is for you, not your ship, relieved as we are to see it. We have missed you, and we have missed outsiders. Even the beauty of Sitka can become dull for lack of new faces." He went on to explain that after Zinnovy's failure to capture LaBarge, the Baron had returned and begun all at once to make changes. At first it seemed an effort to increase the efficiency of the operating force on the patrol ships, but soon it became apparent that one safe man after another had been taken from the Castle and replaced by someone obedient only to Zinnovy. Letters from St. Petersburg had convinced Rudakof that Zinnovy was in the driver's seat, and whatever Count Rotcheff might report would be discounted. Rotcheff and his wife were practically prisoners, and all ships coming to or leaving Sitka were checked by Zinnovy's men. At first none of this had been apparent. Zinnovy had either avoided them or been carefully respectful, but he had built carefully to the point where he would have the situation in hand.

"The people of Sitka?"

"Frightened, most of them, but they hate him.

Right now the Baron is worried, I believe. When orders arrived recalling me to St. Petersburg he became very friendly and extremely polite."

"Does he know I'm here?"

"He was furious . . . but even he will be glad to see the wheat this time, and I've told him there was not a ship I'd trust myself in . . . not in Sitka harbor."

Later, Rotcheff returned to his desk and left them alone. When the door closed they stood for a long time looking into each other's eyes.

"Jean, Jean," Helena said, at last, "you've no idea how we've missed you!"

"We?"

"Alexander, too. There have been times when we have thought of you as our only friend. You've no idea what it means to know there is someone, somewhere, who would come if called. Alexander has said as much several times.

"He is . . . he is not so young any more, and could never stand the rigors of a trip in an open boat. Had it not been for that we might have made the attempt."

"Has he mistreated you? Zinnovy, I mean."

"He wouldn't dare. At least, not yet. But wait until you see him. He has changed, too."

"Changed?"

"Perhaps it is just the veneer wearing off, but he has grown more brutal. He is not formal as he was, not so stiff or so neat. He drinks a lot, and goes to the village too often for his own good. Some night one of the Kolush will kill him. Last month he shot an Indian for nothing at all, and he has had several brutally whipped."

"How about you? Would he let you go?"

"Alexander believes he dares do nothing else, but I only wish I were as sure."

Shadows had grown long in the room and LaBarge became worried. His crew had been chosen for their fighting ability as much as for their seamanship; should they encounter any of Zinnovy's men there might be trouble.

"I can't stay," he said, but made no move to go.

"When you return to Russia, what then?"

"We have no idea what will be planned for us in St. Petersburg. Alexander believes much could be done here, but it would take a certain sort of man to do it."

"And I'll never see you again."

She touched the teapot with idle fingers. "No . . . unless you come to St. Petersburg."

He chuckled. "And what would I do there? I'm not a courtier. Although," he smiled, "one American sailor did well enough—a man named Jones."

"John Paul Jones? I think he was a better hand with a ship than an empress." She turned around to face him. "You've never told me about yourself. What was your mother like?"

"How can you answer a question like that? She was a little woman with big brown eyes and she used to take me into the swamp with her and show me the useful plants. I believe she came from a good family, wealthy at one time. She told me about the house they lived in: it had once been beautiful, but became very run-down, I guess."

He paused. "She wanted me to amount to something and was very sure I would, and she used to tell me it wasn't where a man started that mattered, but where he went. She believed the swamp was a good place for a man to begin. She may have been right."

"And you? What do you want, Jean?"

"You have a husband . . . a man I respect."

She brushed the suggestion aside. "I did not mean that. But there must be something you want, that you want very much."

"I suppose there is. It used to be wealth, but it isn't any more. When I first began to learn about Alaska I felt it was a new country, a rich country where a man could become rich in a hurry. But I've done a lot of thinking since then, and I have a friend, Rob Walker, who has given me a different slant. I want to be rich, I suppose, but I keep thinking of Jefferson. I'd like to see Alaska a part of the United States."

"Why?"

"I've heard men curse it. I've heard them talk about the cold, the wolves, the northern lights, but that's not important. I want it for my country because someday my country may need it very much."

The room was now dark and the town only a velvet blackness where a few lights shone like far-off stars. Down upon the bay the harbor lights shot arrows of gold into the black heart of the water.

"What of you, Jean?"

"What I want I can make with these—" He lifted his hands. "Where there's fur I'll have some of it, and where there's gold, I'll take my share. But that's not enough. More and more I want to do something of value, the way Rob Walker is doing."

"Tell me about him."

"He's a little man, the way my mother was a little woman. I doubt if he weighs more than one hundred pounds. But that's the only way he's small. I think he would do anything for his country, and he knows how to bring men together to work, how to use their ambition, their envy, greed, even their hatred. It's funny—I remember him mostly as a shy little boy, and now to think he's become a great man."

A servant entered and lighted the lamps. When he was gone she turned to him again. "You may get what you want, Jean. Strangely, perhaps, it is what Alexander also wants. We must talk to him of this."

"And what of us?"

She put her hand on his sleeve. "You must not ask that, and you must not think of it. There is nothing for us, nor can there be anything for us, except"—she looked up at him—"except to say, I love you."

The door opened and Rotcheff came into the room. "I am sorry, Captain, if I have kept you waiting. You will wish to return to your ship."

22

He was crossing the foyer when a door opened and in the opening stood Paul Zinnovy. LaBarge needed only a quick glance to see that what Helena had told him was true. Zinnovy was a changed man. There was about him now an air of sullen brutality. Little remained of the immaculate perfection in uniform that he had once been. His coat was unbuttoned and his shirt collar gaped wide. He carried a bottle by the neck and in the other hand a half-filled glass, but he was not drunk. He was heavier than when Jean had last seen him. There were red veins in his face and his features seemed somehow thicker.

"So? Our little merchant comes to pick crumbs from the Russian table? Enjoy them while you can, Captain, it will not be for long."

"Perhaps."

"So you will take our Rotcheff back to Russia, will you? And that will be the end of Zinnovy, you think?" He chuckled. "Think again, my friend. I have power here. I have a warehouse filled with furs, I have wealth. Do you think I would lose all that and what it could mean to me in St. Petersburg for one man? Or a dozen men?"

Jean was impatient to be away, but the man fascinated him. It was a rare opportunity to see his enemy at first hand. "Count Rotcheff is a good man," he replied shortly, "and very close to the Czar."

Zinnovy smiled. "Is he now? How long does a man's influence last when he is far away?" He held up two fingers and rubbed them together. "See? I will have this. Gold speaks an eloquent tongue, understood in court or cottage. There are many men who stand between the Czar and any issued order. As for Rotcheff"—he shrugged—"he might be dangerous if he gets back, and as for that little bit—"

Jean swung toward Zinnovy. "I'd not say that if I were you."

Zinnovy's eyes danced with cynical amusement. "Ah? So that is how it is? Oh, do not worry, my American friend, I'll say nothing to offend either you or the lady, but it interests me that you would fight for her. Chivalrous, and all that." His eyes narrowed a little. "It interests me that you will fight at all. You have always seemed more ready to run."

Abruptly, Jean turned to the door. Nothing could be gained here and he had a ship to make ready for the sea. A long voyage lay before him and neither the Bering Sea nor the North Pacific was gentle. He walked out, drawing the door to behind him, conscious of Zinnovy'z eyes.

Outside it was completely dark. Most of the lights in the town had been extinguished. Jean

LaBarge paused at the head of the flight of wooden steps and looked down, not enjoying that descent into blackness. Hadn't there been a light there, at the foot of the steps? He started to step down when a low voice called to him.

"Captain! *Wait!*"

He drew back from the step and turned to find a girl, her head covered with a shawl. "It is I! Dounia! You must not go down the steps. There are Russian sailors waiting for you! They mean to kill you!"

"How many?"

"Nine, perhaps ten. I do not know."

"And my men?"

"They are with the boat."

"Is there another path? Where we can't be seen?"

She caught his sleeve. "Come!" Swiftly she led him through the darkness, past barracks and tannery, to the corner of a storehouse. There they crouched in the shadows, listening.

It was very dark, and very still. The water was gray, with a fringe of white along the rocks. From where they stood he looked along the water's edge toward the landing stage. His ship's boat was clearly visible.

Now that they had come this far the girl waited, knowing he must decide the next move. The building loomed above them, and looking back he could see the Castle outlined darkly against the sky. A few of the Russians would be waiting at the bottom of the stair, growing restive now, and there would be others in the log warehouse, watching the boat.

But they would not be watching closely for they would expect no movement there. It would be sounds from up the street they would be expecting.

As he watched he saw a man move in the boat; and taking a chance, he called softly. Ben Turk was at the boat, and so was Gant. Both men knew the call of the loon, and he made it now. The moving figure stood still, listening. Softly, he called again, and there was a stirring in the boat shadows. For an instant starlight glinted on an oar blade.

He realized suddenly he was holding Dounia by the arm. "What about you?" he whispered. "Will you be all right?"

"I know every path."

"You're sure?"

"I played here as a child."

"Your father should have sent someone else. You shouldn't be out at this hour."

"Nobody sent me. I . . . I just came."

He took her shoulders in his hands and squeezed them gently. "Thanks . . . thanks, Dounia. But you must never do this again, do you hear?"

"I won't."

Suddenly she stood on tiptoe and kissed him fiercely on the lips, then ducked under his arm and was gone in the darkness. He started after her, then realized how futile it would be to pursue someone in such dark and unfamiliar surroundings.

The boat was drawing close, drifting like a darker shadow on the gray water. The oars stopped and it glided through the water with only ripples to make a whisper of sound. "Captain?" It was Gant's voice.

"Here."

At that moment a shot sounded.

Jean LaBarge had stepped down to the water's edge, but now he stood still, listening, ears attuned to the slightest sound. Far away an unhappy coyote yammered his loneliness to the wide sky, the water rippled, water dripped from the suspended oars, and then a faint woman's cry, from the Castle.

"Wait here!" he called to Gant.

Spinning, he dashed into the darkness. How he found his way through the maze of buildings he never knew, but suddenly he was back on the Hill, and when he stepped through the door Count Rotcheff lay on the carpet, blood flowing from a wound in his side. Helena was kneeling beside him and two servants came running into the room.

Jean dropped to his knees. His familiarity with wounds had been bred of emergency, and he worked swiftly now. When he had stopped the flow of blood and sent one of the servants running for the doctor, he got to his feet.

The door to Zinnovy's quarters opened and the Baron came out, looking down at the wounded man. His face showed no expression, yet there was a faint flicker of amusement in his eyes. "It seems you've lost a passenger, Captain. He may recover, but it will take time . . . time." Zinnovy glanced at Helena and then at Jean. "In the meantime he must remain here."

"You shot him! You did!" Helena's face was

white, her eyes enormous. "I will see you shot for this! You . . . you . . . !"

"Naturally, you're hysterical." Zinnovy drew himself up. "And of course, I ignore the accusation. It was some Kolush, no doubt, perhaps believing the Count was myself." He smiled again. "I forgive you, Princess, and assure you I shall see that everything is done, everything, I repeat, to speed his recovery. Of course"—he pursed his lips thoughtfully—"it may take months and months."

Turning to Jean he added, "And of course, LaBarge, there will be no need for your schooner. None at all. Your stay here is over at midnight tomorrow. If you are in Russian waters within four days I'll blow you out of the water."

When he was gone, Rotcheff opened his eyes. He glanced quickly after the Baron to make sure he was unheard, then he whispered, "Take her and go." His eyes were bright and quick. "Take her to the Czar, my friend. I cannot go . . . and he will listen to no one else. You must take her, Captain . . . and you must go at once . . . before they realize."

"But—!"

Helena's protest was brushed aside. The Count's voice was firmer and his eyes clear. "Your things are already aboard the schooner, as are mine. Go now, quickly."

"Leave you?" she protested. "Leave you wounded? Perhaps . . ."

"Perhaps dying? No, I shall not die, but unless you go now we may both be killed. We know now to what lengths he will go . . . for it was Paul. I cannot prove it . . . but it was he.

"If you escape, I shall be safe. If you remain here . . . he will try again and again. With you away, safe with the Czar . . . then he dare do nothing more for fear of repercussions. You are the only chance."

"He's right," Jean told her. "And if we go it must be now, before Zinnovy thinks of this."

He led her, still protesting, to the door. Suddenly she turned and fled to Rotcheff and fell on her knees beside him. For a moment she was there, then she arose and came swiftly to the door. As they stepped out to the terrace the doctor and a servant came in the Castle entrance. Wasting no time, Jean led her to the path he had twice covered that night.

Kohl helped her aboard and whispered to Jean, "Zinnovy went out to the *Lena*. What's that mean?"

"Is the cargo gone?"

"Gone. And we've loaded the furs. The last lighter cleared an hour ago."

"All right. As soon as we're aboard we clear for sea. As quietly as possible."

Ben Turk touched his sleeve. "We aren't the only ones, Cap. Look!"

The canvas of the *Lena* was white against the night as she caught for an instant the reflection of shore light. Phosphorus showed in her wake. Zinnovy was taking the patrol ship out and Jean needed no blueprints as to why she was going. Out upon the dark water the sea would swallow any evidence of what happened to the *Susquehanna*;

here in the harbor there were too many witnesses. Without doubt he intended to sink the *Susquehanna* and end the problem presented by LaBarge, once and for all. Yet he could have no idea they intended to sail this soon, nor could he guess that Helena was aboard.

A wind stirred along the face of the mountains, and clouds drifted in the wide sky. Lights from the town made golden daggers into the heart of the black, glistening water. The patrol ship had taken the Middle Channel between Turning and Kutken Islands, but it was only a little past midnight and the anchor of the schooner was catted and she was moving.

"He can sit out there and wait until we come out," Kohl said unhappily, "and when we're at sea and out of gunshot of the town, he can sink us at will."

Jean LaBarge was not thinking of Zinnovy; that would come in its own good time. Now he was thinking of a channel that led north past the Indian settlement and Channel Rock where the *Susquehanna* had lain at anchor on her first voyage. One of the clumsy Russian ships that lay in the harbor had moved across that opening. Zinnovy must have planned shrewdly, hours before; he seemed to have blocked every exit, leaving only the way the *Lena* had gone.

"Keep moving," he told Kohl. "Let her swing as if we were taking the opening past Aleutski Island, and then at the last minute, point her into that opening past the Russian ship."

The channel where the Russian was moored was not more than one hundred and fifty yards wide, and there were rocks along the shore of Japonski Island, but between those off-lying rocks and the Russian ship there was a space . . . very narrow.

"We can't do it," Kohl protested. "We'd be fools to try."

"You do what I tell you."

The wind off the mountains was picking up, the sails filled, and Kohl went aft and took the wheel from Noble. He watched the approach to the channel past Aleutski. A few Russians loitered along the bulwarks of the moored ship. As Kohl measured the distance sweat broke out on his forehead. It was narrow, far too narrow. He swore bitterly, then setting his jaw, he spun the spokes rapidly and pointed their bows at the Russian ship.

There was a long moment before comprehension dawned on the Russian sailors. Suddenly a man shouted hoarsely at them and running aft began to wave his hands wildly at the schooner which was bearing down as if to ram.

"Steady on!" LaBarge walked away from the rail and stood, his big hands on his hips, watching the narrowing gap. Kohl stared at him. To have seen LaBarge at this moment no man would have guessed that he was gambling his ship, their lives, and at the very least a Russian prison. Kohl could not know that LaBarge's throat was so dry he could not swallow, and his heart was throbbing heavily. Had he kicked an ant's nest there could have been no greater burst of activity than there now was aboard the Russian. Men shouted and waved their arms to warn him off, but the *Susquehanna* plunged on.

"Gant! Boyar! Get forward and stand by with your rifles. If anybody lays a hand on the wheel, drop him where he stands!"

It was close. If anyone touched the wheel on the Russian bark it might be just enough to close off the channel and bring about the collision they feared.

The water gap narrowed. A hundred yards . . . seventy . . . fifty! A man standing at the bulwark suddenly ran to the bow and dove off into the black water, swimming wildly for shore. Lights appeared in doorways and people rushed out, shouting and staring seaward.

Kohl's eyes were riveted on the narrowing distance. "Cap'n!" he pleaded.

The moment seemed to stand still as the schooner closed that distance. Forty-five . . . forty . . .

"Hard aport!" LaBarge shouted. His mouth was so dry his voice sounded choked. "Hard over! *Hard!*"

Kohl swung the spokes and Turk jumped to lend a hand. Jean stood with his legs spread, watching the bow of the schooner swing. He had drawn the line very fine indeed, perhaps too fine. But he knew his ship, and the *Susquehanna* answered smartly to her wheel, answered as if she understood what her master wanted. The bow began to swing faster. Jean chewed on the stick of a match and watched the narrowing space.

Thirty yards . . . twenty-five . . . twenty . . . fifteen. The schooner was forging ahead now, but still swinging. She was . . . she was going to clear. Suddenly added wind filled her sails and she gathered speed, slipping past the stern of the moored ship with less than ten feet to spare.

Close off the port side were the off-lying rocks, but the *Susquehanna* slipped through and lifted her bows proudly to the seas.

"All sail!" LaBarge shouted the command and then walked forward alone so they could not see his hands trembling. He had, in that moment, risked everything. If the wind had fallen the least bit, if the schooner had yawed . . . but she had come through like a thoroughbred.

He turned, after a moment, and walked aft. They were not yet free. If Zinnovy knew they had started and had slipped out of the harbor he might sail north and round Japonski Island to cut them off. Only, it was dark, and while the night lasted there was still a chance.

"Barney." LaBarge stopped beside Kohl, who had turned the wheel over to Larsen. "You told me you once took a boat through Neva Strait."

Kohl was still sweating out the near collision. "But that was in broad daylight!" he protested.

Jean grinned at him. "Next time you see the crowd at the Merchant's Exchange," he told him, "you can tell them you're the only man alive who ever took a schooner through Neva Strait in the dark!"

23

Helena, wrapped in a dark cloak, returned to the deck. She had stood by during part of the escape operation, and now she listened to comments of the crew. This ship, she realized, was operated as though every man aboard had a real share in its success. Rolling along under a good head of sail with a following wind, the crew stood by, alert for whatever might come.

"Neva Strait," Kohl was explaining patiently, "is four miles of pure hell in the daytime. The Whitestone Narrows are maybe forty yards wide, possibly less. In the daylight the dangers are marked by kelp, and some of the rocks are awash. At night you can't see anything."

LaBarge knew that Kohl's first instinct when danger threatened the ship was to hesitate, to object to the risk. His second instinct was to weigh their chances and if the situation warranted it, to go along with the risk.

"And if we get through? What then?"

"Peril Strait around the end of the island, and once in the sound on the other side, we sail north."

"One thing I'll say," Kohl grumbled, "you've got guts."

"A good ship and a good crew," LaBarge added.

Together he and Helena walked to the waist, where a little spray was breaking over the gunwale, and it tasted salt on their lips. They were silent together, listening to the bow-wash about the hull, the whining of wind in the rigging, and the straining of the schooner against sea and wind. These were sounds of the sea, the sounds a man remembers when he lies awake at night on shore, and hears in his blood, feels deep in the convolutions of his brain, the sounds that have taken men back to the sea for these thousands of years. The winds that whispered in the rigging had blown long over the icy steppes and the cold Arctic plains, and over empty, lonely, unknown seas that lay gray under gray clouds.

Neither of them could avoid the realization that if all went well they would be together for months on end. Now, for the first time, they knew they were definitely committed to a long journey together. As their eyes grew accustomed to the darkness they could watch the whitecaps on the dark, glasslike waves, and see the darker, unknown shores that rose abruptly from the water's edge.

"You seemed very calm."

"I wasn't," Jean admitted, "I was scared."

"This story I must tell to my uncle. He will enjoy it." She changed the subject. "The Neva Strait . . . it is bad?"

"Did you ever walk down a dark hallway in a

226

strange house, a hallway scattered at random with chairs? It will be like that."

"You leave it to the mate?"

"I'd better . . . he's twice the sailor I am. Don't be fooled by that business back there: I was gambling that they wouldn't think I'd take such a risk. Also, I've a good ship and a good crew, and I knew they would be ready for anything that might happen. For day-to-day sailing Kohl is much better than I am."

They were silent, watching the water. Helena knew that Zinnovy had gone so far now that withdrawal was impossible. Although the shooting of Rotcheff·could not be proved, if she reached the Czar his position would be at least endangered and might be finished. It was always easier to explain a disappearance than to escape consequences of crime when confronted by a witness. Yet the longer Zinnovy pursued the schooner the better Rotcheff's chances of recovery without hindrance, and Rotcheff would be in touch with Busch. The merchant had as many fighting men as Zinnovy himself and would be no more reluctant to use them.

Long after Helena went below, Jean remained on deck. He walked forward to where Boyar stood lookout in the bow. "You have crossed Siberia, Boyar? How long would it require?"

"Who can say? Three months? Or three years? It is a long trip, nearly six thousand of miles, and the roads are bad, the *troikas* miserable, the people indifferent or criminal."

Three months . . . they could scarcely hope to make it faster even though she was a niece of the

Czar. To secure an escort they must appeal to the very people they wished to avoid. The headquarters of the Russian American Company was in Siberia, and many of the officials were actually in the pay of the Company.

The shores slipped by in darkness. It gave him an eerie feeling to be sliding into these narrow channels, uncharted and largely unknown. How many men might already have lost their lives here, unrecorded by history? Captain Cook had been here, and the Spanish before that, and the Russian ships. The first Russians who had come to these islands had vanished. There was a story in the Tlingit villages that a chief covered with a bearskin had enticed them into the woods and into an ambush. A second boat sent ashore to find the first vanished in the same way. Their ship had waited and waited, then finally sailed away. But Chinese and Japanese fishing boats had been carried to this coast, and some of their crews might have survived. What strange lives they must then have led, with no hope of return to their homes.

"Neva Point ahead, Captain."

"Go aft and report to Mr. Kohl. I'll stand watch."

He tasted the smell of pines on the wind, heard the splash of something falling into water. Behind him the crew were moving about, taking in sail. The Point loomed suddenly on their left, well defined. On their right a breaking rock showed a ruffle of white foam where the angry lips of the sea bared its teeth against the shore.

Kohl came forward and spat across the rail.

"Thank God, she's deep enough. There's four fathoms in the Narrows, and it's deeper beyond."

The Whitestone Narrows closed down on them like the jaws of a trap. It was cooler there, with the forest closer. They could hear the murmur of wind in the pines, but the schooner moved forward confidently. Ahead of them there was faint gray in the sky.

After what seemed a long time of creeping down the dark Narrows the schooner slid into the open water beyond. The Neva lay behind . . . how long had it been?

"Nearly two hours," Kohl said. "There aren't any fast passages of the Neva."

Pope came on deck to take over the watch. He glanced at the graying sky, a thin, silent man who seemed ever discontented with things as they were. He swore bitterly when he realized they had passed the Neva in his sleep, and swore again when he learned he must take her through Peril Strait.

Finally, more tired than he could have believed, Jean stumbled down the companionway and stood in the paneled cabin, watching the brass lamp sway to the ship's movement. Helena was at the table with a freshly brewed pot of tea. "Mr. Kohl took his to his bunk. Sit down. You look exhausted."

Gratefully, he accepted the tea. The warmth went through him slowly, taking the chill from his muscles, the damp from his bones. He was the first to speak and it was of something he had considered for a long time.

"There's something you can do for me," he said. "You can do it if anyone can. I want to see the Czar."

She was startled. "The Czar! But why?"

"Maybe . . . I don't know . . . he might consider selling Alaska to the United States. If he should agree . . . well, Rob Walker could do the rest."

"I can promise nothing, but I can try."

She was silent, and he saw how white were her fingers that pressed the cup, and the shadows under her eyes, shadows he had not been able to see out on the deck under the clouds. "Jean, Jean," she whispered, "I wish I knew how he was."

"He'll be all right."

Rotcheff had made a tough decision but he had made it without hesitation, knowing exactly what must be done. It was another reason for admiring the husband of the woman he loved . . . and Rotcheff had a good chance. Familiar as he was with gunshot wounds, he knew that such a wound, low down on the left side, was more likely only a severe flesh wound. With care and proper food he might make it.

"Where are we going, Jean? What is it we have to do?"

"The quickest way would be through Salisbury Strait to the Pacific, but we might be cut off there, so we're going east up a passage called Peril Strait."

"Is it dangerous?"

"There are tide rips in all these passages, and unexpected currents. Water piles up in these narrow guts, then comes roaring through, and most of the rocks are uncharted. By this time Zinnovy undoubtedly has other ships out from Sitka to cut us off."

Above them the brass lantern swayed and in his bunk behind the small door Kohl snored in an easy rhythm. Jean's head lowered to his arms for a moment of rest and at once he was asleep. The night had been long . . . long.

Outside a small wave broke over the bow and the water ran along the deck rustling into the scuppers where it gurgled solemnly. Helena looked across the table at the black, wavy hair, glistening in the lantern's light, and put out her hand to touch it, then drew it quickly back, frightened by the impulse. After a moment she got to her feet and went into her little cubbyhole of a cabin and closed the door.

She stood then, her back to the door and her eyes closed, while the light from a crack moved slowly back and forth across her face. And then for a long time there was a silence made more silent by the sound of breathing and the lonely ship-sounds in the gray light of a breaking day at sea.

24

For two days the *Susquehanna* crept along through a dense fog that reduced visibility to zero, a cold penetrating fog that wrapped the schooner in a depressing cloud. With Zinnovy somewhere behind there was no chance to heave-to and wait it out, so they continued to creep along, using what little wind there was. With luck they could get into Icy Strait and so to the Pacific.

No sound reached them except that of breaking surf. Fog had come upon them in the vicinity of the Hoggat Reefs along Deadman Reach, and they had crept north to the point, rounded it and sailed southeastward toward Chatham. Every mile was a mile of danger for fog filled the Strait and tidal currents were strong.

During a brief interval when fog cleared they rounded another point and started north, ice becoming more frequent. Then the fog closed in again, thicker and colder than before. Several times, unable to see the floes in time, they were struck with brutal force.

Kohl, wrapped in sweaters and oilskins, joined Jean in the bow while the lookout went below for coffee. "We'd better heave-to, Cap'n. Not even the Russkies will try moving in this fog."

"If it gets colder we'll start icing up," LaBarge said. "Damn it, man, if we get caught in these narrow channels we're through!"

Kohl agreed gloomily. "If we could only get a couple of hours of sunshine and good wind."

"How far do you think we've come since turning into the Strait?"

"Your guess is as good as mine. We've been moving, but with the current against us part of the time, and there hasn't been a rock or a point to take a sight from."

"Do you know these waters?"

"No . . . but Icy Strait can't be far."

Men came and went like wraiths in the gray, clinging fog. Ghostly trailers of fog lay in the rigging and the great sails dripped water to the deck. Nowhere was there anything by which to gauge their progress, and much of the time they could not see beyond the bowsprit.

Yet they could not heave-to. Even now ships might be awaiting them off every passage to the sea, but if they could get through Icy Strait and Cross Sound the opening was wide enough for them to slip by . . . if they did not go past it in the fog and end up in one of the deadend, ice-breeding inlets north of the Strait.

Jean held up a hand. "I thought I heard something, Barney. Listen. . . . "

At first there was only the ship sounds, the strain of rigging, the creaking of ship's timbers, a faint stir of unseen movement, and then they heard it dead ahead. The beat of surf against a rocky shore.

Unmoving, they listened for a clearer sound. Not far off was a shore upon which waves were breaking. "I wish I dared fire a shot." Jean was worried. "The echo might help us."

"Not in this fog. Besides, I think Point Augusta is a low shore."

Miraculously, the fog thinned and they glimpsed momentarily a low shore on which a light sea was breaking, a sea that hustled and whispered among the black rocks. Jean studied it, trying to remember what little information he had about the area. He seemed to recall that the point they must turn into Icy Strait was more abrupt, yet there was clear water ahead of them and as far as they could see on the starb'rd side. "All right," he said, "let's try it."

When he went below Helena was reading. She looked up quickly, and seeing his expression, said, "You're worried."

"Yes . . . we changed course and I'm not sure we should have."

"If we could only get some news!" She closed her book. "I've done all I can to keep from worrying, but I can't help it. Jean, I never should have left Alexander."

"You would have both been trapped. He was right to make you go, Helena."

He accepted a cup of tea. It was scalding hot and very strong. He had never appreciated tea until he started coming into northern waters, but there they all drank it.

Kohl stepped down the ladder. "Cap'n? It was a wrong turn. There's land off the starb'rd beam."

"Close?"

"It isn't the strait."

He went on deck and stood there, his fists balled in his pockets. "It's narrow," he said, "it would be a risk to attempt a turn with the tide running."

"It wouldn't be worth it."

Any decision was better than none. "Drop the hook and we'll wait it out. When the fog lifts we'll get the hell out of here."

"I've seen these fogs last two weeks."

"All right. Get a boat into the water and we'll explore a little. See? There's about four feet of clearance between the water and the fog."

They were taking a chance, he realized that. With the onset of darkness finding the ship again might be difficult. Still, there was no place it could go, and they had only to come back up the strait to find it. Strait? More likely an inlet. They shoved off and let the longboat drift along close to the shore.

Nearly a half hour had passed when Boyar, who was in the bow, lifted a warning hand. At the signal all rested on their oars, and then they all heard it. Somewhere not far off a man was whistling. Then something dropped on a deck and a man swore in Russian.

The boat still drifted, and then, plain to all of them, from beneath the fog they saw the gray hull of the patrol ship. She lay fair across the mouth of the inlet, blocking any escape.

A voice spoke in Russian. "I saw slops from a ship in the opening of the inlet. We've only to wait until the fog lifts and then go in after them. This is Tenakee Inlet and there is no other way out, I know the place well."

At a signal from Jean the oars dipped gently and turning the boat they started back the way they had come. His own ship was up the inlet and out of hearing of the Russian.

Tenakee Inlet . . . there was something he should remember about Tenakee. He scowled into the fog . . . it had been a half-breed who had come down the coast with old Joshua Flintwood, the Bedford whaler. Once on the schooner's deck he wasted no time. "We'll go to the head of the inlet. There may be a way out."

"If there is," Kohl said skeptically, "we'd best find it. Once the fog lifts the *Lena* is coming in, which leaves us like a duck in a shooting gallery."

"We've got that long." Duncan Pope spat over the rail. "He'd be a fool to come in here before the fog lifts."

All the long day through they crept up the inlet through fog like gray cotton, holding as close to shore as feasible, taking soundings as they proceeded. Twice they passed small openings but each proved to be a bay, and it was not until almost dusk that the fog thinned close to shore and they glimpsed the head of the inlet, fronting a mud flat.

Wanting time, Jean had the hook dropped and the schooner swung to anchor.

"Any chance of slipping by?" Kohl wondered.

"No . . . not with his guns. He's just inside the opening of the inlet where he can cover the passage."

At the shore the fog was thinner. It drifted in ghostly wraiths among the dark sentinel pines. A break in the line of trees caught Jean's eye, and he had a sudden hunch. "Drop the boat over, Barney. Then pick four men and we'll go ashore."

Leaving the boat on the gravel beach, Jean LaBarge led the way toward the break in the trees. To the right and left the forest was a solid wall of virgin timber, dripping with damp from the fog, but before them the opening gaped wide and they stumbled into a narrow path that led into it.

It was very still. There was no movement of wind or animal. Only water dripping from the trees and the gray mystery of the fog. There had been a wider track here at one time, and only a few large trees in the opening, although some of the bordering pines were magnificent trees. When they had walked about fifty yards they found themselves looking out over another arm of the sea. Jean walked down to the edge and tasted the water. It was salt.

It was an arm of the sea of some size and it ran in a northwesterly direction. Boyar shifted his rifle to his other arm, and got out his chewing tobacco. "That there," he said, "must open into Icy Strait."

The water was obviously quite deep only a few feet out from shore. He had an idea and it scared him. If a man could catch a spring tide ... or even without it. But it was a fool idea.

He seated himself on a rock and stoked his pipe. The shore was flat and this was an old Indian portage where they had carried their canoes and *bidarkas* from one inlet to the other for many years. The water was deep off both sides, and at no place was the level of the portage more than six feet above the water level. There were indications that the sea had once been higher. No doubt the level of the water had fallen with years, but at present the distance was a bare sixty yards from inlet to inlet. Yet a schooner was not a canoe that one could pick up and carry across a neck of land.

Getting to his feet he strolled slowly back toward the *Susquehanna*, studying the ground with care. The big question was the fog. How long would it hold? How long would Zinnovy be content to wait him out? A slight change in the wind, or even a rise in wind strength, and the fog would be blown out to sea, leaving them naked and exposed. They had but one gun, although of very good range, and the patrol ship had ten guns and Zinnovy was a naval officer accustomed to handling ships under fire. If it came to a fight they would have absolutely no chance; the superior maneuverability of the schooner was useless in the narrow inlet.

The portage was wide enough, and they would have to fell some trees, anyway. Did he dare take the gamble? The Vikings used to take their ships over narrow necks of land, and there had been a pirate in the West Indies who had ... Closer to home,

Jean had himself seen the Missouri River steamboats "grasshoppered" over sand bars, an occurrence common to nearly every trip upriver.

"All right, Barney," he said finally, "break out that heavy tackle. Get twelve men ashore with axes and make it fast! We're going to take the *Susquehanna* over the portage!"

25

The forest rang with the sound of axes and the torchlight cast weird, dancing shadows upon the backdrop of fog and forest. The first of the skids was in place and the two most expert axmen in the crew were beveling the edges, trimming them as smooth as if planed. The anchor trees had been selected and the brush cleared. The skids were run down into the water and as it was nearly high tide the bow of the schooner was being eased up to the skids.

Six men with poles on either side of the bow were helping to guide her into the troughlike, opening of the skid. The smoothed-off sides of the skids were heavily coated with grease and a wire rope ran to the big tree well inland through two huge blocks with snatch blocks attached to trees along the portage to exert greater pull. The bow eased into the skid opening and the men dropped their poles and scrambled up the bow chains to the deck to join the others at the capstan. Setting their capstan bars in place they began to walk around and take up the slack. Twelve men leaned their strength into the bars and two more slapped grease on the skids. Slowly, the schooner began to inch up the skids.

"I've been thinking," Pope said suddenly, "—that other inlet over there. I think that's the same inlet where Hoonah village is. The directions line up right, and Hoonah is Chief Katlecht's village. He hates Russians."

LaBarge thought a minute. He knew of Katlecht; he was, in fact, one of the chiefs to whom he had sent presents, and from whose village had come some of the best furs he had been buying in the past years.

"I had an idea," Pope added, "one of us might go to see him. We could use thirty or forty of those husky lads of his right now."

"Do you know him?"

"I should hope to smile." Pope chuckled. "Spent a couple of months in the village, even had me a Kolush wife. Maybe I should have stayed."

"Take Boyar and get on over there. Get what information you can, and if you can get some help, bring them on the jump."

The schooner was moving slowly, but it was moving. The rigging of the snatch block had increased the strength of the pull by several times and the schooner was inching up on the skids. The remainder of the crew were trimming felled trees for skids to be used further along.

Jean walked along the line of travel with a rifle under his arm, but from time to time he took an ax and spelled one of the crewmen. Kohl was himself taking a place at the capstan . . . day would soon be breaking. Would the fog lift?

With the schooner high and dry they would have no choice but to abandon it and take to the woods, and that would mean destruction of the schooner and their chance of escape as well.

Not far from the schooner was a promontory covered with forest and easily ascended from the shore side. Taking several men from the crew, Jean had their one gun lowered over the side and hauled to a position among the trees on that promontory. From its position it commanded the approach to the head of the inlet. A few shells might stand off the patrol ship for a short time at least.

By daybreak the schooner was completely clear of the water, holding its position with guy wires running to trees on either side of the portage. The hauling tackle was shifted then to a new set of trees and the men resumed their position at the capstan bars. Gant struck up a chantey and slowly and steadily they plodded around the capstan, and inch by slow inch the schooner began to move once more.

At midmorning there was a sudden shout from the woods, followed by a cheer from the crew. Led by Duncan Pope and Boyar a swarm of husky Tlingit Indians hustled toward the schooner. In the van was Katlecht himself, grinning broadly. He thrust out his hand as he had seen white men do, and with the fingers of the other plucked at the red flannel shirt LaBarge had sent him from San Francisco a year before. He also carried a bowie knife Jean had sent and displayed it proudly.

The exhausted sailors resigned their places at the capstan to the Tlingits, and twenty powerful Indians took over. Others hauled and pushed at the hull while still others cleared brush ahead of the moving schooner.

And the fog held, gray, drifting streamers of it lurking among the trees like lost ghosts. The air was damp and cold.

Helena had joined the cook in making tea and serving Tlingit and seaman alike, working from a fire beside the portage. By noon, with the fog showing no change, the schooner had advanced its full length out of the water.

Sweating and tired, Jean accepted a cup gratefully. Holding it in both hands he warmed his numbed fingers, his breath forming a little fog of its own. "You're all woman, Helena," he said. "I never thought I'd see a princess serving tea to my crew."

"Why should a princess not care for her" —she had started to say "man" but caught herself in time—"men as well as any other woman?"

She walked around the fire to him. "Jean, can we do it? How does it look now?"

"If the fog breaks we're in trouble. Otherwise . . . well, we're making progress. I think we can do it or I'd not have tried."

"Was there another choice?"

"No."

The schooner moved at a steadier pace. The Indians had brought grease from their camp, barrels of it that came in their *bidarkas*, and they were slapping it liberally on the skids. The *Susquehanna*, unnaturally tall now that she was out of her natural element, towered above them. Once a small gust of wind came through the pines and the fire guttered, and all waited, holding their breath, but the wind disappeared and the fog held.

Jean returned to the capstan and took his place, plodding steadily for an hour. When Kohl relieved him, he returned to superintending the shifting of the tackle and the guy wires. Also, with apprehension for what might happen, he had two tall poles cut to make a shears in the event they needed to grasshopper the schooner. He had never seen it attempted with a craft of this size but as a boy he had seen the heavy river schooners grasshoppered over sand bars on more than one occasion, and knew that at last resort this would be the method to use.

Yet once the schooner reached the far side of the portage they must skid it into the water. Mentally he calculated the times of the tides. They worked within narrow limits of time and their only hope lay in the fog. If the fog held they could do it, but if it did not. . . .

Small men trooped to the fires for tea and warmth. Twice Jean had rum broken out and laced their coffee when the switch was made to that beverage. During the late afternoon Katlecht sat by the fire sipping his coffee and rum when he suddenly looked up at LaBarge who had stumbled wearily to the fire. "Fog go," Katlecht said. "Fog go soon."

Jean glanced at Kohl, and their faces were grim.

Indians were excellent judges of weather; if Katlecht was right their time was short. He sent a messenger to the men at the gun to stand by for trouble, then had guns brought from the ship's armory and passed around to the men to be kept close to hand in the event of attack.

Despite their weariness the men returned to their labors with a rush. The water ahead of them meant escape and freedom; to be caught here meant death or worse, a Siberian prison camp. The Tlingits, filled with their age-old hatred of Russians, fell to with a will and to the tune of chanteys they shoved and pushed on the capstan bars. It was slow, painstaking, backbreaking labor, but the schooner moved and the water lay ahead of them, only a short distance away now.

But the fog was thinning. . . . Jean glanced up and saw a star . . . then other stars. "Pope," he said, "take the gunner, Gant and Turk, and go out and relieve the men at the gun. Don't take any unnecessary risks, but do what damage you can." He hesitated. "Wait until she's close, Pope, and for God's sake, hurt her."

Within the hour the fog was gone and darkness had come. Once more torches were lighted and the heavy blocks were shifted again, new anchor trees had been chosen and marked out. The shifting of the gear took less time now that the movements had become familiar. Once again the capstan was manned. The schooner was moving.

Taking his rifle, LaBarge started back toward the Tenakee side, Helena walking beside him. Bundled in furs against the penetrating chill of the night, she walked easily beside him, showing little of the exhaustion she must feel.

"Can we get into the water before daylight?"

"If the men hold out. They're weary now; how they keep going I can't guess, and Indians never work like this, anyway."

The skids had been torn up and taken to the opposite side to use again, and there was little evidence of what had been done except the cut brush and the trampled earth. Standing together they looked out upon the dark and silent water. There was no sound but the soft rustle of the water on the shore, and above them the vast sky, studded with stars. The sounds of working men, the creak of tackle, the groaning of the schooner's timbers and occasional cries of the men seemed farther away than they actually were. A coolness came off the water. Somewhere out on the inlet a fish splashed.

"Even if we make it here," Jean said, "we've far to go."

"I'll be in my own country, and I'll be safe."

"Siberia is not Russia," Jean replied bluntly. "You know that as well as I do. It's full of thieves and renegades with a corrupt administration to whom it won't matter at all that you're a niece of the Czar . . . if they believe you they'll be afraid of what you might report."

"There's still no reason for you to come."

"I'm coming, so don't bother your head about it."

They stood hand in hand watching the stars

above the dark rim of the pines. There had been too few moments like this, and life without them was nothing. Their love was like no other love, for they could not speak of it, and each was on guard against desire. A word, a touch, it would take so little.

Nearing the lighted area, LaBarge suddenly quickened his step. "Something's wrong," he said.

The men stood about, muscles heavy with weariness, their faces showing their despair.

Kohl came toward them. "Captain," he said, "we're in trouble. Fifteen feet short of the downhill side and she won't budge an inch. We just don't have the power to take her over the hump. We're stuck!"

He led the way up through the cut-down brush and trampled ground to where the hulk loomed black against the night, the towering masts like leafless trees, stark and strong against the sky.

It was what Jean had feared. The power of the capstan and the arrangement of the blocks had enabled the men by their slow, steady push to move the schooner, inch by inch, out of the water and along the skids, heavily greased to aid them. The huge blocks and careful rigging had more than quadrupled the power they could exert; but now, near the highest point above the water, their combined strength was not enough to move the schooner farther.

"We can't budge her," Kohl said. "We broke a couple of capstan bars trying."

Glancing at the stars he could see they still had

several hours of darkness remaining, but the men were exhausted. He believed he knew what to do, but he would need rested men to do the work that lay ahead. Despite the fact that the fog was gone, that the coming of the patrol ship was imminent, there was but one thing to do. "Barney," he said, after a moment, "have everybody turn in and get some rest. I'll stand by the gun myself. I'll want two men to stand watch here at the ship; the rest to sleep until four A.M."

"Lord knows they need the rest," Kohl said, "but what about the *Susquehanna?* The *Lena* will be along at daybreak."

"If she heaves her hook at daybreak it will take her all of three hours to get this far. I'll be standing by the gun. If you hear a shot, turn the men to and rig those shears as I told you. And send four men to me."

Kohl put his cap back on his head and started to turn away, then stopped. "Cap'n," he said slowly, "I figured I was a better man than you, that I should be master of this ship, but believe me, I've learned better. You've pulled off things this trip that I'd never had tackled."

"Thanks, Barney."

LaBarge turned to Helena. "You'd better get some sleep. You'll need the rest."

"I'm coming with you."

"But, look—"

"I'm coming with you."

Together, they walked to the promontory where the gun had been placed, pointing its dark muzzle down the channel. The men arose as they approached. "Nothing yet, Cap'n."

"Turn in . . . you'll be turning to again at four A.M."

When they had gone he made a place for Helena between the trails of the gun, folding some blankets and placing them over a pile of evergreen boughs. When she was settled he lit his pipe and settled himself for the long hours of waiting. He was tired, but he forced himself to remain awake.

Somewhere out in the forest a pine cone fell, and upon the water a fish jumped, while far over the trees a night bird called. The rest was silence and the darkness.

The earth was soft beneath him with a deep carpet of pine needles and damp from the fog. A vagrant wind stirred in the pines and he could hear the far-off rushing of wind, a strange, lonely, wonderful sound that is a part of every evergreen forest. He listened, liking it, and listened to the water along the rocks below. These were old sounds, familiar sounds.

"It's a grand country," he said.

"I love it. I shall always love it."

"I've always lived close to the forest," he said. "I'm at home there. I like the wild lands."

Far off in the forest a wind began. It had started somewhere in the pines along the rim of the world and it came down, awakening new ranks of trees to stirring life, moving the pine needles, brushing the arms of the spruce. It came down across Alaska and moved through the forests and then scattered itself among the coastal islands. It was a long, long wind and it was cold.

The wind rustled the pines above Tenakee Inlet and talked among the trees over the manless beds of Hoonah village, then fell its way along the bare flanks of the *Susquehanna*, so unnaturally naked without the shielding water.

Jean listened to the wind. "You'd better sleep," he told Helena, "we're going to have snow."

26

Jean came sharply awake, aware instantly that something had happened. Snow was falling gently and steadily through the pines, but it was not this that had disturbed him. Silently, so as not to awaken Helena, he got to his feet and rubbed his legs to restore the circulation.

When he could move quietly, he walked away from the gun and stood in a small opening in the forest, listening. There had been many such times when he waited in complete stillness, ears keyed to the slightest sound . . . and now he heard it.

It came from far off, but it was a noise not of the forest. The forest's sounds he had known since boyhood, and this was no murmur among the trees, this was the steady advance of a large number of men.

On still cold nights sound travels amazingly, and the men were several miles away. They were not Indians, for even a large body of Indians would not have been heard; these men were unaccustomed to travel at night in the forest.

LaBarge quickly realized what the movement implied: Zinnovy was sure of taking the *Susquehanna*;

men had been put ashore to prevent the escape of himself or his crew. Undoubtedly the *Lena* was now moving upstream and had landed these men to take up posts on shore. The attack was to be both by sea and by land, and there were to be no survivors.

It was the one thing he had not anticipated, for which he had no plan, and he must move swiftly. An attack now, on the ground, could immobilize the *Susquehanna* and prevent further movement. From the trees his men could be picked off at will as they worked.

He went quickly to the gun and, stooping, touched Helena's shoulder. She opened her eyes at once, completely aware. He explained quickly. "We must go back now, and we must hurry!"

She was on her feet, straightening her clothing. "You go. I'll stay. The *Lena* may come in sight while you are gone and I could fire the cannon. It might stop her."

"You? Fire a cannon?"

She laughed at him. "You forget, Jean. I am a daughter of the Romanoffs, the Honorary Colonel of a regiment of artillery. Several times I have fired salutes with cannon. Is it loaded?"

"Yes."

"Then all I must do is get on the target and pull the lanyard."

He hesitated. "All right, but when the men arrive, you come back. Do you hear?"

She came to attention and saluted. "Yes, Commander! I return at once!"

Jean LaBarge plunged through the brush toward the now-dying fire. Quickly, he shook Kohl awake. The alerted guards awakened the crew and the Indians.

"They'll make a reconnaissance first. When they get close they'll hear the sounds of our work party and send men in to find out what is happening. My guess is that Zinnovy stayed aboard, in which case before they launch an attack they'll communicate with him."

Even with the Indians they would be outnumbered. If the patrol ship reached the head of the inlet before the *Susquehanna* could be launched it could blow the schooner to fragments. Nor did they have men enough to protect the gun from shore attack, although the gun was their only hope to slow the approach of the *Lena*.

How many men had been landed they could not guess, but it was likely that the number exceeded their own.

"We've one chance and one only," LaBarge told them after a moment. "We've got to get the schooner into the water and get the hell out of here. Kohl, take twelve men and get those poles sunk into the ground, make a shears of them, and get the rigging in place. If we can grasshopper her over the hump the rest will be easy."

LaBarge had previously explained the process to Kohl, who had never seen it done. Two long poles, as long as the masts of the ship and heavier, were hastily dragged from their resting places and holes were sunk just ahead of the schooner's bow and almost at the crest of the slight rise. The tackle was rigged and the men manned the capstan. Jean took six of the Tlingit warriors to the gun's position, and Katlecht took another twelve into the forest to intercept the landing party.

Leaving two men with the gun, Jean took the other four and moved up through the forest to aid Katlecht. The gun crew had already relieved Helena and she had returned to stand by the *Susquehanna*.

For a moment there was silence. At the crest of a small rise in the forest, a position that enabled them to look down various lanes between the trees, LaBarge and his Tlingits silently waited the approaching party. Only yards away was Katlecht with his group, scattering across the front and down the flank of the Russians. From behind him LaBarge could hear the hammer blows of the working men.

Suddenly men began to emerge from the trees into view. The first were *promyshleniki*, at least a dozen. Skilled woodsmen these, and dangerous fighting men. Quickly, Jean passed the word along to the Tlingits to select these targets first. In the forest they would be dangerous antagonists.

The *promyshleniki* were an advance party and now they waited the approach of the men from the *Lena's* crew. Then, quite suddenly there was a dull boom of a cannon, their own gun. The Tlingits took the signal as one to fire, and squeezed off as one man. His own shot was only an instant behind theirs. Four of the *promyshleniki* dropped and one seaman, but Katlecht's men were firing, too. The Russians dissolved into the woods but not before LaBarge wounded another man with a shot from his turret rifle. Instantly the Russians began a hot and determined return fire.

The Tlingits were eager to attack, but Jean ordered them to fall back on the gun's position. As they started to retreat, the cannon boomed again and then there was the tremendous crash of a broadside from the *Lena*. The shells were high, and whistled through the forest, cutting off limbs and sending down a shower of leaves.

A Tlingit near Jean, a man with a scarred face and a lean, hard body, was doing yeoman work with his rifle. As Jean watched he saw the Indian fire at what seemed to be a wall of brush and a *promyshleniki* fell face forward from the trees, hit the ground. He started to rise, but the scarred Tlingit nailed him to the earth with a shot through the top of the skull.

Then for a time there was silence. The Tlingits needed no advice when it came to woods fighting, and his own Indians scattered out and took good positions where they could cover every approach to the gun. Jean slipped back to lower ground and ran, crouching as he moved, to the gun position.

Lying flat he looked over the crest of a knoll to see the *Lena*, at least four hundred yards off, swung broadside across the inlet. From her position the portage was not visible; the disappearance of the schooner must have come as a tremendous surprise. One shell from his own cannon had struck her foretop and dropped a spar to the deck. Even as he sighted the patrol ship another shell struck it and sheered away a piece of the bulwark, scattering fragments in every direction. There was a scream of anguish from the ship's deck.

The landing party were, by the sound of the small arms fire, falling back under the carefully aimed shooting of the Tlingits, who were skilled woodsmen to a man. Of the ten or twelve *promyshleniki* in the landing party at least five were out of action, and it had become obvious to the others that they were marked targets. To men who fought purely for money this was not an especially happy thought.

The *Lena* was shelling the woods now, but most of the fire was directed at the shore position of the gun with a view toward knocking it out of action. The gun's position, well behind the hummock with only her muzzle lifted over the top, was excellent.

Returning to the schooner Jean scrambled up the rope ladder that hung from her amidships bulwark and threw his weight behind a capstan bar. Slowly, under the pull of the huge blocks, the schooner's bow began to lift just as the bows of the river boats had lifted on the Missouri. As it lifted it moved forward, drawn toward the shears. Inch by inch, foot by foot it crept forward, then was dropped to the skid.

Holes had been dug for a new position and swiftly the big poles were transferred, and the men went to work to rig the grasshoppering at the new position. Glancing back down the portage, Jean knew their time was short. Sweat stood out on his brow despite the coolness of the day. If the *Lena* moved up to the head of the inlet she would have the *Susquehanna* at point-blank range and entirely without protection.

"Grease your skids, Barney. This hop should put it over the hump."

Moving swiftly, LaBarge gathered his crew and sent them to the schooner. He found Katlecht lying in the brush, his rifle tucked against his cheek. "You come with us? We must go now."

Katlecht shook his head. "We go mountains. All move now so they find nobody."

Jean gathered those of the crew who were not busy on deck and they moved down the portage ready to repel any attempted landing at that point. Under cover of brush near the end of the portage they watched the patrol ship and waited. Behind them they could hear the creak of the blocks and the complaining of the heavy lines as they took the strain.

The *Lena*, now that no more shells had been fired, was heading toward the head of the inlet. A man in uniform moved near the rail and Jean laid his rifle over a fallen log and took careful aim. He drew a long breath, then let it out easily, his finger tightening on the trigger. The rifle sprang in his hands, and the report laid a lash of sound across the suddenly silent morning. The man on the deck jerked, grabbed the rigging to hold himself erect, then slowly slid from sight.

Immediately, all the crew opened fire on the *Lena*. The man at the wheel, caught in the fire of several rifles, was knocked back and then he fell forward to the deck, the wheel spinning. Another man sprang to the wheel but the *Lena* yawed sharply just as she let go a broadside and the shells were wasted in empty forest. Behind them there was a hail from Kohl, and Jean sprang to his feet. "On the double!" he yelled. "Move it!"

One man only lay still, and LaBarge ducked to his side. It was Larsen; the big Swede's shirt under his jacket was soaked with blood. He looked up at Jean. "It was a good fight."

Jean looked down in the usually florid features of the Swede. "You made every voyage with me, Lars. I'm taking you along on this one."

"You run . . . they soon come."

LaBarge looked up, hastily taking in the situation. He could hear the boatfalls on the *Lena*, which meant a landing party and immediate attack. He bent to lift the Swede and saw that he was dead.

An instant he stared at the dead sailor, and then at a shout from the schooner he was up and running. As he came abreast, the men working at the shears, lowering away, allowed the ropes to slip and the shears fell, the V astride of the skids. Even as it happened, the schooner groaned and creaked as she started to slide down the ways.

The men sprang away, frightened. An instant and all hung in the balance. If the schooner struck the shears it would be thrown on its side or the runway torn and the ship would slide off into the ground.

LaBarge glimpsed it all as he ran. Dropping his

rifle he grabbed an ax from the nearest man and with a leap sprang astride the skid. Swinging the ax with all his great strength he struck the wire rope that bound the two poles of the shears together. As the ax struck he heard a shout of warning. The runway creaked as it took the schooner's weight, now only a few feet away and gaining momentum. He swung the ax again and again. Somewhere abaft the ship he heard shooting. The bow loomed above him. The ax fell for the last time and the wires parted. He fell rather than sprang aside and dropping the ax, stumbled to pick up his fallen rifle.

The last of the crew was running beside the dangling rope ladder. Scattered in a skirmish line, running toward them, were Zinnovy and his landing party. From the schooner's deck a sporadic fire began. The schooner eased forward, moving at a speed just faster than a walk. The log of the shears was pushed easily aside and fell off the skid to the ground. Jean took a shot at the advancing men, and sprang for the rope ladder. He caught it and started to climb, pausing halfway to lay his rifle across his forearm and fire. He gripped the ladder with his left hand more tightly, leveled the rifle again, felt a smashing blow in his side, then fired.

He felt suddenly weak. He grabbed a rung higher and pulled himself up. Hands that seemed desperately far away reached for him. Now the schooner was moving fast. He gathered his strength and pulled himself a rung higher. Somebody caught at his rifle, to which he had clung, held insecurely in front of his body. The hands grabbed at him, caught his sleeve and pulled.

Above him the sun was shining, and then it faded out, and he heard rifle fire mingled with a sound as of rushing water. He felt himself lowered to the deck, and then he remembered nothing at all for a long time.

27

Under a gray sky the gray water was ruffled by a wind raw with cold. The bare masts of the schooner and the bare roofs of the houses along a bare shore offered no comfort from the wind. On deck Jean LaBarge, still pale from blood lost by his wound, stood waiting for the gear to be lowered into the longboat.

"Take the furs to Canton," he advised Kohl. "You don't have a full cargo, but the furs are good and you should make a nice profit. Then return to San Francisco and report to Hutchins. You're in command."

"And you?"

"I'll make my plans as there's need for them. When I've escorted Princess de Gagarin to St. Petersburg there will be time to plan. I may return by this route, and may go across the Atlantic to the east coast."

Kohl did not like it, and said so. "Begging the lady's pardon, Cap'n, you can't trust them. These are a suspicious people, and Baron Zinnovy has friends ashore here. If he doesn't come after you

261

himself he'll send a ship with orders for your arrest."

"I can take care of that eventuality," Helena said. "I believe we can also cope with Baron Zinnovy."

"I hope so." Kohl was gloomy. "You'd better take Boyar, Cap'n. He'd like to visit Poland, and he knows much of this country."

LaBarge glanced at Boyar. "Do you want to come?"

"If I can . . . yes."

"Get your gear on deck, and make it quick."

Snow lay in splotches on the gray slopes back of the town, and on the shaded sides of the buildings just back from the waterfront. Duncan Pope, suddenly gracious, helped Helena into the boat. His sour face anguished, he struggled to find words. "I . . . I never knew a princess before," he finally managed to say, "and . . . and you act like a princess."

She gave him a dazzling smile. "Thank you, Mr. Pope! Thank you very much!"

All the crew had gathered to say goodbye. One by one they bobbed their heads at her. Only Ben Turk was more formal, muttering something indistinguishable as he stepped back.

"Take care of the boys, Barney," LaBarge told Kohl, "and of the *Susquehanna*. And there's a letter on my desk for Robert Walker. Mail it, will you?"

The water was choppy but the men at the oars pulled strongly and the longboat headed for shore. Gant, who was in charge of the boat, glanced at Boyar. "Be careful, man. Remember you're a Pole."

"I'd do better here," Boyar said dryly, "to forget it."

Jean LaBarge looked back at the *Susquehanna*, experiencing once more the thrill he had felt when he first saw her lying on the waters of Frisco bay.

The shore offered nothing, just a gray slate shore with its patches of snow, and the weather-beaten buildings. This was Okhotsk, on the coast of Siberia, and the end of the world. Before them lay a journey of more than five thousand miles to St. Petersburg, and much of that distance was fraught with danger.

The boat grated on the gravel of the beach and a sailor jumped in and drew the boat higher. Jean sprang down to the gray sand and helped Helena from the boat.

He turned to the crew and shook hands all around. "Take her back, boys, and take care of the schooner for me."

Several people, bundled in shapeless clothing, had paused to watch the arrivals but they did not offer to approach. When the boat shoved off and left the three standing on the beach the observers walked away, apparently no longer interested. Taking Helena's arm, Jean started up the shelving beach toward the muddy street lined with its haggard buildings of logs or unpainted lumber, all equally dismal and unattractive. There was no evidence of warmth or welcome.

Helena had papers she often used when traveling incognito, which identified her as Helena Mirov, governess, of St. Petersburg. She had her own papers, but as she explained to Jean, "Nobody would believe a niece of the Czar could travel without entourage or luggage. They would certainly hold us for investigation, and that could take months and might lead to no end of trouble. And it would certainly alert all of Baron Zinnovy's allies here."

"Then you must use the other papers."

"Jean" —Helena looked up at him—"there is another thing. It would be better, I think, if it was believed I was your wife—recently married, to account for the names on the papers. There would be fewer questions."

"I agree with Madame," Boyar said. "And unless Madame intends to ask for an armed escort, I would suggest the sooner we start the better for us."

A square-built man in a heavy gray coat stopped across the street some distance away and watched them. Boyar glanced at him nervously, then picked up their bags and started hastily up the street. The man watched them without apparent change until they entered the office of the post.

Boyar paused in the door and watched the man cross the street and enter police headquarters. Boyar looked around the bare, uncomfortable room in which they stood. There was no one behind the counter and no one in sight. "Wait here," he said, and slipped out of the door and down the street.

The moments ticked slowly by. The fire in the potbellied stove gave off little heat. They looked at each other, saying nothing. For once, Jean felt out of his element. There was so much he did not understand. Shivering in the still cold of the post station, they waited for someone to come. A half hour passed before Boyar suddenly opened the door and motioned to them. "Come quickly!" he called. "We leave at once!"

Boyar caught up their bags and started out the door. He went down the street a few steps, then turned into a dismal alley to a low-roofed barn where a man was hitching three horses to an odd-looking vehicle.

"These are *volni*," Boyar explained, low-voiced. "They are 'free horses,' unattached to the post system. The driver is a peasant farmer willing to make some extra money."

The vehicle was a *tarantas*, a heavy, boat-shaped carriage mounted on four wheels with a heavy hood that could be closed in bad weather. The body of the carriage was mounted on two poles which connected the front and rear axles and served as rude springs to break the jolts on the always rough roads. The usual procedure was for the traveler to stow his luggage in the bottom, cover it with straw, and then to cover the straw with blankets and robes. On this he reclined, leaning against pillows. The driver sat on the front end of the carriage and drove the three horses hitched side by side with four reins.

Hastily, they stowed their luggage, and Boyar brought from the house some blankets and an odorous bearskin rug. Climbing in, they spread these out and then Boyar got to a seat beside the driver and the latter gathered the reins and shouted, *"Nu rodniya!"*

Eager to be off, the horses started with a rush. As they turned down the street the police official they had earlier seen glanced their way in an uninterested manner. He stepped to the door of the post station and entered. Instantly he was out on the street, shouting after the *tarantas.*

Boyar noticed but the driver did not, and Boyar lifted a finger to his lips. With the jangling harness, bumping of wheels over the rutted road and the ringing of bells over the horses' backs, the driver heard nothing.

Once on the road the man whipped up his horses. Their hoofs pounded smartly on the half-frozen road as they dashed off into the emptiness before them. Yet this emptiness would not remain with them for many miles. Beyond that lay the *taiga*, the world's greatest stand of virgin timber, a wild, lonely region of forest and swamp, inhabited by peasants and exiles, escaped convicts and outlaws.

This road was the famous *tracht*, leading from Siberia to Perm, at the edge of Russia proper. Travel by post road was easy, although subject to interference and questioning by the police. All that was needed for travel on the post road was the priceless *padarozhnaya*—the order for horses. The same carriage might be kept all the way through and only the horses changed. However, travel by *volni* was often best, for the farmers' horses were better fed and the travel faster.

It was cold. Not a piercing cold but the chill of late spring. The country over which they drove was a vast marshy plain scattered with clumps of alder and willow, stunted growths more like brush than trees. Helena moved closer to him and they leaned back against a duffel bag Jean had placed as a back rest, reclining rather than sitting.

Boyar turned his head to tell them they were headed, not for the post station, but for a farm where the driver knew free horses were also available. In this way, with luck, they might travel the entire distance without approaching a post station.

The curtains of the carriage were open and they could watch the country as it slipped behind them. Occasionally a cold blast of wind whipped the curtains and Helena snuggled deeper into the blankets and closer to Jean. From time to time they dozed, talked, watched the miles go by.

The farm at which they finally arrived had a high wooden gate, behind which were several log buildings, much less impressive than the gate that led to them. As they drove up two huge dogs ran out, barking wildly. The gate swung back and a man emerged, accompanied by a boy.

They were served a meal, hastily prepared, coarse black bread, pickled mushrooms, boiled salmon, wild strawberries and tea.

"He eats too well, this one." Boyar spoke in an undertone to Jean. "We must be careful."

Their host was a stocky, powerful man with a heavy beard. His smile was wide but the look in his eyes was hard and calculating. Those eyes took in their warm clothing, the bags in the vehicle, and several times his eyes returned to Helena, lively with curiosity. He spoke to Boyar in Russian, and Boyar commented, "He suggests we stay the night . . . I think it would be unwise."

"Thank him," Jean said, "and tell him we have no time."

When they rose from the table to return to their carriage, their host was talking to a stranger who must have come up after their arrival. He also said something to their driver. This was a new driver, a boy scarcely sixteen, with a sallow, vicious face and shifty eyes. His hair was uncut and his clothing was grimy and evil-smelling. Once, after the carriage was moving, he turned and glanced back at them with such an expression of malignancy that Helena shuddered. "I don't like it, Jean," she whispered. "I am afraid!"

Before them the narrow dirt road dipped into a forest of scattered pines that grew thicker and thicker as they rolled and rocked over the rutted road. The lowering clouds grew darker and a wind blew through the pines, skittering the dried leaves along the frozen ground. Off the road the forest was thick with an unrevealing gloom. Helena had fallen asleep against Jean's shoulder and slowly he himself relaxed and began to sleep fitfully, jolted awake again and again by the roughness of the road and the capacity of the *tarantas* to bounce around. . . .

He was awakened by a persistent shaking of his foot. He opened his eyes, aware that the vehicle was moving at a walk and something was pressing against him. The he heard Boyar's whisper and realized that the weight against his side was the Polish hunter. "Captain, sir?"

"Yes?"

"We're in trouble. Our driver . . . I think he fixes to meet someone."

Wide awake, Jean eased himself into a sitting position. He whispered briefly into Boyar's ear, and the Pole moved back to his former seat. Outside a spatter of rain fell, then ceased. There was no sound but the creak of harness and of the carriage itself. Jean slid his pistol from under his coat and waited, listening. Suddenly the *tarantas* stopped moving.

Boyar asked a question and the boy replied, his voice surly. Boyar ordered him to keep going but the boy became belligerent. In the vague light Jean caught a gleam on a pistol barrel and then the *tarantas* began moving again. In the moment before it started Jean heard a rush of hoofs, somewhere in the forest behind them. The carriage gathered speed. Helena stirred, awake now and listening.

As if on order there was a rift in the clouds and the moon shone through. Closing in around the carriage was a group of horsemen.

Jean held his fire. It would not do to fire into a troop of Cossacks or a party of innocent travelers. A voice shouted, the voice of the innkeeper at their last stop. Boyar spoke sharply and must have emphasized his command with a thrust of the gun barrel for the whip cracked and the horses began to run.

There was an angry shout from the riders. LaBarge lifted his pistol and took as careful aim as was possible with the *tarantas* bouncing from stone to rut to stone again. He aimed at a bulky rider somewhat to the right of the others, who might be the innkeeper. He aimed, hesitated, then fired. The rider jerked in the saddle, fell headlong into the road in front of the following horses. Promptly, LaBarge fired twice more into the dark mass of riders, bunched by the timber lining the road.

The pursuers fell back, astonished by the sudden burst of firing, and in drawing back they lost the race. LaBarge reloaded his pistol, taking his time. He carried another pistol and a two-barreled derringer as well, the latter in his sleeve holster.

The driver was frightened and sullen but he drove hard. Still it was well after midnight when the *tarantas* reached the wooden gate of their next stop. Jean got stiffly to the ground and Boyar closed in beside him.

Men with lanterns gathered around and Boyar ordered them to change teams and be quick. He had neglected to holster his pistol, and the sight of it lent emphasis to his directions. From time to time the men stared at the boy who stood to one side watching LaBarge and Boyar. One of the men ventured a whisper but the boy snapped a one-syllable reply, his tone ugly.

Once inside the farmhouse Jean chose a seat against the wall that commanded the door, and drawing his pistol, placed it on the table beside his plate. The people outside were acquaintances or allies of those who had attempted the attack, and he wanted them to know he was ready for anything.

The room was long and low with a rough board floor and beamed ceiling. To one side there was a fireplace; the house might have been taken right from western America. Food was brought to them, and hot tea. The man who served them was obviously much interested in the pistol: his eyes glistened with envy. "Such a gun!" he exclaimed. "I have not seen such a gun before!"

"I carry two," Jean replied, "and it was fortunate."

"Fortunate?" The man's thin face seemed to grow still. He looked at LaBarge. "There was trouble?"

"We were attacked by robbers."

There were three men in the room now, and the boy driver as well. Nothing more was said until Jean asked about horses.

The proprietor shrugged. "I am sorry. We will have no horses until morning, but it is better that you stay here. We—"

"We leave tonight." Jean looked across the table at the man and lifted his cup with his left hand. "And you had better harness the team at once, and with your best horses."

"It is impossible!" The proprietor was voluble with protest. "It is—!"

"If you believe those men who attacked us are following," LaBarge said coolly, "you're mistaken. Their leader is dead."

"Dead?" The proprietor looked with quick concern at the boy, whose face showed white under the dirt.

They stared at him, shocked to immobility. LaBarge put down his teacup and picked up the pistol. Immediately the room broke into movement. "You," LaBarge said to the proprietor, "come with us. The rest of you stay here. Think hard before you come outside. We don't care how many you bury here."

Boyar took the man to the stables and returned with three gray horses, in fine condition. Hastily they were harnessed and then Jean told the proprietor to call his driver. The last they saw was a small cluster of people standing in the road, staring after them.

Ahead the road wound over rough country but the gray horses galloped cheerfully on, their breath steaming in the chill air, their feet making a lively clatter on the hard ground. When they had been on the road about an hour, it began to snow.

28

Crowded together as they were, Helena and Jean bumped and jarred against each other as the *tarantas* jolted over roads made rough by traffic as well as by lumps of ice, frozen earth and ridges of snow. Their bodies twisted and jerked with the motion until every muscle ached. And all the while the driver kept up a din of shouts, yells, whipcracking and cursing which mingled with the jangling bells that hung from the bow over the shaft horse.

Occasionally they would emerge from the forest to race along between stubbled fields and clatter through peaceful villages where every dog within hearing rushed out baying and barking, only to be scattered helter-skelter by the charging team. Inside the passengers were pitched, tossed, heaved and battered.

At last, in the cold gray of earliest dawn, they drove into the streets of still another village. The street was a mere alleyway of ruts a foot deep or more, lined on either side by buildings of logs or unpainted lumber, their gable ends turned to the road, each with a huge wooden gate beside it. Near the end of the street the horses turned of their own volition toward one of these gates.

Then began a period of shouts from the driver and faint replies from within, protesting argument, and finally after an interminable period, the gates swung back and they drove into a court flanked by a low-roofed stable covered with sod and an open-faced shed containing a bunch of decrepit carts, a weird and amazing assortment of vehicles, relics of some vanished era too remote to be guessed.

Jean fell rather than stepped down from the *tarantas* and straightened his bruised and aching muscles. Shin Boyar's face was sullen with cold, showing its weariness, and when Jean helped Helena from the carriage she looked up at him with a glance of mingled despair and amusement at their situation. Painfully they walked toward the small door that offered little but a promise of warmth.

As the door opened under his hand a blast of odorous air struck them in the face. For a moment they hesitated, but the bitter cold left them no choice. They went inside.

Three small windows, their glass gray with dirt, looked out upon the road they had just left. Against the wall on the inner side was a long wooden bench, fastened to the wall. Before it was a heavy table and several stools lined the table's opposite side. In the corner opposite was a huge stove built of whitewashed brick, and from the top of the stove to the wall was a shelf some eight feet wide that was also built of the same whitewashed brick.

On this *palati* the family slept at night, as well as any guests who might be present.

A buxom girl with two thick blond braids entered and began putting dishes on the table. On Boyar's advice they had brought their own tea and sugar, the custom of travelers in Russia, for the tea along the *tracht* was scarcely drinkable. The food on the table consisted of eggs, black bread, some thick green soup which was very hot, and butter.

"I think we should drive on," Boyar advised. "I am sure these are honest people here, but if Madame is not tired—?"

Helena looked up, smiling. "If you can ride farther, I can also!"

"How soon will you try to contact your friends?"

"At Perm . . . and that is a long way yet."

Outside the cold was bitter. The *tarantas* started with a rush, then settled down to a steady jog. The village fell behind and they entered upon a vast plain scattered with clumps of trees. The sky had turned gray and sullen, and as the miles went by the driver glanced again and again at the sky. Turning on his seat, he called back to them. *"Purga!"*

The clouds, a flat mass above the tops of the trees, seemed to press down upon them, and the cold increased. Helena pressed close to him, her face against his arm. There were no buildings, anywhere, and the trees grew thicker, the country wilder and more desolate. Here the land was swept by great winds that had left the trees twisted into grotesque shapes. Snow began to fall, a few flakes at first, then increasing until all was shut out by a white, moving curtain. Boyar drew the leather curtains and the *tarantas* was black inside. It was like riding in a moving cave. The wind whipped under the curtains, however, and the cold could not be kept out. The driver sat hunched and silent, seemingly impervious to the temperature.

Jean leaned toward Boyar. "We've got to find shelter! This will get worse!"

The *tarantas* had slowed to a walk; the driver was having trouble staying on the road. LaBarge knew the *purga* was the dreaded black blizzard of Siberia which could uproot trees or blow the roof off a house. Travel in such a storm would be impossible. The temperature was already far below zero and growing colder. Yet the driver was apparently headed for some place of which he knew. Finally, just when the wind seemed to become a full gale, he swung the horses into a dark avenue of trees through which the storm roared in a mighty blast. Treetops bent, glimpsed through a momentary lifting of the curtain. Behind them a tree crashed, blown down by the wind. Occasionally a blast of wind would seem to lift the carriage off the ground, but the horses were running now, and then they were in the lee of a hill and drawing up before a window which showed a feeble glow of light.

There were two doors in a log wall built against the side of a rocky hill, one for people and a larger one for the carriage and animals. With Helena clinging to his arm, Jean LaBarge opened the smaller door and they stepped inside.

They found themselves standing in the mouth of

a cave. Beyond a log partition they could hear Boyar and the driver stabling the horses. A small fire dying in a huge fireplace provided the only light. There was a table, a few stools, some broken harness and on one of several bunks, a man was lying.

Finding a stump of candle, Jean struck a match to the wick. The flame leaped up, swaying like a dancer in the breeze from the chimney. The room was icy cold and there was no fuel. Crossing to the bunk, Jean lifted the candle and looked down at the man who lay there.

The man's face was white, the skin drawn tight against the skull, his eyes, wide open, were sunk deep within their sockets. For a moment he believed the man dead, and then he saw his lips move.

A door in the partition opened and Boyar came through with the driver. Boyar had his arms full of supplies, the tea, sugar, biscuits and some other articles with which they had provided themselves against emergency. "Get the tea on," LaBarge told Boyar. "We've a man here who's in a bad way."

"No!" The driver caught LaBarge's arm. He spoke in hoarse Russian. "The man is a convict! An escaped prisoner!"

For the first time Jean noticed the loop of chain descending from under the ragged blanket. Lifting the blanket, he saw that iron bands enclosed the man's legs around each ankle, each thigh, and just above each knee. The bands were joined by a heavy chain suspended from a belt.

Holding the candle close, LaBarge removed the blanket and examined the man. His dirty shirt was stained with blood; he had been shot twice. The first was only a graze along the ribs, although it had bled severely; the other was a wound through the chest. There had been a bad flow of blood from that wound but the blood had no bubbles in it and the lung did not appear to have been penetrated.

"You must do nothing!" the driver insisted. "If you are caught it is hard labor in the salt mines. Let him die."

"The hell with that." LaBarge turned. "Shin, how's the tea coming?"

"Soon . . . and there will be hot water enough for the wounds."

Gratefully, the escaped prisoner accepted the scalding tea. He tried it gingerly, then sipped again. With a clean cloth LaBarge bathed the wounds. Obviously, the second bullet had gone clear through, yet aside from lost blood no harm seemed to be done. Still, without care the man would bleed to death, and without fuel he would freeze.

Twice Boyar slipped into the night and each time returned with a huge armful of wood. Soon the fire was roaring. It was almost an hour before LaBarge completed his job of bathing, treating the wounds and bandaging them. By that time Boyar had prepared soup and Helena had broken bread into it. With a large spoon she fed the man, who scarcely took his eyes from her face, and then only to stare at LaBarge.

The driver sat hunched near the fire, his gaze

averted, wanting no part in the crime. Yet from time to time he replenished the fire, and went with Boyar to gather more fuel. Finally, the driver went to a bunk and rolling up in his greatcoat, was asleep in a moment. Boyar gathered more fuel, ate a little, then followed him.

The prisoner dropped off to sleep and Helena joined LaBarge beside the crackling fire. Covering themselves with a blanket, his arm about her shoulders, they sat and watched the flames in silence. The cave room was warm now; the wind roared outside. Snow fell and hissed in the flames, and occasionally the wind guttered the fire, but there was no other sound but the snores of sleeping men.

Under the blanket Helena reached for and found Jean's hand, and so they sat, and so, propped against a chair turned on its side, they slept.

29

Three days the storm blew without letup, but within the cave the fire kept them warm. There was fuel within a few steps of the door, yet each day found the driver, Liakov, more frightened. Obviously he wished to be far from the cave before a searching party would come for Marchenko, which, they discovered, was the prisoner's name. He had escaped, he told them, by ducking away from a column of prisoners in a blinding snowstorm, but not before he was struck by two bullets. With his last strength he had dragged himself to the cave.

"I knew of it as a boy," he told them. "It was a place where outlaws came." His eyes went to Helena. "That was before I served in the Army."

"With what regiment?" Helena asked.

"The Semyonovsky, Madame. I often stood guard at the Peterhof and the Winter Palace."

He knew her then, which explained the peculiar way he had looked at her when he had seen her that first night. He had probably recognized her at once.

"It is imperative," she told him quietly, "that I reach St. Petersburg." She kept her voice low so that the driver would not hear. "It is even more important that I reach there unknown to Siberian officials."

The pitifully thin lips smiled. "I am a poor convict, Madame. I have seen no one . . . only a wandering hunter who bandaged my wounds and went away . . . who knows where?"

By the evening of the third day the wind had died and LaBarge directed Liakov to make the *tarantas* ready for travel at daylight.

Liakov glanced at the convict. "What of him?" he asked. "We will turn him over to the police?"

"The safest thing for all concerned is to say nothing. This is police business. The police will ask many questions. They will be pleased at no one for interfering."

The morning dawned gray and cold. While Boyar aided Liakov with the harness, LaBarge stood by the bunk. He handed Marchenko a fistful of rubles. "These will help. My advice to you is to get away from here, even if you have to lie in the snow. I've left some tea on the table, and a bit of cheese and bread."

Outside the cold was piercing. The carriage started stiffly, but the horses were eager to go after their confinement and soon they had broken into a run. Several times they were forced to stop and remove trees blown across the road, and fifteen miles from the cave they came to their first halt where they quickly changed horses and started off with a fresh team and driver. Glancing back as they pulled away, LaBarge saw Liakov staring after them.

"You are worried about Marchenko?"

"I hope he escapes, Helena. I hope he does."

"He is very weak."

"But his heart is strong."

With such a one there was always a chance. How about himself? Would he have the fortitude to stand what Marchenko had stood? Could he survive? Would he lose his will to escape? If Liakov went to the police . . .

As if to atone for the past, the clouds drifted away and the sun appeared. It was spring and here and there the hillsides showed a bit of green under the grays and browns. Twice they stopped to change horses, each time remaining with the *volni* system of free horses. The free drivers were known to the police, of course, but a man was harder to trace by that method than by the post system. Often the *volni* drivers were weeks in returning to their home villages, which meant weeks before they could be questioned.

The villages were as alike as peas, gray lumber and weather-beaten logs, a hint of decoration at the eaves. The few people who moved about were bundled to the eyes in odds and ends of clothing.

The steppe had changed to pale green with here and there the golden yellow of wild mustard or buttercups. The driver pulled off the muddy road to the prairie and drove more swiftly, crushing grass and flowers under the spinning wheels. He was a younger man, this driver, and filled with good spirits. He sang as he drove, and seemed to know everyone along the road. He shouted at them and they shouted back. Several times they raced past trains of wagons whose drivers plodded beside them, and several times they raced for miles over plains that were blue with a carpet of forget-me-nots. Distant hillsides were thick with the slim white trunks of birch, and always the villages kept appearing, shutters hanging loose, gates sagging. They drove on and on with a succession of teams and drivers until all sense of time was lost and all was forgotten but their own spinning wheels, and the never-ending shouts of drivers who raged, cajoled, praised, petted and swore at their teams.

From Tiumen to Ekaterinburg the road was bordered on either side by a double row of splendid birches nearly eighty feet tall, set so closely their branches arched over the road and shut out the sun with their green canopy. This was known, Helena told him, as "Catherine's Alley," for the trees had been planted by the order of Catherine II, and now, almost a hundred years later, they offered shade to the traveler.

The peasants' huts were alike in their cheerlessness except for occasional flowers in the windows. Rarely was there a tree or blade of grass in any of the villages, but in the windows one saw geraniums, oleanders, tea roses, cinnamon pinks or fuchsias.

Then came the night when they slept in a two-story brick house near the river where the owner advertised "rooms for arrivers." LaBarge was awakened in the first gray of dawn to find a rough hand on his shoulder and bending above him the thin, cadaverous face of an utter stranger. He sat up quickly and the man stepped back. LaBarge glanced toward the connecting door to Helena's room.

"It's all right," the man said. "I tell you, mate, I've touched nothing, and as for the lady, I'd bother no lady, mate. Not I."

"What are you doing here? How did you get in?"

The fellow stood with his feet apart, grinning. His nose was a great beak, his red, wrinkled neck like that of a buzzard, and his eyes, small and blue, twinkled with a cynical humor. "How did I get in, you ask? Through the door, mate, through that very door. Locks, you know, I've no time for them, and I'd no wish to go knocking about on your door at this hour of the morning. Start folks looking, you know, and maybe start them thinking."

"What do you want?"

"Now that's more like it. I like a man who comes to the point. But it ain't so much what I want, mate, as what you need. It's the police, mate, and they're hunting you. You, the lady, and the sailorman who's with you."

"Sailor?"

"Aye . . . spotted him at once, I did. And you likewise, mate. I've seen a bit of the sea myself, seven year aboard a lime-juicer out of Liverpool. It's where I learned my English. But if I were you I'd be getting myself up."

Jean rolled out and dressed quickly. He had no

idea who the man was, but a warning was a warning, and that the police were looking for him was more than likely.

"What is it?" LaBarge asked. "What makes you think the police are looking for me?"

"This is the way of it, mate. I've no love for the law, not to speak of, I ain't. Time to time they've given me a bit of trouble, so when I seen the man in the black coat, seen the wide jaws and bullethead of him, I says to myself, it's the law. So I listen. . . .

"Inquiring, he is, for people of your description. Now I'd seen you arrive, knew where you'd gone and, thinks I, this man and his lady would like to know, so I've come."

"Where's the officer now?"

"Eating, he is. Eating better than I've eaten these many weeks, stuffing his fat jowls in the town, and when he's finished that, had a bit of tea and picked his teeth, then most like, he'll be after you."

"We'll need a team for our *tarantas*."

"They'll be ready for you, mate. Leave it be. A boat's better, and I've spoke to a man for you. He's owner of a barge, and he's made room for us."

"Us?"

"Look, mate. I've nothing here I can't leave behind, and I'd best be leaving it, too. With a bit of cash I might make it, and if I come along with you, I might be helping you." He winked. "I'm one who says it will never go wrong with a man to help the gentry."

Coolly, Jean checked his pistols. To be taken now was not part of his plan. He slid the pistols into his waistband.

The man with the great nose and twinkling eyes glanced at the pistols and then looked up at Jean LaBarge. He had a sudden feeling that he would not like to face a pistol backed by those eyes and in those hands.

"Gentry, you said?"

"Did you think I'd not notice the lady? And a beauty too, if I may say so. . . . "

Helena came through the door, dressed for travel. She looked gay and excited. "Why, thank you! That was nicely said!"

The ruffian bowed, his eyes twinkling. "A lady, I said, and you, sir, anybody can see you're a gent." He canted his head at him. "And maybe a soldier, too, but a fighting man in any course. Take that from me, as one who knows."

When Boyar entered the room, LaBarge explained their situation hurriedly and the man led them out the back way, across the court and into one of the sheds that surrounded it. Here he lifted a board and they all emerged into an alleyway that ended in a field bordering the river. Walking along a path, half-concealed by a line of trees, they reached the stream and boarded the barge.

A man seated on a bollard got to his feet, knocked out his pipe and came aboard. He cast off while the red-faced man hauled in the plank that served as gangway.

"I'd go below," he told LaBarge. "You're dressed a bit well for barge folk."

The cabin was cramped but clean, and there was a samovar with a fire under it. When they were well into the stream, their guide came below and took cups from the cupboard and began to make tea.

"Murzin, they call me," he said. "It's a good name, short and handy-like." He was a long, bony man, slightly stooped in the shoulders and his body was so lean that every rib must show, but his thin hands were dexterous and swift. "A thief, they call me, and they are right. I steal from travelers."

"You have not stolen from us," Helena commented. Jean could see that she liked the man, and he did himself.

Murzin chuckled and grinned wickedly. "Because the police are after you. I'm not one to foul my own nest, to rob my own kind.

"Oh, I know! You two are gentry, although that one"—he pointed a finger at LaBarge—"would have made a fine thief. Maybe that's another reason I didn't steal from you. He would kill a man if he needed killing. He would kill a man very quickly, I think." He glanced sharply at LaBarge. "Is that why they want you?"

He decided to be frank. "Madame and I have enemies who would like to prevent us from reaching St. Petersburg. That could be it, although I think we lost them, but it may be another thing. Back there" —he jerked his head toward the Siberia that lay behind—"we helped an escaped convict. Our driver might have informed on us."

"That could be it . . . they don't like that, not one bit do they like it."

He gulped his tea. "St. Petersburg, is it? Aye, and I'm your man. I can help." He swallowed more tea.

"We've ways of our own, you know. Ways of getting about that the police don't know."

"How much?"

"The bargeman will want fifty rubles, but you can give me what you like when we get there."

He looked slyly from one to the other. "And when you are there, where will you go?"

"We will have a place," Helena said.

"Where then? I say—"

Helena looked straight into Murzin's eyes. "There is a story that King Richard trusted a thief, and I shall. We go to the Peterhof."

Murzin's eyes were bright. "I know that story. Robin Hood, wasn't it? So you go to the Peterhof? Yes . . . yes, that would be it." His eyes lighted with savage, cynical amusement. "The Peterhof! What a place for a thief! What a place from which to steal!"

30

Moonlight lay cold upon the Neva as their carriage rolled through the silent streets. Long ago they had left the barge behind, and since then had changed their means of travel several times. Now there was no sound but the *clop-clop-clop* of their horses' hoofs.

Sitting back against the cushions of the carriage in which they now rode, Jean LaBarge looked about him at the wide avenues and stately buildings, wondering that he, born in the swamps of the Susquehanna, grown to a fur trader among the northwest islands, should have come to this place. He rode now in the streets of the city of Peter the Great, riding beside a niece of the Czar, and within a few days, a few weeks at most, he would see the Czar himself.

At last they dismounted from their carriage before the palace of the Rotcheffs. A strange group: Shin Boyar, the Polish *promyshleniki* from Alaska, Murzin, the wandering thief, Jean LaBarge, merchant adventurer, and the Princess Gagarin, wife of Count Rotcheff and said by some to be the most beautiful woman in Russia.

It was her hand that rang the bell. They waited, saying nothing, and for a long time there was no sound within. Finally, after the third ring, the door opened slightly.

"Alexis! Open the door! It is I!"

The old man opened the door with fumbling haste, bowing and backing away, his face covered with a smile. Yet when he looked past her at the three men, he hesitated. "The Master? Is he all right?"

"He is in Sitka, Alexis, and wounded. He sent me home to see His Imperial Majesty, and these men have brought me safely here. We will want food, Alexis, and beds for these men. Quickly now, for we are cold."

The old man hurried away and somewhere in its vast depths the building began to stir and breathe as it came to life. When Boyar and Murzin had been shown to the servants' quarters, Helena led Jean to a sitting room where a fire was blazing. Food was brought to them there, and tea. Jean watched the firelight playing on her face, finding lights in her dark hair. "I suppose I'll see little of you now," he said unhappily.

"There will be time." He had walked to the fireplace with his brandy, and she followed, standing beside him. How tall he was! "Jean, we must work quickly. There is no telling what they will do, so I must arrange an audience with Uncle Alexander at once. Once that is done I shall try to arrange an interview for you. It will not be easy, Jean, for he is a busy man. I believe I can do it."

"I'll need some clothes. Tomorrow I'll hunt up a tailor."

She laughed. "You need not go to a tailor, Jean. We will have him come here. I will tell Alexis and the tailor will come at whatever hour you wish."

She left the room and he was alone with the portraits on the walls and the fire that crackled cheerfully on the wide hearth. The ceiling was high, and the flickering light played upon the faces of the pictured men. The food had been excellent, slices of cold beef, cheese, and a bottle of claret. It was all strange and very different here.

When she returned she joined him at the fireplace again. "So . . . at last we are here."

"Did you doubt we'd make it?"

"Not really. Yet sometimes. . . . Jean, I shall keep Murzin with me. I like him."

"He's a thief."

"Of course. But somehow I do not believe he will steal while he works for me. He has his own pride, I think."

"Yes, I've known men like that. They're rare though."

"Jean." Helena hesitated. "I shall never forget what you have done for me . . . for us. You have no idea how far Sitka seemed from here, even though it is part of Russia. It is like the end of the world. Without you we might both have failed, Alexander and I."

"That makes it harder . . . a man can't steal the wife of a friend. My kind of man can't."

"You couldn't steal me, Jean. He is my husband."

They were silent, watching the fire. "It's hard to believe that when I leave St. Petersburg I'll never see you again."

"I shall return to Sitka. I must go back to Alexander."

"Don't do it, Helena. You can't. Believe me, if you destroy Zinnovy, he'll end by destroying you. I know. The man I looked at that last night would stop at nothing. You can't put yourself in his hands again—you can't."

"I must . . . I must return to my husband."

"Someday," LaBarge said slowly, "some day I think I'll kill Zinnovy . . . or be killed by him."

"Then kill him. I do not want you to die."

"What use is it to live and not have the woman I love?" He spoke angrily. "I'm a fool, Helena. A double-dyed fool."

They stood together, staring down into the fire. The flames were smaller now, the bed of coals glowing and red, shimmering with changing color. They turned to face each other, looking into each other's eyes, then Jean drew her close and they stood for a long time, held in a tight embrace. Finally she stepped back, out of his arms. "Good night, darling," she spoke softly. "Good night, I—" She turned quickly and walked from the room.

A month passed. The Czar was in the Crimea and would soon return; until then there was nothing to do but wait. There were balls and parties and despite his restlessness Jean enjoyed St. Petersburg.

Helena had started the wheels moving to bring

about the return of Paul Zinnovy. There had been no word from Count Rotcheff but his friends were also active. It was soon obvious, however, that Baron Zinnovy had powerful friends, at least one of them highly placed in the Ministry. Her statement that Baron Zinnovy had attempted to murder her husband met with polite disbelief, even among her intimate acquaintances. Officials were courteous, but whatever might be done seemed to die somewhere in the chains of bureaux and offices that lay between an order and its execution. The powerful influence of the Russian American Company blocked every move she could make.

No delays are more infuriating than the delays of officialdom. She knew that many officials regarded her as a pretty woman interfering in matters that did not concern her. The reports she brought back awaited the Czar's return; until then there was nothing to be done.

"They know who you are, Jean," she warned him, "and they will do all they can to prevent you from seeing the Czar. Be careful, for the Baron's friends are shrewd and powerful. They will stop at nothing."

Russia, under Czar Alexander II, was restless with impending change. The Czar was studying a plan to abolish corporal punishment in the armed services as well as in civilian life. He knew the time had come to institute social reforms and bring his country to the level of other western nations in that respect, yet it was necessary to move slowly. Many feared loss of prestige even more than income losses, others opposed change as they opposed anything that interfered with the *status quo*, with every stratagem at their command.

The Russian American Company's stockholders were among the elements he must win over, and they were well aware of the bargaining position they held. They used this position to avoid any change in the situation in Russian America, and indicated that faraway Sitka could wait until much was done at home.

Alexander II knew he must proceed with care. He had abolished many of the restrictions on the Jews, and had suggested the restoration of home rule for the Finns, but oddly enough, his greatest opposition came from the Liberals who demanded he do more and do it faster. Nothing would satisfy them but dramatic change and such a change was impossible under the circumstances.

Of these facts Jean LaBarge had been only dimly aware when he arrived in Russia, but Helena soon acquainted him with the situation. Then they received their first break.

Helena met him as he entered the palace one afternoon. "Jean! He's here! The Czar is back and he has permitted an audience!"

"When?"

"The night after tomorrow. It will be very late, and he will see us at the Peterhof, in a private audience."

It was, he knew, a rare privilege, and without the help of Helena it could never have been managed. Now they could do something for Rotcheff and there was a chance he might have time to talk of Alaska itself.

A half mile away a slim, erect man with iron-gray hair and cold eyes shielded by square-cut glasses sat behind a desk. He was tall; even seated he seemed tall. His desk was bare of all but one sheet of paper and from time to time he glanced at it. There was a knock at the door.

"Come in!"

A young man in a naval officer's uniform stepped into the room and closed the door carefully behind him, walked to a position before the desk, clicked his heels and saluted.

"Lieutenant Kovalski"—the man behind the desk studied the officer as he spoke—"I am informed that you have killed three men in duels with a pistol, two with the saber."

"Yes, sir."

"Lieutenant, there is a man in this city who is very dangerous to Russia. He interferes in Russian affairs and he endangers the position of a naval officer who is very important to Russia. The man I refer to has arranged to have a private audience with the Czar. It is not wise that such an audience take place, yet the Czar has given his word. You understand?"

Lieutenant Kovalski understood perfectly, just as he had understood when a superior officer had suggested his coming to this address. There were enemies of the state who must be destroyed and it was often inconvenient to bring them to trial. He was also aware that the man before him controlled many avenues to power and prestige, and that a word from him . . .

"The man to whom I refer is called Jean LaBarge. He is an American and at present resides at the Rotcheff palace."

Kovalski's eyes flickered. He knew the man in question by sight. A tall, dark man with a scar . . . there was something about him . . . for the first time he felt uneasy at the prospect of a duel, yet it was foolish to be disturbed. He was one of the finest pistol shots in all Russia. Before coming here he had been informed that he would be transferred to the Army and given the temporary rank of Colonel, and that might be only the beginning.

"It must be done at once, you understand? The audience is for the night after tomorrow."

"Thank you, sir. Is that all?"

"Only this." The man behind the desk took a long envelope from a drawer and handed to Kovalski. "Examine this in private when you are gone from here."

The man removed his glasses and placed them on the sheet of paper, taking the bridge of his nose between his thumb and forefinger for an instant.

"One thing, Lieutenant. You must not fail. Do you understand?"

"Of course." Kovalski snapped to attention, did an about-face and walked from the room. When he reached the street he paused briefly opposite a lighted window and drew the papers from the envelope. The first was a deed for a small estate in

Poland, a place he knew well. He glanced at the date and saw it was for several days in advance, and below was a note to the effect that to be valid the deed must be presented at the estate by Colonel Kovalski, in person.

He smiled wryly. "And if I'm dead . . . ?" The answer was obvious.

He shrugged. No matter. He would not be dead. It would not be the first time he killed a man on instructions.

31

The place chosen for the duel was near a small castle outside of St. Petersburg. Jean stepped down from the carriage and strolled casually across the grass under the trees into the small open park that lay beyond. Beside him was Count Felix Novikoff, who had consented to act as his second.

The challenge had been an obviously arranged affair. In company with Novikoff, who was a friend of Helena and the Rotcheff family, he had gone to a fashionable café. Several Russians in uniform had entered, and in passing, one of them deliberately bumped him. Then, turning, the officer looked LaBarge right in the eye and said, "Swine!"

Novikoff started to speak, but LaBarge was smiling. "Swine?" he questioned. "How do you do, Mr. Swine? My name is LaBarge."

For an instant the Russian stood very still, blood rushing to his face. Then someone laughed and the Russian's face stiffened with anger. He raised his hand to slap LaBarge, but Jean was in no mood to be slapped, so he struck first and hard, knocking Kovalski to the floor, half stunned.

There was silence in the café. The officers who had entered with Kovalski were shocked. Novikoff caught Jean's sleeve. "Come!" he whispered. "We must go ... *now!*"

He had recognized Kovalski at once, knew the man's reputation, and what the sequel must be. Novikoff realized the quarrel had been deliberately provoked and was intended to result in a legal assassination.

Jean turned to go when Kovalski staggered to his feet. "Wait!" he shouted hoarsely. "Wait, damn you!"

LaBarge turned to face him. Kovalski drew himself up. He was wearing the uniform of a colonel in the Russian Army. "My seconds—"

"Send them. Send them, Colonel, and I'll tell them what I tell you now. If you challenge me the choice of weapons is mine, and I choose revolvers, at thirty paces. We walk toward each other at the command and cease firing only when one or both of us is unable to continue."

Kovalski opened his mouth to speak, then closed it. This was all wrong. LaBarge, he had been informed, was an American businessman, not accustomed to duels. He ... with a shock the terms of the duel came home to him. They were to walk toward each other, firing! He had never fired a pistol while walking in his life.

"Will you act as my second, Felix?" LaBarge asked.

"Gladly, Jean! Gladly!"

Appalled by Kovalski's challenge, Novikoff had seen the shock of LaBarge's terms, and realized at once that Kovalski was disturbed. It had, perhaps, been LaBarge's sudden acceptance, his immediate dictation of terms, and his coolness. Also, it had been as obvious to Kovalski as to Novikoff that if the two men went toward each other shooting, one of them was sure to die. Many a man who is a fine marksman in firing at a fixed target is helpless in firing at a moving target while moving himself. And to know at each step that his own danger would be greater. . . . Many a duelist who is master of his weapon can act with complete composure as long as he is sure he is master, but at close quarters even a novice would have a chance.

Later, leaving the café, Novikoff, who was twenty-five, watched LaBarge with unstinted admiration. "Have you used a pistol? In a duel, I mean?"

"In western America every boy begins to carry a pistol as soon as he becomes a man, usually at fifteen or sixteen. I've had duels, but on the spur of the moment, without warning, and always with men used to the pistol."

Count Felix Novikoff was excited. From Shin Boyar he learned more about Jean LaBarge, learned about his life in the west as Boyar had heard it, and about the fur poaching in Alaskan waters. LaBarge overheard Novikoff repeating the stories to friends, and did not mind. He knew that before long the stories would reach Kovalski.

When they had walked through the trees to the open park in the middle, Jean paused a moment, his eyes glancing over the area across which they must walk. He did not wish to step into an unexpected hole or trip over some unforeseen obstacle. The grass was smooth and well trimmed. He figured that if Kovalski was accustomed to firing from a stance he would without doubt attempt to score with his first shot from the original position.

Kovalski was jumpy and irritable. LaBarge looked to him almost like a professional duelist, although the terms he had proposed were ones no professional in his right mind would suggest. For the first time since he could remember, Kovalski had not slept well.

The distance was paced off and the two men took their positions, some thirty yards apart.

Colonel Balacheff stood at attention midway between the two and well out of the line of fire. "Does either gentleman wish to extend an apology?"

"No." LaBarge's voice was calm. "I do not."

He stood very still, waiting. His stomach felt hollow, his mouth dry. This was the worst part, this waiting. But he knew exactly what he was going to do.

"No." Kovalski's voice was steady.

"I will count." Balacheff spoke clearly. "I will count to three. At the count of three you will commence firing and will move toward each other firing at will. You will not cease to fire until one of you is unable to continue. Am I understood?"

Both men nodded.

The sun was not yet above the trees; there was still dew on the grass. Somewhere a bird rustled in the leaves and off across the fields a raven cawed hoarsely into the still, clear morning.

"One!"

Jean felt a trickle of sweat start down the back of his neck. Kovalski stood sidewise to him, his pistol raised in the orthodox position. He would shoot as the pistol came level, and Jean would be stepping out with that shot. If he led off with his right foot and Kovalski fired, his step would carry him a bit out of line with the bullet . . . he hoped.

"Two!"

The raven called suddenly, and Jean saw Kovalski twitch, almost as if he had started to fire, then caught himself. Jean could feel the sweat on his brow; he hoped it would not trickle into his eyes. A muscle in his leg started to jerk.

"Three!"

Jean LaBarge stepped off with his right foot and felt the whip of the bullet. Kovalski could shoot, but he had missed.

Holding his own gun slightly above belt height, Jean walked swiftly toward the Russian. The morning was very still and he could feel the grass against his shoes. A bead of sweat was trickling down his cheek and the stillness of the morning was slashed by a second shot. Only a split second had passed, yet he was moving. He felt the second shot go by him, then realized it must have been the third shot because he had already heard the report of the second.

He was walking fast but he was counting his steps and when he had taken seven steps he was going to fire. He felt the shock of the bullet as it struck him and the air lash of two more as they missed, and then his foot came down on the seventh step and he fired.

He fired his shot from hip level, the gun thrust out with his elbow close to the hip to steady it, the trigger squeezed off gently. He felt the gun leap in his fist and thumbed back the hammer for the second shot.

Kovalski wavered, then buckled at the knees and began to fall. As he fell the pistol dropped from his hand and when his body hit the turf his feet rebounded, fell hard, and he was dead.

LaBarge looked at the man who had been sent to kill him. He lowered the hammer on his pistol and from habit thrust it into his waistband. Novikoff rushed to him, hand outstretched. "Wonderful! Wonderful!" Novikoff was excited. "I never saw anything like it! He kept firing, and you—!"

Balacheff had picked up Kovalski's pistol. He glanced at the cylinder. *"Empty!"* He looked at LaBarge with unbelieving eyes. "Sir, let me congratulate you! I have never seen a braver thing! *Never*, sir!"

"Thank you."

Jean held himself stiffly against the beginning pain. There was a dampness of blood within his shirt.

When they were seated in the carriage, Jean said, "Right home, and don't stop!"

Novikoff stared at him, arrested by something in his tone, then abruptly, he felt alarm. "You're hurt! You've been shot!"

"Just get me home."

When the carriage drew up at the curb, Jean descended and walked stiffly to the door. He heard Novikoff paying the driver and then the door opened and he stepped blindly into the great hall. Then his legs buckled under him and he felt himself falling. From the stair there was a scream. The last thing he remembered was Helena rushing to him.

Lying in the canopied bed he looked up into the vague darkness above him. When he turned his head Helena was sitting across the room under a shaded light, reading. For a long time he lay watching her, tracing the way her lips were shaped and the proud lines of her face, softened now by shadows as they were sometimes softened by sunlight. He did not speak, nor feel like speaking, but lay still, thinking of her and of all that had transpired since their first meeting on the rain-wet dock in San Francisco. All that seemed far away now, all the distant Pacific, the wastes of Siberia, all of it. It had been months since they had left Alexander Rotcheff wounded in Baranof Castle, and now he himself was wounded, and for the same reasons.

"How bad was I hit?"

Helena dropped her book and rushed to him. "Jean! Oh, Jean! You're awake!"

"Seems that way. I wasn't hard hit, was I?"

"No . . . the bullet went through you and nobody knew, nobody even guessed you were hit. The doctor says it is only a flesh wound, but you lost a lot of blood, your clothing was soaked with it, underneath. But nobody knew."

"And they must not know. What day is today?"

"The same . . . it is almost midnight. I was waiting until you became conscious before I sent word to the Czar."

"There's no need to send word. We'll go."

"But you're hurt! You can't possibly go!"

"Want to bet?" He grinned at her. "And if you think I'm not capable, just try sitting down beside me."

She drew back quickly. "Jean! You mustn't talk like that." She looked down at him with excited, happy eyes. "You frightened me so! When you fell I thought you were dying."

"May I have some brandy? I could use it."

"Of course! What have I been thinking of! But then you must rest."

Nowhere in the world were there so many fountains, nor fountains of so many varieties, and when turned on simultaneously, as they were now, all the splendid parks were filled with a wondrous and mysterious splashing of water, making a strange music all its own. From the front of the old palace, where Helena and Jean paused on the wide terrace, a broad avenue of fountains and cascades led all the way to the seashore. And everywhere the scent of lilacs.

As they mounted the steps a Beethoven German dance was being played on the terrace by the Court orchestra. From the terrace where they had paused the view was magnificent, gilded statues mingling with the sparkling silver of the fountains. Pausing by the balustrade, neither wished to speak, they stood absorbed in the beauty of the moment. Behind them the Peterhof was ablaze with lights. They turned from the display of fountains, to watch the arrivals. Tall old men in mutton-chop whiskers, resplendent in uniforms, younger men with handsome mustaches, officers of the armed services and members of the nobility.

The audience arranged with the Czar was to take place privately, but during the grand ball. Standing beside the balustrade, Jean watched the colorful sight before him and was glad it had happened this way. He would never again see such a sight. He listened to the low-voiced comments and greetings, and was introduced to people whose names he never managed to distinguish but who were alike in extraordinary titles. All of them were anxious to talk to the Princess Gagarin of her experiences in Alaska, all curious about Count Rotcheff, and equally curious, he realized, as to his presence there.

Conscious of the beautiful girl beside him, more than ever conscious of her position, conscious of the music, the fountains and the scent of the lilacs, he could not help but draw a comparison between this place and the deck of the *Susquehanna* as she had been, gliding through the dark waters of Peril Strait. Nor could he forget the old man who lay wounded in Baranof Castle, and whose future as well as his life might rest on the interview that lay before them.

"Do you feel all right, Jean?" Helena looked at him anxiously. "Maybe we should not have come."

"Nonsense. I've never felt better." And he did not lie. True, the bullet had gone through him, and there was a stiffness in his chest muscles and his side. But he had suffered much more from slighter wounds, and weak though he might be, his enormous vitality and the strength built into him by years of outdoor living made the wound of little moment. He smiled a little, thinking of Hugh Glass crawling his miles upon miles across the plains of Nebraska after being clawed by a grizzly, and of a trapper he knew who had survived two weeks in the wilds when unable to walk from wounds and a broken leg he had set himself.

Count Novikoff crossed the terrace to them, clad in a blue and gold uniform, accompanied by a tall young Hussar in white and gold with a scarlet dolman flung over his shoulder.

"Captain LaBarge? I should like to present my friend, Prince Wolkonski."

A remarkably handsome young man, the Prince was scarcely more than a boy, with smooth blond hair and the face of a Greek god, and he was excited. "I am honored, sir! All St. Petersburg is talking of your duel with Colonel Kovalski, and how you allowed him to empty his pistol before you fired a shot! And while walking toward him! Remarkable, sir! Remarkable!"

"Thank you." Embarrassed, Jean took Helena and slipped away as quickly as possible. When alone for a moment, he turned to her.

"They believe I did it because of honor," he said dryly, "that I deliberately gave him every chance. I don't like to appear under false banners. I took my time because I wanted to fire one shot and kill him when I fired."

"Nevertheless, you gave him every chance."

"Helena," he smiled gently, "I don't want you to misunderstand me. I didn't give him any chance I could withhold. These boys, they make a hero of me because they believe I acted the way I did as a matter of honor. Actually, from the minute of the challenge every move I made was calculated to put him at a psychological disadvantage. His trouble was that his marksmanship was better than his strategy."

Even among the two thousand guests present, eyes turned again and again to Jean LaBarge. His height, the great breadth of his shoulders, the dark, piratical face with its scar, all were calculated to draw attention to the man who had killed the noted duelist.

The Emperor and the Empress opened the ball with a formal polonaise, and soon, despite his wound, Jean was dancing also. He felt good . . . shaky in the legs, but good. Yet soon at a tug from Helena's fingers, he followed her from the floor and into the great park.

The shaded walks were silent except for the distant music and the play of the waters in the fountains. They walked, arm in arm, under the dark trees.

"Jean, we shall be seeing His Majesty in just a

few minutes. When we were changing partners during the last dance I was told to be ready. We are to meet him in a little pavilion built by Peter the Great."

The park was empty of people. Jean moved carefully, not liking the shadows, suspecting danger everywhere.

As they walked up the path to the pavilion a man came down the steps to greet them. He was tall, bearded, and in uniform. He glanced quickly, sharply, at LaBarge. "Follow me, please."

They followed him through a small door and Jean found himself in a long room with a large fireplace and several pictures at which he merely glanced. Before him stood Alexander II, Czar of all the Russias.

"So, Captain LaBarge, you celebrate your arrival in my capital by killing one of my officers!"

Jean LaBarge bowed slightly. "Only, Your Majesty, because he would have prevented my audience with you!"

32

Alexander's tone was ironic as he said to Helena, "We must keep this gentleman with us, Princess. He talks as well as he shoots."

The Czar, a tall man with keen gray eyes, studied Jean thoughtfully for a moment, then said, "You have visited our Pacific colonies, sir. What do you think of them?"

"I think they are too far from St. Petersburg, Your Majesty."

"In other words, you agree with the report forwarded to me by Count Rotcheff?"

"I haven't seen the report, Your Majesty, only Russian America. And I believe that when a private company runs a territory for its exclusive profit it will give more thought to the profit than to the welfare of the territory."

Alexander seated himself abruptly. "Sit down, Captain." He gestured to a chair, "Helena?" When they were seated, he said, "Now, sir, tell us of your experiences in Alaska."

LaBarge thought quickly. He could lie, and paint Alaska as a territory no one would want; he knew this was the opinion of many of those in important positions in Russia as well as in the United States. Or he could tell the truth, relying upon the Czar's own intelligence to realize that a rich colony in an exposed position invited seizure. He decided that frankness was the best policy. It was likely, anyway, that the Czar knew a great deal about Alaska.

He began with his first awareness of Alaska, led his listeners quickly through the buying of furs, his first information in regard to fisheries, lumber and coal. He also mentioned the costs of exploitation, the distance from markets, and his own ventures into the area. The only thing he did not mention was gold.

"You traded in Russia against the orders of the Russian American Company?" demanded the Czar. His features were cold, revealing nothing.

"Yes, Sire."

Alexander raised an eyebrow and glanced at Helena, who restrained a smile. "You fired on a Russian warship? You evaded her demands to heave-to?"

"I did, Your Majesty, in the belief that the warship was acting upon Company orders rather than your own. Also," he added it without more than the merest trace of a smile, "because I believed I could outsail him."

Alexander laughed. "You are frank, sir."

"What's to be gained by lying? I trust to your judgment, Your Majesty, and also to your realization that the captain of a ship is often in the same position as the head of a state. He has to accept the risks of his position, and sometimes he has to act boldly."

Alexander tapped his fingers on the table. Jean had a feeling that the Czar agreed with him in principle, and might be reasoned with. He decided to speak out.

"Your Majesty, it's said in the United States that you are Europe's most enlightened monarch; it's said you plan to free your serfs. Did you know that the Indians in Alaska, who were free from the beginning of time until the Russian American Company came to Alaska, are greater slaves than your own serfs?"

He paused momentarily. "I deal in furs. I know the income from those furs. I know that on every trip to Alaska I have made a very substantial profit. Still I understand that the Alaska Company has to ask appropriations from the government of Russia to keep operating."

Alexander's face hardened. "Are you suggesting that the stockholders are being cheated? That the government is being robbed?"

"I'm only saying that each of my trips was successful. The trips of dozens of other traders whose furs I bought were successful. But the Russian American Company, which is on the ground, is losing money."

Alexander got to his feet and walked slowly across the room and back. Then he stopped and asked LaBarge about the matter of the wheat. Jean explained in as few words as possible, told of the burning of the wheat but without any suggestions or accusations. Then his own ride north and the delivery of wheat that resulted. The Czar asked many questions about the ride, the terrain crossed, and dangers.

"Obviously, Captain LaBarge," he said finally, "you honored your agreement with Count Rotcheff at great personal risk to yourself." He hesitated. "You are staying long in St. Petersburg, Captain?"

"No, Your Majesty, I'll return now. My only wish was to see the Princess safely returned to her home, and if possible to speak to you."

"I see . . . and what did you hope to gain by speaking to me?"

"I hoped to suggest, Your Majesty, that Russia sell Alaska to the United States."

If the Czar was surprised, he gave no evidence of it. Perhaps Helena had mentioned it, perhaps he had seen it coming, or there might have been some such suggestion in the report forwarded by Count Rotcheff.

"And you, a private citizen, are in a position to negotiate?"

"No, Your Majesty. But," Jean added, "I have a friend in Washington who might be. His name is Robert J. Walker, and he is former Secretary to the Treasury of the United States, and former Senator from Mississippi. I know he favors such a plan, and is in touch daily with others who do."

Alexander changed the subject and they talked quietly for nearly an hour on conditions in Alaska, the rapid westward expansion of the United States, and of the building of railways.

He arose suddenly. "Captain, I have taken much of your time. I thank you for coming to see me, and especially for assuring the safe return of the Princess, my niece."

"Thank you, Your Majesty."

"As for your suggestion, I shall give it much thought. It remains a possibility."

Outside in the park it was cool and pleasant. They stood for a long time watching the play of light among the sparkling waters of the fountains, and listening to the cascades as they ran down to the sea. From the palace came the sound of music. The dance continued still, although it seemed forever that they had been gone.

"And now?"

"San Francisco. But I believe this time I'll cross the Atlantic and see Rob Walker."

"I shall return to Sitka."

He turned sharply around. "Helena, you . . ."

"You think I am a fool? But Alexander is there, and my first duty is to him. Would you think more of me if I remained here?"

"Less, maybe, of your loyalty, more of your judgment. It isn't safe, Helena."

"No matter, I must go back."

33

Jean LaBarge picked his way across the rutted, muddy street. He had arrived in Washington scarcely an hour before and was shocked by the appearance of the capital. Heavy army wagons had furrowed the streets and plowed the avenues into rivers of mud. Here and there Negroes walked about with planks and for a consideration aided passengers alighting from vehicles to reach the sidewalks, or pedestrians to cross the streets. Hacks were few and hard to find, and often became stalled in the street where their passengers must remain marooned or wade through mud to the sidewalks.

Without waiting for a cab he picked his way through the streets and at last reached the impressive mansion on the tree-bordered square where Robert Walker made his temporary home. He walked up the steps and scraped the mud from his feet on the door scraper, then pulled the bell.

The Negro who answered the door was a short, stocky man who recognized the name at once. "Mistuh LaBarge, suh? Mr. Robert, he's sho' gonna be pleased! He sho'ly is."

The man who sat behind the desk in the high-ceilinged room was short and slender. He looked up from his desk as the door opened, then came suddenly to his feet. "Jean!" he said. "Jean LaBarge!"

"Hello, Rob."

They gripped hands for an instant, smiling at each other. It had been a long time.

"When did you get in?"

"Less than an hour ago. I took a room at the Willard."

"You needn't have done that."

They walked on into the room and Jean handed his hat and cloak to the Negro. Rob glanced at LaBarge's wide shoulders and the perfectly tailored suit.

"Whiskey?"

"Please. . . . "

Rob poured the drinks. "To the Honey Tree!"

Jean grinned at him. "The Honey Tree!"

He downed half his drink, then put his glass down. "I've often wondered about it, wondered if anyone ever got all that honey."

"I have no idea, Jean, but I do know there has been some talk of draining the swamp and logging it off."

"Then I don't want to go back."

For a half hour they talked of various topics, then Rob lit a cigar. "All right, Jean, tell me about it. Tell me about Russia. . . . "

It was growing light when Rob suddenly got to his feet. "Jean, you're tired. Can you come for dinner tomorrow night?" He glanced at his watch. "I mean, tonight? I want you to meet some friends of mine."

"Sure."

"You should have told me you were coming. The Willard is all right, but—"

"It's best for me. I'm lunching with a friend tomorrow. You may know him. Senator Bill Stewart."

"Of Nevada? I know of him, and a very able man."

"He was a cattle drover for a while as a boy, drove them right along Mill Creek Road once, he told me."

"How does he stand?"

"On Alaska? He's for it, I'm sure. He came early to California and is in favor of opening up new country."

"Sumner is the man you must meet. He's been against us, but I believe he is wavering a little. Jean, I want you to talk to him, I want you to tell him about Alaska.

"There's been no question about Seward. He's been for it from the beginning, perhaps even before I was, and he has been taking the brunt of the ridicule while I've been gathering the support. The papers refer to it as Seward's Folly, Seward's Icebox, but he found many of the arguments offered against Alaska were the same as those offered against the Louisiana Purchase. Seward dug up all those old arguments and has published the lot."

"Will it go through, Rob? Will they buy Alaska?"

He shrugged. "Who knows? I believe we will. I believe, in spite of the opposition, that the treaty will be ratified, but we've got a fight on our hands. Sumner is lukewarm, unconvinced but willing to listen, but I will tell you something about him, Jean. He likes facts. He likes to *know*, and when he speaks, he likes to deliver facts. Given the proper ammunition, I think he'll be with us."

The streets were dark and silent. When the door closed behind him Jean LaBarge walked slowly up the street. Several times he paused in his walking, feeling the mistlike rain on his face, looking up a broad avenue. The mud was obscured by darkness, and the tree-lined streets were softly beautiful.

Robert Walker did not go to bed. The excitement of seeing his old friend was joined with another realization: it was Jean LaBarge, if anyone, who could swing the balance toward ratification. His actual presence here, the chance to talk to a man who knew the country. LaBarge's own dramatic personality was sure to do much to convince a few laggards. He spoke easily and well, and above all, he seemed to know everything there was to know about Alaska.

Seated at his desk, Robert Walker considered the situation that faced him. Pleased as he was to see his old friend, he knew at once he must utilize his presence, and he knew that LaBarge would have been the first to agree. A less colorful person would have been less valuable, but the dark, handsome LaBarge with his romantic scar, his stories of the fur trade and the islands, his recent visit to the Czar's court and the duel that preceded it, these were sure to make their impression.

From the beginning of his political career Robert J. Walker had devoted himself to his country. He was an American who was filled with the ideas that filled many Americans at the time. He wanted to see the United States possess the entire continent, and the subjugation of a continent seemed a small task for men who had crossed the plains in covered wagons, who scouted the first trails and built towns where none before existed.

Walker had not made the westward trek, yet he had lived much of it with Jean LaBarge. He had not helped organize a mining village into a law-abiding community but he knew how it had been done, and to the little man from the banks of the Susquehanna it was vastly exhilarating.

The United States was bound to grow, as Muraviev had foreseen. In Walker's files there was a letter Muraviev had written to the Emperor:

... It was impossible not to foresee the swift expansion of the United States power in North America; it was impossible not to foresee that these States, having secured a foothold on the Pacific, would soon surpass all other powers, and acquire the whole northwest coast of America. ... We need have no regrets that we did not establish ourselves in California twenty years ago. Sooner or later we should have lost it ... it is foolish not to realize that we should, sooner or later, have to surrender our North American possessions. It is also inevitable for Russia to hold sway over the whole of eastern Asia.

* * *

Walker looked thoughtfully at his dead cigar. It was strange that a man like LaBarge, with no apparent interest in politics, had yet become a key figure. This man, sure to be forgotten in the march of history, at this important moment possessed the information that might swing the vote, and a personality dramatic enough to convince.

He, Walker, had been called a genius of party management. To many outside the understanding of world affairs, the term might seem less than flattering, yet Walker preferred it to any other. He knew how to line up the votes, knew what the states and territories needed, and he knew that statecraft consists of a reconciling of viewpoints, and to be a superior statesman one must also be a superior politician. It was not enough to have vision, to have a program. It was not enough to be strong, sincere, honest. In a democracy one also needed votes, and to put over a program one must find a way to win the votes of those with less vision and possibly even less loyalty to country.

The United States must have Alaska, not only as a possession, but as a state. To win a land is not to possess it; the land must be populated and held.

The first person Jean saw when he entered the room was Seward. From descriptions he recognized him at once, standing near the fireplace chewing an unlighted cigar. His limp gray hair was rumpled and untidy, and some cigar ash had scattered itself over his satin-faced waistcoat.

Seward acknowledged the introduction with a

brief, limp handshake and a glance from his shrewd, appraising eyes. "You are much spoken of these days, Mr. LaBarge." He rolled the cigar in his teeth. "You have the advantage of us, sir. You have seen Alaska."

"And I have talked to the Czar."

"You have assumed a lot, Mr. LaBarge. By whose authority did you speak?"

Despite the words, his voice held no animosity. Jean replied quickly, smiling as he spoke. "By yours, of course, sir. Mr. Walker tells me that in a speech at St. Paul a few years ago you said, speaking to the Russians, 'Go on and build your outposts all along the coast to the Arctic Ocean, they will yet become the outposts of my own country.'"

Seward's eyes flickered for an instant with humor. "Mr. Walker's memory is very convenient for you, Mr. LaBarge."

Jean sensed rather than saw that other men had joined them. One of these he was sure was Charles Sumner, for Seward then said, "Tell us about Alaska, LaBarge. Tell us what you saw."

Robert Walker glanced quickly around the room. Here, in this room, were a dozen of the key men in the Senate, men who might make or break ratification of the treaty. So much depended on the next few minutes. Suddenly he found himself wishing that Fessenden were here. One of the ablest speakers in the Senate, Fessenden was a bitter opponent of the purchase of Alaska.

LaBarge had turned, almost casually, with his back to the fire. What he was to say now need not convince Seward, for Seward had been a consistent fighter for Alaska from the beginning; it was the others he must win. Charles Sumner was a man who dearly loved to present facts, to speak with authority, and he was a man whose words carried weight.

"What can any man say of a land the size of Alaska in a few minutes? I've seen its furs, its miles upon miles of forest, its gold, its iron, its fish. I have hunted in woods teeming with wild game, and seen valleys as fertile as any upon earth."

From his vest pocket Jean took a small lump wrapped in skin. It was the nugget he had bought, long ago, from the trapper. "See this? Gold . . . and there is more of it there. But believe me, Gentlemen, gold is the least of Alaska's riches."

For an hour LaBarge talked, replied to questions, and told stories of his experiences in Russian America. He told of the cruelties of the *promyshleniki*, and gave figures on the fur shipments. In forty years the Russian American Company had shipped over 51,000 sea otter skins, 291,000 fox pelts, 319,000 beaver and 831,000 fur seal hides.

"And that, Gentlemen, says nothing of what our own ships took out, nor the British. My own ship has taken out more than 100,000 skins, much whalebone, walrus, ivory, Tlingit blankets and some gold."

It was late before the party broke up and at last Walker and LaBarge sat down together.

"I think," Walker said, "you've won some allies

for us, and certainly you've given our backers some ammunition. What are your plans?"

"I'll leave for the coast at once. I have the *Susquehanna* to think of." He glanced up at Walker. "When do you think this can be done?"

"The purchase?" Walker shrugged. "Congress rarely does anything swiftly, Jean, and there are enemies to the plan. Some think it a waste of money, and General Ben Butler is bringing up the old matter of the Perkins claims. He says he will use their claim against Russia to stall ratification of the treaty. It may take months yet, even years."

"I see." Jean got up. "Rob, I'll write from San Francisco. I'm anxious to get back."

"The Princess de Gagarin has returned to Sitka, you said?"

"I'm worried, Rob. I must get back there. If Zinnovy was willing to risk shooting Rotcheff, he won't hesitate to rid himself of them both. As you say, politics isn't always a fast business, and although the Princess turned her husband's reports over to the Czar, it may be months before anything can be done. There will be delays, hesitations, arguments . . . you know more about that than I . . . and in the meantime, they are there."

For a moment the two men stood together, and then Walker put his hand on the younger man's arm. "Jean . . . take care of yourself."

"You do the same."

It was snowing when he reached the street, a light, unseasonal snow that melted as it hit the pavement. Jean LaBarge walked quickly away into the darkness.

Robert Walker returned to his study. Now he could move, now he had ammunition, facts, figures, arguments. And Sumner, he thought, was won. And Sumner would dearly love a debate with Fessenden.

So tomorrow. . . .

34

Baron Edouard Stoeckl had arrived in New York from St. Petersburg on February 15th, 1867. As he was recovering from a severe injury to his leg he remained in New York for two weeks, but during this time he was in touch with Robert Walker. His purpose in returning was to negotiate the sale of Alaska.

A draft of the treaty was before the cabinet by March 15th, and on March 29th, Stoeckl received word from the Czar that the treaty was approved. Although it was very late when the news came to him, he at once joined Robert Walker and together they went to see William Seward, Secretary of State. All night they worked.

As the *Susquehanna* prepared for sea, Jean LaBarge read in the *Alta Californian* that the treaty "will hardly be considered at this session, but will go over to next winter."

Seward increased his campaign of education. The papers rarely came out now without some information on Alaska, and by letter, Jean continued to supply information on various parts of the

Russian-held area. On April 4th it was reported that there was no chance of the treaty being ratified. But a letter from Rob was optimistic, and with that final word, the *Susquehanna* sailed.

For several days a fast-sailing sloop had been lying alongside a wharf near Clark's Point, and during none of those days had a man been ashore. Within the hour after the *Susquehanna* cleared the Golden Gate, Royle Weber dropped into Denny O'Brien's bar.

Much had changed. Yankee Sullivan, under threat of lynching by the Vigilantes, had committed suicide. Charley Duane had been escorted to a ship and sent off to New York, and O'Brien had much to worry about. But his memory was long, and the night when he had stood at his own bar with his pants around his heels with the click of his vest buttons on the floor in his ears was not easy to forget.

Crossing the room he dropped into a chair opposite Weber. Weber shifted his weight on the chair seat and smiled. "Well, Denny, we've waited a long time!"

"It's now?"

"The *Susquehanna* cleared port this afternoon."

Denny turned and motioned to a dark-skinned man who loitered at the bar, and when the man leaned over, spoke to him. Instantly, the man was out of the door and running. Less than an hour later the sailing sloop slid away from the dock and pointed herself north for Sitka.

"I'd like to be there," Denny O'Brien said. "I'd like to see his face."

The *Susquehanna's* second port of call was at Kootznahoo Inlet. The information LaBarge had received was clear. No ship had called at Kootznahoo since his own last trip, and there were many furs. It would be a rich cargo to pick up. When the *Susquehanna* dropped the hook off Kootznahoo head the *bidarkas* were swift to come.

A few days before the fast-sailing sloop had put into Sitka harbor, but had not gone near the dock. Rather, it had gone at once to the *Lena* and tied up alongside. Within an hour both the *Lena* and the *Kronstadt* slipped out of Sitka harbor, the *Lena* sailing north and around the island through Peril Strait, while the *Kronstadt* sailed south, rounded Point Ommaney and started north. The sloop, taking water and provisions from the *Lena*, never even docked at Sitka for fear the grapevine would carry word across the islands, but sailed immediately back to the United States.

The weather was good. Ben Turk, Gant and Boyar had gone ashore to hunt in the hills back of the inlet. Kohl was also ashore. Trading had been brisk that morning, but now it had begun to lag. Jean LaBarge went below and stretched out in his bunk.

He was half-asleep when from the deck there was a sudden wild yell, then a tremendous explosion. Leaping from his bunk he was thrown off balance by a second concussion. Lunging for the companionway he heard screams of agony from the deck, then a concussion from aft. He sprang out into a cloud of smoke and flame. Something forward was burning. The forem'st lay in a welter of tangled ropes and splintered wood. After, Duncan Pope and Ben Noble were working the gun, and near them, sprawled in the wreck of the helm, lay one of the Indians in a pool of blood.

Across the mouth of the bay lay the *Lena*. At a glance, LaBarge knew the situation was hopeless. There was no other way out of the inlet, and inside, the water was not deep enough to take the schooner. She would be shot to wreckage before they could get moving.

"Cut loose the anchor," he yelled. "Get a jib on her!"

A shell screamed overhead and lost itself somewhere in the woods. The schooner was moving slowly now. If they could get around Turn Point. . . . He had no hopes of saving the ship, what he wanted now was a chance for the crew to take to the hills. Once there, with the friendly Indians, they could hide out for weeks until they might reach the mainland.

Pope fired their own gun again, and LaBarge had the satisfaction of seeing the shell burst amidships, smashing the whaleboat to splinters and ripping sails and rigging. Now the *Lena* moved closer, getting into position to rip the *Susquehanna* with another broadside.

Enough of the wheel remained to swing the schooner and LaBarge started to put it over when a

shell struck forward and he felt the ship stagger
under a wicked blow in the hull. Then the shelling
stopped. Their own gun had ceased to fire and
turning he saw Duncan Pope sprawled on the deck,
his skull blown half away. Noble caught his arm.

"We'd better run for it, sir!" he shouted. "They'll
be alongside in a few minutes!"

Two boats were in the water, pulling strongly toward the wreck of the *Susquehanna*.

Dazed, he glanced around. Pope was dead, and
another man lay sprawled amidships. The
schooner was drifting helplessly, but the current,
slight as it was, was taking them deeper into the
inlet. The tidal currents there, he recalled, were
fearfully strong.

The way was blocked. The *Lena* lay fairly across
the only entrance and her boats were drawing near.
There was nothing else for it.

"Abandon ship," he said. "Get for shore, all of
you."

"What about you?" Noble protested.

"I'll come," he said. "Get going!"

He turned to the companionway and went
swiftly down the ladder. For the first time he realized how badly hulled they were: water stood on
the deck of the saloon. He slipped a pistol behind
his belt, caught up a coat. Alongside he heard
splashes and yells as the crew jumped over the
side. The shore here was nowhere over fifty yards
away.

He went swiftly up the ladder and reaching the
rail, turned back for a last long look. The forem'st

was gone, trailing over the side in a mass of wreckage. The stern was a wreck and the deck was literally a shambles. Pope and Sykes were definitely gone, both killed in those few minutes of shelling. Luckily, most of the crew had been ashore. Yet . . . the *Susquehanna* . . . it was like deserting an old friend. He sprang to the rail.

Below him and not twenty yards away was the Russian longboat, and in it were a dozen men, six of whom covered him with rifles. In the stern sat Baron Paul Zinnovy, smiling.

To jump was to die, and he was not ready to die.

The boat came alongside and the Russians swarmed aboard. Two men seized him and bound his hands behind him, stripping him of his pistol.

Zinnovy scarcely glanced at him, walking about the ship, looking her over curiously. Other men had gone below to inspect the cargo.

As he was seated in the boat one of the men spoke to the other and indicating LaBarge, said, "*Katorzhniki.*"

It was a word that stood for a living death, it was the term applied to hard-labor convicts in Siberia.

May had come and gone before the news reached Robert Walker, and he acted with speed. The purchase of Alaska hung in the balance and the Baron Edouard Stoeckl was worried. He wanted to be back in Russia, or to have an assignment in Paris or Vienna, and everything depended on this mission. Now this LaBarge affair had to come up, and the man involved had to be a personal friend, a very close friend of Walker himself, known moreover to Seward, Sumner, all of them.

Ratification of the treaty was not enough. The appropriation must be made. He had watched Congress in action long enough to know that the whole sale of Alaska might fail right there. And if any man could get out the necessary vote, it was Walker. Why couldn't that confounded Zinnovy have kept his ships in Sitka?

He sat now, in Walker's home, and the little man with the wheezy voice glanced over at him. "Is there any news of LaBarge?"

The Baron's face shadowed a little. He had hoped the subject would not arise. "We have done our best, but—"

"Could it be possible," Walker suggested, "to arrange for the transfer of such a prisoner? Supposing he is in Siberia?"

"There is no record of such a prisoner," Stoeckl protested, "nor of any such capture. I am sure the whole affair is the figment of someone's imagination."

"Sir," Walker's voice was stiff, "the man whose letter lies on my desk is a man of honor, LaBarge's partner and my friend. Not only was an American vessel shelled but its cargo was taken. This, sir, savors of piracy."

Baron Stoeckl had friends in the Russian American Company, but Baron Zinnovy was not one of these. However, he had a very good idea as to Zinnovy's duties in Sitka, and it would not do to have such news reach the ears of the Czar. Stoeckl knew that following the return of Princess Helena there had been a great fuss, which had been calmed down only after some time. At this moment orders for a complete shake-up at Sitka were carefully pigeonholed in the Ministry of the Interior. A *revisor* was to be appointed to investigate, but so far this had not been done.

"I cannot see what good it would do to have the prisoner transferred if he remained a prisoner."

Walker brushed the question aside. "I have heard, correct me if I am wrong, that some convict labor is used in Sitka?"

Baron Stoeckl almost smiled. So that was what the fox was thinking! Maybe this man was married to Benjamin Franklin's granddaughter with some reason . . . a prisoner transferred to Alaska on the evening of the sale would most certainly be freed when the Americans took over.

It was a very sensible idea . . . and this he, Baron Stoeckl, might arrange. There were people, the superiors of Zinnovy, in the Ministry of the Interior who wanted LaBarge to remain a prisoner. Yet a prisoner might be transferred without incurring the displeasure of these people. It was something that might be done without endangering his own future prospects.

There was one thing Walker did not know and which Stoeckl had no intention of telling him. There was every prospect that Zinnovy himself would be appointed *revisor* at Sitka.

"It is, as you suggest, a possibility that another shipment of convicts might be sent to Sitka. . . .

How do the votes stand, Mr. Walker, for the appropriation?"

They talked far into the night, weighing the pros and cons and Stoeckl nursed his injured leg and cursed under his breath.

It was bad luck that Zinnovy had gone to Siberia without putting in at Sitka, and the prisoners had been landed there and turned over to the police. Probably not even he knew what had become of LaBarge by now. It was several days before he saw Walker again. They met briefly, over a glass of sherry.

"By the way"—Stoeckl was on his feet ready to go—"I understand a shipment of twenty prisoners will leave Okhotsk on the last of the month."

"I shall hope for further news. Are any prisoners I know involved?"

"At least one," Stoeckl replied, "that I am sure of."

They parted and the Baron walked away. There was no reason why he should feel guilty. It was too bad for LaBarge, and the Baron felt real regret for Robert Walker. A good man, this Walker, a genius at managing things like this treaty. Seward might be the key figure, but it was Walker who lined up the vote, did the lobbying, the entertaining, and the leg work to arrange the purchase.

Walker must be content with that. For the rest of it, there was no hope. Prisoner Jean LaBarge was going out of the Siberian frying pan into the Sitka fire.

35

From the window of her room in Baranof Castle, Helena looked out over the city and harbor where sunlight lay bright upon the water, and gleamed from the serene loveliness of Mount Edgecumbe. The Castle was no longer the gloomy place it had been. In the capable hands of Prince Maksoutof and his wife it had become warm, comfortable, even gay.

The same eighty cannon looked grimly over the city from the parapet below. But there was more shipping in the bay, and several of them were American ships.

She had been a fool to come, yet if Rob Walker's hint in his letter to her had been founded upon fact, Jean LaBarge might soon be arriving here. If she could not free him she could at least, through Prince Maksoutof, relieve his imprisonment a little.

So few words had actually passed between them, yet she knew how he had felt, and she also knew, only too well, her own feelings. But what would prison have done to him? She had seen men who returned from Siberia, some of them scarcely human after the hard labor and punishments. Yet there was something about Jean that seemed indestructible.

There had been so little. The warmth in his eyes, the pressure of his hand, their bodies close together in the bouncing, jouncing *tarantas*.

She had loved a man for the first time, and she had lost him. Her husband had always been more like a kind father, tender, thoughtful, and considerate, and she had loved him for this. But it was nothing like her feeling for the tall, dark, dangerous-looking man with the scar whom she had loved with a love that bridged the bitter months and made them seem an age.

If this was being a fool, then she was a fool, and she had come across Siberia again, and across the ocean, merely on the hope that he would be here, and that he would still care.

Prince Maksoutof was questioning himself as to why she was here. Both the Prince and Princess had tried to find some clue from her conversation or her guarded replies to questions.

The Russian American Company still operated in Sitka although its charter had not been renewed. Something was impending, some change of which she could find out nothing. So far as she had been able to discover, the plan to sell Alaska had failed at the last minute. There were rumors of negotiations and rumors of the collapse of negotiations.

From the beginning of Jean's disappearance she had corresponded with Robert Walker. In his last letter he had hinted that Jean, as a convict, might be transferred to Sitka. She knew from here an escape might be arranged and she was perfectly prepared to do her part in making the arrangements.

A schooner that had come in only last night had brought news that a Russian ship was due in today, and Murzin was down in town even now making friends. If anyone could help Jean escape it was the former thief, that wiry, narrow-faced man who had never left her service since that meeting on the trip across Siberia with Jean.

At breakfast she had been gay, chatting cheerfully of St. Petersburg, the court, that handsome Count Novikoff, and the last ball at the Peterhof. She had told them of San Francisco and its warm green hills, sometimes misted with rain. She had talked of everything but the ship that hour after hour, minute after minute, was drawing nearer to Sitka. Even now it might be coming up the bay through those beautiful islands that resembled so much the islands of the Adriatic. A warmer sea, but never a more lovely one than this.

She went down the steps slowly, not wishing to reveal her excitement. If Jean was aboard she must help him escape, and that before the *revisor* came on his inspection trip. Maksoutof had told her the man was coming, but nobody knew when.

"Helena," Princess Maksoutof suggested, "why don't we go to the teahouse and watch the people land from the ship? They will come up the street and if we get in the right position we can see them leave the dock."

She got up, almost too quickly. "I'd like a walk," she said. "I'd like it very much."

Although from the teahouse they could see little, Helena forced herself to wait quietly, knowing whatever news there was would first be known here, long before it was heard on the Hill.

The waitress was excited. "They are bringing convicts ashore! They are to work here!"

"Irina"—Helena could wait no longer—"let's go down and watch them come in!"

They came, preceded by soldiers, in a column of twos, the gray-clad prisoners marching in slow, even steps, swaying as though to a soundless rhythm.

The first two were a red-bearded giant and a slender man with a twisted face. They blinked their eyes against the light after standing for some time in the shadowed warehouse. There was one man, tall, whose head was bowed. It could be Jean.

"Helena!" Irina caught her arm. "Look! Isn't he magnificent!"

He stood straight and tall, and he wore his chains in this town where he was remembered as another man might have worn a badge of honor. His face was shaggy with beard and his hair was long . . . he was much, much thinner! But he stood tall and he walked tall. He carried his head up and his eyes were clear. How could she ever have imagined they could break or tame him? He was one of the untamed, and so he would ever be.

He walked beside a shorter man who was also bearded, but Helena had eyes only for Jean. She moved to the edge of the walk, hoping he would see her, hoping he would know she was here to help.

"Jean!" She must have whispered it, for Irina turned suddenly to look at her.

"Do you know him?" Irina's eyes were bright with excitement and curiosity.

"Yes . . . yes, I know him. I know him well. I love him."

"You needn't have told me that. I can see." Irina looked at Jean again. "Yes, without so much beard, and if his hair was cut—" She glanced around at Helena. "Is that why you came? Did you know about this?"

"I came on hope," she said.

Jean hunched his shoulders inside the thin coat. His eyes swung to the crowd, and suddenly he saw Helena.

An instant, a step only, he paused. Their eyes met across the heads of the people and suddenly there was a great smile on his face and Helena started forward. Irina caught her arm. "No! No, Helena! You mustn't! I'll arrange—"

"Whatever you arrange"—the voice was cool, amused—"do it quickly. He goes on trial tomorrow."

Baron Paul Zinnovy was heavier, his thick neck had grown still thicker. There was in his eyes more cynicism and cruelty than Helena remembered.

"What are you doing here?" she demanded. He had been ordered back to Siberia, to Yakutsk. She remembered that. It could have been only a few months after Jean was captured.

"Why, I am the *revisor*," he said, "here to rectify mistakes, conduct trials and discharge incompetent officials, but most particularly, to conduct trials."

"Haven't you done enough to him? And to me?"

"To you?" His eyebrow lifted. "To you, Princess?"

"You murdered my husband." She spoke deliberately, coldly, and heard Irina's startled gasp. "I shall not be able to prove it, but you murdered him, and we both know it."

"It is a weakness of women to be overly imaginative, but if you wish to see reality, you may come as my guest to the trial of Jean LaBarge for theft, for smuggling, and for murder."

36

The room was packed with spectators. As Sitka had little entertainment, the prospect of a trial conducted by Baron Zinnovy as *revisor* held an unusual interest. And the man on trial was as well known to them, by name at least, as the Baron himself.

LaBarge was seated, still in chains, inside a small enclosure. He had been allowed to shave, and his clothing had been carefully brushed. Here and there in the crowd he saw familiar faces, but there was no welcome on those faces, no expression of sympathy. He was alone here.

Yet he had seen Helena. Did that mean that Count Rotcheff had never left Sitka? Or had he too returned again as Zinnovy had?

He had seen American ships in the harbor but there was no activity around them, and he had seen no Americans ashore in the town.

His thoughts returned to Rotcheff. If he was here he could do nothing, for LaBarge had been long enough in Siberia to know the power of the *revisor*. Appeal from his judgments could be made only to the Minister of the Interior or the Czar himself, and all such appeals were reviewed by the Ministry.

Siberia had made him suffer, but it had been a few months only, and this recall to Sitka had given him hope. If he could do nothing else, he could kill Zinnovy. He needed no weapon but his hands, and once those hands were on Zinnovy's throat nothing, nothing at all would stop him. He would kill Paul Zinnovy.

It would be absurdly easy. He could see where Zinnovy must sit, and he, LaBarge, must rise to receive sentence. His guards would be behind him, but the distance he must travel was short and they would not dare shoot at first for fear of hitting Zinnovy. Afterwards they would shoot him, but it would be better than Siberia again. Or the knout. He kept thinking of that.

Yet somewhere Rob Walker would be trying. By now he would know what had happened and Rob would move swiftly. No doubt he was working even now, and had been working, but it was too late. It was up to him, LaBarge, to do what he could.

He saw Prince Maksoutof and the Princess take their places, and Helena with them. Her face was pale, the circles under her eyes testifying to the sleepless night. Maksoutof had been pointed out to Jean by one of the guards. He was now the company director here, and governor of the colony. But even he could be removed by a *revisor*. The prison grapevine had a rumor that the Company had sent Zinnovy as *revisor*, appointed by somebody in the Ministry of the Interior who was a stockholder, to wipe out all evidence of the graft, cruelty and outright theft the Company officials had been perpetrating here.

Jean's mouth was dry. He was tired and the room was warm. His clothing stank of prisons and of unbathed bodies. This was an end of it then, the end of all his dreams, hopes, and ambitions. Rotcheff, the only friend he might have expected here, was not present. Helena could not help him, and Busch was not present: the merchant must have returned to Siberia. He was alone . . . alone.

What could be done? Being familiar with Russian courts, he knew that a trial was actually no trial at all but merely a hearing to air the crimes of the accused and pronounce sentence. The very fact that a trial was called meant the prisoner had been convicted.

The voices in the large room stilled, the clerk stood, then the spectators. Baron Zinnovy, resplendent in a magnificent uniform, entered and seated himself behind the desk. "Proceed with the trial," he said.

The clerk stood, then cleared his throat. The crowd leaned forward, the better to hear.

"The prisoner will stand!"

Jean LaBarge got to his feet, the chains clanking in the silent room.

"You, Jean LaBarge, are accused; you are accused of illegal trading with Tlingit people in Russian territory;

"You are accused of refusing to obey a command to heave-to given by a patrol ship of His Imperial Majesty;

"You are accused of evading capture;

"You are accused of firing on the patrol ship *Lena* while it was in the service of His Imperial Majesty;

"You are accused of firing upon and killing three members of the crew of His Imperial Majesty's ship, *Lena*;

"You are accused of the theft of furs belonging to the Russian American Company;

"You are accused of resisting capture. . . . "

The clerk's monotonous voice rolled on with the long list of accusations, some carrying at least a grain of truth, most completely false, yet the voice droned on and on.

Behind the judge's desk Baron Zinnovy filled his pipe and considered the clerk a dull stick and a fool, but it was something that must be done. Zinnovy stifled a yawn. It was warm in the overcrowded room. He had expected this to be a triumph, but LaBarge showed no weakening, no fear as yet. The whole affair was a confounded bore. He should have shot the man when captured, then he could have saved himself this.

Helena listened, her eyes half-closed against the sight she dreaded, against the heaviness of the room and the heat of the crowded bodies. From such an array of charges there could be no appeal, no hope of escape. The droning voice ended. There was silence in the room.

From the back of the crowd a voice said, "It's a pack o' lies!"

Baron Zinnovy did not lift his voice. "Arrest that man," he said, then turned his heavy-lidded eyes on LaBarge.

"Has the prisoner any statement to make before sentence is passed?"

There had been a knothole, long ago, through which came the first gray light of morning. It had been a long, long night but he had never doubted that help would come because his friend Rob Walker had gone for help, and Rob would not fail him. There was a knothole here, high near the eaves of the building, and a ray of light fell through it too. He stared at it, remembering that morning so long ago. He began to smile.

Behind his desk Zinnovy's eyes tightened a little and a line appeared between them. Why was the fool smiling? Had he gone insane? Could he not realize what sentence would mean? That there was no appeal? LaBarge got slowly to his feet.

"You ask for a statement." He spoke in a dull heavy voice that gained in strength as he spoke. "Whatever I might say in denial of your false accusations would be ignored. To some of the charges I admit my guilt." He smiled broadly. "I admit to buying furs from the Tlingit and paying honest prices; I admit to evading the patrol ship because it was absurdly easy to do; but—" His eyes strayed to the beam of light from the knothole near the eaves. . . .

Puzzled by LaBarge's expression, Zinnovy followed the line of his gaze to the knothole, puzzled even more when he realized at what LaBarge was staring.

Suddenly, Jean knew he was going to take a chance, a daring chance, but one through which he could lose nothing.

"I admit the truth to some of the statements," he repeated, "but I deny they are crimes, Baron Zinnovy. I deny your right, as a Russian official, to conduct a trial *on the territory of the United States!*"

"*What?*" Zinnovy came half out of his chair. "What nonsense is this?"

"People of Sitka!" LaBarge turned suddenly to face the crowd. "You stand now on the free soil of the United States of America! The treaty of purchase has been ratified and signed by the Czar, and this territory now belongs to the United States of America, and the Czar has proclaimed an amnesty, freeing all prisoners at present held in Sitka!"

The audience rose to their feet, cheering. Zinnovy was shouting, his face swollen with anger. Soldiers ran along the aisles, threatening the crowd. Slowly they subsided. Jean LaBarge remained on his feet, his heart pounding heavily. He had attempted a colossal bluff and now he must carry it through.

There were American ships in the outer harbor, and those ships had given him the idea. He knew that shipping men have a nose for developments, and that coupled with his great faith in his friend inspired him to the gamble.

The room was quiet and Zinnovy straightened in his chair. "Prisoner, I sentence—"

"You are without jurisdiction, Baron Zinnovy." Jean's voice was clam, but it carried to every corner of the room. "Sitka is now a territory of the United States and if sentence is carried out on me, you will yourself be liable to prosecution under the laws of the United States."

Zinnovy hesitated. He was trembling with fury, but he was never an incautious man, and now a beam of cool sanity penetrated his rage. LaBarge was too positive, too sure. If the sale *had* gone through, and especially if the money was not yet paid, and he passed sentence on an American citizen, he was buying himself a ticket to Siberia from which even his friends could not save him. And the Princess Helena was right here to report every detail, so he could never deny he did not know.

The room was filled with excited whispering; he was enraged to see with what excitement the news had been greeted. Here and there was a solemn face, but all too many had been made happy. Some of the smiles were from loyal Russians who were pleased to see him thwarted. This was nonsense . . . yet, suppose it were true?

The thought was an unpleasant one; he knew even his powerful friends would sacrifice him if it became necessary . . . but how would a prisoner know if such a treaty had been ratified?

Even as he denied the possibility he answered the question himself. It was with prisoners as with the army: many times they knew things in the rank and file before the colonels of regiments knew. It was the grapevine, that word of mouth telegraph that could not be shut off or stopped. Perhaps—

"Sentence will be passed tomorrow afternoon," he commanded abruptly, rising to his feet. "Return the prisoner to his cell."

37

When he awakened it was night. Returned to his cell he had fallen across his bunk and slept like a man drugged, but he now lay wide awake, listening to the night sounds, for his was the hunter's brain, always tuned to the little sounds, the creeping sounds. He got up and walked to the narrow window.

Out there were the stars, the same he had watched long ago from the Great Swamp. Was he a fool to trust in a man so far away? Outside a night bird called, and a wind talked gently among the pines and whispered of far-off mountains, a wind that came from distant glaciers, caressed the restless waters and blew into his small window.

There was a rustle in the corridor, a rustle of movement. He turned quickly, knowing that sound. A key grated in the lock and the door opened, and in the instant before it swung wide he caught a whiff of perfume.

"Jean? . . . Jean!"

She was in his arms then and they clung to each other, clung with a strength that hurt. "Jean! Oh, Jean! I've been so frightened!"

Helena drew back suddenly, the guard was still in the door, but he had politely turned his back. "Jean, is it true? Has the United States bought Sitka?"

"Helena"—he spoke softly so the guard would not hear—"I don't know anything more than you. It was a bluff.

"Of course," he added, "I know Rob. I know he has made this thing go through if anyone could, and when I saw those American ships out there, just lying there waiting . . . well, what could I lose?"

She hesitated, fearing to tell him. "Jean, Rob Walker has been writing to me, and they have tried everything to find you and free you. It was because of that that I am here, but at the last minute it all came to nothing. The treaty was not ratified."

He shook his head stubbornly. "I can't believe that. If the treaty was written, if a price was agreed upon, then Walker would get out the vote. No, Helena, if that treaty was written and submitted to the Senate it was ratified."

"But it wasn't, Jean! You mustn't depend on that! You must escape!"

"No, I think Zinnovy wants me to attempt an escape . . . if I do I'll be shot and his problem is solved. Don't you realize he would expect you to see me? That he might deliberately make it easy believing you would bring me something, a weapon? No, I'll stay. If Count Rotcheff can help, then—"

"Jean?" Her throat found difficulty with the words. "Jean, Alexander has been dead for nearly a year. He died before I returned to Sitka."

"Dead?" The word did not make sense. If he was dead then she was free . . . free.

Free . . . they could be together. They could belong to each other. Nothing would stand between them. Only tomorrow he would be returned to Siberia . . . or hanged.

The improvised courtroom was jammed. The clerk took his place. Opposite Jean, Helena sat where her eyes could see his, and beside her were Prince and Princess Maksoutof. The crowd was large, and contained many familiar faces. His eyes stopped a full second.

Barney Kohl . . . his face was solemn, but there was an obvious bulge at his waistband. Beside him was the square, tough face of Gant.

Suddenly, Jean was filled with excitement. They had escaped then . . . none of them were known to Zinnovy, and they were here. That meant they had been able to hide out after the attack on the *Susquehanna*.

His eyes searched the crowd . . . Ben Turk . . . beside him was Sin Boyar. There were several other men he did not know but he was sure they were Americans; they looked like Frisco seamen, right off the waterfront. And they were scattered, scattered in a perimeter around the room. Kohl was seated right behind a guard. Boyar was beside another. That meant they intended to break him out, which meant shooting unless they had a plan, a good plan. Baron Paul Zinnovy came into the room. He walked to the desk and seated himself. He was cool, composed, sure. If he noticed the strange faces in the crowd he gave no evidence of it.

The clerk got to his feet. "Jean LaBarge, stand and receive sentence!"

Jean LaBarge got to his feet, and Baron Zinnovy looked over the papers he held in his hand. He smiled at LaBarge, finding pleasure in the moment.

Suddenly there was a rustle of movement at the door, a shoving, a whisper, a shout, and then the door pushed open and a man in civilian clothes entered followed by a line of American bluejackets.

The man passed LaBarge by without speaking and stopped before Zinnovy, whose face had turned ashen.

"Baron Zinnovy? I am Brigadier General Lovell H. Rousseau, United States Commissioner to accept the Territory of Alaska from the government of Russia."

A Russian officer walked from the door to a place beside the general. He stood at attention and bobbed his head. "Captain Alexei Petchouroff," he said. "Special Emissary of His Imperial Majesty the Czar of all the Russias!"

Baron Paul Zinnovy leaned back in his chair, his face without expression.

Captain Petchouroff extended an envelope to Zinnovy. "My orders, sir, and yours. You are to return to Okhotsk to await His Imperial Majesty's pleasure."

Zinnovy got to his feet. "Of course, but we have a trial here, and—"

Petchouroff waved a gesture of dismissal. "In honor of this great day, His Imperial Majesty has declared a general amnesty. A pardon for all on trial and all awaiting trial in Russian America. They are free, and you are freed of this disagreeable duty!"

Jean LaBarge turned to meet Helena as she ran to him from across the room, and then the crew of the *Susquehanna* moved in around him.

The morning was bright and clear. Brigadier General Rousseau and General Jefferson C. Davis, backed by a solid square of two hundred American sailors, soldiers and marines, stood at attention. Across from them stood one hundred Russian soldiers in their gray, red-trimmed uniforms. The music began, and officers on both sides mounted the steps of the Castle where Prince Maksoutof awaited them. They turned and faced the square, Captain Petchouroff descending to a place beside General Rousseau.

As the Russian flag was lowered, Princess Maksoutof sobbed gently. Among the Russian civilians several were openly crying.

The American flag climbed the staff and out on the bay the guns of the U.S.S. *Ossipee* boomed a salute.

Behind the gathered civilians Jean LaBarge stood

beside Helena, and as the flag climbed the staff, Jean whispered, "Do you know what I'm thinking of now? I'm remembering a boy who grew up back on the Susquehanna, a boy who was smaller than any of us, but bigger in a lot of ways than any of us would ever be. In the future they may forget, or they may say cruel things about him. But what he did was not small, and there will always be a few who will not forget."

Helena squeezed his hand. "What about the other boy?"

"He now has"—he took her arm gently—"all he could ever want."

They stood together, watching the flag flutter at the masthead, and listened to the dull boom of the guns out on the bay, and heard the echoes thrown back by the mountains, while on the ageless slopes of Mountain Edgecumbe the sun made a moment of glory.

DICK FRANCIS

BONE-CRACK

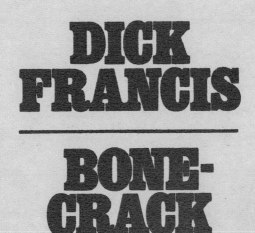

POCKET BOOKS

New York   London   Toronto   Sydney   Tokyo   Singapore

POCKET BOOKS, a division of Simon & Schuster Inc.
1230 Avenue of the Americas, New York, NY 10020

Copyright © 1971 by Dick Francis

ISBN: 0-671-74671-5

First Pocket Books printing November 1978

21 20 19 18 17 16 15 14 13

POCKET and colophon are registered trademarks of
Simon & Schuster Inc.

Printed in the U.S.A.

BONECRACK

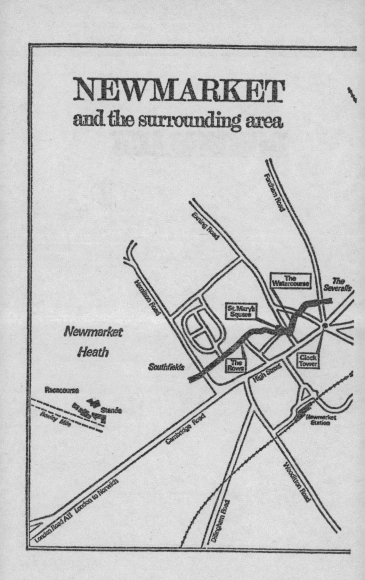

NEWMARKET
and the surrounding area

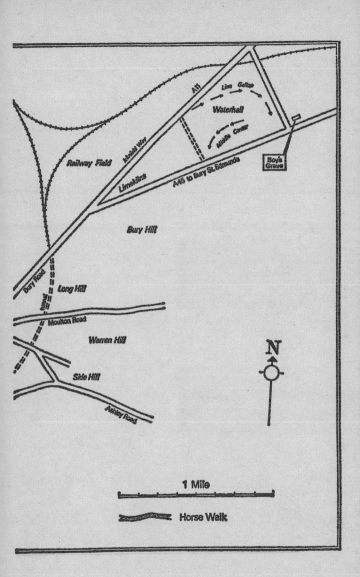

and then walking up again toward the house.

1

They both wore thin rubber masks.

Identical.

I looked at the two identical faceless faces in tingling disbelief. I was not the sort of person to whom rubber-masked individuals, up to no good, paid calls at twenty to midnight. I was a thirty-four-year-old sober-minded businessman quietly bringing up to date the account books at my father's training stables in Newmarket.

The pool of light from the desk lamp shone squarely upon me and the work I had been doing, and the two rubber faces moved palely against the near-black paneling of the dark room like alien moons closing in on the sun. I had looked up when the latch clicked, and there they were, two dim figures calmly walking in from the hall of the big house, silhouetted briefly against the soft lighting behind them and then lost against the paneling as they closed the door. They moved without a squeak, without a scrape, on the bare polished floor. Apart from the unhuman faces, they were black from head to foot.

9

I picked up the telephone receiver and dialed the first of three nines.

One of the men closed in fast, swung his arm, and smashed downward on the telephone. I removed my finger fractionally in time, with the second nine all but complete, but no one was ever going to achieve the third. The black-gloved hand slowly disentangled a heavy police truncheon from the mangled remains of the post office's property.

"There's nothing to steal," I remarked.

The second man had reached the desk. He stood on the far side of it, looking down at me. He produced an automatic pistol, without silencer, which he pointed unwaveringly at the bridge of my nose. I could see quite a long way into the barrel.

"You," he said. "You will come with us."

His voice was flat, without tone, deliberate. There was no identifiable accent, but he wasn't English.

"Why?"

"You will come."

"Where to?"

"You will come."

"I won't, you know," I said pleasantly, and reached out and pressed the button which switched off the desk lamp.

The sudden total darkness got me two seconds' advantage. I used them to stand up, pick up the heavy angled lamp, and swing the base of it round in an arc in the general direction of the mask which had spoken.

There was a dull thump as the lamp connected, and a grunt. Damage, I thought, but no knockout.

Mindful of the truncheon on my left, I was out from behind the desk and sprinting toward the door. But no one was wasting time batting away in the darkness in the hope of hitting me. A beam of torchlight snapped out from his hand, swung round and dazzled on my face, and bounced as he came after me.

I swerved. Dodged. Lost my straight line to the door

10

and saw sidewise that the rubber face I'd hit with the lamp was purposefully on the move.

The torch beam flickered away, circled briefly, and steadied like a rock on the light switch beside the door. Before I could reach it, the black-gloved hand swept downward and clicked on the five double wall brackets, ten naked candle bulbs coldly lighting the square wood-lined room.

There were two windows with green floor-length curtains. One rug from Istanbul. Three unmatched William and Mary chairs. One sixteenth-century oak chest. One flat walnut desk. Nothing else. An austere place, reflection of my father's austere and Spartan soul.

I had always agreed that the best time to foil an abduction was at the moment it started; that merely obeying marching orders could save present pain but not long-term anxiety; that abductors might kill later but not at the beginning; and that if no one else's safety was at risk, it would be stupid to go without a fight.

Well, I fought.

I fought for all of ninety seconds more, during which time I failed to switch off the lights, to escape through the door, or to crash out through the windows. I had only my hands and not much skill against the truncheon of one of them and the threat of a crippling bullet from the other. The identical rubber faces came toward me with an unnerving lack of human expression, and although I tried, probably unwisely, to rip one of the masks off, I got no further than feeling my fingers slip across the tough slippery surface.

The men favored infighting, with their quarry pinned against the wall. As there were two of them, and they appeared to be experts in their craft, I got such a hammering in that eternal ninety seconds that I soundly wished I had not put my abduction-avoiding theories into practice.

It ended with a fist in my stomach, the pistol slamming into my face, my head crashing back against the paneling, and the truncheon polishing the whole thing off somewhere behind my right ear. When I was next conscious of anything, time had all too clearly passed. Otherwise I should not have been lying face down along the back seat of a moving car with my hands tied crampingly behind my back.

For a good long time, I believed I was dreaming. Then my brain came further awake and made it clear that I wasn't. I was revoltingly uncomfortable and also extremely cold, as the thin sweater I had been wearing indoors was proving a poor barrier to a freezing night.

My head ached with a throb like a steam hammer. Bang, bang, bang. If I could have raised the mental energy, I would have been furious with myself for having proved such a pushover. As it was, only uncomplicated responses were getting anywhere, like dumb unintelligent endurance and a fog-like bewilderment. Of all the candidates for abduction, I would have put myself among the most unlikely.

There was a lot to be said for a semiconscious brain in a semiconscious body. *Mens blotto in corpore ditto.* . . . The words dribbled inconsequentially through my mind, and a smile started along the right nerve, but didn't get as far as my mouth. My mouth anyway was half in contact with some imitation leather upholstery which smelled of dogs. They say many grown men call out for their mothers in moments of fatal agony, and then upon their God: but I hadn't had a mother since I was two, and from then until seven I had believed God was someone who had run off with her and was living with her somewhere else. ("God took your mother, dear, because he needed her more than you do"), which had never endeared him to me; and in any case this was no fatal agony, this was just a thumping concussion and some very sore places and maybe a grisly future at the end of the ride. The ride meanwhile went on and on. Nothing about it improved. After several years, the car stopped with a jerk. I nearly fell forward off the seat. My brain came alert with a jolt and my body wished it hadn't.

The two rubber faces loomed over me, lugged me out, and literally carried me up some steps and into a house. One of them had his hands under my armpits and the other held my ankles. My hundred and sixty pounds seemed to be no special burden.

The sudden light inside the door was dazzling, which seemed as good a reason as any for shutting one's eyes. I shut them. The steam hammer had not by any means given up.

They dumped me presently down on my side, on a wooden floor. Polished. I could smell the polish. Scented. Very nasty. I opened my eyes a slit, and verified. Small intricately squared parquet, modern. Birch veneer, wafer thin. Nothing great.

A voice awakening toward fury and controlled with audible effort spoke from a short distance above me.

"And who exactly is this?"

There was a long pin-dropping silence during which I would have laughed if I could. The rubber faces hadn't even pinched the right man. All that battering for bloody nothing. And no guarantee they would take me home again, either.

I squinted upward against the light. The man who had spoken was sitting in an upright leather armchair with his fingers laced rigidly together over a swelling paunch. His voice was much the same as rubber mask's: without much accent, but not English. His shoes, which were more on my level, were supple, handmade, and of Genoese leather.

Italian shape. Not conclusive: they sell Italian shoes from Hong Kong to San Francisco.

One of the rubber faces cleared his throat. "It is Griffon."

The remains of laughter died coldly away. Griffon was indeed my name. If I was not the right man, they must have come for my father. Yet that made no more sense; he was, like me, in none of the abduction-prone professions.

13

The man in the armchair, with the same reined-in anger, said through his teeth, "It is not Griffon."

"It is," persisted rubber face faintly.

The man stood up out of his armchair and with his elegant toe rolled me over onto my back.

"Griffon is an old man," he said. The sting in his voice sent both rubber faces back a pace as if he had physically hit them.

"You didn't *tell* us he was old," the first one protested. "You didn't describe him. You just told us to bring the trainer from Rowley Lodge."

The other rubber face backed up his colleague in a defensive whine and a different accent. This time, down-the-scale American. "We watched him all evening. He went around the stables, looking at the horses. At every horse. The men, they treated him as boss. He is the trainer. He is Griffon."

"Griffon's assistant," he said furiously. He sat down again and held on to the arms with the same effort as he was holding on to his temper.

"Get up," he said to me abruptly.

I struggled up nearly as far as my knees, but the rest was daunting, and I thought, Why on earth should I bother, so I lay gently down again. It did nothing to improve the general climate.

"Get up," he said furiously.

I shut my eyes.

There was a sharp blow on my thigh. I opened my eyes again in time to see the American-voiced rubber face draw back his foot for another kick. All one could say was that he was wearing shoes and not boots.

"Stop it." The sharp voice arrested him in mid-kick. "Just put him in that chair."

American rubber face picked up the chair in question and placed it six feet from the armchair, facing it. Mid-Victorian, I assessed automatically. Mahogany. Probably once had a caned seat, but was upholstered now in pink flowered glazed chintz. The two rubber faces lifted me up bodily and draped me around so that

14

my tied wrists were behind the back of the chair. When they had done that, they stepped away, just as far as one pace behind each of my shoulders.

From that elevation, I had a better view of their master, if not of the total situation.

"Griffon's assistant," he repeated. But this time, the anger was secondary; he'd accepted the mistake and was working out what to do about it.

It didn't take him long.

"Gun," he said, and rubber face gave it to him.

He was plump and bald, and I guessed he would take no pleasure from looking at old photographs of himself. Under the rounded cheeks, the heavy chin, the folds of eyelids, there lay an elegant bone structure. It still showed in the strong clear beak of the nose and in the arch above the eye sockets. He had the basic equipment of a handsome man, but he looked, I thought fancifully, like a Caesar gone self-indulgently to seed, and one might have taken the fat as a sign of mellowness had it not been for the ill will that looked unmistakably out of his narrowed eyes.

"Silencer," he said acidly. He was contemptuous, irritated, and not suffering his rubber-faced fools gladly.

One rubber face produced a silencer from his trouser pocket and Caesar began screwing it on. Silencers meant business where naked barrels might not. He was about to bury his employees' mistake.

My future looked decidedly dim. Time for a few well-chosen words, especially if they might prove to be my last.

"I am not Griffon's assistant," I said. "I am his son."

He had finished screwing on the silencer and was beginning to raise it in the direction of my chest.

"I am Griffon's son," I repeated. "And just what is the point of all this?"

The silencer reached the latitude of my heart.

"If you're going to kill me," I said, "you might at least tell me why."

My voice sounded more or less all right. He couldn't see, I hoped, that all my skin was prickling into sweat.

I stared at him; he stared back. I waited. Waited while the tumblers clicked over in his brain, waited for three thumbs down to slot into a row on the fruit machine.

Finally, without lowering the gun a millimeter, he said, "Where is your father?"

"In hospital."

Another pause.

"How long will he be there?"

"I don't know. Two or three months, perhaps."

"Is he dying?"

"No."

"What is the matter with him?"

"He was in a car crash. A week ago. He has a broken leg."

Another pause. The gun was still steady. No one, I thought wildly, should die so unfairly. Yet people did die unfairly. Probably only one in a million deserved it. All death was intrinsically unfair; but in some forms more unfair than in others. Murder, it forcibly seemed to me, was the most unfair of all.

In the end, all he said, and in a much milder tone, was "Who will train the horses this summer if your father is not well enough?"

Only long experience of wily negotiators who thundered big threats so that they could achieve their real aims by presenting them as a toothless anticlimax kept me from stepping straight off the precipice. I nearly, in relief at so harmless an inquiry, told him the truth: that no one had yet decided. If I had done, I discovered later, he would have shot me, because his business was exclusively with the resident trainer at Rowley Lodge. Temporary substitutes, abducted in error, were too dangerous to leave chattering around.

So from instinct I answered, "I will be training them myself," although I had not the slightest intention of doing so for longer than it took to find someone else.

It had indeed been the crucial question. The frightening black circle of the silencer's barrel dipped a fraction; became an ellipse; disappeared altogether. He lowered the gun and balanced it on one well-padded thigh.

A deep breath trickled in and out of my chest in jerks, and the relief from immediate tension made me feel sick. Not that total safety loomed very loftily on the horizon. I was still tied up in an unknown house, and I still had no idea for what possible purpose I could be a hostage.

The fat man went on watching me. Went on thinking. I tried to ease the stiffness which was creeping into my muscles, to shift away the small pains and the throbbing headache, which I hadn't felt in the slightest when faced with a bigger threat.

The room was cold. The rubber faces seemed to be snug enough in their masks and gloves, and the fat man was insulated and impervious, but the chill was definitely adding to my woes. I wondered whether he had planned the cold as a psychological intimidation for my elderly father, or whether it was simply accidental. Nothing in the room looked cozily lived in.

In essence, it was a middle-class sitting room in a smallish middle-class house, built, I guess, in the nineteen-thirties. The furniture had been pushed back against striped cream wallpaper to give the fat man clear space for maneuver: furniture which consisted of an uninspiring three-piece suite swathed in pink chintz, a gate-leg table, a standard lamp with parchment-colored shade, and a display cabinet displaying absolutely nothing. There were no rugs on the highly polished birch parquet, no ornaments, no books or magazines, nothing personal at all. As bare as my father's soul, but not to his taste.

The room did not in the least fit what I had so far seen of the fat man's personality.

"I will release you," he said, "on certain conditions."

I waited. He considered me, still taking his time.

17

"If you do not follow my instructions exactly, I will put your father's training stables out of business."

I could feel my mouth opening in astonishment. I shut it with a snap.

"I suppose you doubt that I can do it. Do not doubt. I have destroyed better things than your father's little racing stables."

He got no reaction from me to the slight in the word "little." It was years since I had learned that to rise to slights was to be forced into a defensive attitude which only benefited my opponent. In Rowley Lodge, as no doubt he knew, stood eighty-five aristocrats whose aggregate worth topped six million pounds.

"How?" I asked flatly.

He shrugged. "What is important to you is not how I would do it, but how to prevent me from doing it. And that, of course, is comparatively simple."

"Just run the horses to your instructions?" I suggested neutrally. "Just lose to order?"

A spasm of renewed anger twisted the chubby features and the gun came six inches off his knee. The hand holding it relaxed slowly, and he put it down again.

"I am not," he said heavily, "a petty crook."

But you do, I thought, rise to an insult, even to one that was not intended, and one day, if the game went on long enough, that could give me an advantage.

"I apologize," I said without sarcasm. "But those rubber masks are not top level."

He glanced up in irritation at the two figures standing behind me. "The masks are their own choice. They feel safer if they cannot be recognized."

Like highwaymen, I thought; who swung in the end.

"You may run your horses as you like. You are free to choose entirely . . . save in one special thing."

I made no comment. He shrugged, and went on.

"You will employ someone who I will send you."

"No," I said.

"Yes." He stared at me unwinkingly. "You will employ this person. If you do not, I will destroy the stable."

"That's lunacy," I insisted. "It's pointless."

"No, it is not," he said. "Furthermore, you will tell no one that you are being forced to employ this person. You will assert that it is your own wish. You will particularly not complain to the police, either about tonight or about anything else which may happen. Should you act in any way to discredit this person, or to get him evicted from your stables, your whole business will be destroyed." He paused. "Do you understand? If you act in any way against this person, your father will have nothing to return to when he leaves the hospital."

After a short intense silence, I asked, "In what capacity do you want this person to work for me?"

He answered with care. "He will ride the horses," he said. "He is a jockey."

I could feel the twitch round my eyes. He saw it, too. The first time he had really reached me.

It was out of the question. He would not need to tell me every time he wanted a race lost. He had simply to tell his man.

"We don't need a jockey," I said. "We already have Tommy Hoylake."

"Your new jockey will gradually take his place."

Tommy Hoylake was the second-best jockey in Britain and among the top dozen in the world. No one could take his place.

"The owners wouldn't agree," I said.

"You will persuade them."

"Impossible."

"The future existence of your stable depends on it."

There was another longish pause. One of the rubber faces shifted on his feet and sighed as if from boredom, but the fat man seemed to be in no hurry. Perhaps he understood very well that I was getting colder and more uncomfortable minute by minute. I would have asked him to untie my hands if I hadn't been sure he would count himself one up when he refused.

Finally, I said, "Equipped with your jockey, the stable would have no future existence anyway."

He shrugged. "It may suffer a little, perhaps, but it will survive."

"It is unacceptable," I said.

He blinked. His hand moved the gun gently to and fro across his well-filled trouser leg.

He said, "I see that you do not entirely understand the position. I told you that you could leave here upon certain conditions." His flat tone made the preposterous sound reasonable. "These conditions are that you employ a certain jockey, and that you do not seek aid from anyone, including the police. Should you break either of these agreements, the stable will be destroyed. But"—he spoke more slowly, and with emphasis—"if you do not agree to these conditions in the first place, you will not be freed."

I said nothing.

"Do you understand?"

I sighed. "Yes."

"Good."

"Not a petty crook, I think you said."

His nostrils flared. "I am a manipulator."

"And a murderer."

"I never murder unless the victim insists."

I stared at him. He was laughing inside at his own jolly joke, the fun creeping out in little twitches to his lips and tiny snorts of breath.

This victim, I supposed, was not going to insist. He was welcome to his amusement.

I could believe, all at once, that he was no ordinary crook. Crooked, yes; but something else besides. Something undefinable, unrecognizable, alien. Something . . . *crazy*.

I moved my shoulders slightly, trying to ease them. He watched attentively and offered nothing.

"Who, then, is this jockey?" I said.

He hesitated.

"He is eighteen," he said.

"Eighteen . . ."

He nodded. "You will give him the good horses to ride. He will ride Archangel in the Derby."

Impossible. Totally impossible. I looked at the gun lying so quiet on the expensive tailoring. I said nothing. There was nothing to say.

When he next spoke, there was the satisfaction of victory in his voice alongside the careful non-accent.

"He will arrive at the stable tomorrow. You will hire him. He has not yet much experience in races. You will see he gets it."

An inexperienced rider on Archangel . . . ludicrous. So ludicrous, in fact, that he had used abduction and the threat of murder to make it clear he meant it seriously.

"His name is Alessandro Rivera," he said.

After another interval for consideration, he added the rest of it.

"He is my son."

2

When I next woke up, I was lying face down on the bare floor of the oak-paneled room in Rowley Lodge. Too many bare boards everywhere. Not my night.

Facts oozed back gradually. I felt woolly, cold, semi-conscious, anesthetized. . . .

Anesthetized.

For the return journey, they had had the courtesy not to hit my head. The fat man had nodded to the American rubber face, but instead of flourishing the truncheon he had given me a sort of quick pricking thump in the upper arm. After that, we had waited around for about a quarter of an hour during which no one said anything at all, and then quite suddenly I had lost consciousness. I remembered not a flicker of the journey home.

Creaking and groaning, I tested all articulated parts. Everything present, correct, and in working order. More or less, that is, because having clanked to my feet, it became advisable to sit down again in the chair

22

by the desk. I put my elbows on the desk and my head in my hands, and let time pass.

Outside, the beginnings of a damp dawn were turning the sky to gray flannel. There was ice round the edges of the windows, where condensed warm air had frozen solid. The cold went through to my bones.

In the brain department, things were just as chilly. I remembered all too clearly that Alessandro Rivera was that day to make his presence felt. Perhaps he would take after his father, I thought tiredly, and would be so overweight that the whole dilemma would fold its horns and quietly steal away. On the other hand, if not, why should his father use a sledgehammer to crack a peanut? Why not simply apprentice his son in the normal way? Because he wasn't normal, because his son wouldn't be a normal apprentice, and because no normal apprentice would expect to start his career on a Derby favorite.

I wondered how my father would now be reacting had he not been slung up in traction with a complicated fracture of tibia and fibula. He would not, for certain, be feeling as battered as I was, because he would, with supreme dignity, have gone quietly. But he would nonetheless have also been facing the same vital questions: which were, firstly, did the fat man seriously intend to destroy the stable if his son did not get the job, and secondly, how could he do it?

And the answer to both was a king-sized blank.

It wasn't my stable to risk. They were not my six million pounds' worth of horses. They were not my livelihood, or my life's work.

I could not ask my father to decide for himself; he was not well enough to be told, let alone to reason out the pros and cons.

I could not now transfer the stable to anyone else, because passing this situation to a stranger would be like handing him a grenade with the pin out.

I was already due back at my own job and was late for my next assignment, and I had only stopgapped at the stable at all because my father's capable assistant, who had been driving the Rolls when the lorry jack-knifed into it, was now lying in the same hospital in a coma.

All of which added up to a fair-sized problem. But then problems, I reflected ironically, were my business. The problems of sick businesses were my business.

Nothing at that moment looked sicker than my prospects at Rowley Lodge.

Shivering violently, I removed myself bit by bit from the desk and chair, went out to the kitchen, and made myself some coffee. Drank it. Moderate improvement only.

Inched upstairs to the bathroom. Scraped off the night's whiskers and dispassionately observed the dried blood down one cheek. Washed it off. Gun-barrel graze, dry and already healing.

Outside, through the leafless trees, I could see the lights of the traffic thundering as usual up and down Bury Road. Those drivers in their warm moving boxes, they were in another world altogether, a world where abduction and extortion were something that only happened to others. Incredible to think that I had in fact joined the others.

Wincing from an all-over feeling of soreness, I looked at my smudge-eyed reflection and decided that for a little while at least I would do what the fat man dictated. Partly out of curiosity, partly out of serious concern for the stable, I would wait to see what happened before mounting what might prove to be a self-destructive counterattack. A quieter way out, a profitable solution, would probably reveal itself in the end. It usually did. Meanwhile I would emulate the saplings which bent before the storm . . . and lived to grow into oaks.

Long live oaks.

I swallowed some aspirins, stopped shivering, tried to marshal a bit more sense into my shaky wits, and struggled into jodhpurs, boots, two more pullovers, and a windproof jacket. Whatever had happened that night, or whatever might happen in the future, there were still those eighty-five six million quids' worth downstairs waiting to be seen to.

They were housed in a yard that had been an inspiration of spacious design when it was built in 1870 and which still, a hundred-plus years later, worked as an effective unit. Originally there had been two blocks facing each other, each block consisting of three bays, and each bay being made up of ten boxes. Across the far end, forming a wall joining the two blocks, were a large feed storeroom, a pair of double gates, and an equally large tack room. The gates had originally led into a field, but early on in his career, when success struck him, my father had built on two more bays, which formed another small enclosed yard of twenty-five boxes. More double gates opened from these now into a small railed paddock.

Four final boxes had been built facing toward Bury Road, onto the outside of the short west wall at the end of the north block. It was in the farthest of these four boxes that a full-blown disaster had just been discovered.

My appearance through the door which led directly from the house to the yard galvanized the group which had been clustered round the outside boxes into returning into the main yard and advancing in ragged but purposeful formation. I could see I was not going to like their news. Waited in irritation to hear it. Crises, on that particular morning, were far from welcome.

"It's Moonrock, sir," said one of the lads anxiously. "Got cast in his box and broke his leg."

"All right," I said abruptly. "Get back to your own horses, then. It's nearly time to pull out."

"Yes, sir," they said, and scattered reluctantly round the yard to their charges, looking back over their shoulders.

"Damn and bloody hell," I said aloud, but I can't say it did much good. Moonrock was my father's hack,

25

a pensioned-off star-class steeplechaser of which he was uncharacteristically fond. The least valuable inmate of the yard in many terms, but the one he would be most upset to lose. The others were insured. No one, though, could insure against painful emotion.

I plodded round to the box. The elderly lad who looked after him was standing at the door with the light from inside falling across the deep worried wrinkles in his tortoise skin and turning them to crevices. He looked round toward me at my step. The crevices shifted and changed like a kaleidoscope.

"Ain't no good, sir. He's broke his hock."

Nodding, I reached the door and went in. The old horse was standing up, tied in his usual place by his head-collar. At first sight, there was nothing wrong with him: he turned his head toward me and pricked up his ears, his liquid black eyes showing nothing but his customary curiosity. Five years in headline limelight had given him the sort of presence which only intelligent, highly successful horses seem to develop—a sort of consciousness of their own greatness. He knew more about life and about racing than any of the golden youngsters in the main yard. He was fifteen years old and had been a friend of my father's for five.

The hind leg on his near side, toward me, was perfect. He bore his weight on it. The off-hind looked slightly tucked up.

He had been sweating; then were great dark patches on his neck and flanks, but he looked calm enough at that moment. Pieces of straw were caught in his coat, which was unusually dusty.

Soothing him with her hand, and talking to him in a common-sense voice, was my father's head stable hand, Etty Craig. She looked up at me with regret on her pleasant weather-beaten face.

"I've sent for the vet, Mr. Neil."

"Of all damn things," I said.

She nodded. "Poor old fellow. You'd think he'd know better after all these years."

26

I made a sympathetic noise, went in and fondled the moist black muzzle, and took as good a look at his hind leg as I could without moving him. There was absolutely no doubt: the hock joint was out of shape.

Horses occasionally rolled around on their backs in the straw in their boxes. Sometimes they rolled over with too little room and wedged their legs against the wall, then thrashed around to get free. Most injuries from getting cast were grazes and strains, but it was possible for a horse to twist or lash out with a leg strongly enough to break it. Incredibly bad luck when it happened, which luckily wasn't often.

"He was still lying down when George came in to muck him out," Etty said. "He got some of the lads to come and pull the old fellow into the center of the box. He was a bit slow, George says, standing up. And then of course they could see he couldn't walk."

"Bloody shame," George said, nodding in agreement.

I sighed. "Nothing we can do, Etty."

"No, Mr. Neil."

She called me Mr. Neil religiously during working hours, though I'd been plain Neil to her in my childhood. Better for discipline in the yard, she said to me once, and on matters of discipline I would never contradict her. There had been quite a stir in Newmarket when my father had promoted her to head lad, but as he had explained to her at the time, she was loyal, she was knowledgeable, she would stand no nonsense from anyone. She deserved it from seniority alone, and had she been a man the job would have been hers automatically. He had decided, as he was a just and logical person, that her sex was immaterial. She became the only female head lad in Newmarket—where girl lads, anyway, were rare—and the stable had flourished through all the six years of her reign.

I remembered the days when her parents used to turn up at the stables and accuse my father of ruining her life. I had been about ten when she first came to the yard, and she was nineteen and had been privately educated at an expensive boarding school. Her parents with increasing bitterness had complained that the stable was spoiling her chances of a nice suitable marriage; but Etty had never wanted marriage. If she had ever experimented with sex, she had not made a public mess of it, and I thought it likely that she had found the whole process uninteresting. She seemed to like males well enough, but she treated them as she did her horses, with brisk friendliness, immense understanding, and cool unsentimentality.

Since my father's accident, she had to all intents been in complete charge. The fact that I had been granted a temporary license to hold the fort made mine the official say-so, but both Etty and I knew I would be lost without her.

It occurred to me, as I watched her capable hands moving quietly across Moonrock's bay hide, that the fat man might think me a pushover, but as an apprentice his son Alessandro was going to run into considerable difficulties with Miss Henrietta Craig.

"You better go out with the string, Etty," I said. "I'll stay and wait for the vet."

"Right," she said, and I guessed she had been on the point of suggesting it herself. As a distribution of labor, it was only sense, for the horses were well along in their preparation for the coming racing season, and she knew better than I what each should be doing.

She beckoned to George to come and hold Moonrock's head-collar and keep him soothed. To me she said, stepping out of the box, "What about this frost? It seems to me it may be thawing."

"Take the horses over to Warren Hill and use your own judgment about whether to canter."

She nodded. "Right." She looked back at Moonrock, and a momentary softness touched her mouth. "Mr. Griffon will be sorry."

"I won't tell him yet."

"No." She gave me a small businesslike smile and

28

walked off into the yard, a short neat figure, hardy and competent.

Moonrock would be quiet enough with George. I followed Etty back into the main yard and watched the horses pull out: thirty-three of them in the first lot. The lads led their charges out of the boxes, jumped up into the saddles, and rode away down the yard, through the first double gates, across the lower yard, and out through the far gates into the collecting paddock beyond. The sky lightened moment by moment, and I thought Etty was probably right about the thaw.

After ten minutes or so, when she had sorted them out as she wanted them, the horses moved away out beyond the paddock, through the trees and the boundary fence, and straight out onto the Heath.

Before the last of them had gone, there was a rushing scrunch in the drive behind me and the vet halted his dusty Land-Rover with a spray of gravel. Leaping out with his bag, he said breathlessly, "Every bloody horse on the Heath this morning has got colic or ingrowing toenails. You must be Neil Griffon. Sorry about your father. Etty says it's old Moonrock. Still in the same box?" Without drawing breath, he turned on his heel and strode along the outside boxes. Young, chubby, purposeful, he was not the vet I had expected. The man I knew was an older version, slower, twinkly, just as chubby, and given to rubbing his jaw while he thought things over.

"Sorry about this," Dainsee, the young vet, said, having given Moonrock three full seconds of examination. "Have to put him down, I'm afraid."

"I suppose that hock couldn't just be dislocated?" I suggested, clinging to straws.

He gave me a brief glance full of the expert's forgiveness for a layman's ignorance. "The joint is shattered," he said succinctly.

He went about his business, and splendid old Moonrock quietly folded down onto the straw. Packing his bag again, the vet said, "Don't look so depressed. He

29

had a better life than most. And be glad it wasn't Archangel."

I watched his chubby back depart at speed. Not so very unlike his father, I thought. Just faster.

I went slowly into the house and telephoned to the people who removed dead horses. They would come at once, they said, sounding cheerful. And within half an hour, they came.

Another cup of coffee. Sat down beside the kitchen table and went on feeling unwell. Abduction didn't agree with me in the least.

The string came back from the Heath without Etty, without a two-year-old colt called Lucky Lindsay, and with a long tale of woe.

I listened with increasing dismay while three lads at once told me that Lucky Lindsay had whipped round and unshipped little Ginge over by Warren Hill, and had then galloped off loose and seemed to be making for home, but had diverted down Moulton Road instead, and had knocked over a man with a bicycle and had sent a woman with a pram into hysterics, and had ended up by the clock tower, disorganizing the traffic. The police, added one boy, with more relish than regret, were currently talking to Miss Etty.

"And the colt?" I asked. Because Etty could take care of herself, but Lucky Lindsay had cost thirty thousand guineas and could not.

"Someone caught him down the High Street outside Woolworth's."

I sent them off to their horses and waited for Etty to come back, which she presently did, riding Lucky Lindsay herself and with the demoted and demoralized Ginge slopping along behind on a quiet three-year-old mare.

Etty jumped down and ran an experienced hand down the colt's chestnut legs.

"Not much harm done," she said. "He seems to have a small cut there. . . . I think he probably did it on the bumper of a parked car."

"Not on the bicycle?" I asked.

She looked up, and then straightened. "Shouldn't think so."

"Was the cyclist hurt?"

"Shaken," she admitted.

"And the woman with the pram?"

"Anyone who pushes a baby and drags a toddler along Moulton Road during morning exercise should be ready for loose horses. The stupid woman wouldn't stop screaming. It upset the colt thoroughly, of course. Someone had caught him at that point, but he backed off and broke free and went down into the town."

She paused and looked at me. "Sorry about all this."

"It happens," I said. I stifled the small inward smile at her relative placing of colts and babies. Not surprising. To her, colts were, in sober fact, more important than humans.

"We had finished the canters," she said. "The ground was all right. We went right through the list we mapped out yesterday. Ginge came off as we turned for home."

"Is the colt too much for him?"

"Wouldn't have thought so. He's ridden him before."

"I'll leave it to you, Etty."

"Then maybe I'll switch him to something easier for a day or two." She led the colt away and handed him over to the lad who did him, having come as near as she was likely to admitting she had made an error in putting Ginge on Lucky Lindsay. Anyone, any day, could be thrown off. But some were thrown off more than others.

Breakfast. The lads put straight the horses they had just ridden, and scurried round to the hostel for porridge, bacon sandwiches, and tea. I went back into the house and didn't feel like eating.

It was still cold indoors. There were sad mounds of fir cones in the fireplaces of ten dust-sheeted bedrooms, and a tapestry fire screen in front of the hearth in the drawing room. There was a two-tier electric fire in the cavernous bedroom my father used and an undersized convector heater in the oak-paneled room where he sat at his desk in the evenings. Not even the kitchen was warm, as the cooker fire had been out for repairs for a month. Normally, having been brought up in it, I did not notice the chill of the house in winter; but then normally I did not feel so physically wretched.

A head appeared round the kitchen door. Neat dark hair coiled smoothly at the base, to emerge in a triumphant arrangement of piled curls on the crown.

"Mr. Neil?"

"Oh . . . good morning, Magaret."

A pair of fine dark eyes gave me an embracing once-over. Narrow nostrils moved in a small quiver, testing the atmosphere. As usual, I could see no further than her neck and half a cheek; my father's secretary was as economical with her presence as with everything else.

"It's cold in here," she said.

"Yes."

"Warmer in the office."

The half head disappeared and did not come back. I decided to accept what I knew had been meant as an invitation, and retraced my way toward the corner of the house which adjoined the yard. In that corner were the stable office, a cloakroom, and the one room furnished for comfort, the room we called the owners' room, where owners and assorted others were entertained on casual visits to the stable.

The lights were on in the office, bright against the gray day outside. Margaret was taking off her sheepskin coat, and hot air was blowing busily out of a mushroom-shaped heater.

"Instructions?" she asked briefly.

"I haven't opened the letters yet."

She gave me a quick comprehensive glance.

"Trouble?"

I told her about Moonrock and Lucky Lindsay. She listened attentively, showed no emotion, and asked how I had cut my face.

"Walked into a door."

Her expression said plainly, "I've heard that one before," but she made no comment.

In her way, she was as unfeminine as Etty, despite her skirt, her hairdo, and her efficient make-up. In her late thirties, three years widowed, and bringing up a boy and a girl with masterly organization, she bristled with intelligence and held the world at arm's length from her heart.

Margaret was new at Rowley Lodge, replacing mouselike old Robinson, who had finally scratched his way at seventy into unwilling retirement. Old Robinson had liked his little chat, and had frittered away hours of working time telling me in my childhood about the days when Charles II rode in races himself, and made Newmarket the second capital of England, so that ambassadors had to go there to see him, and how the Prince Regent had left the town forever because of an inquiry into the running of his colt Escape, and refused to go back even though the Jockey Club apologized and begged him to, and how in 1905 King Edward VII was in trouble with the police for speeding down the road to London—at forty miles an hour on the straight bits.

Margaret did old Robinson's work more accurately and in half the time, and I understood after knowing her for six days why my father found her inestimable. She demanded no human response, and he was a man who found most human relationships boring. Nothing tired him quicker than people who constantly demanded attention for their emotions and problems, and even social openers about the weather irritated him. Margaret seemed to be a matched soul, and they got on excellently.

I slouched down in my father's revolving office armchair and told Margaret to open the letters herself. My father never let anyone open his letters, and was obsessive about it. She simply did as I said without comment, either spoken or implied. Marvelous.

The telephone rang. Margaret answered it.

"Mr. Bredon? Oh, yes. He'll be glad you called. I'll put you on to him."

She handed me the receiver across the desk, and said, "John Bredon."

"Thanks."

I took the receiver with none of the eagerness I would have shown the day before. I had spent three intense days trying to find someone who was free at short notice to take over Rowley Lodge until my father's leg mended, and of all the people helpful friends had suggested, only John Bredon, an elderly recently retired trainer, seemed to be of the right experience and caliber. He had asked for time to think it over and had said he would let me know as soon as he could.

He was calling to say he would be happy to come. I thanked him and uncomfortably apologized as I put him off. "The fact is that after thinking it over I've decided to stay on myself. . . ."

I set the receiver down slowly, aware of Margaret's astonishment. I didn't explain. She didn't ask. After a pause, she went back to opening the letters.

The telephone rang again. This time, with schooled features, she asked if I would care to speak to Mr. Russell Arletti.

Silently I stretched out a hand for the receiver.

"Neil?" a voice barked. "Where the hell have you got to? I told Grey & Cox you'd be there yesterday. They're complaining. How soon can you get up there?"

Grey & Cox, in Huddersfield, were waiting for Arletti, Incorporated, to sort out why their once profitable business was going down the drain. Arletti's sorter was sitting disconsolately in a stable office in Newmarket wishing he was dead.

"You'll have to tell Grey & Cox that I can't come."

"You *what?*"

"Russell . . . count me out for a while. I've got to stay on here."

"For God's sake, why?"

"I can't find anyone to take over."

34

"You said it wouldn't take you more than a week."

"Well, it has. There isn't anyone suitable. I can't go and sort out Grey & Cox and leave Rowley Lodge rudderless. There is six million involved here. Like it or not, I'll have to stay."

"Damn it, Neil . . ."

"I'm really sorry."

"Grey & Cox will be livid." He was exasperated.

"Go up there yourself. It'll only be the usual thing. Bad costing. Underpricing their product at the planning stage. Rotten cash flow. They say they haven't any militants, so it's ninety percent to a cornflake that it's lousy finance."

He sighed. "I don't have quite your talent. Better ones, mind you. But not the same." He paused for thought. "Have to send James, when he gets back from Shoreham. If you're sure?"

"Better count me out for three months at least."

"Neil!"

"Better say, in fact, until after the Derby. . . ."

"Legs don't take that long," he protested.

"This one is a terrible mess. The bones were splintered and came through the skin, and it was touch and go whether they amputated."

"Oh, *hell.*"

"I'll give you a call," I said. "As soon as I look like being free."

After he had rung off, I sat with the receiver in my hand, staring into space. Slowly I put it back in its cradle.

Margaret sat motionless, her eyes studiously downcast, her mouth showing nothing. She made no reference at all to the lie I had told.

It was, I reflected, only the first of many.

3

Nothing about that day got any better.

I rode out with the second lot on the Heath and found there were tender spots I hadn't even known about. Etty asked if I had a toothache. I looked liked it, she said. Sort of drawn, she said.

I said my molars were in good crunching order and how about starting the canters. The canters were started, watched, assessed, repeated, discussed. Archangel, Etty said, would be ready for the Guineas.

When I told her I was going to stay on myself as the temporary trainer, she looked horrified.

"But you *can't.*"

"You are unflattering, Etty."

"Well, I mean . . . you don't know the horses." She stopped and tried again. "You hardly ever go racing. You've never been really interested, not since you were a boy. You don't know enough about it."

"I'll manage," I said, "with your help."

But she was only slightly reassured, because she was not vain, and she never overestimated her own abilities.

She knew she was a good head lad. She knew there was a lot to training that she wouldn't do so well. Such self-knowledge in the sport of kings was rare, and facing it rarer still. There was always thousands of people who knew better, on the stands.

"Who will do the entries?" she asked astringently, her voice saying quite clearly that I couldn't.

"Father can do them himself when he's a bit better. He'll have a lot of time."

At this she nodded with more satisfaction. The entering of horses in races suited to them was the most important skill in training. All the success and prestige of a stable started with the entry forms, where for each individual horse the aim had to be not too high, not too low, but just right. Most of my father's success had been built on his judgment of where to enter and when to run each horse.

One of the two-year-olds pranced around, lashed out, and caught another two-year-old on the knee. The boys' reactions had not been quick enough to keep them apart, and the second colt was walking lame. Etty cursed them coldly and told the second boy to dismount and lead his charge home.

I watched him following on foot behind the string, the horse's head ducking at every tender step. The knee would swell and fill and get hot, but with a bit of luck it would right itself in a few days. If it did not, someone would have to tell the owner. The someone would be me.

That made one horse dead and two damaged in one morning. If things went on at that rate, there would soon be no stable left for the fat man to bother about.

When we got back, there was a small police car in the drive and a large policeman in the office. He was sitting in my chair and staring at his boots, and rose purposefully to his feet as I came through the door.

"Mr. Griffon?"

"Yes."

He came to the point without preliminaries.

"We've had a complaint, sir, that one of your horses knocked over a cyclist on the Moulton Road this morning. Also a young woman has complained to us that this same horse endangered her life and that of her children."

He was a uniformed sergeant, about thirty, solidly built, uncompromising. He spoke with the aggressive politeness that in some policemen is close to rudeness, and I gathered that his sympathies were with the complainants.

"Was the cyclist hurt, Sergeant?"

"I understand he was bruised, sir."

"And his bicycle?"

"I couldn't say, sir."

"Do you think that a—er—a settlement out of court, so to speak, would be in order?"

"I couldn't say, sir," he repeated flatly. His face was full of the negative attitude which erects a barrier against sympathy or understanding. Into my mind floated one of the axioms that Russell Arletti lived by. In business matters with trade unions, the press, or the police, never try to make them like you. It arouses antagonism instead. And never make jokes; they are anti-jokes.

I gave the sergeant back a stare of equal indifference and asked if he had the cyclist's name and address. After only the slightest hesitation, he flicked over a page or two of notebook and read it out to me. Margaret took it down.

"And the young woman's?"

He provided that, too. He then asked if he might take a statement from Miss Craig, and I said certainly, Sergeant, and took him out into the yard. Etty gave him a rapid adding-up inspection and answered his questions in an unemotional manner. I left them together and went back to the office to finish the paperwork with Margaret, who preferred to work straight through the lunch hour and leave at three to collect her children from school.

"Some of the account books are missing," she observed.

"I had them last night," I said. "They're in the oak room. . . . I'll go and fetch them."

The oak room was quiet and empty. I wondered what reaction I would get from the sergeant if I brought him in and said that last night two faceless men had knocked me out, tied me up, and removed me from my home by force. Also they had threatened to kill me, and had punched me full of anesthetic to bring me back.

"Oh, yes, sir? And do you want to make a formal allegation?"

I smiled slightly. It seemed ridiculous. The sergeant would produce a stare of top-grade disbelief, and I could hardly blame him. Only my depressing state of health and the smashed telephone lying on the desk made the night's events seem real at all.

The fat man, I reflected, hardly needed to have warned me away from the police. The sergeant had done the job for him. It would have been sensible, I supposed, to have enlisted help—if not from the sergeant, at least from one of his superiors. I knew it wasn't only the risk to the stable which stopped me, or the sergeant's off-putting manner, but something more obscure and internal, some urge to deal with the situation myself. To calm things down, rather than stir them up. Wait and see, I thought. Wait and see.

Etty came into the office fuming while I was returning the account books to Margaret.

"Of all the pompous clods!"

"Does this sort of thing happen often?" I asked.

"Of course not," Etty said positively. "Horses get loose, of course, but things are usually settled without all this fuss. And I told that old man that you would see he didn't suffer. Why he had to go complaining to the police beats me."

"I'll go and see him this evening," I said.

"Now, the old sergeant, Sergeant Chubb," Etty said forcefully, "he would have sorted it out himself. He wouldn't have come round taking down statements. But this one—this one is new here. They've posted him here from Ipswich, and he doesn't seem to like it. Just promoted, I shouldn't wonder. Full of his own importance."

"The stripes were new," Margaret murmured in agreement.

"We always have good relations with the police here," Etty said gloomily. "Can't think what they're doing, sending the town someone who doesn't understand the first thing about horses."

The steam had all blown off. Etty breathed sharply through her nose, shrugged her shoulders, and produced a small resigned smile.

"Oh, well . . . worse things happen at sea."

She had very blue eyes, and light brown hair that went frizzy when the weather was damp. Middle age had roughened her skin without wrinkling it, and as with most undersexed women there was much in her face that was male. She had thin dry lips and bushy unkempt eyebrows, and the handsomeness of her youth was only something I remembered. Etty seemed a sad, wasted person to many who observed her, but to herself she was fulfilled, and was busily content.

She stamped away in her jodhpurs and boots, and we heard her voice raised at some luckless boy caught in wrongdoing.

Rowley Lodge needed Etty Craig. But it needed Alessandro Rivera like a hole in the head.

He came late that afternoon.

I was out in the yard looking round the horses at evening stables. With Etty alongside, I had got as far as bay five, from where we would go round the bottom yard before walking up again toward the house.

One of the fifteen-year-old apprentices nervously appeared as we came out of a box and prepared to go into the next.

"Someone to see you, sir."

"Who?"

"Don't know, sir."

"An owner?"

"Don't know, sir."

"Where is he?"

"Up by the drive, sir."

I looked up, over his head. Beyond the yard, out on the gravel, there was parked a large white Mercedes with a uniformed chauffeur standing by the bonnet.

"Take over, Etty, would you?" I said.

I walked up through the yard and out into the drive. The chauffeur folded him arms and his mouth like barricades against fraternization. I stopped a few paces away from him and looked toward the inside of the car.

One of the rear doors, the one nearest to me, opened. A small black-shod foot appeared, and then a dark trouser leg, and then, slowly straightening, the whole man.

It was clear at once who he was, although the resemblance to his father began and ended with the autocratic beak of the nose and the steadfast stoniness of the black eyes. The son was emaciated instead of chubby. He had sallow skin that looked in need of a sun tan, and strong thick black hair curving in springy curls round his ears. Over all he wore an air of disconcerting maturity, and the determination in the set of his mouth would have done credit to a steel trap. Eighteen he might be, but it was a long time since he had been a boy.

I guessed that his voice would be like his father's: definite, unaccented, and careful.

It was.

"I am Rivera," he announced. "Alessandro."

41

"Good evening," I said, and intended it to sound polite, cool, and unimpressed.

He blinked.

"Rivera," he repeated. "I am Rivera."

"Yes," I agreed. "Good evening."

He looked at me with narrowing attention. If he expected from me a lot of groveling, he was not going to get it. And something of this message must have got across to him from my attitude, because he began to look faintly surprised and a shade more arrogant.

"I understand you wish to become a jockey," I said.

"Intend."

I nodded casually. "No one succeeds as a jockey without determination," I said, and made it sound patronizing.

He detected the flavor immediately. He didn't like it. I was glad.

"I am accustomed to succeed," he said.

"How very nice," I replied dryly.

It sealed between us an absolute antagonism. I felt him shift gear into overdrive, and it seemed to me that he was mentally gathering himself to fight on his own account a battle he believed his father had already won.

"I will start at once," he said.

"I am in the middle of evening stables," I said matter-of-factly. "If you will wait, we will discuss your position when I have finished." I gave him the politeness of an inclination of the head which I would have given to anybody, and without waiting around for him to throw any more of his slight weight about, I turned smoothly away and walked without haste back to Etty.

When we had worked our way methodically round to the whole stable, discussing briefly how each horse was progressing, and planning the work program for the following morning, we came finally to the four outside boxes, only three busy now, and the fourth full of Moonrock's absence.

The Mercedes still stood on the gravel, with both

Rivera and the chauffeur sitting inside it. Etty gave them a look of regulation curiosity and asked who they were. "New customer," I said economically.

She frowned in surprise. "But surely you shouldn't have kept him waiting!"

"This one," I reassured her with private, rueful irony, "will not go away."

But Etty knew how to treat new clients, and making them wait in their car was not it. She hustled me along the last three boxes and anxiously pushed me to return to the Mercedes. Tomorrow, no doubt, she would not be so keen.

I opened the rear door and said to him, "Come along into the office."

He climbed out of the car and followed me without a word. I switched on the fan heater, sat in Margaret's chair behind the desk, and pointed to the swivel armchair in front of it. He did as I suggested.

"Now," I said, in my best interviewing voice, "you want to start tomorrow."

"Yes."

"In what capacity?"

He hesitated. "As a jockey."

"Well, no," I said reasonably. "There are no races yet. The season does not start for about four weeks."

"I know that," he said stiffly.

"What I meant was, do you want to work in the stable? Do you want to look after two horses, as the others do?"

"Certainly not."

"Then what?"

"I will ride the horses at exercise two or three times a day. Every day. I will not clean their boxes or carry their food. I wish only to ride."

Highly popular, that was going to be, with Etty and the other lads. Apart from all else, I was going to have a shop floor-management confrontation—or, in plain old terms, a mutiny—on my hands in no time at all. None of the other lads was going to muck out and groom a horse for the joy of seeing Rivera ride it.

However, all I said was "How much experience, exactly, have you had so far?"

"I can ride," he said flatly.

"Race horses?"

"I can ride."

This was getting nowhere. I tried again. "Have you ever ridden in any sort of race?"

"I have ridden in amateur races."

"Where?"

"In Italy, and in Germany."

"Have you won any?"

He gave me a black stare. "I have won two."

I supposed that that was something. At least it suggested that ·he could stay on. Winning itself, in his case, had no significance. His father was the sort to buy the favorite and nobble the opposition.

"But you want now to become a professional?"

"Yes."

"Then I'll apply for a license for you."

"I can apply myself."

I shook my head. "You will have to have an apprentice license, and I will have to apply for it for you."

"I do not wish to be an apprentice."

I said patiently, "Unless you become an apprentice, you will be unable to claim a weight allowance. In England in flat races, the only people who can claim weight allowances are apprentices. Without a weight allowance, the owners of the horses will all resist to the utmost any suggestion that you should ride. Without weight allowance, in fact, you might as well give up the whole idea."

"My father—" he began.

"Your father can threaten until he's blue in the face," I interrupted. "I cannot *force* the owners to employ you. I can only persuade. Without a weight allowance, they will never be persuaded."

44

He thought it over, his expression showing nothing.

"My father," he said, "told me that anyone could apply for a license and that there was no need to be apprenticed."

"Technically, that is true."

"But practically, it is not." It was a statement more than a question; he had clearly understood what I had said.

I began to speculate about the strength of his intentions. It certainly seemed possible that if he read the Deed of Apprenticeship and saw to what he would be binding himself, he might simply step back into his car and be driven away. I fished around in Margaret's tidy desk drawers, and found a pile of copies of the printed agreement.

"You will need to sign this," I said casually, and handed one over.

He read it without a flicker of an eyelid, and, considering what he was reading, that was remarkable. The familiar words trotted through my mind ". . . the Apprentice will faithfully, diligently and honestly serve the Master and obey and perform all his lawful commands . . . and will not absent himself from the service of the Master, nor divulge any of the secrets of the Master's business . . . and shall deliver to the Master all such monies and other things that shall come into his hands for work done . . . and will in all matters and things whatsoever demean and behave himself as a good true and faithful Apprentice ought to do. . . ."

He put the form down on the desk and looked across at me.

"I cannot sign that."

"Your father will have to sign it as well," I pointed out.

"He will not."

"Then that's an end to it," I said, relaxing back in my chair.

He looked down at the form. "My father's lawyers will draw up a different agreement," he said.

I shrugged. "Without a recognizable apprenticeship deed, you won't get an apprentice's license. That form there is based on the articles of apprenticeship common to all trades since the Middle Ages. If you alter its intentions, it won't meet the licensing requirements."

After a packed pause, he said, "That part about delivering all monies to the Master . . . does that mean I would have to give to you all money I might earn in races?" He sounded incredulous, as well he might.

"It does say that," I agreed, "but it is normal nowadays for the Master to return half of race earnings to the apprentice. In addition, of course, to giving him a weekly allowance."

"If I win the Derby on Archangel, you would take half. Half of the fee and half of the present?"

"That's right."

"It's wicked!"

"You've got to win it before you start worrying," I said flippantly, and watched the arrogance flare up like a bonfire.

"If the horse is good enough, I will."

You kid yourself, mate, I thought; and didn't answer.

He stood up abruptly, picked up the form, and without another word walked out of the office, and out of the house, out of the yard, and into his car. The Mercedes purred away with him down the drive, and I stayed sitting back in Margaret's chair, hoping I had seen the last of him, wincing at the energy of my persisting headache, and wondering whether a triple brandy would restore me to instant health.

I tried it.

It didn't.

There was no sign of him in the morning, and on all counts the day was better. The kicked two-year-old's knee had gone up like a football but he was walking pretty sound on it, and the cut on Lucky Lindsay was as superficial as Etty had hoped. The elderly cyclist, the evening before, had accepted my apologies and ten pounds for his bruises and had left me with the impression that we could knock him down again, any time, for a similar supplement to his income. Archangel worked a half-speed six furlongs on the Side Hill gallop, and in me a night's sleep had ironed out some creases.

But Alessandro Rivera did come back.

He rolled up the drive in the chauffeur-driven Mercedes just as Etty and I finished the last three boxes at evening stables, timing it so accurately that I wondered if he had been waiting and watching from out on Bury Road.

I jerked my head toward the office, and he followed me in. I switched on the heater and sat down, as before; and so did he.

He produced from an inner pocket the apprenticeship form and passed it toward me across the desk. I took it and unfolded it, and turned it over.

There were no alterations. It was the deed in the exact form he had taken it. There were, however, four additions.

The signatures of Alessandro Rivera and Enso Rivera, with an appropriate witness in each case, sat squarely in the spaces designed for them.

I looked at the bold heavy strokes of both the Riveras' signatures and the nervous elaborations of the witnesses. They had signed the agreement without filling in any of the blanks: without even discussing the time the apprenticeship was to run for, or the weekly allowance to be paid.

He was watching me. I met his cold black eyes.

"You and your father signed it like this," I said slowly, "because you have not the slightest intention of being bound by it."

47

His face didn't change. "Think what you like," he said.

And so I would. And what I thought was that the son was not as criminal as his father. The son had taken the legal obligations of the apprenticeship form seriously. But his father had not.

4

The small private room in the North London hospital where my father had been taken after the crash seemed to be almost entirely filled with the frames and ropes and pulleys and weights which festooned his high bed. Apart from all that, there was only a high-silled window with limp floral curtains and a view of half the back of another building and a chunk of sky, a chest-high washbasin with lever-type taps designed to be turned on by elbows, a bedside locker upon which reposed his lower teeth in a glass of water, and an armchair of sorts, for the use of visitors.

There were no flowers glowing against the margarine-colored walls, and no well-wishing cards brightening the top of the locker. He did not care for flowers, and would have dispatched any that came straight along to the other wards, and I doubted that anyone at all would have made the error of sending him a glossy or amusing get-well, which he would have considered most frightfully vulgar.

The room itself was meager compared with what he

would have chosen and could afford, but to me during the first critical days the hospital itself had seemed effortlessly efficient. It did after all, as one doctor had casually explained to me, have to deal constantly with wrecked bodies prized out of crashes on the A1. They were used to it. Geared to it. They had a higher proportion of accident cases than of the normally sick.

He had said he thought I was wrong to insist on private treatment for my father and that he would find time hanging less heavy in a public ward where there was a lot going on, but I had assured him that he did not know my father. He had shrugged and acquiesced, but said that the private rooms weren't much. And they weren't. They were for getting out of quickly, if one could.

When I visited my father that evening, he was asleep. The ravages of the pain he had endured during the past week had deepened and darkened the lines round his eyes and tinged all his skin with gray, and he looked defenseless in a way he never did when he was awake. With his teeth out, the dogmatic set of his mouth was relaxed, and with his eyes shut he no longer seemed to be disapproving of nineteen-twentieths of what occurred. A lock of gray-white hair curved softly down over his forehead, giving him a friendly gentle look which was hopelessly misleading.

He had not been a kind father. I had spent most of my childhood fearing him and most of my teens loathing him, and only in the past very few years had I come to understand him. The severity with which he had used me had not, after all, been rejection and dislike, but lack of imagination and an inability to love. He had not believed in beating, but he had lavishly handed out other punishments of deprivation and solitude, without realizing that what would have been trifling to him was torment to me. Being locked in one's bedroom for three or four days at a time might not have come under the heading of active cruelty, but it had dumped me into agonies of humiliation and shame;

50

and it had not been possible, although I had tried until I was the most repressed child in Newmarket, to avoid committing anything my father could interpret as a fault.

He had sent me to Eton, which in its way had proved just as callous, and on my sixteenth birthday I ran away.

I knew that he had never forgiven me. An aunt had relayed to me his furious comment that he had provided me with horses to ride and taught me obedience, and what more could any father do for his son?

He had made no effort to get me back, and through all the years of my commercial success we had not once spoken to each other. During that time, I had of course read about him often in the newspapers, and in fact had seen him from a distance several times, as I had never lost my inborn interest in racing, and had occasionally been to race meetings where he had runners. In the end, after fourteen years of avoiding him, I had gone to Ascot knowing that he would be there and wanting finally to make peace.

When I said, "Mr. Griffon . . . ," he had turned to me from a group of people, raised his eyebrows, and looked at me inquiringly. His eyes were cool and blank. He hadn't known me.

I had said, with more amusement than awkwardness, "I am your son. . . . I am Neil."

Apart from surprise, he had shown no emotion whatsoever, and on the tacit understanding that none would be expected on either side, he had suggested that any day I happened to be passing through Newmarket, I could call in and see him.

I had called three or four times every year since then, sometimes for a drink, sometimes for lunch, but never staying; and I had come to see him from a much saner perspective in my thirties than I had at fifteen. His manner to me was still for the most part forbidding, critical, and punitive, but as I no longer depended solely upon him for approval, and as he could no longer lock me in my bedroom for disagreeing with him, I found a perverse sort of pleasure in his company.

I had thought when I was called in a hurry to Rowley Lodge after the accident that I wouldn't sleep again in my old bed, that I'd choose any other. But in fact in the end I did sleep in it, because it was the room that had been prepared for me, and there were dust sheets still over all the rest.

Too much had crowded back when I looked at the unchanged furnishings and the fifty-times-read books on the small bookshelf; and, smile at myself as cynically as I would, on that first night back I hadn't been able to lie in there in the dark with the door shut.

I sat down in the armchair and read the copy of the *Times* which rested on his bed. His hand, yellowish, freckled, and with thick knotted veins, lay limply on the sheets, still half entwined in the black-framed spectacles he had removed before sleeping. I remembered that when I was seventeen I had taken to wearing frames like those, with plain glass in them, because to me they stood for authority, and I had wanted to present an older and weightier personality to my clients. Whether it was the frames or not which did the trick, the antiques business had flourished.

He stirred, and groaned, and the lax hand closed convulsively into a fist with almost enough force to break the lenses.

I stood up. His face was screwed up with pain, and beads of sweat stood out on his forehead, but he sensed that there was someone in the room and opened his eyes sharp and wide as if there were nothing the matter.

"Oh . . . it's you."

"I'll fetch a nurse," I said.

"No. Be better . . . in a minute."

But I went to fetch one anyway, and she looked at the watch pinned upside down on her bosom and remarked that it was time for his pills, near enough.

After he had swallowed them and the worst of it had passed, I noticed that during the short time I was out of the room he had managed to replace his lower teeth. The glass of water stood empty on the locker. A great one for his dignity, my father.

"Have you found anyone to take over the license?" he asked.

"Can I make your pillows more comfortable?" I suggested.

"Leave them alone," he snapped. "Have you found anyone to take charge?" He would go on asking, I knew, until I gave him a direct answer.

"No," I said. "There's no need."

"What do you mean?"

"I've decided to stay on myself."

His mouth opened, just as Etty's had done, and then shut again with equal vigor.

"You can't. You don't know a damn thing about it. You couldn't win a single race."

"The horses are good, Etty is good, and you can sit here and do the entries."

"You will not take over. You will get someone who is capable, someone I approve of. The horses are far too valuable to have amateurs messing about. You will do as I say. Do you hear? You will do as I say."

The pain-killing drug had begun to act on his eyes, if not yet on his tongue.

"The horses will come to no harm," I said, and thought of Moonrock and Lucky Lindsay and the kicked two-year-old, and wished with all my heart I could hand the whole lot over to Bredon that very day.

"If you think," he said with a certain malice, "that because you can sell antiques you can run a racing stable, you are overestimating yourself."

"I no longer sell antiques," I pointed out calmly. As he knew perfectly well.

"The principles are different," he said.

"The principles of all businesses are the same."

"Rubbish."

"Get the costs right and supply what the customer wants."

"I can't see you supplying winners." He was contemptuous.

"Well," I said moderately, "I can't see why not."

"Can't you?" he asked acidly. "Can't you, indeed?"

"Not if you will give me your advice."

He gave me instead a long wordless stare while he searched for an adequate answer. The pupils in his gray eyes had contracted to micro-dots. There was no tension left in the muscles which had stiffened his jaw.

"You must get someone else," he said; but the words had begun to slur. I made a noncommittal movement of my head halfway between a nod and a shake, and the argument was over for that day. He asked after that merely about the horses. I told him how they had each performed during their workouts, and he seemed to forget that he didn't believe I understood what I had seen. When I left him, a short while later, he was again on the edge of sleep.

I rang the doorbell of my own flat in Hampstead, two long and two short, and got three quick buzzes back, which meant come on in. So I fitted my key into the latch and opened the door.

Gillie's voice floated disembodiedly across the hall. "I'm in your bedroom."

"Convenient," I said to myself with a smile. But she was painting the walls.

"Didn't expect you tonight," she said when I kissed her. She held her arms away from me, so as not to smear yellow ocher onto my jacket. There was a yellow streak on her forehead and a dusting of it on her shining chestnut hair and she looked companionable and easy. Gillie at thirty-six had a figure no model would have been seen dead in, and an attractive lived-in face with wisdom looking out of gray-green eyes. She was sure and mature and much traveled in spirit, and had left behind her one collapsed marriage and one dead child. She had answered an advertisement for a tenant which I had put in the *Times,* and for two and a half years she had been my tenant and a lot else.

"What do you think of this color?" she said. "And we're having a cinnamon carpet and green and shocking-pink striped curtains."

"You can't mean it."

"It will look ravishing."

"Ugh," I said, but she simply laughed. When she had taken the flat, it had had white walls, polished furniture, and blue fabrics. Gillie had retained only the furniture, and Sheraton and Chippendale would have choked over their new settings.

"You look tired," she said. "Want some coffee?"

"And a sandwich, if there's any bread."

She thought. "There's some crisp bread, anyway."

She was permanently on diets, and her idea of dieting was not to buy food. This led to a lot of eating out, which completely defeated the object.

Gillie had listened attentively to my wise dictums about laying in suitable protein like eggs and cheese, and then continued happily in the same old ways, which brought me early on to believe that she really did not lust after a beauty-contest figure, but was content as long as she did not burst out of her forty-inch-hip dresses. Only when they got tight did she actually shed half a stone. She could if she wanted to. She didn't obsessively want to.

"How is your father?" she asked as I crunched my way through a sandwich of rye-crisp bread and slices of raw tomato.

"It's still hurting him."

"I would have thought they could have stopped that."

"Well, they do, most of the time. And the sister in charge told me this evening that he will be all right in a day or two. They aren't worried about his leg any more. The wound has started healing cleanly, and it should all be settling down soon and giving him an easier time."

"He's not young, of course."

"Sixty-seven," I agreed.

"The bones will take a fair time to mend."

"Mm."

"I suppose you've found someone to hold the fort."

"No," I said, "I'm staying there myself."

"Oh boy, oh boy," she said, "I might have guessed."

I looked at her inquiringly with my mouth full of bits.

"Anything which smells of challenge is your meat and drink."

"Not this one," I said with feeling.

"It will be unpopular with the stable," she diagnosed, "and apoplectic to your father, and riotous success."

"Correct on the first two, way out on the third."

She shook her head, with the glint of a smile. "Nothing is impossible for the whiz kids."

She knew I disliked the journalese term, and I knew she liked to use it. "My lover is a whiz kid," she said once into a hush at a sticky party; and the men mobbed her.

She poured me a glass of the marvelous Château Lafite 1961, which she sacrilegiously drank with anything from caviar to baked beans. It had seemed to me when she moved in that her belongings consisted almost entirely of fur coats and cases of wine, all of which she had precipitiously inherited from her mother and father respectively when they died together in Morocco in an earthquake. She had sold the coats, because she thought they made her look fat, and had set about drinking her way gradually through the precious bins that wine merchants were wringing their hands over.

"That wine is an *investment*," one of them had said to me in agony.

"But *someone's* got to drink it," said Gillie reasonably, and pulled out the cork on the second of the Cheval Blanc '61.

Gillie was so rich, because of her grandmother, that she found it more pleasing to drink the super-duper than to sell it at a profit and develop a taste for Brand X. She had been surprised that I had agreed, until I had pointed out that that flat was filled with precious pieces where painted deal would have done the same job. So we sat sometimes with our feet up on a six-teenth-century Spanish walnut refectory table which had brought dealers sobbing to their knees and drank her wine out of eighteenth-century Waterford glass, and laughed at ourselves, because the only safe way to live with any degree of wealth was to make fun of it.

Gillie had said once, "I don't see why that table is so special, just because it's been here since the Armada. Just look at those moth-eaten legs." She pointed to four feet, which were pitted, stripped of polish, and worn untidily away.

"In the sixteenth century, they used to sluice the stone floors with beer because it whitened them," I said. "Beer was fine for the stone, but a bit unfortunate for any wood which got continually splashed."

"Rotten legs proves it's genuine?" she said.

"Got it in one."

I was fonder of that table than of anything else I possessed, because on it had been founded all my fortunes. Six months out of Eton, on what I had saved out of sweeping the floors at Sotheby's, I set up in business on my own pushing a barrow round the out-skirts of flourishing country towns and buying any-thing worthwhile that I was offered. The junk I sold to secondhand shops and the best bits to dealers, and by the time I was seventeen I was thinking about a shop.

I saw the Spanish table in the garage of a handy-man from whom I had just bought a late-Victorian chest of drawers. I looked at the wrought-iron crossed spars bracing the solid square legs under the four-inch-thick top, and felt unholy butterflies in my guts.

He had been using it as a trestle for paperhanging, and it was littered with pots of paint.

"I'll buy that, too, if you like," I said.

"It's only an old worktable."

"Well . . . how much would you want for it?"

He looked at my barrow, onto which he had just helped me lift the chest of drawers. He looked at the twenty pounds I had paid him for it, and he looked at my shabby jeans and jerkin, and he said kindly, "No, lad, I couldn't rob you. And anyway, look, its legs are all rotten at the bottom."

"I could afford another twenty," I said doubtfully. "But that's about all I've got with me."

He took a lot of persuading, and in the end would only let me give him fifteen. He shook his head over me, telling me I'd better learn a bit more before I ruined myself. But I cleaned up the table and repolished the beautiful slab of walnut, and I sold it a fortnight later to a dealer I knew from the Sotheby days for two hundred and seventy pounds.

With those proceeds swelling my savings, I opened the first shop, and things never looked back. When I sold out twelve years later, to an American syndicate, there was a chain of eleven stores, all bright and clean and filled with treasures.

A short time afterward, on a sentimental urge, I traced the Spanish table and bought it back. And I sought out the handyman with his garage and gave him two hundred pounds, which almost caused a heart attack; so I reckoned if anyone was going to put his feet up on that expensive plank, no one had a better right than I.

"Where did you get all those bruises?" Gillie said, sitting up in the spare-room bed and watching me undress.

I squinted down at the spatter of mauve blotches.

"I was attacked by a centipede."

She laughed. "You're hopeless."

"And I've got to be back at Newmarket by seven tomorrow morning."

"Stop wasting time, then. It's midnight already."

I climbed in beside her, and lying together in naked companionship we worked our way through the *Times* crossword.

It was always better like that. By the time we turned off the light, we were relaxed and entwined, and we turned to each other for an act that was a part but not the whole of a relationship.

"I quite love you," Gillie said. "Believe it or not."

"Oh, I believe you," I said modestly. "Thousands wouldn't."

"Stop biting my ear, I don't like it."

"The books say the ear is an A-1 erogenous zone."

"The books can go stuff themselves."

"Charming."

"And all those women's lib publications about 'The Myth of the Vaginal Orgasm.' So much piffle. Of course it isn't a myth."

"This is not supposed to be a public meeting," I said. "This is supposed to be a spot of private passion."

"Oh, well . . . if you insist."

She wriggled more comfortably into my arms.

"I'll tell you something, if you like," she said.

"If you absolutely must."

"The answer to four down isn't hallucinated, it hallucinogen."

I shook. "Thanks very much."

"Thought you'd like to know."

I kissed her neck and laid my hand on her stomach.

"That makes it a 'g,' not a 't,' in twenty across," she said.

"Stigma?"

"Clever old you."

"Is that the lot?"

"Mm."

After a bit, she said, "Do you really loathe the idea of green and shocking-pink curtains?"

"Would you mind just concentrating on the matter in hand?"

I could feel her grin in the darkness.

"O.K.," she said.

And concentrated.

She woke me up like an alarm clock at five o'clock. It was not so much the pat she woke me up with, but where she chose to plant it. I came back to the surface laughing.

"Good morning, little one," she said.

She got up and made some coffee, her chestnut hair in a tangle and her skin pale and fresh. She looked marvelous in the mornings. She stirred a dollop of heavy cream into the thick black coffee and sat opposite me across the kitchen table.

"Someone really had a go at you, didn't they?" she said casually.

I buttered a piece of rye crunch and reached for the honey.

"Sort of," I agreed.

"Not telling?"

"Can't," I said briefly. "But I will when I can."

"You may have a mind like teak," she said, "but you've a vulnerable body, just like anyone else."

I looked at her in surprise, with my mouth full. She wrinkled her nose at me.

"I used to think you mysterious and exciting," she said.

"Thanks."

"And now you're about as exciting as a pair of old bedroom slippers."

"So kind," I murmured.

"I used to think there was something magical about the way you disentangled all those nearly bankrupt businesses . . . and then I found out that it wasn't magic but just uncluttered common sense."

"Plain, boring old me," I agreed, washing down the crumbs with a gulp of coffee.

"I know you well now," she said. "I know how you tick. And all those bruises. . . ." She shivered suddenly in the warm little room.

"Gillie," I said accusingly, "you are suffering from intuition," and that remark in itself was a dead giveaway.

"No, from interpretation," she said. "And just you watch out for yourself."

"Anything you say."

"Because," she explained seriously, "I do not want to have the bother of hunting for another ground-floor flat with cellars to keep the wine in. It took me a whole month to find this one."

5

It was drizzling when I got back to Newmarket. A cold wet horrible morning on the Heath. Also, the first thing I saw when I turned in to the drive of Rowley Lodge was the unwelcome white Mercedes.

The uniformed chauffeur sat behind the wheel. The steely young Alessandro sat in the back. When I stopped not far away from him, he was out of his car faster than I was out of mine.

"Where have you been?" he demanded, looking down his nose at my silver-gray Jensen.

"Where have you?" I said equably, and received a full freeze of the Rivera specialty in stares.

"I have come to begin," he said fiercely.

"So I see."

He wore superbly cut jodhpurs and glossy brown boots. His waterproof anorak had come from an expensive ski shop and his string gloves were clean and pale yellow. He looked more like an advertisement in *Country Life* than a working rider.

"I have to go in and change," I said. "You can begin when I come out."

"Very well."

He waited again in his car and emerged from it immediately I reappeared. I jerked my head at him to follow, and went down into the yard wondering just how much of a skirmish I was going to have with Etty.

She was in a box in bay three helping a very small lad to saddle a seventeen-hand filly, and with Alessandro at my heels I walked across to talk to her. She came out of the box and gave Alessandro a widening look of speculation.

"Etty," I said matter-of-factly, "this is Alessandro Rivera. He has signed his indentures. He starts today. Er, right now, in fact. What can we give him to ride?"

Etty cleared her throat. "Did you say *apprenticed?*"

"That's right."

"But we don't need any more lads," she protested.

"He won't be doing his two. Just riding exercise."

She gave me a bewildered look. "All apprentices do their two."

"Not this one," I said briskly. "How about a horse for him?"

She brought her scattered attention to bear on the immediate problem.

"There's Indigo," she said doubtfully. "I had him saddled for myself."

"Indigo will do beautifully." I nodded. Indigo was a quiet ten-year-old gelding which Etty often rode as lead horse to the two-year-olds, and upon which she liked to give completely untrained apprentices their first riding lessons. I stifled the urge to show Alessandro up by putting him on something really difficult; couldn't risk damaging expensive property.

"Miss Craig is the head lad," I told Alessandro. "And you will take your orders from her."

He gave her a black unfathomable stare, which she returned with uncertainty.

"I'll show him where Indigo is," I reassured her. "Also the tack room, and so on."

"I've given you Cloud Cuckoo-land this morning, Mr. Neil," she said hesitantly. "Jock will have got him ready."

"Fine," I said with a smile, but I didn't get one back.

I pointed out the tack room, feed room, and the general layout of the stable to Alessandro and led him back toward the drive.

"I do not take orders from a woman," he said.

"You'll have to," I said without emphasis.

"No."

"Goodbye, then."

He walked one pace behind me in fuming silence, but he followed me round to the outside boxes and did not peel off toward his car. Indigo's box was the one next to Moonrock's, and the horse stood patiently in his saddle and bridle, resting his weight on one leg and looking round lazily when I unbolted his door.

Alessandro's gaze swept him from stem to stern and he turned to me with unrepressed anger.

"I do not ride nags. I wish to ride Archangel."

"No one lets an apprentice diamond cutter start on the Kohinoor," I said.

"I can ride any race horse on earth. I can ride exceptionally well."

"Prove it on Indigo, then, and I'll give you something better for second lot."

He compressed his mouth. I looked at him with complete lack of feeling that always seemed to calm tempers in industrial negotiations, and after a moment or two it worked on him as well. His gaze dropped away from my face; he shrugged, untied Indigo's head-collar, and led him out of his box. He jumped with ease up into the saddle, slipped his feet into the stirrups, and gathered up the reins. His movements were precise and unfussy, and he settled onto old Indigo's back with an appearance of being at home. Without another word, he started walking away down the yard, shortening the stirrup leathers as he went, for Etty rode long.

Watching his back view, I followed him on foot, while from all the bays the lads led out the horses for the first lot. Down in the collecting paddock, they circled round the outer cinder track while Etty, on the grass in the center, began the ten-minute task of swapping some of the riders. The lads who did the horses did not necessarily ride their own charges out at exercise; each horse had to be ridden by a rider who could at least control him and at the most improve him. The lowliest riders usually got the task of walking any unfit horses round the paddock at home; Etty seldom let them loose in canters on the Heath.

I joined her in the center as she referred to her list. She was wearing a bright yellow sou'wester down which the drizzle trickled steadily, and she looked like a diminutive American fisherman. The scrawled list in her hand was slowly degenerating into pulp.

"Ginge, get up on Pulitzer," she said.

Ginge did as he was told in a sulk. Pulitzer was a far cry from Lucky Lindsay, and he considered that he had lost face.

Etty briefly watched Alessandro plod round on Indigo, taking in with a flick of a glance that he could at least manage him with no problems. She looked at me in a baffled questioning way, but I merely steered her away from him by asking who she was putting up on our problem colt, Traffic.

She shook her head in frustration. "It'll still have to be Andy. . . . He's a right little devil, that Traffic. All that breed, you can't trust one of them." She turned and called on him "Andy, get up on Traffic."

Andy, middle-aged, tiny, wrinkled, could ride the sweetest of training gallops; but my father had mentioned that when, years before, Andy had been given his chance in races, his wits had flown out of the window, and his grasp of tactics was nil. He was given a leg up onto the dark irritable two-year-old, which jigged and fidgeted and buck-jumped under him without remission.

Etty had switched herself to Lucky Lindsay, who wore a shield over the cut knee and, although sound, would not be cantering; in Cloud Cuckoo-land she had given me the next best to a hack, a strong five-year-old handicapper up to a man's weight. With everyone mounted, the gates to the Heath were opened, and the whole string wound out onto the walking ground, colts as always in front, fillies behind.

Bound for the Southfield Gallops beside the racecourse, we turned right out of the gate and walked down behind the other stables which were strung out along the Bury Road. Passed the Jockey Club notice board announcing which training areas could be used that day. Crossed the A 11, holding up heavy lorries with their windscreen wipers twitching impatiently. Wound across the Severalls, along the Watercourse, through St. Mary's Square, along the Rows, and so finally to Southfields. No other town in England provided a special series of roads upon which the only traffic allowed was horses; but one could go from one end of Newmarket to the other, only yards behind its bustling High Street, and spend just a fraction of the journey on the public highway.

We were the only string on Southfields that morning, and Etty wasted no time in starting the canters. Up on the road to the racecourse stood the two usual cars, with two men standing out in the damp in the unmistakable position which meant they were watching us through binoculars.

"They never miss a day," Etty said sourly. "And if they think we've brought Archangel down here, they're in for a disappointment."

The touts watched steadfastly, though what they could see from half a mile away through unrelenting drizzle was anyone's guess. They were employed not by bookmakers but by racing columnists, who relied on their reports for the wherewithal to fill their pages. I thought it might be a very good thing if I could keep Alessandro out of their attention for as long as possible.

He could handle Indigo right enough, though the gelding was an undemanding old thing within the powers of the Pony Club. All the same, he sat well on him and had quiet hands. "Here, you," Etty said, beckoning to him with her whip. "Come over here."

To me she said, as she slid to the ground from Lucky Lindsay, "What is his name?"

"Alessandro."

"Aless—? Far too long."

Indigo was reined to a halt beside her. "You, Alex," she said. "Jump down and hold this horse."

I thought he would explode. His furious face said plainly that no one had any right to call him Alex, and that no one, but no one, was going to order him about. Especially not a woman.

He saw me watching him and suddenly wiped all expression from his own face as if with a sponge. He shook his feet out of the irons, swung his leg agilely forward over Indigo's withers, and slid to the ground facing us. He took the reins of Lucky Lindsay, which Etty held out to him, and gave her those of Indigo. She lengthened the stirrup leathers, climbed up into the saddle, and rode away without comment to give a lead to the six two-year-olds we had brought with us.

Alessandro said, like a throttled volcano, "I am not going to take any more orders from that woman."

"Don't be so bloody silly," I said.

He looked up at me. The fine rain had drenched his black hair so that the curls had tightened and clung close to his head. With the arrogant nose, the back-tilted skull, the close-curling hair, he looked like a Roman statue come to life.

"Don't talk to me like that. No one talks to me like that."

Cloud Cuckoo-land stood patiently, pricking his ears up to watch some sea gulls fly across the Heath.

I said, "You are here because you want to be. No one asked you to come, no one will stop you going. But just so long as you do stay here, you will do what Miss Craig says, and you will do what I say, and you will do it without arguing. Is that clear?"

"My father will not let you treat me like this." He was rigid with the strength of his outrage.

"Your father," I said coldly, "must be overjoyed to have a son who needs to shelter behind his skirts."

"You will be sorry," he threatened furiously.

I shrugged. "Your father said I was to give you good horses to ride in races. Nothing was mentioned about bowing down to a spoiled little tin god."

"I will tell him—"

"Tell him what you like. But the more you run to him, the less I'll think of you."

"I don't care what you think of me," he said vehemently.

"You're a liar," I said flatly, and he gave me a long tight-lipped stare until he turned abruptly away. He led Lucky Lindsay ten paces off, and stopped and watched the canters that Etty was directing. Every line of the slender shape spoke of injured pride and flaming resentment, and I wondered whether his father would indeed think that I had gone too far. And if I had, what was he going to do about it?

Mentally shrugging off the evil until the day thereof, I tried to make some assessment of the two-year-olds' relative abilities. Scoff as people might about me taking over my father's license, I had found that childhood skills came back after nineteen years as naturally as riding a bicycle; and few lonely children could grow up in a racing stable without learning the trade from the muckheap up. I'd had the horses out-of-doors for company, and the furniture indoors, and I reckoned if I could build one business out of the deadwood I could also try to keep things rolling with the live muscles. But for only as long, I reminded myself, as it took me to get rid of Alessandro.

Etty came back after the canters and changed horses again.

"Give me a leg up," she said briskly to Alessandro; for Lucky Lindsay like most young thoroughbreds did not like riders climbing up to mount them.

For a moment, I thought the whole pantomime was over. Alessandro drew himself up to his full height, which topped Etty's by at least two inches, and dispatched at her a glare which should have cremated her. Etty genuinely didn't notice.

"Come on," she said impatiently, and held out her leg backward, bent at the knee.

Alessandro threw a glance of desperation in my direction, then took a visibly deep breath, looped Indigo's reins over his arm, and put his two hands under Etty's shin. He gave her quite a respectable leg up, though I wouldn't have been surprised if it was the first time in his life that he had done it.

I carefully didn't laugh, didn't sneer, didn't show that I thought there was anything to notice. Alessandro swallowed his capitulation in private. But there was nothing to indicate that it would be permanent.

We rode back in the rain through the town and into the yard, where I gave Cloud Cuckoo-land back to Jock and walked into the office to see Margaret. She had the mushroom heater blowing full blast, but I doubted that I would have properly dried through by the time we pulled out again for second lot.

"Morning," she said economically.

I nodded, half smiled, slouched into the swivel chair. "I've opened the letters again—was that right?" she said.

"Absolutely. And answer them yourself, if you can."

She looked surprised. "Mr. Griffon always dictates everything."

"Anything you have to ask about, ask. Anything I need to know, tell me. Anything else, deal with it yourself."

"All right," she said, and sounded pleased.

I sat in my father's chair and stared down at his books, which I had usurped, and thought seriously about what I had seen in his account books. Alessandro wasn't the only trouble the stable was running into.

There was a sudden crash as the door from the yard was forcibly opened, and Etty burst into the office like a stampeding ballistic missile.

"That bloody boy you've taken on— He'll have to go. I'm not standing for it. I'm not."

She looked extremely annoyed, with eyes blinking fiercely and her mouth pinched into a slit.

"What has he done?" I asked resignedly.

"He's gone off in that stupid white car and left Indigo in his box still with his saddle and bridle on. George says he just got down off Indigo, led him into the box, and came out and shut the door, and got into the car and the chauffeur drove him away. Just like that!" She paused for breath. "And who does he think is going to take the saddle off and dry the rain off Indigo and wash out his feet and rug him up and fetch his hay and water and make his bed?"

"I'll go out and see George," I said. "And ask him to do it."

"I've asked him already," Etty said furiously. "But that's not the point. We're not keeping that wretched little Alex. Not one more minute."

She glanced at me with her chin up, making an issue of it. Like all head lads, she had a major say in the hiring and firing of the help. I had not consulted her over the hiring of Alessandro, and clear as a bell she was telegraphing that I was to acknowledge her authority and get rid of him.

"I'm afraid that we'll have to put up with him, Etty," I said sympathetically. "And hope to teach him better ways."

"He must go," she insisted vehemently.

"Alessandro's father," I lied sincerely, "is paying through the nose to have his son taken on here as an apprentice. It is very much worth the stable's while financially to put up with him. I'll have a talk with him when he comes back for second lot and see if I can get him to be more reasonable."

"I don't like the way he stares at me," Etty said, unmollified.

"I'll ask him not to."

"Ask!" Etty said exasperatedly. "Whoever heard of *asking* an apprentice to behave with respect to the head lad!"

"I'll tell him," I said.

"And tell him to stop being so snooty with the other lads—they are already complaining. And tell him he is to put his horse straight after he has ridden it, the same as all the others."

"I'm sorry, Etty. I don't think he'll put his horse straight. We'll have to get George to do it regularly. For a bonus, of course."

Etty said angrily, "It's not a yard man's job to act as a—a—*servant*—to an *apprentice*. It just isn't right."

"I know, Etty," I said. "I know it isn't right. But Alessandro is not an ordinary apprentice, and it might be easier all round if you could let all the other lads know that his father is paying for him to be here, and that he has some romantic notion of wanting to be a jockey, which he'll get out of his system soon enough, and when he has gone, we can all get back to normal."

She looked at me uncertainly. "It isn't a proper apprenticeship if he doesn't look after his horses."

"The details of an apprenticeship are a matter for agreement between the contracting parties," I said regretfully. "If I agree that he doesn't have to do his two,

71

then he doesn't have to. And I don't really approve of him not doing them, but there you are, the stable will be richer if he doesn't."

Etty had calmed down but she was not pleased. "I think you might have consulted me before agreeing to all this."

"Yes, Etty. I'm very sorry."

"And does your father know about it?"

"Of course," I said.

"Oh, well, then." She shrugged. "If your father wants it, I suppose we must make the best of it. But it won't be at all good for discipline."

"The lads will be used to him within a week."

"They won't like it if he looks like getting any chance in races which they think should be theirs."

"The season doesn't start for a month," I said soothingly. "Let's see how he makes out, shall we?"

And put off the day when he got the chances however bad he was, and however much they should have gone to someone else.

Etty put him on a quiet four-year-old mare which didn't please him but was a decided step up from old Indigo. He had received with unyielding scorn my request that he should stop staring so disquietingly at Etty, and sneered at my suggestion that he should let it be understood that his father was paying for him to be there.

"It is not true," he said superciliously.

"Believe me," I said with feeling, "if it were true, you wouldn't be here tomorrow. Not if he paid a pound a minute."

"Why not?"

"Because you are upsetting Miss Craig and upsetting the other lads, and a stable seething with resentment is not going to do its best by its horses. In fact, if you want the horses here to win races for you, you'll do your best to get along without arousing ill feeling in the staff."

He had given me the black stare and hadn't answered, but I noticed that he looked steadfastly at the ground when Etty detailed him to the mare. He rode her quietly along toward the back of the string and completed his allotted half-speed four-furlong canter without incident. On our return to the yard, George met him and took the mare away to the box, and Alessandro without a backward glance walked into his Mercedes and was driven away.

The truce lasted for two more mornings. On each of them, Alessandro arrived punctually for the first exercise, disappeared presumably for breakfast, came back for the second lot, and departed for the rest of the day. Etty gave him middling horses to ride, all of which he did adequately enough to wring from her the grudging comment "If he doesn't give us any more trouble, I suppose it could be worse."

But on his fourth morning, which was Saturday, the defiant attitude was not only back but reinforced. We survived through both lots without a direct confrontation between him and Etty only because I purposely kept parting them. For the second lot, in fact, I insisted on taking him with me and a party of two-year-olds along to the special two-year-old training ground while Etty led the bulk of the string over to Warren Hill.

We got back before Etty so that he should be gone before she returned, but instead of striding away to his Mercedes he followed me to the office door.

"Griffon," he said behind me.

I turned, regarded him. The arrogant stare was much in evidence. His eyes were blacker than space.

"I have been to see my father," he said. "He says that you should be treating me with deference. He says I should not take orders from a woman and that you must arrange that I do not. If necessary, Miss Craig must leave. He says I must be given better horses to ride, and in particular, Archangel. He says that if you do not see to these things immediately, he will show you that he meant what he said. And he told me to give you this. He said it was a promise of what he could do."

He produced a flat tin box from an inner pocket of his anorak, and held it out to me.

I took it. I said, "Do you know what it contains?"

He shook his head, but I was sure he did know.

"Alessandro," I said, "whatever your father threatens, or whatever he does, your only chance of success is to leave the stable unharmed. If your father destroys it, there will be nothing for you to ride."

"He will make another trainer take me," he asserted.

"He will not," I said flatly, "because should he destroy this stable I will put all the facts in front of the Jockey Club and they will take away your license and stop you riding in any races whatsoever."

"He would kill you," he said matter-of-factly. The thought of it did not surprise or appall him.

"I have already lodged with my solicitor a full account of my interview with your father. Should he kill me, they will open that letter. He could find himself in great trouble. And you, of course, would be barred for life from racing anywhere in the world."

A lot of the starch had turned to frustration. "He will have to talk to you himself," he said. "You do not behave as he tells me you will. You confuse me. He will talk to you himself."

He turned on his heel and took himself stiffly away to the attendant Mercedes. He climbed into the back, and the patient chauffeur, who always waited in the car all the time that his passenger was on the horses, started the purring engine and, with a scrunch of his Michelins, carried him away.

I took the flat tin with me into the house, through into the oak-paneled room, and opened it there on the desk.

Between layers of cotton wool, it contained a small

carved wooden model of a horse. Round its neck was tied a label, and on the label was written one word: "Moonrock."

I picked the little horse out of the tin. It was necessary to lift it out in two pieces, because the off-hind leg was snapped through at the hock.

6

I sat for quite a long time turning the little model over in my hands, and its significance over in my mind, wondering whether Enso Rivera could possibly have organized the breaking of Moonrock's leg, or whether he was simply pretending that what had been a true accident was all his own work.

I did not on the whole believe that he had destroyed Moonrock. What did become instantly ominous, though, was his repeated choice of the word "destroy."

Almost every horse which broke a leg had to be destroyed, as only in exceptional cases was mending them practicable. Horses could not be kept in bed. They would scarcely ever even lie down. To take a horse's weight off a leg meant supporting him in slings. Supporting him in slings for the number of weeks that it took a major bone to mend incurred debility and gut troubles. Race horses, always delicate creatures, could die of the inactivity, and if they survived were never as good afterward; and only in the case of valuable stallions and brood mares was any attempt normally made to keep them alive.

If Enso Rivera broke a horse's leg, it would have to be destroyed. If he broke enough of them, the owners would remove their survivors in a panic, and the stable itself would be destroyed.

Alessandro had said his father had sent the tin as a promise of what he could do.

If he could break horses' legs, he could indeed destroy the stable.

But it wasn't as easy as all that to break a horse's leg.

Fact or bluff.

I fingered the little maimed horse. I didn't know, and couldn't decide, which it represented. But I did decide at least to turn a bit of my own bluff into fact.

I wrote a full account of the abduction, embellished with every detail I could remember. I packed the little wooden horse back into its tin and wrote a short explanation of its possible significance. Then I enclosed everything in a strong manila envelope, wrote on it the time-honored words "To be opened in the event of my death," put it into a larger envelope with a covering letter, and posted it to my London solicitor from the main post office in Newmarket.

"You've done *what?*" my father exclaimed.

"Taken on a new apprentice."

He looked in fury at all the junk anchoring him to his bed. Only the fact that he was tied down prevented him from hitting the ceiling.

"It isn't up to you to take on new apprentices. You are not to do it. Do you hear?"

I repeated my fabrication about Enso paying well for Alessandro's privilege. The news percolated through my father's irritation and the voltage went out of it perceptibly. A thoughtful expression took over, and finally a grudging nod.

He knows, I thought. He knows that the stable will before long be short of ready cash.

I wondered whether he was well enough to discuss it, or whether, even if he was well enough, he would be able to talk to me about it. We had never in our lives discussed anything; he had told me what to do, and I either had or hadn't done it. The divine right of kings had nothing on his attitude, which he applied also to most of the owners. They were all in varying degrees in awe of him and a few were downright afraid; but they kept their horses in his stable because year after year he brought home the races that counted.

He asked how the horses were working. I told him at some length, and he listened with a skeptical slant to his mouth and eyebrows, intending to show doubt of the worth of any or all of my assessments. I continued without rancor through everything of any interest, and at the end he said, "Tell Etty I want a list of the work done by each horse, and its progress."

"All right," I agreed readily. He searched my face for signs of resentment and seemed a shade disappointed when he didn't find any. The antagonism of an aging and infirm father toward a fully grown healthy son was a fairly universal manifestation throughout nature, and I wasn't fussed that he was showing it. But all the same I was not going to give him the satisfaction of feeling he had scored over me; and he had no idea of how practiced I was at taking the prideful flush out of people's ill-natured victories.

I said merely, "Shall I take a list of the entries home, so that Etty will know which races the horses are to be prepared for?"

His eyes narrowed and his mouth tightened, and he explained that it had been impossible for him to do the entries; treatment and X-rays took up so much of his time and he was not left along long enough to concentrate.

"Shall Etty and I have a go, between us?"

"Certainly not. I will do them . . . when I have more time."

"All right," I said. "How is the leg feeling? You are certainly looking more your own self now."

"It is less troublesome," he admitted. He smoothed the already wrinkle-free bedclothes which lay over his stomach, engaged in his perennial habit of making his surroundings as orderly, as dignified, as starched as his soul.

I asked if there was anything I could bring him. "A book," I suggested. "Or some fruit? Or some champagne?" Like most race-horse trainers, he saw champagne as a sort of superior Coca-Cola, best drunk in the mornings if at all, but he knew that as a pick-me-up for the sick it had few equals.

He inclined his head sidewise, considering. "There are some half bottles in the cellar at Rowley Lodge."

"I'll bring some," I said.

He nodded. He would never, whatever I did, say thank you. I smiled inwardly. The day my father thanked me would be the day his personality disintegrated.

Via the hospital telephone, I checked whether I would be welcome at Hampstead and, having received a warming affirmative, headed the Jensen along the eight miles further south.

Gillie had finished painting the bedroom, but its furniture was still stacked in the hall.

"Waiting for the carpet," she explained. "Like Godot."

"Godot never came," I commented.

"That," she agreed with exaggerated patience, "is what I mean."

"Send up rockets, then."

"Firecrackers have been going off under backsides since Tuesday."

"Never mind," I said soothingly. "Come out to dinner."

"I'm on a grapefruit day," she objected.

"Well, I'm not. Positively not. I had no lunch and I'm hungry."

"I've got a really awfully nice grapefruit recipe. You put the halves in the oven doused in saccharin and kirsch and eat it hot. . . ."

"No," I said definitely. "I'm going to the Empress."

That shattered the grapefruit program. She adored the Empress.

"Oh, well . . . it would be so boring for you to eat alone," she said. "Wait a mo while I put on my tatty black."

Her tatty black was a long-sleeved St. Laurent dress that made the least of her curves. There was nothing approaching tatty about it, very much on the contrary, and her description was inverted, as if by diminishing its standing she could forget her guilt over its price. She had recently developed some vaguely Socialist views, and it had mildly begun to bother her that what she had paid for one dress would have supported a ten-child family throughout Lent.

Dinner at the Empress was its usual quiet, spacious, superb self. Gillie ordered curried prawns to be followed by chicken in a cream-and-brandy sauce, and laughed when she caught my ironic eye.

"Back to the grapefruit," she agreed. "But not until tomorrow."

"How are the suffering orphans?" I asked. She worked three days a week for an adoption society which, because of the Pill and easy abortion, was running out of its raw materials.

"You don't happen to want two-year-old twins, Afro-Asian boys, one of them with a squint?" she said.

"Not all that much, no."

"Poor little things." She absent-mindedly ate a bread roll spread with enjoyable chunks of butter. "We'll never place them. They don't look even averagely attractive."

BONECRACK

"Squints can be put right," I said.

"Someone has to care enough first, to get it done."

We drank a lesser wine than Gillie's but better than most.

"Do you realize," Gillie said, "that a family of ten could live for a week on what this dinner is costing?"

"Perhaps the waiter has a family of ten," I suggested. "And if we didn't eat it, what would they live on?"

"Oh . . . blah," Gillie said, but looked speculatively at the man who brought her chicken.

She asked how my father was. I said better, but by no means well.

"He said he would do the entries," I explained, "but he hasn't started. He told me it was because he isn't given time, but the sister says he sleeps a great deal. He had a frightful shaking and his system hasn't recovered yet."

"What will you do, then, about the entries? Wait until he's better?"

"Can't. The next lot have to be in by Wednesday."

"What happens if they aren't?"

"The horses will go on eating their heads off in the stable when they ought to be out on a racecourse trying to earn their keep. It's now or never to put their names down for some of the races at Chester and Ascot and the Craven meeting at Newmarket."

"So you'll do them yourself," she said matter-of-factly. "And they'll all go and win."

"Almost any entry is better than no entry at all." I sighed. "And by the law of averages, some of them must be right."

"There you are, then. No more problems."

But there were two more problems, and worse ones, sticking up like rocks on the fairway. The financial problem, which I could solve if I had to; and that of Alessandro, which I didn't yet know how to.

*　　*　　*

The following morning, he arrived late. The horses for first lot were already plodding round the cinder track, while I stood with Etty in the center as she changed the riders, when Alessandro appeared through the gate from the yard. He waited for a space between the passing horses and then crossed the cinder track and came toward us.

The finery of the week before was undimmed. The boots shone as glossily, the gloves as palely, and the ski jacket and jodhpurs were still immaculate. On his head, however, he wore a blue-and-white striped woolly cap with a pompon, the same as most of the other lads; but on Alessandro this cozy protection against the stinging March wind looked as incongruous as a bowler hat on the beach.

I didn't even smile. The black eyes regarded me with their customary chill from features that were more gaunt than delicate. The strong shape of the bones showed clearly through the yellowish skin, and more so, it seemed to me, than a week ago.

"What do you weigh?" I asked abruptly.

He hesitated a little. "I will be able to ride at six stone seven when the races begin. I will be able to claim all the allowances."

"But now? What do you weigh now?"

"A few pounds more. But I will lose them."

Etty fumed at him but forbore to point out to him that he wouldn't get any rides if he wasn't good enough. She looked down at her list to see which horses she had allotted him, opened her mouth to tell him, and then shut it again, and I literally saw the impulse take hold of her.

"Ride Traffic," she said. "You can get up on Traffic."

Alessandro stood very still.

"He doesn't have to," I said to Etty; and to Alessandro, "You don't have to ride Traffic. Only if you choose."

He swallowed. He raised his chin and his courage, and said, "I choose."

With a stubborn set to her mouth, Etty beckoned to Andy, who was already mounted on Traffic, and told him of the change.

"Happy to oblige," Andy said feelingly, and gave Alessandro a leg up into his unrestful place. Traffic lashed out into a few preliminary bucks, found he had a less hard-bitten customer than usual on his back, and started off at a rapid sidewise trot across the paddock.

Alessandro didn't fall off, which was the best that could be said. He hadn't the experience to settle the sour colt to obedience, let alone to teach him to be better, but he was managing a great deal more efficiently than I could have done.

Etty watched him with disfavor and told everyone to give him plenty of room.

"That nasty little squirt needs taking down a peg," she said in unnecessary explanation.

"He isn't doing too badly," I commented.

"Huh." There was a ten-ton lorry-load of scorn in her voice. "Look at the way he's jabbing him in the mouth. You wouldn't catch Andy doing that in a thousand years."

"Better not let him out on the Heath," I said.

"Teach him a lesson," Etty said doggedly.

"Might kill the goose, and then where would we be for the golden eggs?"

She gave me a bitter glance. "The stable doesn't need that sort of money."

"The stable needs any sort of money it can get."

But Etty shook her head in disbelief. Rowley Lodge had been in the top division of the big league ever since she had joined it, and no one would ever convince her that its very success was leading it into trouble.

I beckoned to Alessandro and he came as near as his rocking horse permitted.

"You don't have to ride him on the Heath," I said.

Traffic turned his quarters toward us and Alessandro called over his shoulder, "I stay here. I choose."

Etty told him to ride fourth in the string and everyone else to keep out of his way. She herself climbed into Indigo's saddle, and I into Cloud Cuckoo-land's, and George opened the gates. We turned right onto the walking ground, bound for the canter on Warren Hill, and nothing frantic happened on the way except that Traffic practically backed into an incautious tout when crossing Moulton Road. The tout retreated with curses, calling the horse by name. The Newmarket touts knew every horse on the Heath by sight. A remarkable feat, as there were about two thousand animals in training there, hundreds of them two-year-olds which altered shape as they developed month by month. Touts learned horses as headmasters learned new boys, and rarely made a mistake. All I hoped was that this one had been too busy getting himself to safety to take much notice of the rider.

We had to wait our turn on Warren Hill, since we were the fourth stable to choose to work there that morning. Alessandro walked Traffic round in circles a little way apart—or at least tried to walk him. Traffic's idea of walking would have tired a bucking bronco.

Eventually, Etty sent the string off up the hill in small clusters, with me sitting halfway up the slope on Cloud Cuckoo-land, watching them as they swept past. At the top of the hill, they stopped, peeled off to the left, and went back down the central walking ground to collect again at the bottom. Most mornings each horse cantered up the hill twice, the sharpish incline getting a lot of work into them in a comparatively short distance.

Alessandro started up the hill in the last bunch, one of only four.

Long before he drew level with me, I could see that of the horse and rider it was the horse who had control. Galloping was hard labor up Warren Hill, but no one had given Traffic the message.

As he passed me, he was showing all the classic signs of the bolter in action: head stretched horizontally forward, bit gripped between his teeth, eyes showing the whites. Alessandro, with as much hope of dominating the situation as a virgin in a troopship, hung grimly on to the neck strap and appeared to be praying.

The top of the rise meant nothing to Traffic. He swerved violently to the left and set off sidewise toward Bury Hill, not even having the sense to make straight for the stable but swinging too far north and missing it by half a mile. On he charged, his hoofs thundering relentlessly over the turf, carrying Alessandro inexorably away in the general direction of Lowestoft.

Stifling the unworthy thought that I wouldn't care all that much if he plunged straight on into the North Sea, I reflected with a bit more sense that if Traffic damaged himself, Rowley Lodge's foundations would feel the tremor. I set off at a trot after him as he disappeared into the distance, but when I reached the Bury St. Edmunds Road there was no sign of him. I crossed the road and reined in there, wondering which direction to take.

A car came slowly toward me with a shocked-looking driver poking his head out of the window.

"Some bloody madman nearly plowed straight into me," he yelled. "Some bloody madman on the road on a mad horse."

"How very upsetting," I shouted back sympathetically, but he glared at me balefully and nearly ran into a tree.

I went on along the road, wondering whether it would be a dumped-off Alessandro I saw first, and if so, how long it would take to find and retrieve the wayward Traffic.

From the next rise, there was no sign of either of them; the road stretched emptily ahead. Beginning to get anxious, I quickened Cloud Cuckoo-land until we were trotting fast along the soft ground edging the tarmac.

Past the end of the Limekilns, still no trace of Alessandro. The road ran straight, up and down its inclines. No Alessandro. It was a good two miles from the training ground that I finally found him.

He was standing at the crossroads, dismounted, holding Traffic's reins. The colt had evidently run himself to a standstill, as he drooped there with his head down, his sides heaving, and sweat streaming from him all over. Flecks of foam spattered his neck, and his tongue lolled exhaustedly out.

I slid down from Cloud Cuckoo-land and ran my hand down Traffic's legs. No tenderness. No apparent strain. Sighing with relief, I straightened up and looked at Alessandro. His face was stiff, his eyes expressionless.

"Are you all right?" I asked.

He lifted his chin. "Of course."

"He's a difficult horse," I remarked.

Alessandro didn't answer. His self-pride might have received a body blow, but he was not going to be so soft as to accept any comfort.

"You'd better walk back with him," I said. "Walk until he's thoroughly cooled down. And keep him out of the way of the cars."

Alessandro tugged the reins and Traffic sluggishly turned, not moving his legs until he absolutely had to.

"What's that?" Alessandro said, pointing to a mound in the grass at the corner of the crossroads where he had been standing. He shoved Traffic farther away so that I could see; but I had no need to.

"It's the Boy's Grave," I said.

"What boy?" He was startled. The small grave was known to everyone in Newmarket, but not to him. The mound, about four feet long, was outlined with overlapping wire hoops, like the edges of lawns in parks. There were some dirty-looking plastic daffodils entwined in the hoops, and a few dying flowers scattered in the center. Also a white plastic drinking mug which someone had thrown there. The grave looked forlorn yet, in a futile sort of way, cared for.

"There are a lot of legends," I said. "The most likely is that he was a shepherd boy who went to sleep in charge of his flock. A wolf came and killed half of them, and when he woke up he was so remorseful that he hanged himself."

"They used to bury suicides at crossroads," Alessandro said, nodding. "It is well known."

There didn't seem to be any harm in trying to humanize him, so I went on with the story.

"The grave is always looked after, in a haphazard sort of way. It is never overgrown, and fresh flowers are often put there. No one knows exactly who puts them there, but it's supposed to be the gypsies. And there is also a legend that in May the flowers on the grave are in the colors that will win the Derby."

Alessandro stared down at the pathetic little memorial.

"There are no black flowers," he said slowly: Archangel's colors were black, pale blue, and gold.

"The gypsies will solve that if they have to," I said dryly, and thought that they would opt for an easier nap selection.

I turned Cloud Cuckoo-land in the direction of home and walked away. When presently I looked back, Alessandro was walking Traffic quietly along the side of the road, a thin straight figure in his clean clothes and bright blue-and-white cap. It was a pity, I thought, that he was as he was. With a different father, he might have been a different person.

But with a different father, so would I. And who wouldn't.

I thought about it all the way back to Rowley Lodge. Fathers, it seemed to me, could train, feed, or warp their young plants, but they couldn't affect their basic nature. They might produce a stunted oak or a luxuriant weed, but oak and weed were inborn qualities, which would prevail in the end. Alessandro, on such a horticultural reckoning, was like a cross between holly and deadly nightshade; and if his father had his way the red berries would lose out to the black.

Alessandro bore Etty's strongly implied scorn with a frozen face, but few of the other lads teased him on his return, as they would have done to one of their own sort. Most of them seemed to be instinctively afraid of him, which to my mind showed their good sense, and the other, less sensitive types had drifted into the defense mechanism of ignoring his existence.

George took Traffic off to his box, and Alessandro followed me into the office. His glance swept over Margaret, sitting at her desk in a neat navy-blue dress with the high curls piled as elaborately as ever, but he saw her as no bar to giving me the benefit of the thoughts that he evidently had also had time for on the way back.

"You should not have made me ride such a badly trained horse," he began belligerently.

"I didn't make you. You chose to."

"Miss Craig told me to ride it to make a fool of me."

True enough.

"You could have refused," I said.

"I could not."

"You could have said that you thought you needed more practice before taking on the worst ride in the yard."

His nostrils flared. So self-effacing an admission would have been beyond him.

"Anyway," I went on, "I personally don't think riding Traffic is going to teach you much. So you won't be put on him again."

"But I insist," he said vehemently.

"You insist what?"

"I insist I ride Traffic again." He gave me the haughtiest of his selection of stares, and added, "Tomorrow."

"Why?"

"Because if I do not, everyone will think it is because I cannot, or that I am afraid to."

"So you do care what the others think of you," I said matter-of-factly.

"No, I do not." He denied it strongly.

"Then why ride the horse?"

He compressed his strong mouth stubbornly. "I will answer no more questions. I will ride Traffic tomorrow."

"Well, O.K.," I said casually. "But I'm not sending him on the Heath tomorrow. He'll hardly need another canter. Tomorrow he'll only be walking round the cinder track in the paddock, which will be very boring for you."

He gave me a concentrated, suspicious, considering stare, trying to work out if I was meaning to undermine him. Which I was, if one can call taking the point out of a Grand Gesture undermining.

"Very well," he said grudgingly. "I will ride him round the paddock."

He turned on his heel and walked out of the office. Margaret watched him go with a mixed expression I couldn't read.

"Mr. Griffon would never stand for him talking like that," she said.

"Mr. Griffon doesn't have to."

"I can see why Etty can't bear him," she said. "He's insolent. There's no other word for it. Insolent." She handed me three opened letters across the desk. "These need your attention, if you don't mind." She reverted to Alessandro: "But all the same, he's beautiful."

"He's no such thing," I protested mildly. "If anything, he's ugly."

She smiled briefly. "He's absolutely loaded with sex appeal."

I lowered the letters. "Don't be silly. He has the sex appeal of a bag of rusty nails."

"You wouldn't notice," she said judiciously. "Being a man."

I shook my head. "He's only eighteen."

"Age has nothing to do with it," she said. "Either you've got it, or you haven't got it, right from the start. And he's got it."

I didn't pay much attention; Margaret herself had so little sex appeal that I didn't think her a reliable judge. When I'd read through the letters and agreed with her how she should answer them, I went along to the kitchen for some coffee.

The remains of the night's work lay littered about: the various dregs of brandy, cold milk, coffee, and masses of scribbled-on bits of paper. It had taken me most of the night to do the entries, a night I would far rather have spent lying warmly in Gillie's bed.

The entries had been difficult, not only because I had never done them before, and had to read the conditions of each race several times to make sure I understood them, but also because of Alessandro. I had to make a balance of what I would have done without him and what I would have to let him ride if he was still there in a month's time.

I was continuing to take his father's threats seriously. Part of the time, I thought I was foolish to do so; but that abduction a week ago had been no playful joke, and until I was certain Enso would not let loose a thunderbolt it was more prudent to go along with his son. I still had nearly a month before the Flat season started, still nearly a month to see a quick way out. But, just in case, I had put down some of the better prospects for apprentice races, and had duplicated the entries in many open races, because if two ran there would be one for Alessandro. Also I entered a good many in the lesser meetings, particularly those in the north; whether he liked it or not, Alessandro was not going to start his career in a blaze of limelight. After all that, I dug around in the office until I found the book in which old Robinson had recorded all the previous years' entries, and I checked my provisional list against what my father had done. After subtracting about twenty names, because I had been much too lavish, and shuffling things around a little, I made the total number of entries for the week approximately the same as those for the year before, except that I still had more in the north. Then I wrote the final list onto the official yellow form, in block letters as requested, and double-checked again to make sure I hadn't entered two-year-olds in handicaps, or fillies in colts-only, and made any other such giveaway gaffes.

When I gave the completed form to Margaret to record and then post, all she said was "This isn't your father's writing."

"No," I said. "He dictated the entries. I wrote them down."

She nodded noncommittally, and whether she believed me or not I had no idea.

Alessandro rode Pulitzer competently next day at first lot, and kept himself to himself. After breakfast he returned with a stony face that forbade comment, and when the main string had started out onto the Heath, was given a leg up onto Traffic. Looking back from the gate, I saw the fractious colt kicking away at shadows, as usual, and noticed that the two other lads detailed to stay in and walk their charges were keeping well away from him.

When we returned an hour and a quarter later, George was holding Traffic's reins, the other lads had dismounted, and Alessandro was lying on the ground in an unconscious heap.

7

"Traffic just bucked him off, sir," one of the lads said. "Just bucked him clean off, sir. And he hit his head on the paddock rail, sir."

"Just this minute, sir," added the other anxiously.

They were both about sixteen, both apprentices, both tiny, neither of them very bold. I thought it unlikely they would have done anything purposely to upset Traffic further and bring the stuck-up Alessandro literally down to earth, but one never knew. What I did know was that Alessandro's continuing health was essential to my own.

"George," I said, "put Traffic away in his box, and, Etty"—she was at my shoulder, clicking her tongue but not looking over-sorry—"is there anything we can use as a stretcher?"

"There's one in the tack room," she said, nodding, and told Ginge to go and get it.

The stretcher turned out to be a minimal affair of a piece of grubby green canvas slung between two uneven-shaped poles, which looked as though they might once have been a pair of oars. By the time Ginge returned with it, my heartbeat had descended from Everest: Alessandro was alive and not in too deep a coma, and Enso's pistol would not yet be popping me off in revenge to kingdom come.

As far as I could tell, none of his bones were broken, but I took exaggerated care over lifting him onto the stretcher. Etty disapproved; she would have had George and Ginge lift him up by his wrists and ankles and sling him on like a sack of corn. I, more moderately, told George and Ginge to lift him gently, carry him down to the house, and put him on the sofa in the owners' room. Following, I detoured off into the office and asked Margaret to telephone for a doctor.

Alessandro was stirring when I went into the owners' room. George and Ginge stood looking down at him, one elderly and resigned, one young and pugnacious, neither of them feeling any sympathy with the patient.

"O.K.," I said to them. "That's the lot. The doctor's coming for him."

Both of them looked as if they would like to say something, but they left without speaking and aired their opinions in the yard.

Alessandro opened his eyes, and for the first time looked a little vulnerable. He didn't know what had happened, didn't know where he was or how he had got there. The puzzlement formed new lines on his face, made it look younger and softer. Then his eyes focused on my face, and in one bound a lot of memory came back. The dove dissolved into the hawk. It was like watching the awakening of a spastic, from loose-limbed peace up to tightness and jangle.

"What happened?" he asked.

"Traffic threw you."

"Oh," he said more weakly than he liked. He shut his eyes and through his teeth emitted one heartfelt word. "Sod."

There was a sudden commotion at the door and the chauffeur plunged into the room with Margaret trying to cling to one arm. He threw her effortlessly out of his way and shaped up to do the same to me.

"What has happened?" he demanded threateningly. "What are you doing to the son?" His voice sent a shiver up my spine. If he wasn't one of the rubber faces, he sounded exactly like it.

Alessandro spoke from the sofa with tiredness in his voice; and he spoke in Italian, which, thanks to a one-time girl friend, I more or less understood.

"Stop, Carlo. Go back to the car. Wait for me. The horse threw me. Neil Griffon will not harm me. Go back to the car, and wait for me."

Carlo moved his head to and fro like a baffled bull, but finally subsided and did as he was told. Three *sotto-voce* cheers for the discipline of the Rivera household.

"A doctor is coming to see you," I said.

"I do not want a doctor."

"You're not leaving that sofa until I'm certain there is nothing wrong with you."

He sneered. "Afraid of my father?"

"Think what you like," I said; and he obviously did.

The doctor, when he came, turned out to be the same one who had once diagnosed my mumps, measles, and chicken pox. Old now, with overactive lachrymal glands and hesitant speech, he did not in the least appeal to his present patient. Alessandro treated him rudely, and got back courtesy where he deserved a smart kick.

"Nothing much wrong with the lad" was the verdict. "But he'd better stay in bed today, and rest tomorrow. That'll put you right, young man, eh?"

The young man glared back ungratefully and didn't answer. The old doctor turned to me, gave me a tolerant smile, and said to let him know if the lad had any aftereffects, like dizziness or headaches.

"Old fool," said the lad audibly as I showed the doctor out; and when I went back Alessandro was already on his feet.

"Can I go now?" he asked sarcastically.

"As far and for as long as you like," I agreed.

His eyes narrowed. "You are not getting rid of me."

"Pity," I said.

After a short furious silence, he walked a little unsteadily past me and out the door. I went into the office and with Margaret watched through the window while the chauffeur bustled around, settling him comfortably into the back seat of the Mercedes; and presently, without looking back, he drove "the son" away.

"Is he all right?" Margaret asked.

"Shaken, not stirred," I said flippantly, and she laughed. But she followed the car with her eyes until it turned left down Bury Road.

He stayed away the following day but came back on the Thursday morning in time for the first lot. I was up in the top part of the yard talking to Etty when the car arrived. Her pleasant expression changed to the one of tight-lipped dislike which she always wore when Alessandro was near her, and when she saw him erupting athletically from the back seat and striding purposefully toward us, she discovered something that urgently needed seeing to in one of the bays farther down.

Alessandro noted her flight with a twist of scorn on his lips, and widened it into an irritating smirk as a greeting to me. He held out a small flat tin box, identical with the one he had presented before.

"Message for you," he said. All the cockiness was back *fortissimo,* and I would have known even without the tin that he had again been to see his father. He had recharged his malice like a battery plugged into the mains.

"Do you know what is in it, this time?"

He hesitated. "No," he said. And I believed him, because his ignorance seemed to annoy him. The tin was fastened round the edge with adhesive tape. Alessandro, with the superior smirk still in place, watched me pull it off. I rolled the tape into a small sticky ball and put it in my pocket; then carefully I opened the tin.

There was another little wooden horse between two thin layers of cotton wool.

It had a label round its neck.

It had a broken leg.

I didn't know what exactly was in my face when I looked up at Alessandro, but the smirk deteriorated into a half-anxious bravado.

"He said you wouldn't like it," he remarked defiantly.

"Come with me, then," I said abruptly. "And see if you do." I set off up the yard toward the drive, but he didn't follow; and before I reached my destination I was met by George hurrying toward me with a distressed face and worried eyes.

"Mr. Neil, Indigo's got cast and broken a leg in his box—same as Moonrock. You wouldn't think it could happen, not to two old'uns like them, not ten days apart."

"No, you wouldn't," I said grimly, and walked back with him into Indigo's box, stuffing the vicious message in its tin into my jacket pocket.

The nice-natured gelding was lying in the straw trying feebly to stand up. He kept lifting his head and pushing at the floor with one of his forefeet, but all strength seemed to have left him. The other forefoot lay uselessly bent at an unnatural angle, snapped through just above the pastern.

I squatted down beside the poor old horse and patted his neck. He lifted his head again and thrashed to get back onto his feet, then flopped limply back into the straw. His eyes looked glazed, and he was dribbling.

"Nothing to be done, George," I said. "I'll go and telephone the vet." I put only regret into my voice and kept my boiling fury to myself. George nodded resignedly but without much emotion; like every older stableman, he had seen a lot of horses die.

The young chubby Dainsee got out of his bath to answer the telephone.

"Not another one!" he exclaimed when I told him.

"I'm afraid so. And would you bring with you any gear you need for doing a blood test?"

"Whatever for?"

"I'll tell you when you get here."

"Oh." He sounded surprised, but willing to go along. "All right, then. Half a jiffy while I swap the bath towel for my natty suiting."

He came in jeans and his dirty Land-Rover twenty minutes later. Bounced out onto the gravel, nodded cheerfully, and turned at once toward Indigo's box. George was along there with the horse, but the rest of the yard stood quiet and empty. Etty, showing distress at the imminent loss of her lead horse, had taken the string down to Southfields on the racecourse side, and Alessandro presumably had gone with her, as he was nowhere about, and his chauffeur was waiting as usual in the car.

Indigo was up on his feet. George, holding him by the head-collar, said that the old boy just suddenly seemed to get his strength back and stood up, and he'd been eating some hay since then, and it was a right shame he'd got cast, that it was. I nodded and took the head-collar from him, and told him I'd see to Indigo, and he could go and get on with putting the oats through the crushing machine ready for the morning feeds.

"He makes a good yard man," Dainsee said. "Old George, he was deputy head gardener once at the Viceroy's palace in India. It accounts for all those tidy flower beds and tubs of pretty shrubs which charm the owners when they visit the yard."

I was surprised. "I didn't know that."

"Odd world." He soothed Indigo with a touch, and peered closely at the broken leg. "What's all this about a blood test?" he asked, straightening up and eying me with speculation.

"Do vets have a keep-mum tradition?"

His gaze sharpened into active curiosity. "Professional secrets, like doctors and lawyers? Yes, sure we do. As long as it's not a matter of keeping quiet about a spot of foot-and-mouth."

"Nothing like that." I hesitated. "I'd like you to run a private blood test. Could that be done?"

"How private? It'll have to go to the Equine Research Labs. I can't do it myself, haven't got the equipment."

"Just a blood sample, with no horse's name attached."

"Oh, sure. That happens all the time. But you can't really think anyone *doped* the poor old horse!"

"I think he was given an anesthetic," I said. "And that his leg was broken on purpose."

"Oh, glory." His mouth was rounded into an O of astonishment, but the eyes flickered with the rapidity of his thoughts. "You seem sane enough," he said finally, "so let's have a look-see."

He squatted down beside the affected limb and ran his fingers very lightly over the skin. Indigo shifted under his touch and ducked and raised his head violently.

"All right, old fellow," Dainsee said, standing up again and patting his neck. He raised his eyebrows at me. "Can't say you're wrong, can't say you're right." He paused, thinking it over. The eyebrows rose and fell several times, like punctuations. "Tell you what," he said, at length. "I've got a portable X-ray machine back home. I'll bring it along, and we'll take a picture. How's that?"

"Very good idea," I said, pleased.

"Right." He opened his case, which he had parked just inside the door. "Then I'll just freeze that leg, so he'll be in no discomfort until I come back." He brought out a hypodermic and held it up against the light, beginning to press the plunger.

"Do the blood test first," I said.

"Eh?" He blinked at me. "Oh, yes, of course. Golly,

yes, of course. Silly of me." He laughed gently, laid down the first syringe, and put together a much larger one, empty.

He took the sample from the jugular vein, which he found and pierced efficiently first time of asking. "Bit of luck," he murmured in self-deprecation, and drew half a tumblerful of blood into the syringe. "Have to give the lab people enough to work on, you know," he said, seeing my surprise. "You can't get reliable results from a thimbleful."

"I suppose not."

He packed the sample into his case, shot the freezing local into Indigo's near fore, nodded and blinked with undiminished cheerfulness, and smartly departed. Indigo, totally unconcerned, went back contentedly to his haynet, and I with bottled anger went into the house.

The label on the little wooden horse had "INDIGO" printed in capitals on one side of it, and on the other, also in capitals, a short sharp message: "TO HURT MY SON IS TO INVITE DESTRUCTION."

Neither George nor Etty saw any sense in the vet going away without putting Indigo down.

"Er . . . ," I said. "He found he didn't have the humane killer with him, after all. He thought it was in his bag, but it wasn't."

"Oh," they said, satisfied, and Etty told me that everything had gone well on the gallop and that Lucky Lindsay had worked a fast five furlongs and afterward wouldn't have blown out a candle.

"I put that bloody little Alex on Clip Clop and told him to take him along steadily, and he damn well disobeyed me. He shook him into a full gallop and left Lancat standing, and the touts' binoculars were working overtime."

"Stupid little fool," I said. "I'll speak to him."

"He takes every opportunity he can to cross me," she complained. "When you aren't there, he's absolutely insufferable." She took a deep, troubled breath, considering. "In fact, I think you should tell Mr. Griffon that we can't keep him."

"Next time I go to the hospital, I'll see what he says," I said. "What are you giving him to ride second lot?"

"Pulitzer," she replied promptly. "It doesn't matter so much if he doesn't do as he's told on that one."

"When you get back, tell him I want to see him before he leaves."

"Aren't you coming?"

I shook my head. "I'll stay and see to Indigo."

"I rather wanted your opinion of Pease Pudding. If he's to run in the Lincoln, we ought to give him a trial this week or next. The race is only three weeks on Saturday, don't forget."

"We could give him a half-speed gallop tomorrow and see if he's ready for a full trial," I suggested, and she grudgingly agreed that one more day would do no harm.

I watched the trim jodhpured figure walk off toward her cottage for breakfast, and would have felt flattered that she wanted my opinion had I not known why. Under an umbrella, she worked marvelously; out in the open, she felt rudderless. Even though in her heart she knew she knew more than I did, her shelter instinct had cast me as decision maker. What I needed now was a crash course in how to tell when a horse was fit. And that old joke about a crash course for pilots edged itself into a corner of my mind, like a thin gleam in the gloom.

Dainsee came back in his Land-Rover when the string had gone out for second lot, and we ran the cable for the X-ray machine through the office window and plugged it into the socket which served the mushroom heater. There seemed to be unending reinforcements of cable; it took four lengths plugged together to reach to Indigo's box, but their owner assured me that he could manage a quarter of a mile, if pushed.

He took three X-rays of the dangling leg, packed everything up again, and, almost as a passing thought, put poor old Indigo out of his troubles.

"You'll want evidence for the police," Dainsee said, shaking hands and blinking rapidly.

"No. I shan't bother the police. Not yet, anyway." He opened his mouth to protest, so I went straight on, "There are very good reasons. I can't tell you them, but they do exist."

"Oh, well, it's up to you." His eyes slid sidewise toward Moonrock's box, and his eyebrows asked the question.

"I don't know," I said. "What do you think? Looking back."

He thought for several seconds, which meant he was serious, and then said, "It would have taken a good heavy blow to smash that hock. Wouldn't have thought anyone would bother, while a pastern like Indigo's would be simple."

"Moonrock just provided the idea for Indigo?" I suggested.

"I should think so." He smiled grimly. "Mind it doesn't become an epidemic."

"I'll mind," I said thinly; and knew I would have to.

Alessandro showed no sign that Etty had given him my message about wanting to see him. He strode straight out of the yard toward his waiting car, and it was only because I happened to be looking out the office window that I caught him.

I opened the window and called to him. "Alessandro, come here a minute."

He forged straight on as if he hadn't heard, so I added, "To talk about your first races."

He stopped in one stride with a foot left in the air in indecision, then changed direction and came slowly toward the window.

"Go round into the owners' room," I said. "Where you were lying on the sofa." I shut the window, gave

Margaret a whimsically rueful placating smile, which could mean whatever she thought it did, and removed myself from earshot.

Alessandro came unwillingly into the owners' room, knowing that he had been hooked. I played fair, however.

"You can have a ride in an apprentice race at Catterick in four weeks. On Pulitzer. And on condition that you don't go bragging about it in the yard and antagonizing all the other boys."

"I want to ride Archangel," he said flatly.

"It sometimes seems to me that you are remarkably intelligent and, with a great deal of application, might become a passable jockey," I said and, before his self-satisfaction smothered him, added, "and sometimes, like today, you behave so stupidly, and with such little understanding of what it takes to be what you want to be, that your ambitions look pathetic."

The thin body stiffened rigidly and the black eyes glared. Since I undoubtedly had his full attention, I made the most of it.

"These horses are here to win races. They won't win races if their training program is hashed up. If you are told to do a half-speed gallop on Clip Clop and you work him flat out and tire him beyond his capacity, you are helping to make sure he takes longer to prepare. You won't win races unless the stable does, so it is in your own interest to help train the horses to the best of your ability. Disobeying riding orders is therefore just plain stupid. Do you follow?"

The black eyes looked blacker and sank into the sockets. He didn't answer.

"Then there is this fixation of yours about Archangel. I'll let you ride him on the Heath as soon as you show you are good enough, and in particular responsible enough, to look after him. Whether you ever ride him in a race is up to you more than me. But I'm doing you a favor in starting you off on less well-known horses at smaller meetings. You may think you are brilliant, but you have only ridden against amateurs. I am giving you a chance to prove what you can do against professionals in private, and lessening the risk of you falling flat on your face at Newbury or Kempton."

The eyes were unwavering. He still said nothing.

"And Indigo," I went on, taking a grip on my anger and turning it out cold and biting, "Indigo may have been of no use to you because he no longer raced, but if you cause the death of any more of the horses, there will be just one less for you to win on."

He moved his jaw as if with an effort.

"I didn't—cause the death of Indigo."

I took the tin out of my pocket and gave it to him. He opened it slowly, compressed his mouth at the contents, and read the label.

"I didn't want . . . I didn't mean him to kill Indigo." The supercilious smile had all gone. He was still hostile, but defensive. "He was angry because Traffic had thrown me."

"Did you mean him to kill Traffic, then?"

"No, I did not," he said vehemently. "As you said, what would be the point of killing a horse I could win a race on?"

"But to kill harmless old Indigo because you bumped your head off a horse you yourself insisted on riding," I said with bitter sarcasm.

His gaze, for the first time, switched to the carpet. He was not too proud of himself.

"You didn't tell him," I guessed. "You didn't tell him that you insisted on riding Traffic."

"Miss Craig told me to," he said sullenly.

"Not the time he threw you."

He looked up again, and I would have sworn he was unhappy. "I didn't tell my father I was knocked out."

"Who did?"

"Carlo. The chauffeur."

"You could have explained that I did not try to harm you."

The unhappiness turned to a shade of desperation.

"You have met my father," he said. "It isn't always possible to tell him things, especially when he is angry. He will give me anything I ask for, but I cannot talk to him."

He went away and left me speechless.

He couldn't talk to his father.

Enso would give Alessandro anything he wanted, would smash a path for him at considerable trouble to himself, and would persist as long as Alessandro hungered, but they couldn't talk.

And I . . . I could lie and scheme and walk a tightrope to save my father's stables for him.

But talk with him, no, I couldn't.

8

"Did you know," Margaret said, looking up casually from her typewriter, "that Alessandro is living down the road at the Forbury Inn?"

"No, I didn't," I said. "But it doesn't surprise me. It goes with a chauffeur-driven Mercedes, after all."

"He has a double room to himself with a private bathroom, and doesn't eat enough to keep a bird alive."

"How do you know all this?"

"Susie brought a friend home from school for tea yesterday, and she turned out to be the daughter of the resident receptionist at the Forbury Inn."

"Any more fascinating intimate details?" I asked.

She smiled. "Alessandro puts on a track suit every afternoon and goes off in a car, and when he comes back he is all sweaty and has a very hot bath with nice smelly oil in it."

"The receptionist's daughter is how old?"

"Seven."

"Proper little snooper."

"All children are observant. . . . And she also said

that he never talks to anyone if he can avoid it except to his chauffeur in a funny language—"

"Italian," I murmured.

". . . and that nobody likes him very much because he is pretty rude, but they like the chauffeur still less because he is even ruder."

I pondered. "Do you think," I said, "that via your daughter, via her school chum, via her receptionist parent, we could find out if Alessandro gave any sort of home address when he registered?"

"Why don't you just ask him?" she said reasonably.

"Ah," I said. "But our Alessandro is sometimes a mite contrary. Didn't you ask him when you completed his indentures?"

"He said they were moving, and had no address."

"Mm." I nodded.

"How extraordinary. . . . I can't see why he won't tell you. Well, yes, I'll ask Susie's chum if she knows."

"Great," I said, and pinned little hope on it.

Gillie wanted to come and stay at Rowley Lodge.

"How about the homeless orphans?" I said.

"I could take some weeks off. I always can. You know that. And now that you've stopped wandering round industrial towns living in one hotel after another, we could spend a bit more time together."

I kissed her nose. Ordinarily I would have welcomed her proposal. I looked at her with affection.

"No," I said. "Not just now."

"When, then?"

"In the summer."

She made a face at me, her eyes full of intelligence. "You never like to be cluttered when you are deeply involved in something."

"You're not clutter." I smiled.

"I'm afraid so. That's why you've never married. Not like most bachelors because they want to be free to sleep with any offered girl, but because you don't like your mind distracted."

"I'm here," I pointed out, kissing her again.

"For one night in seven. And only then because you had to come most of the way to see your father."

"My father gets visited because he's on the way to you."

"Liar," she said agreeably. "The best you can say is that it's two cats with one stone."

"Birds."

"Well, birds, then."

"Let's go eat," I said; opened the front door and closed it behind us, and packed her into the Jensen.

"Did you know that Aristotle Onassis had earned himself a whole million by the time he was twenty-eight?"

"No, I didn't know," I said.

"He beat you," she said. "By four times as much."

"He's four times the man."

Her eyes slid sidewise toward me and a smile hovered in the air. "He may be."

We stopped for a red light and then turned left beside a church with a notice board saying, "These doth the Lord hate: a proud look, a lying tongue. Proverbs 6:16–17."

"Which proverb do you think is the most stupid?" she asked.

"Um. . . . Bird in the hand is worth two in the bush."

"Why ever?"

"Because if you build a cage round the bush, you get a whole flock."

"As long as the two birds aren't both the same sex."

"You think of everything," I said admiringly.

"Oh, I try. I try."

We went up to the top of the Post Office Tower and revolved three and a half times during dinner.

"It said in the *Times* today that that paper firm you advised last autumn has gone bust," she said.

"Well. . . ." I grinned. "They didn't take my advice."

"Silly old them. What was it?"

"To sack ninety percent of the management, get

some new accountants, and make peace with the unions."

"So simple, really." Her mouth twitched.

"They said they couldn't do it, of course."

"And you said?"

"Prepare to meet thy doom."

"How Biblical."

"Or words to that effect."

"Think of all those poor people thrown out of work," she said. "It can't be funny when a firm goes bust."

"The firm had hired people all along in the wrong proportions. By last autumn, they had only two productive workers for every one on the clerical, executive, and maintenance staff. Also the unions were vetoing automation, and insisting that every time a worker left another should be hired in his place."

She pensively bit into pâté and toast. "It doesn't sound as if it could have been saved at all."

"Yes, it could," I said reflectively. "But it often seems to me that people in a firm would rather see the whole ship sink than throw out half the crew and stay afloat."

"Fairer to everyone if they all drown?"

"Only the firm drowns. The people swim off and make sure they overload someone else's raft."

She licked her fingers. "You used to find sick firms fascinating."

"I still do," I said, surprised.

She shook her head. "Disillusion has been creeping in for a long time."

I looked back, considering. "It's usually quite easy to see what's wrong. But there's often a stone-wall resistance on both sides to putting it right. Always dozens of reasons why change is impossible."

"Russell Arletti rang me up yesterday," she said casually.

"Did he really?"

She nodded. "He wanted me to persuade you to

leave Newmarket and do a job for him. A big one, he said."

"I can't," I said positively.

"He's taking me out to dinner on Tuesday evening to discuss, as he put it, how to wean you from the gee-gees."

"Tell him to save himself the price of a meal."

"Well, no." She wrinkled her nose. "I might just be hungry again by Tuesday. I'll go out with him. I like him. But I think I'll spend the evening preparing him for the worst."

"What worst?"

"That you won't ever be going back to work for him again."

"Gillie . . ."

"It was only a phase," she said, looking out the window at the sparkle of the million lights slowly sliding by below us. "It was just that you'd cashed in your antique chips and you weren't exactly starving, and Russell netted you on the wing, so to speak, with an interesting diversion. But you've been getting tired of it recently. You've been restless, and too full of—I don't know—too full of power. I think that after you've played with the gee-gees you'll break out in a great gust and build a new empire—much bigger than before."

"Have some wine?" I said ironically.

"And you may scoff, Neil Griffon, but you've been letting your Onassis instinct go to rust."

"Not a bad thing, really."

"You could be creating jobs for thousands of people, instead of trotting round a small town in a pair of jodhpurs."

"There's six million quids' worth in that stable," I said slowly; and felt the germ of an idea lurch, as it sometimes did, across the ganglions.

"What are you thinking about?" she demanded. "What are you thinking about at this moment?"

"The genesis of ideas."

She gave a sigh that was half a laugh. "And that's exactly why you'll never marry me, either."

"What do you mean?"

"You like the *Times* crossword more than sex."

"Not more," I said. "First."

"Do you want me to marry you?"

She kissed my shoulder under the sheet.

"Would you?"

"I thought you were fed up with marriage." I moved my mouth against her forehead. "I thought Jeremy had put you off it for life."

"He wasn't like you."

He wasn't like you. . . . She said it often. Any time her husband's name cropped up. He wasn't like you.

The first time she said it, three months after I met her, I asked the obvious question.

"What was he like?"

"Fair, not dark. Willowy, not compact. A bit taller: six feet two. Outwardly more fun; inwardly infinitely more boring. He didn't want a wife so much as an admiring audience . . . and I got tired of the play." She paused. "And when Jennifer died . . ."

She had not talked about her ex-husband before that, and had always shied painfully away from the thought of her daughter. She went on, in a careful emotionless quiet voice, half muffled against my skin.

"Jennifer was killed in front of me . . . by a youth in a leather jacket on a motorcycle. We were crossing the road. He came roaring round the corner doing sixty in a built-up area. He just . . . plowed into her. . . ." A long shuddering pause. "She was eight . . . and super." She swallowed. "The boy had no insurance. . . . Jeremy raved on and on about it, as if money could have compensated . . . and we didn't need money; he'd inherited almost as much as I had. . . ." Another pause. "So anyway, after that, when he found someone else and drifted off, I was glad, really. . . ."

Though passing time had done its healing, she still

had dreams about Jennifer. Sometimes she cried when she woke up, because of Jennifer.

I smoothed her shining hair. "I'd make a lousy husband."

"Oh. . . ." She took a shaky breath. "I know that. Two and a half years I've known you, and you've blown in every millennium or so, to say hi."

"But stayed awhile."

"I'll grant you."

"So what do you want?" I asked. "Would you rather be married?"

She smiled contentedly. "We'll go on as we are—if you like."

"I do like." I switched off the light.

"As long as you prove it now and again," she added unnecessarily.

"I wouldn't let anyone else hang pink-and-green curtains against ocher walls in my bedroom," I said.

"My bedroom. I rent it."

"You're in arrears. By at least eighteen months."

"I'll pay up tomorrow. . . . Hey, what are you doing?"

"I'm a businessman," I murmured, "getting down to business."

When I saw my father next, he did not make it easy for me to start a new era in father-son relationships.

He told me that as I did not seem to be making much progress in engaging someone else to take over the stable, he was going to find someone himself. By telephone.

He said he had done some of the entries for the next two weeks, and that Margaret was to type them out and send them off.

He said that Pease Pudding was to be taken out of the Lincoln.

He said that I had brought him the '64 half bottles of Bollinger, and he preferred the '61.

"You are feeling better, then," I said into the first real gap of the monologue.

"What? Oh, yes, I suppose I am. Now, did you hear what I said? Pease Pudding is not to go in the Lincoln."

"Why ever not?"

He gave me an irritated look. "How do you expect him to be ready?"

"Etty is a good judge. She says he will be."

"I will not have Rowley Lodge made to look stupid by running hopelessly undertrained horses in important races."

"If Pease Pudding runs badly, people will only say that it shows how good a trainer you are yourself."

"That is not the point," he said repressively.

I opened one of the half bottles and poured the golden bubbles into his favorite Jacobean glass, which I had brought for the purpose. Champagne would not have tasted right to him from a tooth mug. He took a sip and evidently found the '64 was bearable after all, though he didn't say so.

"The point," he explained as if to a moron, "is the stud fees. If he runs badly, his future value at stud is what will be affected."

"Yes, I understand that."

"Don't be silly, how can you? You know nothing about it."

I sat down in the visitors' armchair, leaned back, crossed my legs, and put into my voice all the reasonableness and weight which I had learned to project into industrial discussions, but which I had never before had the sense to use on my father.

"Rowley Lodge is heading for some financial rocks," I said, "and the cause of it is too much prestige-hunting. You are scared of running Pease Pudding in the Lincoln because you own a half share in him, and if he runs badly it will be your own capital investment, as well as Lady Vector's, that will suffer."

He spilled some champagne on his sheet, and didn't notice it.

I went on, "I know that it is quite normal for people to own shares in the horses they train. At Rowley Lodge just now, however, you own too many part shares for safety. I imagine you collected so many because you could not bear to see rival stables acquiring what you judged to be the next crop of world-beaters, so that you probably said to your owners something like 'If Archangel goes for forty thousand at auction and that's too much for you, I'll put up twenty thousand towards it.' So you've gathered together one of the greatest strings in the country, and their potential stud value is enormous."

He gazed at me blankly, forgetting to drink.

"This is fine," I said, "as long as the horses do win as expected. And year after year, they do. You've been pursuing this policy in moderation for a very long time, and it's made you steadily richer. But now, this year, you've overextended. You've bought too many. As all the part owners only pay part training fees, the receipts are not now covering the expenses. Not by quite a long way. As a result, the cash balance at the bank is draining away like bath water, and there are still three weeks to go before the first race, let alone the resale of the successful animals for stud. This dicey situation is complicated by your broken leg, your assistant being still in a coma from which he is unlikely to recover, and your stable apparently stagnating in the hands of a son who doesn't know how to train the horses; and all that is why you are scared silly of running Pease Pudding in the Lincoln."

I stopped for reactions. There weren't any. Just shock.

"You can, on the whole, stop worrying," I said, and knew that things would never again be quite as they had been between us. Thirty-four, I thought ruefully; I had had to be thirty-four before I entered this particular arena on equal terms. "I could sell your half share before the race."

Wheels slowly began to turn again behind his eyes.

He blinked. Stared at his sloping champagne and straightened the glass.

"How—how do you know all this?" There was more resentment in his voice than anxiety.

"I looked at the account books."

"No. . . . I mean, who told you?"

"No one needed to tell me. My job for the last six years has involved reading account books and doing sums."

He recovered enough to take some judicious sips.

"At least you do understand why it is imperative we get an experienced trainer to take over until I can get about again."

"There's no need for one," I said incautiously. "I've been there for three weeks now—"

"And do you suppose that you can learn how to train race horses in three weeks?" he asked with reviving contempt.

"Since you ask," I said, "yes." And before he turned purple, tacked on, "I was born to it, if you remember. I grew up there. I find, much to my own surprise, that it is second nature."

He saw this statement more as a threat than as a reassurance. "You're not staying on after I get back."

"No." I smiled. "Nothing like that."

He grunted. Hesitated. Gave in. He didn't say in so many words that I could carry on, but just ignored the whole subject from that point.

"I don't want to sell my half of Pease Pudding."

"Draw up a list of those you don't mind selling, then," I said. "About ten of them, for a start."

"And just who do you think is going to buy them? New owners don't grow on trees, you know. And half shares are harder to sell. Owners like to see their names in the race cards and in the press."

"I know a lot of businessmen," I said, "who would be glad to have a race horse but who actively shun the publicity. You pick out ten horses, and I'll sell your half shares."

He didn't say he would, but he picked them out, then and there. I ran my eye down the finished list and saw only one to disagree with.

"Don't sell Lancat," I said.

He bristled. "I know what I'm doing."

"He's going to be good as a three-year-old," I said. "I see from the form book that he was no great shakes at two, and if you sell now you'll not get back what you paid. He's looking very well, and I think he'll win quite a lot."

"Rubbish. You don't know what you're talking about."

"All right. . . . How much would you accept for your half?"

He pursed his lips, thinking about it. "Four thousand. You should be able to get four, with his breeding. He cost twelve, altogether, as a yearling."

"You'd better suggest prices for all of them," I said. "If you wouldn't mind."

He didn't mind. I folded the list, put it in my pocket, picked up the entry forms he had written on, and prepared to go. He held out to me the champagne glass, empty.

"Have some of this. . . . I can't manage it all."

I took the glass, refilled it, and drank a mouthful. The bubbles popped round my teeth. He watched. His expression was as severe as ever, but he nodded, sharply, twice. Not as symbolic a gesture as a pipe of peace, but just as much of an acknowledgment, in its way.

On Monday morning, tapping away, Margaret said, "Susie's friend's mum says she has just happened to see Alessandro's passport."

"Which just happened," I said dryly, "to be well hidden away in Alessandro's bedroom."

"Let us not stare at gift horses."

"Let us not," I agreed.

"Susie's friend's mum says that the address on the

passport was not in Italy, but in Switzerland. A place called Bastagnola. Is that any use?"

"I hope Susie's friend's mum won't lose her job."

"I doubt it," Margaret said. "She hops into bed with the manager when his wife goes shopping in Cambridge."

"How do you know?"

Her eyes laughed. "Susie's friend told me."

I telephoned to an importer of cameras who owed me a favor and asked him if he had any contacts in the town of Bastagnola.

"Not myself. But I could establish one, if it's important."

"I want any information anyone can dig up about a man called Enso Rivera. As much information as possible."

He wrote it down and spelled it back. "See what I can do," he said.

He rang two days later and sounded subdued.

"I'll be sending you an astronomical bill for European phone calls."

"That's all right."

"An awful lot of people didn't want to talk about your man. I met an exceptional amount of resistance."

"Is he Mafia, then?" I asked.

"No. Not Mafia. In fact, he and the Mafia are not on speaking terms. On stabbing terms, maybe, but not speaking. There seems to be some sort of truce between them." He paused.

"Go on," I said.

"Well. . . . As far as I can gather—and I wouldn't swear to it—he is a sort of receiver of stolen property. Most of it in the form of currency, but some gold and silver and precious stones from melted-down jewelry. I heard—and it was at third hand from a high-up policeman, so you can believe it or not, as you like—that Rivera accepts the stuff, sells or exchanges it, takes a large commission, and banks the rest in Swiss accounts which he opens up for his clients. They can collect their money any time they like ... and it is believed that he has an almost world-wide connection. But all this goes on behind a supposedly legitimate business as a dealer in watches. They've never managed to bring him to court. They can never get witnesses to testify."

"You've done marvels," I said.

"There's a bit more." He cleared his throat. "He has a son, apparently, that no one cares to cross. Rivera has been known to ruin people who don't immediately do what the son wants. He only has this one child. He is reputed to have deserted his wife. ... Well, a lot of Italian men do that."

"He is Italian, then?"

"By birth, yes. He's lived in Switzerland for about fifteen years, though. Look, I don't know if you're intending to do business with him, but I got an unmistakable warning from several people to steer clear of him. They say he's dangerous. They say if you fall foul of him you wake up dead. Either that, or—well, I know you'll laugh—but there's a sort of superstition that if he looks your way you'll break a bone."

I didn't laugh. Not a chuckle.

Almost as soon as I put the receiver down, the telephone rang again. Dainsee.

"I've got your X-ray pictures in front of me," he said. "But they're inconclusive, I'm afraid. It just looks a pretty ordinary fracture. There's a certain amount of longitudinal splitting, but then there often is with cannon bones."

"What would be the simplest way to break a bone on purpose?" I asked.

"Twist it," he said promptly. "Put it under stress. A bone under stress would snap quite easily if you gave it a bang. Ask any footballer or any skater. Stress, that's what does it."

"You can't see stress on the X-rays. ..."

"Afraid not. Can't rule it out, though. Can't rule it in, either. Sorry."

"It can't be helped."

"But the blood test," he said. "I've had the results, and you were bang on target."

"Anesthetic?"

"Yep. Some brand of promazine. Sparine, probably."

"I'm no wiser," I said. "How would you give it to a horse?"

"Injection," Dainsee said. "Very simple intramuscular injection, nothing difficult. Just punch the needle in anywhere handy. It's often used to shoot into mania patients in mental hospitals when they're raving. Puts them out for hours."

Something about promazine rang a highly personal note.

"Does the stuff work instantly?" I asked.

"If you give it intravenously, it would. But intramuscularly, what it's equally designed for, it would take a few minutes, probably. Ten to fifteen minutes on a human; don't know for a horse."

"If you injected it into a human, could you do it through clothes?"

"Oh, sure. As I said. They use it as a standby in mental hospitals. They wouldn't get people in a manic state to sit nice and quiet and roll their sleeves up."

9

For two weeks, the status of Rowley Lodge remained approximately quo.

I heavily amended my father's entry forms and sent them in, and sold six of the half shares to various acquaintances, without offering Lancat to any of them.

Margaret took to wearing green eye shadow, and Susie's friend reported that Alessandro had made a telephone call to Switzerland and didn't wear pajamas. Also that the chauffeur always paid for everything, as Alessandro didn't have any money.

Etty grew more tense as the beginning of the season drew nearer, and lines of anxiety seldom left her forehead. I was leaving a great deal more to her judgment than my father did, and she was in consequence feeling insecure. She openly ached for his return.

The horses, all the same, were working well. We had no further mishaps except that a two-year-old filly developed severe sinus trouble, and as far as I could judge from watching the performances of the forty-five other stables using Newmarket Heath, the Rowley Lodge string was as forward as any.

Alessandro turned up day after day and silently rode what and how Etty told him to, though with a ramrod spine of protest. He said no more about not taking orders from a woman, and I imagined that even he could see that without Etty there would be fewer winners on the horizon. She herself had almost stopped complaining about him and was watching him with a more objective eye, because there was no doubt that after a month's concentrated practice he was riding better than the other apprentices.

He was also growing visibly thinner, and no longer looked well. Small-framed though he might be, the six stone seven pounds that he was aiming to shrink his body down to was punitive for five foot four.

Alessandro's fanaticism was an awkward factor. If I had imagined that by making the going as rough as I dared he would give up his idle fancy and depart, I had been wrong. This was no idle fancy. It was revealing itself all too clearly as a consuming ambition: an ambition strong enough to make him starve himself, take orders from a woman, and perform what were evidently miracles of self-discipline, considering that it was probably the first time in his life that he had had to use any.

Against Etty's wishes, I put him up one morning on Archangel.

"He's not ready for that," she protested when I told her I was going to.

"There isn't another lad in the yard who will take more care of him," I said.

"But he hasn't the experience."

"He has, you know. Archangel is only more valuable, not more difficult to ride, than the others."

Alessandro received the news not with joy but with an "at last" expression, more scorn than patience. We went down to the Waterhall Center, away from public gaze, and there Archangel did a fast six furlongs and pulled up looking as if he had just walked out of his box.

"He had him balanced," I said to Etty. "All the way."

"Yes, he did," she said grudgingly. "Pity he's such an obnoxious little squirt."

Alessandro returned with an "I told you so" face, which I wiped off by saying he would be switched to Lancat tomorrow.

"Why?" he demanded furiously. "I rode Archangel very well."

"Well enough," I agreed. "And you can ride him again, in a day or two. But I want you to ride Lancat in a trial on Wednesday, so you can go out on him tomorrow, as well, and get used to him. And after the trial I want you to tell me your opinion of the horse and how he went. And I don't want one of your short sneering comments, but a thought-out assessment. It is almost as important for a jockey to be able to analyze what a horse has done in a race as ride it. Trainers depend quite a lot on what their jockeys can tell them. So you can tell me about Lancat, and I'll listen."

He gave me a long concentrating stare, but for once without the habitual superciliousness.

"All right," he said. "I will."

We held the trial on the Wednesday afternoon on the trial ground past the Limekilns, a long way out of Newmarket. Much to Etty's disgust, I had timed the trial to start at exactly the same moment as the Champion Hurdle started at Cheltenham, and she wanted to watch it on television. But the stratagem worked. We achieved the well-nigh impossible, a full-scale trial without an observer or a tout in sight.

Apart from the two Etty and I rode, we took only four horses along; Pease Pudding, Lancat, Archangel, and one of the previous year's most prolific winners, a four-year-old colt called Subito, whose best distance was a mile. Tommy Hoylake drove up from his home in Berkshire to ride Pease Pudding, and we put Andy on Archangel and a taciturn lad called Faddy on the chestnut Subito.

"Don't murder them," I said before they started. "If you feel them falter, just ease off."

Four nods. Four fidgeting colts, glossy and eager.

Etty and I hacked round to within a hundred yards of where the trial ground ended, and when we had pulled up in a useful position for watching, she waved a large white handkerchief above her head. The horses started toward us, moving fast and still accelerating, with the riders crouched forward on their withers, heads down, reins very short, feet against the horses' moving shoulders.

They passed still going all out, and pulled up a little farther on. Archangel and Pease Pudding ran the whole gallop stride for stride, and finished together. Lancat, from starting level, lost ten lengths, made up eight, lost two again, but still moved easily. Subito was ahead of Lancat at the beginning, behind him when he moved up quickly, and alongside when they passed Etty and me.

She turned to me with a deeply worried expression.

"Pease Pudding can't be ready for the Lincoln if Lancat can finish so near him. In fact, the way Lancat finished means that neither Archangel nor Subito are as far on as I thought."

"Calm down, Etty," I said. "Relax. Take it easy. Just turn it the other way round."

She frowned. "I don't understand you. Mr. Griffon will be very worried when he hears—"

"Etty," I interrupted. "Did Pease Pudding, or did he not, seem to you to be moving fast and easily?"

"Well, yes, I suppose so," she said doubtfully.

"Then it may be Lancat who is much better than you expected, not the others who are worse."

She looked at me, her face screwed up with indecision. "But Alex is only an apprentice, and Lancat was useless last year."

"In what way was he useless?"

"Oh . . . sprawly. Babyish. Had no action."

"Nothing sprawly about him today," I pointed out.

"No," she admitted slowly. "You're right. There wasn't."

The riders walked toward us, leading the horses, and Etty and I dismounted to hear what they had to say. Tommy Hoylake, built like a twelve-year-old boy with a forty-three-year-old man's face sitting incongruously on top, said, in his comfortable Berkshire accent, that he had thought that Pease Pudding had run an excellent trial until he saw Lancat pulling up so close behind him. He had ridden Lancat a good deal the previous year, and hadn't thought much of him.

Andy said Archangel went beautifully, considering the Guineas was nearly six weeks away, and Faddy, in his high-pitched finicky voice, said Subito had only been a pound or two behind Pease Pudding last year, in his opinion, and he could have been nearer to him if he had really tried. Tommy and Andy shook their heads. If they had really tried, they, too, could have gone faster.

"Alessandro?" I said.

He hesitated. "I—I lost ground at the beginning because I didn't realize— I didn't expect them to go so fast. When I asked him, Lancat just shot forward— and I could have kept him nearer to Archangel at the end, only he did seem to tire a bit, and you said—" He stopped, his voice, so to speak, on one foot.

"Good," I said. "You did right." I hadn't expected him to be so honest. For the first time since his arrival, he had made an objective self-assessment, but my faint and even slightly patronizing praise was enough to bring back the smirk. Etty looked at him with uncontrolled dislike, which didn't disturb Alessandro one little bit.

"I hardly need to remind you," I said to all of them, ignoring the displayed emotions, "to keep this afternoon's doings to yourselves. Tommy, you can count on Pease Pudding in the Lincoln and Archangel in the

Guineas, and if you'll come back to the office now we'll go through your other probable rides for the next few weeks."

Alessandro's smirk turned sour, and the look he cast on Tommy was pure Rivera. Actively dangerous: in-ured to murder. Any appearance he might have given of being even slightly tamed was suddenly as reliable as sunlight on quicksand. I remembered the unequi-vocal message of Enso's gun pointing at my chest: that if killing seemed desirable, killing would quite casually be done. I had put Tommy Hoylake in jeopardy, and I'd have to get him out.

I sent the others on ahead and told Alessandro to stay for a minute. When the others were too far away to hear, I said, "You will have to accept that Tommy Hoylake will be riding as first jockey to the stable."

I got the full stare treatment, black, wide, and ill-intentioned. I could almost feel the hate which flowed out of him like hot waves across the cool March air.

"If Tommy Hoylake breaks his leg," I said clearly, "I'll break yours."

It shook him, though he tried not to show it.

"Also, it would be pointless to put Tommy Hoylake out of action, as I would then engage someone else. Not you. Is that clear?"

He didn't answer.

"If you want to be a top jockey, you've got to do it yourself. You've got to be good enough. You've got to fight your own battles. It's no good thinking your father will destroy everyone who stands in your way. If you are good enough, no one will stand in your way; and if you are not, no amount of ruining others will make you."

Still no sound. But fury, yes. Signifying all too much.

I said seriously, "If Tommy Hoylake comes to any harm whatsoever, I will see that you never ride in another race. At whatever consequence to myself."

He removed the stare from my face and scattered it over the wide windy spread of the Heath.

"I am accustomed—" he began arrogantly, and then stopped.

"I know what you are accustomed to," I said. "To having your own way at any expense to others. Your own way, bought in misery, pain, and fear. Well, you should have settled for something that could be paid for. No amount of death and destruction will buy you ability."

"All I wanted was to ride Archangel in the Derby," he said defensively.

"Just like that? Just a whim?"

He turned his head toward Lancat and gathered together the reins. "It started like that," he said indistinctly, and walked away from me in the direction of Newmarket.

He came and rode out as usual the following morning, and the days after. News that the trial had taken place got around, and I heard that I had chosen the time of the Champion Hurdle so that I could keep the unfit state of Pease Pudding decently concealed. The antepost price lengthened, and I put a hundred pounds on him at twenty-to-one.

My father shook the *Sporting Life* at me in a rage and insisted that the horse should be withdrawn.

"Have a bit on him instead," I said. "I have."

"You don't know what you're doing."

"Yes, I do."

"It says here . . ." He was practically stuttering with the frustration of not being able to get out of bed and thwart me. "It says here that if the trial was unsatisfactory, nothing more could be expected, with me away."

"I read it," I said. "That's just a guess. And it wasn't unsatisfactory, if you want to know. It was very encouraging."

"You're crazy," he said loudly. "You're ruining the stable. I won't have it. I won't have it, do you hear?"

125

"Do calm down," I said reasonably. "You'll give yourself a heart attack."

He glared at me. A hot amber glare, not a cold black one. It made a change.

"I'll send Tommy Hoylake to see you," I said. "You can ask him what he thinks."

Three days before the racing season started, I walked into the office at two-thirty to see if Margaret wanted me to sign any letters before she left to collect her children, and found Alessandro with her, sitting on the edge of her desk. He was wearing a navy-blue track suit and heavy white running shoes, and his black hair was damp with sweat and had crisped into curls.

She was looking up at him with obvious arousal, her face slightly flushed as if someone had given all her senses a friction rub.

She caught sight of me before he did, as he had his back to the door. She looked away from him in confusion, and he turned to see who had disturbed them.

There was a smile on the thin sallow face. A real smile, warm and uncomplicated, wrinkling the skin round the eyes and lifting the upper lip to show good teeth. For two seconds, I saw an Alessandro I wouldn't have guessed existed, and then the light went out inside and the facial muscles gradually reshaped themselves into the familiar lines of wariness and annoyance.

He slid his slight weight to the floor and wiped away with a thumb some of the sweat that stood out on his forehead and trickled down in front of his ears.

"I want to know what horses I am going to ride this week at Doncaster," he said. "Now that the season is starting, you can give me horses to race."

Margaret looked at him in astonishment, for he had sounded very much the boss. I answered him in a manner and tone carefully lacking in both apology and aggression.

"We have only one entry at Doncaster, which is Pease Pudding in the Lincoln on Saturday, and Tommy

Hoylake rides it," I said. "And the reason we have only one entry"—I went straight on, as I saw the anger stroking up at what he believed to be a blocking movement on my part—"is that my father was involved in a motor accident the week these entries should have been made, and they were never sent in."

"Oh," he said blankly.

"Still," I said, "it would be a good idea for you to go to the races every day, to see what goes on, so that you don't make any crashing mistakes next week."

I didn't add that I intended to do the same myself. It never did to show all your weaknesses to the opposition.

"You can start on Pulitzer on Wednesday at Catterick," I said. "And after that, it's up to you."

There was a flash of menace in the black eyes.

"No," he said, a bite in his voice. "It's up to my father."

He turned abruptly on one toe and, without looking back, trotted out of the office into the yard, swerved left, and set off at a steady jog up the drive toward Bury Road. We watched him through the window, Margaret with a smile tinged with puzzlement and I with more apprehension than I liked.

"He ran all the way to the Boy's Grave and back," she said. "He says he weighed six stone twelve before he set off today, and he's lost twenty-two pounds since he came here. That sounds an awful lot, doesn't it? Twenty-two pounds, for someone as small as him."

"Severe," I said, nodding.

"He's strong, though. Like wire."

"You like him," I said, making it hover on the edge of a question.

She gave me a quick glance. "He's interesting."

I slouched into the swivel chair and read through the letters she pushed across to me. All of them in economic, good English, perfectly typed.

"If we win the Lincoln," I said, "you can have a raise."

"Thanks very much." A touch of irony. "I hear the *Sporting Life* doesn't think much of my chances."

I signed three of the letters and started reading the fourth. "Does Alessandro often call in?" I asked casually.

"First time he's done it."

"What did he want?" I asked.

"I don't think he wanted anything particularly. He said he was going past, and just came in."

"What did you talk about?"

She looked surprised at the question but answered without comment.

"I asked him if he liked the Forbury Inn and he said he did, that it was much more comfortable than a house his father had rented on the outskirts of Cambridge. He said anyway his father had given up that house now and gone back home to do some business." She paused, thinking back, the memory of his company making her eyes smile, and I reflected that the house at Cambridge must have been where the rubber faces took me, and that there was now no point in speculating more about it.

"I asked him if he had always liked riding horses and he said yes, and I asked him what his ambitions were and he said to win the Derby and be Champion Jockey, and I said that there wasn't an apprentice born who didn't want that."

I turned my head to glance at her. "He said he wanted to be Champion Jockey?"

"That's right."

I stared gloomily down at my shoes. The skirmish had been a battle, the battle was in danger of becoming war, and now it looked as if hostilities could crackle on for months. Escalation seemed to be setting in in a big way.

"Did he ask *you* anything?"

"No. At least . . . Yes, I suppose he did." She seemed surprised, thinking about it.

"What?"

"He asked if you or your father owned any of the horses. . . . I told him your father had half shares in some of them, and he said did he own any of them outright. I said Buckram was the only one . . . and he said"—she frowned, concentrating—"he said he supposed it would be insured like the others, and I said it wasn't, actually, because Mr. Griffon had cut back on his premiums this year, so he'd better be extra careful with it on the roads." She suddenly sounded anxious. "There wasn't any harm in telling him, was there? I mean, I didn't think there was anything secret about Mr. Griffon owning Buckram."

"There isn't," I said comfortingly. "It runs in his name, for a start. It's public knowledge that he owns it."

She looked relieved and the lingering smile crept back round her eyes, and I didn't tell her that it was the bit about insurance that I found disturbing.

One of the firms I had advised in their troubles was assemblers of electronic equipment. Since they had, in fact, reorganized themselves from top to bottom and were now delighting their shareholders, I rang up the chief executive and asked for help for myself.

Urgently, I said. In fact, today. And it was half past three already.

A sharp "Phew" followed by some tongue-clicking, and the offer came. If I would drive toward Coventry, their Mr. Wallis would meet me at Kettering. He would bring what I wanted with him, and explain how I was to install it, and would that do?

It would do very well indeed, I said; and did the chief executive happen to be in need of half a race horse?

He laughed. On the salary cut I had persuaded him to take? I must be joking, he said.

Our Mr. Wallis, all of nineteen, met me in a businesslike truck and blinded me with science. He repeated the instructions clearly and twice, and then

129

obviously doubted whether I could carry them out. To him the vagaries of the photoelectric effect were home ground, but he also realized that to the average fool they were not. He went over it again to make sure I understood.

"What is your position with the firm?" I asked at the end.

"Deputy Sales Manager," he said happily. "And they tell me I have you to thank."

I quite easily, after the lecture, installed the early-warning system at Rowley Lodge: basically a photoelectric cell linked to an alarm buzzer. After dark, when everything was quiet, I hid the necessary ultra-violet-light source in the flowering plant in a tub which stood against the end wall of the four outside boxes, and the cell itself I camouflaged in a rosebush outside office window, across the lobby, and into the owners' the office window. The cable from this led through the room, with a switch box handy to the sofa.

Soon after I had finished rigging it, Etty walked into the yard from her cottage for her usual last look round before going to bed, and the buzzer rasped out loud and clear. Too loud, I thought. A silent intruder might just hear it. I put a cushion over it, and the muffled buzz sounded like a bumblebee caught in a drawer.

I switched the noise off. When Etty left the yard, it started again immediately. Hurrah for the Deputy Sales Manager, I thought, and slept in the owners' room with my head on the cushion.

No one came.

Stiffly, at six o'clock, I got up and rolled up the cable, and collected and stowed all the gear in a cupboard in the owners' room; and when the first of the lads ambled yawning into the yard, I headed directly to the coffeepot.

Tuesday night, no one came.

Wednesday, Margaret mentioned that Susie's friend

had reported two Swiss phone calls, one outgoing by Alessandro, one incoming to the chauffeur.

Etty, more anxious than ever, with the Lincoln only three days away, was snapping at the lads, and Alessandro stayed behind after second exercise and asked me if I had reconsidered and would put him up on Pease Pudding in place of Tommy Hoylake.

We were outside in the yard, with the late-morning bustle going on all around. Alessandro looked tense and hollow-eyed.

"You must know I can't," I said reasonably.

"My father says I am to tell you that you must."

I slowly shook my head. "For your own sake, you shouldn't. If you rode it, you would make a fool of yourself. Is that what your father wants?"

"He says I must insist." He was adamant.

"O.K.," I said. "You've insisted. But Tommy Hoylake is going to ride."

"But you must do what my father says," he protested.

I smiled at him faintly but didn't answer, and he did not seem to know what to say next.

"Next week, though," I said matter-of-factly, "you can ride Buckram in a race at Aintree. I entered him there especially for you. He won first time out last year, so he should have a fair chance again this time."

He just stared; didn't even blink. If there was anything to be given away, he didn't give it.

At three o'clock Thursday morning, the buzzer went off with enthusiasm three inches from my eardrum and I nearly fell off the sofa. I switched off the noise, got to my feet, and took a look into the yard through the owners' room window.

Moving quickly through the moonless night went one single small light, very faint, directed at the ground. Then, as I watched, it swung round, paused on some of the numbers of the boxes in bay four, and settled inexorably on the one which housed Buckram.

Treacherous little bastard, I thought. Finding out which horse he could kill without the owner wailing a complaint: an uninsured horse, in order to kick Rowley Lodge the harder in the financial groin.

Telling him Buckram might win him a race hadn't stopped him. Treacherous, callous little bastard.

I was out through the ready left-ajar doors and down the yard, moving silently on rubber shoes. I heard the bolts drawn quietly back and the doors squeak in their hinges, and homed on the small flicking light with far from charitable intentions.

No point in wasting time. I swept my hand down on the switch and flooded Buckram's box with a hundred watts.

I took in at a glance the syringe held, in a stunned second of suspended animation, in the gloved hand, and noticed the truncheon lying on the straw just inside the door.

It wasn't Alessandro. Too heavy. Too tall. The figure turning purposefully toward me, dressed in black from neck to foot, was one of the rubber faces.

In his rubber face.

10

This time, I didn't waste my precious advantage. I sprang straight at him and chopped with all my strength at the wrist of the hand that held the syringe.

A direct hit. The hand flew backward, the fingers opened, and the syringe spun away through the air.

I kicked his shin and punched him in the stomach, and when his head came forward I grabbed hold of it and swung him with a crash against the wall.

Buckram kicked up a fuss and stamped around loose, as rubber face had not attempted to put the head-collar on. When rubber face rushed me with jabbing fists, I caught hold of his clothes and threw him against Buckram, who snapped at him with his teeth.

A muffled sound came through the rubber, which I declined to interpret as an appeal for peace. Once away from the horse, he came at me again, shoulders hunched, head down, arms stretching forward. I stepped straight into his grasp, ignored a bash in my short ribs, put my arm tight round his neck, and banged his head on the nearest wall. The legs turned to latex to match the face, and the lids palely shut inside the eyeholes. I gave him another small crack against the wall to remove any lingering doubts, and stood back a pace. He lay feebly in the angle between floor and wall, one hand twisting slowly forward and backward across the straw.

I tied up Buckram, who by some miracle had not pushed his way out of the unbolted door and roused the neighborhood, and in stepping away from the tethering ring I nearly put my foot right down on the syringe. It lay under the manger, in the straw, and had survived undamaged through the rumpus.

I picked it up, tossed it lightly in my hand, and decided that the gifts of the gods should not be wasted. Pulling up the sleeve of rubber face's black jersey, I pushed the needle firmly into his arm and gave him the benefit of half the contents. Prudence, not compassion, stopped me from squirting in the lot; it might be that what the syringe held was a flattener for a horse but curtains for a man, and murdering was not going to help.

I pulled off rubber face's rubber face. Underneath it was Carlo. Surprise, surprise.

The prizes of war now amounted to one rubber mask, one half-empty syringe, and one bone-breaking truncheon. After a slight pause for thought, I wiped my fingerprints off the syringe, removed Carlo's gloves, and planted his fingerprints all over it; both hands. A similar liberal sprinkling went onto the truncheon; then, using the gloves to hold them with, I took the two incriminating articles up to the house and hid them temporarily in a lacquered box under a dust sheet in one of the ten unused bedrooms.

From the window on the stairs on the way down, I caught the impression of a large pale shape in the drive near the gate. Went to look, to make sure. No mistake: the Mercedes.

Back in Buckram's box, Carlo slept peacefully, totally out. I felt his pulse, which was slow but regular, and looked at my watch. Not yet three-thirty. Extraordinary.

Carrying Carlo to the car looked too much of a chore, so I went and fetched the car to Carlo. The engine started with a click and a purr, and made too little noise in the yard even to disturb the horses. Leaving the engine running, I opened both rear doors and lugged Carlo in backward. I had intended to do him the courtesy of the back seat, since he had done as much for me, but he fell limply off onto the floor. I bent his knees up, as he lay on his back, and gently shut him in.

As far as I could tell, no one saw our arrival at the Forbury Inn. I parked the Mercedes next to the other cars near the front door, switched off the engine and the side lights, and quietly went away.

By the time I had walked the near mile home, collected the rubber mask from Buckram's box and taken off his head-collar, and dismantled the electronic eye and stowed it in the cupboard, it was too late to bother with going to bed. I slept for an hour or so more on the sofa, and woke up feeling dead tired and not a bit full of energy for the first day of the races.

Alessandro arrived late, on foot, and worried.

I watched him, first through the office window and then from the owners' room, as he made his way down into the yard. He hovered in indecision in bay four, and with curiosity overcoming caution, made a crablike traverse over to Buckram's box. He unbolted the top half of the door, looked inside, and then bolted the door again. Unable from a distance to read his reaction, I walked out of the house into his sight without appearing to take any notice of him.

He removed himself smartly from bay four and pretended to be looking for Etty in bay three, but finally his uncertainty got the better of him and he turned to come and meet me.

"Do you know where Carlo is?" he asked without preamble.

"Where would you expect him to be?" I said.

He blinked. "In his room. I knock on his door when I am ready—but he wasn't there. Have you—have you seen him?"

"At four o'clock this morning," I said casually, "he was fast asleep in the back of your car. I imagine he is still there."

He turned his head away as if I'd pushed him.

"He came, then," he said, and sounded hopeless.

"He came," I agreed.

"But you didn't—I mean—kill him?"

"I'm not your father," I said. "Carlo got injected with some stuff he brought for Buckram."

His head snapped back and his eyes held a fury that was for once not totally directed at me.

"I told him not to come," he said angrily. "I told him not to."

"Because Buckram could win for you next week?"

"Yes . . . no . . . You confuse me."

"But he disregarded you and obeyed your father?"

"I told him not to come," he repeated.

"He wouldn't dare disobey your father," I said dryly.

"No one disobeys my father," he stated automatically, and then looked at me in bewilderment. "Except you," he said.

"The knack with your father," I explained, "is to disobey within the area where retaliation becomes progressively less profitable, and to widen that area at every opportunity."

"I don't understand."

"I'll explain it to you on the way to Doncaster," I said.

"I am not coming with you," he said stiffly. "Carlo will drive me in my own car."

"He'll be in no shape to. If you want to go to the races, I think you'll find you either have to drive yourself or come with me."

He gave me an angry stare and didn't admit he couldn't drive. But he couldn't resist the attraction of the races, either, and I had counted on it.

"Very well. I will come with you."

After we had ridden back from the racecourse side with the first lot, I told him to talk to Margaret in the office while I changed into racegoing clothes, and then I drove him up to the Forbury Inn for him to do the same.

He bounded out of the Jensen almost before it stopped rolling and wrenched open one of the Mercedes' rear doors. Inside the car, a hunched figure sitting on the back seat showed that Carlo was at least partially awake, if not a hundred percent receptive to the torrent of Italian abuse breaking over him.

I tapped Alessandro on the back and, when he momentarily stopped cursing, said, "If he feels anything like I did after similar treatment, he will not be taking much notice. Why don't you do something constructive, like getting ready to go to the races?"

"I'll do what I please," he said fiercely, but the next minute it appeared that what pleased him was to change for the races.

While he was indoors, Carlo made one or two remarks in Italian which stretched my knowledge of the language too far. The gist, however, was clear. Something to do with my ancestors.

Alessandro reappeared wearing the dark suit he had first arrived in, which was now a full size too large. It made him look even thinner, and a good deal younger, and almost harmless. I reminded myself sharply that a lowered guard invited the uppercut, and jerked my head for him to get into the Jensen.

When he had closed the door, I spoke to Carlo through the open window of the Mercedes. "Can you hear what I say?" I said. "Are you listening?"

He raised his head with an effort and gave me a look which showed that he was, even if he didn't want to.

"Good," I said. "Now, take this in. Alessandro is coming with me to the races. Before I bring him back, I intend to telephone to the stables to make quite sure that no damage of any kind has been done there—that all the horses are alive and well. If you have any idea of going back today to finish off what you didn't do last night, you can drop it. Because if you do any damage you will not get Alessandro back tonight—or for many nights—and I cannot think that Enso Rivera would be very pleased with you."

He looked as furious as his sorry state would let him.

"You understand?" I said.

"Yes." He closed his eyes and groaned. I left him to it with reprehensible satisfaction.

"What did you say to Carlo?" Alessandro demanded as I swept him away down the drive.

"Told him to spend the day in bed."

"I don't believe you."

"Words to that effect."

He looked suspiciously at the beginning of a smile I didn't bother to repress, and then, crossly, straight ahead through the windscreen.

After ten silent miles, I said, "I've written a letter to your father. I'd like you to send it to him."

"What letter?"

I took an envelope out of my inner pocket and handed it to him.

"I want to read it," he said aggressively.

"Go ahead. It isn't stuck. I thought I would save you the trouble."

He compressed his mouth and pulled out the letter. He read:

Enso Rivera,
The following points are for your consideration.

1. While Alessandro stays, and wishes to stay, at Rowley Lodge, the stable must remain unharmed.

Following any form or degree of destruction, or of attempted destruction, of the stables, the Jockey Club will immediately be informed of everything that has passed, with the result that Alessandro would be banned for life from riding races anywhere in the world.

2. Tommy Hoylake.

Should any harm of any description come to Tommy Hoylake, or to any other jockey employed by the stable, the information will be laid, and Alessandro will ride no more races.

3. Moonrock, Indigo, and Buckram.

Should any further attempts be made to injure or kill any of the horses at Rowley Lodge, information will be laid, and Alessandro will ride no more races.

4. The information which would be laid consists at present of a full account of all pertinent events, together with (a) the two model horses and their hand-written labels; (b) the results of an analysis done at the Equine Research Laboratory on a blood sample taken from Indigo showing the presence of the anesthetic promazine; (c) X-ray pictures of the fracture of Indigo's near foreleg; (d) one rubber mask, worn by Carlo; and (e) one hypodermic syringe containing traces of anesthetic, and (f) one truncheon, both bearing Carlo's fingerprints.

These items are all lodged with a solicitor, who has instructions for their use in the event of my death.

Bear in mind that the case against you and your son does not have to be proved in a court of law, but only to the satisfaction of the Stewards of the Jockey Club. It is they who take away jockeys' licenses. If no further damage is done or attempted at Rowley Lodge, I will agree on my part to give Alessandro every possible opportunity of becoming a proficient and successful jockey.

He read the letter through twice. Then he slowly folded it and put it back in the envelope.

"He won't like it," he said. "He never lets anyone threaten him."

"He shouldn't have tried threatening me," I said mildly.

"He thought it would be your father . . . and old people frighten more easily, my father says."

I took my eyes off the road for two seconds to glance at him. He was no more disturbed by what he had just said than when he had said his father would kill me. Frightening and murdering had been the background to his childhood, and he still seemed to consider them normal.

"Do you really have all those things?" he asked. "The blood-test results . . . and the syringe?"

"I do indeed."

"But Carlo always wear gloves—" He stopped.

"He was careless," I said.

He brooded over it. "If my father makes Carlo break any more horses' legs, will you really get me warned off?"

"I certainly will." ·

"But after that you would have no way of stopping him from destroying the stables in revenge."

"Would he do that?" I asked. "Would he bother?"

Alessandro gave me a pitying, superior smile. "My father would be revenged if someone ate the cream cake he wanted."

"Do you approve of vengeance?" I said.

"Of course."

"It wouldn't get you back your license," I pointed out, "and anyway I doubt whether he could actually do it, because there would then be no bar to police protection and the loudest possible publicity."

He said stubbornly, "There wouldn't be any risk at all if you would agree to my riding Pease Pudding and Archangel."

"It never was possible for you to ride them without any experience, and if you'd had any sense you would have known it. So, although there's always a risk in opposing extortion, in some cases it is the only thing to do. And starting from there, it's just a matter of finding ways of opposing that don't land you in the morgue empty-handed."

There was another long pause while we skirted Grantham and Newark. It started raining. I switched on the wipers and the blades clicked like metronomes over the glass.

"It seems to me," Alessandro said glumly, "as if you and my father have been engaged in some sort of fight to see who is stronger, with me being the one that both of you push around."

I smiled, surprised both at his perception and that he should have said it aloud.

"That's right," I agreed. "That's how it's been from the beginning."

"Well, I don't like it."

"It only happened because of you. And if you give up the idea of being a jockey, it will all stop."

"But I *want* to be a jockey," he said, as if that were the end of it. And as far as his doting father was concerned, it was. The beginning of it, and the end of it.

Ten wet miles farther on, he said, "You tried to get rid of me, when I came."

"Yes, I did."

"Do you still want me to leave?"

"Would you?" I sounded hopeful.

"No," he said. "Because between you, you and my father have made it impossible for me to go to any other stable and start again."

A long pause. "And anyway," he said, "I don't want

to go to any other stable. I want to stay at Rowley Lodge."

"And be Champion Jockey?" I murmured.

"I only told Margaret," he said sharply, and then put a couple of things together. "She told you I asked about Buckram," he said bitterly. "And that's how you caught Carlo."

In justice to Margaret, I said, "She wouldn't have told me if I hadn't directly asked her what you wanted."

"You don't trust me," he complained.

"Well, no," I said ironically. "Wouldn't I be a fool to?"

The rain fell more heavily against the windscreen. We stopped at a red light in Bawtry and waited while a lollipop man shepherded half a school across in front of us.

"That bit in your letter about helping me to be a good jockey—do you mean it?"

"Well, yes, I do," I said. "You ride well enough at home. Better than I expected, to be honest."

"I told you——" he began, lifting the arching nose.

"That you were brilliant," I finished, nodding. "So you did."

"Don't laugh at me." The ready fury boiled up.

"All you've got to do is win a few races, keep your head, show a judgment of pace and an appreciation of tactics, and stop relying on your father."

He was unpacified. "It is natural to rely on one's father," he said stiffly.

"I ran away from mine when I was sixteen."

He turned his head. I could see out of the corner of my eye that he was both surprised and unimpressed.

"Obviously he did not, like mine, give you everything you wanted."

"No," I agreed. "I wanted freedom."

I spent most of the afternoon meeting the people who knew my father: other trainers, jockeys, officials, and some of the owners. They were all without exception helpful and informative, so that by the end of the day I had learned what I would be expected (and, just as importantly, not expected) to do in connection with Pease Pudding for the Lincoln.

Tommy Hoylake, with an expansive grin, put in succinctly, "Declare it, saddle it, watch it win, and stick around in case of objections."

"Do you think we have any chance?"

"Oh, we must have," he said. "It's an open race, anything could win. Lap of the gods, you know. Lap of the gods." By which I gathered that he still hadn't made up his mind about the trial, whether Lancat was good or Pease Pudding bad.

On the drive back to Newmarket, I asked Alessandro how he had got on. As his expression whenever I had caught sight of him during the afternoon had been a mixture of envy and pride, I knew without him telling me that he had been both titillated to be recognizable as a jockey, because of his size, and enraged that a swarm of others should have started the season without him. The look he had given the boy who had won the apprentice race would have frightened a rattlesnake.

"I cannot wait until next Wednesday," he said. "I wish to begin tomorrow."

"We have no runners before next Wednesday," I said calmly.

"Pease Pudding." He was fierce. "On Saturday."

"We've been through all that."

"I wish to ride him."

"No."

He seethed away in the passenger seat. The actual sight and sound and smell of the races had excited him extraordinarily—to the pitch where he could scarcely keep still. The approach to reasonableness which had been made on the way up had all blown away in the squally wind on Doncaster's Town Moor, and the first half of the journey back was a complete waste, as far as I was concerned. Finally, though, the extreme tenseness left him, and he slumped back in his seat in some species of gloom.

I felt it would be all right then to talk to him further. I said, "What sort of a race do you think you should ride on Pulitzer?"

His spine straightened again instantly.

"I looked up his last year's form," he said. "Pulitzer was consistent; he came third or fourth or sixth, mostly. He was always near the front for most of the race but then faded out in the last furlong. Next Wednesday at Catterick, it is seven furlongs. I know that the low numbers are the best to draw, so I would hope for one of those. Then I will try to get away well at the start and take a position next to the rails, or with only one other horse inside me, and I will not go too fast, but not too slow either. I will try to stay not farther back than two and a half lengths behind the leading horse, but I will not try to get to the front until right near the end. The last sixty yards, I think. And I will try to be in front only about fifteen yards before the winning post. I think he does not race his best if he is in front, so he mustn't be in front very long."

To say I was surprised is to get nowhere near the queer excitement which rose sharply and unexpectedly in my brain. I'd had years of practice in sorting the genuine from the phony, and what Alessandro had said rang of pure sterling.

"O.K.," I said casually. "That sounds all right. You ride him just like that. And how about Buckram? You'll be riding him in the apprentice race at Liverpool the day after Pulitzer. Also you can ride Lancat at Teesside two days later, on the Saturday."

"I'll look them up, and think about them," he said seriously.

"Don't bother with Lancat's form," I reminded him.

"He was no good as a two-year-old. Work from what you learned during the trial."

"Yes," he said. "I understand."

I could see at last how to make Enso retract his threats. But it seemed to me very likely that the future would be more dangerous than the past.

11

Every evening during the week before the Lincoln, I spent hours answering the telephone. One owner after another rang up, and without exception sounded depressed. This, I discovered—after the fourth in a row had said, in more or less identical words, "Can't expect much with your father chained to his bed"—was because the invalid in question had been extremely busy on the blower himself.

It seems he had rung them all up, apologized for my presence, told them to expect nothing, and promised them that everything would be restored to normal as soon as he got back. He had also told his co-owner of Pease Pudding, a Major Barnette, that in his opinion the horse was not fit to run; and it had taken me half an hour of my very best persuasive tongue to convince the Major that as my father hadn't seen the horse for the past six weeks, he didn't actually know.

Looking into his activities more closely, I found that my father had also written privately every week to Etty for progress reports and had told her not to tell me she was sending them. I practically bullied this last gem out of her on the morning before the Lincoln, having cottoned on to what was happening only through mentioning that my father had told all the owners the horses were unfit. Something guilty in her expression had given her away, but she fended off my bitterness by claiming that she hadn't actually said they were unfit; that was just the way my father had chosen to interpret things.

I went into the office and asked Margaret if my father had telephoned or written to her for private reports. She looked embarrassed and said that he had.

When I spoke about race tactics to Tommy Hoylake that Friday, he said not to worry, my father had rung him up and given him his instructions.

"And what were they?" I asked, with a great deal more restraint than I was feeling.

"Oh . . . just to keep in touch with the field and not drop out of the back door when he blows up."

"Um. . . . If he hadn't rung you up, how would you have planned to ride?" I said.

"Keep him well up all the time," he said promptly. "When he's fit, he's one of those horses who like to make the others try to catch him. I'd pick him up two furlongs out, take him to the front, and just pray he'd stay there."

"Ride him like that, then," I said. "I've got a hundred pounds on him, and I don't usually bet."

His mouth opened in astonishment. "But your father—"

"Promise you'll ride the horse to win," I said pleasantly, "or I'll put someone else up."

I was insulting him. No one ever suggested replacing Tommy Hoylake. He looked uncertainly at my open expression and came to the conclusion that because of my inexperience I didn't realize the enormity of what I'd said.

He shrugged. "All right. I'll give it a whirl. Though what your father will say . . ."

My father had not finished saying, not by six or more

calls—mostly, it appeared, to the press. Three papers on the morning of the Lincoln quoted his opinion that Pease Pudding had no chance. He'd have me in before the Stewards, I grimly reflected, if the horse did any good.

Among all this telephonic activity, he rang me only once. Although the overpowering bossiness had not returned to his voice, he sounded stilted and displeased, and I gathered that the champagne truce had barely seen me out of the door.

He rang on the Thursday evening after I got back from Doncaster, and I told him how helpful everyone had been.

"Hmph," he said. "I'll ring the Clerk of the Course tomorrow, and ask him to keep an eye on things."

"Have you entirely cornered the telephone trolley?" I asked.

"Telephone trolley? Could never get hold of it for long enough. Too many people asking for it all the time. No, no. I told them I needed my own private extension, here in this room, and after a lot of fuss and delay they fixed one up. I insisted, of course, that I had a business to run."

"And you insisted often?"

"Of course," he said without humor, and I knew from long experience that the hospital had had as much chance as an egg under a steamroller.

"The horses aren't as backward as you think," I told him. "You don't really need to be so pessimistic."

"You're no judge of a horse," he said dogmatically; and it was the day after that that he talked to the press.

Major Barnette gloomed away in the parade ring and poured scorn and pity on my hefty bet.

"Your father told me not to throw good money after bad," he said. "And I can't think why I let you persuade me to run."

"You can have fifty of my hundred, if you like." I

offered it with the noblest of intentions, but he took it as a sign that I wanted to get rid of some of my losses.

"Certainly not," he said resentfully.

He was a spare, elderly man of middle height, who stood, at the slightest provocation, upon his dignity. Sign of basic failure, I diagnosed uncharitably, and remembered the old adage that some owners were harder to train than their horses.

The twenty-nine runners for the Lincoln were stalking long-leggedly round the parade ring, with all the other owners and trainers standing about in considering groups. Strong, cold northwest winds had blown the clouds away, and the sun shone brazenly from a brilliant high blue sky. When the jockeys trickled through the crowd and emerged in a sunburst into the parade ring, their glossy colors gleamed and reflected the light like children's toys.

The old-young figure of Tommy Hoylake in bright green bounced toward us with a carefree aura of play-it-as-it-comes, which did nothing to persuade Major Barnette that his half share of the horse would run well.

"Look," he said heavily to Tommy, "just don't get tailed off. If it looks as if you will be, pull up and jump off, for God's sake, and pretend the horse is lame or the saddle's slipped. Anything you like, but don't let it get around that the horse is no good, or its stud value will sink like a stone."

"I don't think he'll actually be tailed off, sir," Tommy said judiciously, and cast an inquiring glance up at me.

"Just ride him as you suggested," I said, "and don't leave it all in the lap of the gods."

He grinned. Hopped on the horse. Flicked his cap to Major Barnette. Went on his lighthearted way.

The Major didn't want to watch the race with me, which suited me fine. My mouth felt dry. Suppose, after all, that my father was right, that I couldn't tell a fit horse from a letterbox, and that he in his hospital bed was a better judge. Fair enough; if the horse ran stinkingly badly, I would acknowledge my mistake and do a salutary spot of groveling.

Pease Pudding didn't run stinkingly badly.

The horses had cantered a straight mile away from the stands, circled, sorted, lined up, and started back at a flat gallop. I couldn't for a long time see Tommy at all, even though I knew vaguely where to look for him: drawn number twenty-one, almost mid-field. I watched the fast-moving mass making its distant way toward the stands, a multicolored charge dividing into two sections, one each side of the course. Each section narrowed until the center of the track was bare, and it looked as though two separate races were being held at the same time.

I heard his name on the commentary before I spotted the colors.

"And now on the stands' side it's Pease Pudding coming to take it up. With two furlongs to go, Pease Pudding on the rails with Gossamer next and Badger making up ground now behind them, and Willy Nilly on the far side followed by Thermometer, Student Unrest, Manganeta . . ." He rattled off a long string of names to which I didn't listen.

That he had been fit enough to hit the front two furlongs from home was all that mattered. I honestly didn't care from that moment whether he won or lost. But he did win. He won by a short head from Badger, holding his muzzle stubbornly in front when it looked impossible that he shouldn't be caught, with Tommy Hoylake moving rhythmically over the withers and getting out of him the last milligram of balance, of stamina, of utter bloody-minded refusal to be beaten.

In the winner's unsaddling enclosure, Major Barnette looked more stunned than stratospheric, but Tommy Hoylake jumped down with the broadest of grins and said, "Hey, what about that, then? He had the goods in the parcel, after all."

"So he did," I said, and told the discountenanced

pressmen that anyone could win the Lincoln any old day of the week: any old day, given the horse, the luck, the head lad, my father's stable routine, and the second-best jockey in the country.

About twenty people having suddenly developed a close friendship with Major Barnette, he drifted off, more or less at their suggestion, to the bar to lubricate their hoarse-from-cheering throats. He asked me lamely to join him, but as I had caught his eye just when, recovering from his surprise, he had been telling the world that he always knew Pease Pudding had it in him, I saved him embarrassment and declined.

When the crowd round the unsaddling enclosure had dispersed and the fuss had died away, I somehow found myself face to face with Alessandro, who had been driven to Doncaster that day, and the previous day, by a partially revitalized chauffeur.

His face was as white as his yellowish skin could get, and his black eyes were as deep as pits. He regarded me with a shaking, strung-up intensity, and seemed to have difficulty in actually saying what was hovering on the edge. I looked back at him without emotion of any sort, and waited.

"All right," he said jerkily, after a while. "All right. Why don't you say it? I expect you to say it."

"There's no need," I said neutrally. "And no point."

Some of the jangle drained out of his face. He swallowed with difficulty.

"I will say it for you then," he said. "Pease Pudding would not have won if you had let me ride it."

"No, he wouldn't," I agreed.

"I could see," he said, still with a shake in his voice, "that I couldn't have ridden like that. I could see."

Humility was a torment for Alessandro.

I said, in some sort of compassion, "Tommy Hoylake has no more determination than you have, and no better hands. But what he does have is a marvelous judgment of pace and tremendous polish in a tight finish. Your turn will come, don't doubt it."

151

Even if his color didn't come back, the rest of the rigidity disappeared. He looked more dumbfounded than anything else.

He said slowly, "I thought—I thought you would—what is it Miss Craig says?—rub my nose in it."

I smiled at the sound of the colloquialism in his careful accent.

"No, I wouldn't do that."

He took a deep breath and involuntarily stretched his arms out sidewise.

"I want—" he said, and didn't finish it.

You want the world, I thought. And I said, "Start on Wednesday."

When the horse box brought Pease Pudding back to Rowley Lodge that night, the whole stable turned out to greet him. Etty's face was puckered with a different emotion from worry, and she fussed over the returning warrior like a mother hen. The colt himself clattered stiff-legged down the ramp into the yard and modestly accepted the melon-sized grins and the earthy comments ("You did it, you old bugger") which were directed his way.

"Surely every winner doesn't get this sort of reception," I said to Etty after I'd come out of the house to investigate the bustle. I had reached the house half an hour before the horse, and found everything quiet; the lads had finished evening stables and gone round to the hostel for their tea.

"It's the first of the season," she said, her eyes shining in her good plain face. "And we didn't expect— Well, I mean—without Mr. Griffon and everything . . ."

"I told you to have more faith in yourself, Etty."

"It's bucked the lads up no end," she said, ducking the compliment. "Everyone was watching on TV. They made such a noise in the hostel they must have heard them at the Forbury Inn."

The lads were all spruced up for their Saturday evening out. When they'd seen Pease Pudding stowed safely away, they set off in a laughing and cheering bunch to make inroads into the stocks of the Golden Lion; and until I saw the explosive quality of their pleasure, I hadn't realized the extent of their depression. But they had after all, I reflected, read the papers. And they were used to believing my father rather than their own eyes.

"Mr. Griffon will be so pleased," Etty said, with genuine, unsophisticated certainty.

But Mr. Griffon, predictably, was not.

I drove down to see him the following afternoon and found several of the Sunday newspapers in the wastebasket. He greeted me with a face that made agate look like putty, and was watchfully determined that I shouldn't have a chance of crowing.

He needn't have worried. Nothing made for worse future relations in any field whatsoever than crowing over losers; and if I knew nothing else, I knew how to negotiate for the best long-term results.

I congratulated him on the win.

He didn't quite know how to deal with that, but at least it got him out of the embarrassment of having to admit he'd been made to look foolish.

"Tommy Hoylake rode a brilliant race," he stated, and ignored the fact that he had given him directly opposite instructions.

"Yes, he did," I agreed wholeheartedly, and repeated that all the rest of the credit lay with Etty and with his own stable routine, which we had faithfully followed.

He unbent a little, but I found, slightly to my dismay, that in contrast I admired Alessandro for the straightforwardness of his apology, and for the moral courage which had nerved him to offer it. Moral courage was not something I had ever associated with Alessandro before that moment.

Since my last visit, my father's room had taken on the appearance of an office. The regulation bedside locker had been replaced by a much larger table, which pushed around easily on huge wheel casters, like the bed. On the table was the telephone on which he had broadcast so much blight, also a heap of Racing Calendars, copies of the *Sporting Life,* entry forms, a copy of *Horses in Training,* the three previous years' form books, and, half hidden, the reports from Etty in her familiar schoolgirl handwriting.

"What, no typewriter?" I said flippantly, and he said stiffly that he was arranging for a local girl to come in and take dictation sometime in the next week.

"Fine," I said encouragingly, but he refused to be friendly. He saw the winning of the Lincoln as a serious threat to his authority, and his manner said plainly that that authority was not passing to me, or even to Etty, while he could do anything to prevent it.

He was putting himself in a very ambivalent position. Every winner would be to him personally excruciating, yet at the same time he needed it desperately from the financial angle. Too much of his fortune for safety was still invested in half shares; and if the horses all ran as badly as it seemed he would like them to, their value would curl up like dahlias in a frost.

Understanding him was one thing, sorting him out quite another.

"I can't wait for you to get back," I said, but that didn't work either. It seemed that the bones were not mending as fast as had been hoped, and the reminder of the delay simply switched him into a different sort of aggravation.

"Some tommyrot about elderly bones taking longer to knit," he said irritably. "All these weeks, and they can't say when I can get out of all these comfounded pulleys. I told them I want a plaster cast I can walk on. Damn it, enough people have them, but they say there are lots of cases where it isn't possible, and that I'm one of them."

"You're lucky to have a leg at all," I pointed out. "At first they thought they would have to take it off."

"Better if they had." He snorted. "Then I would have been back at Rowley Lodge by now."

I had brought some more champagne, but he refused to drink any. Afraid it might look too much like a celebration, I supposed.

Gillie gave me an uncomplicated hug, and it was she who said, "I told you so."

"So you did," I agreed contentedly. "And, since I won two thousand pounds on your convictions, I'll take you to the Empress."

The tatty black, however, was tight.

"Just look," she wailed, pressing her abdomen with her fingers, "I wore it only ten days ago and it was perfectly all right. And now it's impossible."

"I'm not overaddicted to flat-chested ladies with hip-bones sticking up like Mont Blancs," I said comfortingly.

"No, but voluptuous plenty can go too far."

"Grapefruit, then?"

She sighed, considered, went to fetch a cream trench coat which covered a multitude of bulges, and said cheerfully, "Whoever could do justice to Pease Pudding on a grapefruit?"

We toasted the victory in Château Figeac 1964 but, out of respect for the tatty-black seams, ate melon and steak and averted our eyes strong-mindedly from the puddings.

Gillie said over the coffee that owing to the continued shortage of orphans she was more or less having time off thrust upon her, and couldn't I think again and let her come to Newmarket.

"No," I said, more positively than I intended.

She looked a little hurt, which was unusual enough in her to bother me considerably.

"You remember those bruises I had, about five weeks ago?" I said.

"Yes, I do."

"Well, they were the beginning of a rather unpleasant argument I am still having with a man who has a strong

155

line in threats. So far I have resisted some of the threats, and at present there's a sort of stalemate." I paused. "I don't want to upset that balance. I don't want to give him any levers. I've no wife, no children, and no near relatives except a father well protected in hospital. There's no one the enemy can threaten—no one for whose sake I will do anything he says. But, you see, if you come to Newmarket, there would be."

She looked at me a long time, taking it in, but the hurt went away at once.

Finally, she said, "Archimedes said that if he could find somewhere to stand he could shift the world."

"Huh?"

"With a lever," she said, smiling. "You uneducated goose."

"Let's not give Archimedes a foothold."

"No." She sighed. "Set your tiny mind at rest. I'll pay you no visits until invited."

Back at the flat, lying side by side in bed and reading the Sunday papers in companionable quiet, she said, "You do see what follows from allowing him no levers?"

"What?"

"More bruises."

"Not if I can help it."

She rolled her head on the pillow and looked at me. "You know damn well. You're no great fool."

"It won't come to that," I said.

She turned back to the *Sunday Times*. "There's an advertisement here for travel on a cargo boat to Australia. Would you feel safer if I went on a cruise on a cargo boat to Australia? Would you like me to go?"

"Yes, I would," I said. "And no, I wouldn't."

"Just an offer."

"Declined."

She smiled. "Don't leave this address lying about, then."

"I haven't."

She put the paper down. "Just how much of a lever do you suppose I am?"

I threw the *Observer* onto the floor. "I'll show you, if you like."

"Please do," she said; and switched off the light.

12

"I would like you to come in my car to the races," I said to Alessandro on Wednesday morning when he turned up for the first lot. "Give Carlo a day off."

He looked back dubiously to where Carlo sat in the Mercedes, staring watchfully down the yard.

"He says I talk with you too much. He will object."

I shrugged. "All right," I said, and walked off to mount Cloud Cuckoo-land. We took the string down to Waterhall, where Alessandro rode a pipe-opener on Buckram and Lancat, and Etty grudgingly said that they both seemed to be going well for him. The thirty or so others that we took along didn't seem to be doing so badly, either, and the Lincoln booster was still fizzing around in grins and good humor. The whole stable, that week, had come alive.

Pulitzer had set off to Catterick early in the smaller of the stable's two horse boxes, accompanied by his own lad and the traveling head lad, Vic Young, who supervised the care of the horses while they were away from home. Second in command to Etty, he was a resourceful, quick-witted Londoner grown too heavy in middle age to ride most of the young stable inmates; but the weight came in useful for throwing around. Vic Young was a great one for getting his own way, and it was just good luck that his own way was usually to the stable's advantage. He was, like all the best older lads, deeply partisan.

When I went out after changing, ready to follow to the races, I found Alessandro waiting beside the Jensen, with Carlo glowering in the Mercedes six feet away.

"I will come in your car," announced Alessandro firmly. "But Carlo will follow us."

"Very well," I said, nodding.

I slid down into the driving seat and waited while he got in beside me. Then I started up, moved down the drive, and turned out of the gate with Carlo following in convoy.

"My father ordered him to drive me everywhere," Alessandro explained.

"And he doesn't care to disobey your father," I finished for him.

"That is right. My father also ordered him to make sure I am safe."

I slid a glance sidewise.

"Don't you feel safe?"

"No one would dare to hurt me," he said simply.

"It would depend what there was to gain," I said, speeding away from Newmarket.

"But my father . . ."

"I know," I said. "I know. And I have no wish to harm you. None at all."

Alessandro subsided, satisfied. But I reflected that levers could work both ways, and Enso, unlike me, did have someone for whose sake he could be forced to do things against his will.

Alessandro was impatient for the journey to be over, but was otherwise calmer than I had expected. Determination, however, shouted forth from the arrogant carriage of his head down to the slender hands which clenched and unclenched at intervals on his knees.

I avoided an oncoming oil tanker, whose driver seemed to think he was in France, and said casually, "You won't be able to threaten the other apprentices with reprisals if you don't get it all your own way. You understand that, don't you?"

He looked almost hurt. "I will not do that."

"The habits of a lifetime," I said without censure, "are apt to rear their ugly heads at moments of stress."

"I will ride to win," he asserted.

"Yes. . . . But do remember that if you win by pushing someone else out of the way, the Stewards will take the race away from you, and you'll gain nothing."

"I will be careful," he said, with his chin up.

"That's all that is required," I confirmed. "Generosity is not."

He looked at me with suspicion. "I do not always know if you are meaning to make jokes."

"Usually," I said.

We drove steadily north.

"Did it never occur to your father to buy you a Derby prospect, rather than to insert you into Rowley Lodge by force?" I inquired conversationally as we sped past Weatherby.

He looked as if the possibility were new to him. "No," he said. "It was Archangel I wanted to ride. The favorite. I want to win the Derby, and Archangel is the best. And all the money in Switzerland would not buy Archangel."

That was true, because the colt belonged to a great sportsman, an eighty-year-old merchant banker, whose lifelong ambition it had been to win the great race. His horses had, in years gone by, finished second and third, and he had won every other big race in the Calendar, but the ultimate peak had always eluded him. Archangel was the best he had ever had, and time was running short.

"Besides," Alessandro added, "my father would not spend the money if a threat would do instead."

As usual, when referring to his father's *modus operandi*, he took it entirely for granted and saw nothing in it but logic.

"Do you ever think objectively about your father?" I asked. "About how he achieves his ends, and about whether the ends themselves are of any merit?"

He looked puzzled. "No . . ." he said hesitantly.

"Where did you go to school, then?" I said, changing tack.

"I didn't go to school," he said. "I had two teachers at home. I did not want to go to school. I did not want to be ordered about and have to work all day."

"So your two teachers spent a lot of time twiddling their thumbs?"

"Twiddling—? Oh, yes. I suppose so. The English one used to go off and climb mountains and the Italian one liked the local girls." There was no humor in his voice. There never was. "They both left when I was fifteen. They left because I was then riding my two horses all day long, and my father said there was no point in paying for two tutors instead of one riding master, so he hired one old Frenchman who had been an instructor in the cavalry, and he showed me how to ride better. I used to go and stay with a man my father knew and go hunting on his horse and that is when I rode a bit in races. Four or five races. There were not many for amateurs. I liked it, but I didn't feel as I do now. . . . And then, one day at home when I was saying I was bored, my father said, 'Very well, Alessandro, say what you want and I will get it for you,' and into my head came Archangel, and I just said—just like that, without really thinking—'I want to win the English Derby on Archangel.' And he just laughed, how he sometimes does, and said, so I should." He paused. "After that, I asked him if he meant it, because the more I thought about it the more I knew there was nothing on the earth I wanted more. Nothing on the earth I wanted at all. He kept saying all in good time, but I was impatient to come to England and start, so when he had finished some business, we came."

For about the tenth time, he twisted round in his seat to look out the back window. Carlo was still there, faithfully following.

"Tomorrow," I said, "he can follow us again, to Liverpool. After Buckram for you tomorrow, we have four other horses running at the meeting, and I'm staying there for the three days. I won't be coming with you to Teesside for Lancat."

He opened his mouth to protest, but I said, "Vic Young is going up with Lancat. He will do all the technical part. It's the big race of the afternoon, as you know, and you'll be riding against very experienced jockeys. But all you've got to do is get quietly up on that colt, point it in the right direction, and tell it where to accelerate. And if it wins, for God's sake don't brag about how brilliant you are. There's nothing puts backs up quicker than a boastful jockey, and if you want the press on your side, which you most certainly do, you will give the credit to the horse. Even if you don't feel in the least modest, it will pay to act it."

He digested this thoughtfully.

I went on, "Don't despair if you make a right mess of any race. Everyone does, sometime. Just admit it to yourself. Never fool yourself, ever. Don't get upset by criticism. . . . And don't get swollen-headed from praise. . . . And keep your temper on a racecourse, all the time. You can lose it as much as you like on the way home."

After a while, he said, "You have given me more instructions on behavior than on how to win races."

"Well, you see, I trust your social manners less than your horsemanship."

He worked it out, and didn't know whether to be pleased or not.

After the glitter of Doncaster, Catterick Bridge racecourse disappointed him. His glance raked the simple stands, the modest weighing room, the small-meeting atmosphere, and he said bitterly, "Is this—all?"

"Never mind," I said, though I hadn't myself known what to expect. "Down there on the course are seven important furlongs, and they are all that matters."

The parade ring itself was attractive, with trees dotted all around. Alessandro came out in yellow and blue silks, one of a large bunch of apprentices, most of whom looked slightly smug or self-conscious or nervous, or all three at once.

Alessandro didn't. His face held no emotion whatsoever. I had expected him to be excited, but he wasn't. He watched Pulitzer plod round the parade ring as if it were of no more interest to him than a herd of cows. He settled into the saddle casually, and without haste gathered the reins to his satisfaction. Vic Young stood holding Pulitzer's rug and gazing up at Alessandro doubtfully.

"Jump him off, now," he said admonishingly. "You've got to keep him up there as long as you can."

Alessandro met my eyes over Vic's head. "Ride the way you've planned," I said, and he nodded.

He went away without fuss onto the course, and Vic Young, watching him go, exclaimed to me, "I never did like that snooty little sod, and now he doesn't look as though he's got his heart in the job."

"Let's wait and see," I said soothingly. And we waited. And we saw.

Alessandro rode the race exactly as he'd said he would. Drawn number five of sixteen runners, he made his way over to the rails in the first two furlongs, stayed steadfastly in fifth or sixth place for the next three, moved up slightly after that, and in the last sixty yards found an opening and some response from Pulitzer, and shot through the leading pair of apprentices not more than ten strides from the post. The colt won by a length and a half, beginning to waver.

He hadn't been backed and he wasn't much cheered, but Alessandro didn't seem to need it. He slid off the horse in the unsaddling enclosure and gave me a cool stare quite devoid of the arrogant self-satisfaction I had been expecting. Then, suddenly, his face dissolved into the smile I'd only seen him give that once to Margaret, a warm, confident, uncomplicated expression of delight.

"I did it," he said, and I said, "You did it beautifully," and he could certainly see that I was as pleased as he was.

Pulitzer's win was not popular with the lads. No one had had a penny on it, and when Vic got back and reported that the old horse must have developed a lot with age as Alessandro hadn't ridden to instructions, they were all quick to deny him any credit. As he seldom talked to any of them, however, I doubted whether he knew.

He was highly self-contained when he came to Rowley Lodge the following morning. Etty had gone down to the Flat on the racecourse side with the first lot to give them some longish steady canters, which, because of the distance I had to drive, I couldn't stay to watch. She seemed content to be left in charge for the three days, and had assured me that Lancat and Lucky Lindsay (bound for a two-year-old five furlongs with an experienced northern jockey) would arrive safely at Teesside on the Saturday.

Alessandro came to Aintree with me in the Jensen, with Carlo following as before. On the way, we mostly discussed the tactics he would need on Buckram and Lancat, and again there was an odd lack of excitement, only this time more marked. Where I would have expected him to be strung up and passionate, he was totally relaxed. Now that he was actually racing, it seemed as if his impatient fever had evaporated.

Buckram didn't win for him, but not because he didn't ride the race he had meant to. Buckram finished third because two other horses were faster, and Alessandro accepted it with surprising resignation.

"He did his best," he explained simply. "But we couldn't get there."

"I saw," I said; and that was that.

During the rest of the three-day meeting, I came to know a great many more racing people and began to get the feel of the industry. I saddled our other four runners, which Tommy Hoylake rode, and congratulated him when one of them won.

"Funny thing," he said. "The horses are as forward this year as I've ever known them."

"Is that good or bad?" I asked.

"Are you kidding? But the next trick will be to keep them going till September."

"My father will be back to do that," I assured him.

"Oh . . . yes. I suppose he will," Tommy said, without the enthusiasm I would have expected, and took himself off to weigh out for the next race.

On Saturday, Lancat cruised home by four lengths at Teesside at twenty-five-to-one, which increased my season's winnings from two thousand to four thousand five hundred. And that, I imagined, would be the last of the easy pickings; Lancat was the fourth winner from the stable out of eight runners, and no one was any longer going to suppose that Rowley Lodge was in the doldrums.

Alessandro's and Vic Young's accounts of what had happened at Teesside were predictably different.

Alessandro said, "You remember, in the trial, that I made up a lot of ground—but I did it too soon, because I had been left behind, and then he got tired. Well, he did produce that burst of speed again, just as we thought, and it worked well. I got him going a little before the last furlong pole and he simply zoomed past the others. It was terrific."

But Vic Young said, "He left it nearly too late. Got shut in. The others could ride rings round him, of course. That Lancat must be something special, winning in spite of being ridden by an apprentice having only his third race."

During the next week, we had eight more runners, of which Alessandro rode three. Only one of his was in an apprentice race, and none of them won. In one race, he was quite clearly outridden in a tight finish by the Champion Jockey, but all he said about that was that he would improve, he supposed, with practice.

The owners of all three horses turned up to watch, and raised not a grumble among them. Alessandro behaved toward them with sense and civility, though I gathered from an unguarded sneer he let loose when he thought no one was looking that he was acting away like crazy.

One of the owners was an American who turned out to be a subscriber to the syndicate which had bought out my antique shops. It amused him greatly to find I was Neville Griffon's son, and he spent some time in the parade ring before the race telling Alessandro that this young fellow here—meaning me—could teach everyone he knew a thing or two about how to run a business.

"Never forgot how you summed up your recipe for success when we bought you out. 'Put an eye-catcher in the window, and deal fair.' We'd asked you, remember? And we were expecting a whole dose of the usual management-school jargon, but that was all you said. Never forgot it."

It was his horse on which Alessandro lost by a head, but he had owned race horses for a long time and knew what he was seeing, and he turned to me in the stands immediately they had passed the post, and said, "Never a disgrace to be beaten by the champion. . . . And that boy of yours, he's going to be good."

The following week, Alessandro rode in four races and won two of them, both against apprentices. On the second occasion, he beat the previous season's star apprentice discovery on the home ground at Newmarket, and the press began to ask questions. Four wins in three weeks had put him high on the apprentice list. Where had he come from, they wanted to know. One or two of them spoke to Alessandro himself, and to my relief he answered them quietly. Strictly eyes down, even if tongue in cheek. The old habitual arrogance was kept firmly out of sight.

He usually came to the races in the Jensen, but Carlo never gave up following. The arrangement had become routine.

He talked quite a lot on the journeys. Talked naturally, un-self-consciously, without strain. Mostly we discussed the horses and their form and possibilities in relation to the opposition, but sometimes I had another glimpse or two of his extraordinary home life.

He had not seen his mother since he was about six, when she and his father had had a last appalling row which had seemed to him to go on for days. He said he had been frightened because they were both so violent, and he hadn't understood what it was all about. She kept shouting one word at his father, taunting him, he said, and he had remembered it, though for years he didn't know what it meant. Sterile, that had been the word. His father was sterile. He had had some sort of illness shortly after Alessandro's birth, to which his mother had constantly referred. He couldn't remember her features, only her voice beginning sentences to his father, bitterly and often, with "Since your illness . . ."

He had never asked his father about it, he added. It would be impossible to ask.

I reflected that if Alessandro was the only son Enso could ever have, it explained in some measure the obsessive side of his regard for him. Alessandro was special to Enso in a psychologically disturbing way, and Enso, with well-developed criminal characteristics, was not a normal character in the first place.

As Alessandro's riding successes became more than coincidences, Etty unbent to him a good deal; and Margaret unbent even more. For a period of about four days, there was an interval of peaceful, constructive teamwork in a friendly atmosphere. Something which, looking back to the day of his arrival, one would have said was as likely as snow in Singapore.

Four days, it lasted. Then he arrived one morning with a look of apprehension, and said that his father was coming to England. Was flying over that same afternoon. He had telephoned, and he hadn't sounded pleased.

13

Enso moved into the Forbury Inn, and the very next day the prickles were back in Alessandro's manner. He refused to go to Epsom with me in the Jensen; he was going with Carlo.

"Very well," I said calmly, and had a distinct impression that he wanted to say something, to explain, to entreat—perhaps something like that—but that loyalty to his father was preventing it. I smiled a bit ruefully at him and added, "But any day you like, come with me."

There was a flicker in the black eyes, but he turned away without answering and walked off to where Carlo was waiting; and when we arrived at Epsom I found that Enso had traveled with him as well.

Enso was waiting for me outside the weighing room, a shortish chubby figure standing harmlessly in the April sunshine. No silenced pistol. No rubber-faced henchmen. No ropes round my wrists, needles in my arm. Yet my scalp contracted and the hairs on my legs rose on end. An indefinable quality of abnormality pervaded the atmosphere around him.

He held in his hand the letter I had written him, and the hostility in his puffy-lidded eyes beat anything Alessandro had ever conjured up by a good twenty lengths.

"You have disobeyed my instructions," he said, in the sort of voice which would have sent bolder men than I scurrying for shelter. "I told you that Alessandro was to replace Hoylake. I find that he has not done so. You have given my son only crumbs. You will change that."

"Alessandro," I said, with as unmoved an expression as I could manage, "has had more opportunities than most apprentices get in their first six months."

The eyes flashed with a thousand-kilowatt sizzle. "You will not talk to me in that tone. You will do as I say. Do you understand? I will not tolerate your continued disregard of my instructions."

I considered him. Where on the night he had abducted me he had been deliberate and cool, he was now fired by some inner strong emotion. It made him no less dangerous. More, possibly.

"Alessandro is riding a very good horse in the Dean Swift Handicap this afternoon," I said.

"He tells me this race is not important. It is the Great Metropolitan which is important. He is to ride in that race as well."

"Did he say he wanted to?" I asked curiously, because our runner in the Great Met was the runaway Traffic, and even Tommy Hoylake regarded the prospect without joy.

"Of course," Enso insisted, but I didn't wholly believe him. I thought he had probably bullied Alessandro into saying it.

"I'm afraid," I said with insincere regret, "that the owner could not be persuaded. He insists that Hoylake should ride. He is adamant."

Enso smoldered, but abandoned the lost cause. He said instead, "You will try harder in future. Today I will overlook. But there is to be no doubt, no shadow of doubt—do you understand?—that Alessandro is to ride this horse of yours in the Two Thousand Guineas. Next week he is to ride Archangel, as he wishes. Archangel."

I said nothing. It was still as impossible for Alessandro to be given the ride on Archangel as ever it was, even if I wanted to, which I didn't. The merchant banker was never going to agree to replacing Tommy Hoylake with an apprentice of five weeks' experience, not on the starriest Derby prospect he had ever owned. And for my father's sake also, Archangel had to have the best jockey he could. Enso took my continuing silence for acceptance, began to look less angry and more satisfied, and finally turned his back on me in dismissal.

Alessandro rode a bad race in the Handicap. He knew the race was the Derby distance, and he knew I was giving him practice at the mile and a half because I hoped he would win the big apprentice race of that length two days later; but he hopelessly misjudged things, swung really wide at Tattenham Corner, failed to balance his mount in and out of the dip, and never produced the speed that was there for the asking.

He wouldn't meet my eyes when he dismounted, and after Tommy Hoylake won the Great Met (as much to Traffic's surprise as to mine) I didn't see him for the rest of the day.

Alessandro rode four more races that week, and in none of them showed his former flair. He lost the apprentices' race at Epsom by a glaringly obvious piece of mistiming, letting the whole field slip him half a mile from home and failing to reach third place by a neck, though traveling faster than anything else at the finish.

At Sandown on the Saturday, the two owners he rode for both told me, after he trailed in mid-field on their fancied and expensive three-year-olds, that they did not agree that he was as good as I had made out, that my father would have known better, and that they would like a different jockey next time.

I relayed these remarks to Alessandro by sending into the changing room for him and speaking to him in the weighing room itself. I was now given little opportunity to talk to him anywhere else. He was wooden in the mornings and left the instant he dismounted, and at the races he was continuously flanked by Enso and Carlo, who accompanied him everywhere like guards.

He listened to me with desperation. He knew he had ridden badly, and made no attempt to justify himself. All he said, when I was finished, was "Can I ride Archangel in the Guineas?"

"No," I said.

"Please," he said with distress. "Please say I can ride him. I beg you."

I shook my head.

"You don't understand." It was an entreaty; but I wouldn't and couldn't give him what he wanted.

"If your father will give you anything you ask," I said slowly, "ask him to go back to Switzerland and leave you alone."

It was he then who shook his head, but helplessly, not in disagreement.

"Please," he said again, but without any hope in his voice, "I must—ride Archangel. My father believes that you are going to let me, even though I told him you wouldn't. . . . I am so afraid that if you don't, he really will destroy the stable—and then I will not be able to race again—and I can't—bear—" He limped to a stop.

"Tell him," I suggested without emphasis, "that if he destroys the stable you will hate him forever."

He looked at me numbly. "I think I would," he said.

"Then tell him so, before he does it."

"I'll—" He swallowed. "I'll try."

He didn't turn up to ride out the next morning, the first he had missed since his bump on the head. Etty suggested it was time some of the other apprentices had more chances than the very few I had given them, and indicated that their earlier ill feeling toward Alessandro had all returned with interest.

I agreed with her for the sake of peace, and drove off for my Sunday visit south.

My father was bearing the stable's successes with fortitude and finding some comfort in its losses. He did, however, seem genuinely to want Archangel to win the Guineas, and told me he had had long telephone talks with Tommy Hoylake about how it should be ridden.

He said that his assistant trainer was finally showing signs of coming out of his coma, though the doctors feared irreparable brain damage. He thought he would have to find a replacement.

His own leg also was mending properly at last, he said. He hoped to be home in time for the Derby; and he wouldn't be needing me after that.

The hours spent with Gillie were the usual oasis of peace and amusement, and bedtime was even more satisfactory than usual.

Most of the newspapers that day carried summings-up of the Guineas, with varying assessments of Archangel's chances. They all agreed that Hoylake's big-race temperament was a considerable asset.

I wondered if Enso read the English papers.

I hoped he didn't.

There were to be no race meetings for the next two days, not until Ascot and Catterick on Wednesday, followed by the Newmarket Guineas meeting on Thursday, Friday, and Saturday.

Monday morning, Alessandro appeared on leaden feet with charcoal shadows round his eyes, and said his father was practically raving because Tommy Hoylake was still down to ride Archangel.

"I told him," he said, "that you wouldn't let me ride him. I told him I understood why you wouldn't. I told him I would never forgive him if he did any more harm here. But he doesn't really listen. I don't know. . . . He's different, somehow. Not how he used to be."

But Enso, I imagined, was what he had always been. It was Alessandro himself who had changed.

I said merely, "Stop fretting over it and bend your mind to a couple of races you had better win for your own sake."

"What?" he said vaguely.

"Wake up, you silly nit. You're throwing away all you've worked so hard for. It soon won't matter a damn if you're warned off for life; you're riding so atrociously you won't get any rides anyway."

He blinked, and the old fury made a temporary comeback. "You will not speak to me like that."

"Want to bet?"

"Oh. . . ." he said in exasperation. "You and my father, you tear me apart."

"You'll have to choose your own life," I said matter-of-factly. "And if it still includes being a jockey, mind you win at Catterick. I'm running Buckram there in the apprentice race, and I should give one of the other lads the chance, but I'm putting you up again, and if you don't win they will likely lynch you."

He tried to lift his flagging spirits. His heart was no longer in it.

"And on Thursday, here at Newmarket, you can ride Lancat in the Heath Handicap. It's a straight mile, for three-year-olds only, and I reckon he should win it, on his Teesside form. So get cracking, study those races, and know approximately what the opposition might do. And you bloody well win them both. Understand?"

He gave me a long stare in which there was all of the old intensity but none of the old hostility.

"Yes," he said finally. "I understand. I am to bloody well win them both." It was the first attempt at a joke I had ever heard him make.

Etty was rigidly angry over Buckram. My father would not approve, she said; and another private report was clearly on its way.

I sent Vic Young up to Catterick and went myself

with three other horses to Ascot, telling myself that I was in duty bound to escort the owners at the bigger meeting, and that it had nothing to do with wanting to avoid Enso.

Out on the Heath, during the wait at the bottom of Side Hill for two other stables to complete their canters, I discussed with Alessandro the tactics he proposed using. Apart from the shadows which persisted round his eyes, he seemed to have regained some of his former race-day icy calm. It had yet to survive a long drive in his father's company, but it was a hopeful sign.

Buckram finished second. I felt distinctly disappointed when I saw his name on the "Results from Other Meetings" board at Ascot, but when I got back to Rowley Lodge Vic Young was just returning with Buckram, and he was, for him, enthusiastic.

"He rode a good race," he said, nodding. "Intelligent, you might say. Not his fault he got beat. Not like those stinking efforts last week. He didn't look the same boy, not at all."

The boy walked into the Newmarket parade ring the following afternoon with all the inward-looking self-possession I could want.

"It's a straight mile," I said. "Don't get tempted by the optical illusion that the winning post is much nearer than it really is. You'll know where you are by the furlong posts. Don't pick him up until you've passed the one with two on it, by the bushes, even if you think it looks wrong."

"I won't," he said seriously. And he didn't.

He rode a copybook race, cool, well paced, unflustered. From looking boxed-in two furlongs out, he suddenly sprinted through a split-second opening and reached the winning post an extended length ahead of his nearest rival. With his five-pound apprentice allowance and his Teesside form, he had carried a lot of public money, and he earned his cheers.

When he slid down from Lancat in the winner's unsaddling enclosure, he gave me again the warm rare smile, and I reckoned that, as well as too much weight and too much arrogance, he was going to kick the problem of too much father.

But his focus shifted to somewhere behind me, and the smile changed and disintegrated, first into a deprecating smirk and then into plain apprehension.

I turned round.

Enso stood inside the small white-railed enclosure. Enso stared at me.

I had offered Alessandro a life of his own away from his father, set him on the way to success in the job he craved, and shown him that his father's values were not the only ones possible, and that others were saner.

To turn Alessandro gradually from a threat to an ally had been my solution to the problem. A quiet, productive outcome, because once Alessandro was totally committed to the stable, he would never allow his father to destroy it.

Alessandro was halfway across the bridge. And Enso guessed it. Enso was not going to allow me to take his son. Not if he could help it.

I stared back. Nothing else to do.

I was afraid.

I daresay it was asking for trouble to work at the desk in the oak room after I'd seen round the stables and poured myself a modest Scotch. But this time it was a fine light evening on the last day in April, not midnight in a freezing March.

The door opened with an aggressive crash and Enso walked through it with his two men behind him, the stony-faced familiar Carlo and another with a long nose, small mouth, and no evidence of loving-kindness.

Enso was accompanied by his gun, and the gun was accompanied by its silencer.

"Stand up," he said.

I slowly stood.

He waved the gun toward the door.

"Come," he said.

I didn't move.

The gun steadied on the central area of my chest. He handled the wicked-looking thing as coolly, as familiarly, as a toothbrush.

"I am close to killing you," he said in such a way that I saw no reason not to believe him. "If you do not come at once, you will go nowhere."

This time, there were no little jokes about only killing people if they insisted. But I remembered; and I didn't insist. I moved out from behind the desk and walked woodenly toward the door.

Enso moved back to let me pass, too far away from me for me to jump him. But with the two now barefaced helpers at hand, I would have had no chance at all if I had tried.

Across the large central hall of Rowley Lodge, the main front door stood open. Outside, through the lobby and the farther doors, stood a Mercedes. Not Alessandro's. This one was maroon, and a size larger.

I was invited inside it. The American ex-rubber face drove. Enso sat on my right side in the back, and Carlo on the left. Enso held his gun in his right hand, balancing the silencer on his rounded knee, and his finger never relaxed. I could feel the angry tension in all his muscles whenever the moving car swayed his weight against me.

The American drove the Mercedes northward along the Norwich road, but only for a short distance. Just past the Limekilns and before the bridge over the railway line, he swung off to the left into a small wood, and stopped as soon as the car was no longer in plain sight of the road.

He had stopped on one of the regular and often highly populated walking grounds. The only snag was that as all horses had to be off the Heath by four o'clock every afternoon, there was unlikely to be anyone at that hour along there to help.

"Out," Enso said, and I did as he said.

There was a short pause while the American, who seemed to be known as Cal to his friends, walked around to the back of the car and opened the boot. From it he took first a canvas grip, which he handed to Carlo. Next he produced a long darkish gray gabardine raincoat, which he put on although the weather was as good as the forecast. Finally he picked out with loving care a Lee Enfield .303.

Protruding from its underside was a magazine for ten bullets. He very deliberately worked the bolt to bring the first of them into the breech. Then he pulled back the short lever which locked the firing mechanism in the safety position.

I looked at the massive rifle which he handled so carefully yet with such accustomed precision. It was a gun to frighten with as much as to kill, though from what I knew of it, a bullet from it would blow a man to pieces at a hundred yards, would pierce the brick walls of an average house like butter, would penetrate fifteen feet into sand, and, if unimpeded, would carry accurately for five miles. Compared with a shotgun, which wasn't reliably lethal at a range of more than thirty yards, the Lee Enfield .303 was a dam-buster to a peashooter. Compared with the silenced pistol, which couldn't be counted on even as far as a shotgun, it gave making a dash for it over the Heath as much chance of success as a tortoise in the Olympics.

I raised my eyes from the source of these unprofitable thoughts and met the unwinking gaze of its owner. He was obscurely amused, enjoying the effect his pet had had on me. I had never, as far as I knew, met an assassin before; but without any doubt, I knew them.

"Walk along there," Enso said, pointing with his pistol up the walking ground. So I walked, thinking that a Lee Enfield made a lot of noise. The only thing was the bullet traveled one and a half times as fast as sound, so that you'd be dead before you heard the bang.

Cal had calmly put the big gun under the long raincoat and was carrying it upright with his hand through what was clearly a slit, not a pocket. From even a very short distance away, one would not have known he had it with him.

Not that there was anyone to see. My gloomiest assessments were quite right: we emerged from the little wood onto the narrow end of the Railway Field, and there wasn't a horse or a rider in sight.

Across the field, alongside the railway, there was a fence made of wooden posts with a wooden top rail and plain wire strands below. There were a few bushes bursting green round about, and a calm peaceful spring evening sunshine touching everything with red gold.

When we reached the fence, Enso said to stop.

I stopped.

"Fasten him up," he said to Carlo and Cal; and he himself stayed quietly pointing his pistol at me while Cal laid his deadly treasure flat on the ground and Carlo unzipped the canvas holdall.

From it he produced nothing more forbidding than two narrow leather belts, with buckles. He gave one of them to Cal, and without allowing me the slightest hope of escape, they turned my back toward the fence and each fastened one of my wrists to the top wooden rail.

It didn't seem much. It wasn't even uncomfortable; the rail was barely more than waist high. It just seemed professional, as I couldn't even turn my hands inside the straps, let alone slide them out.

They stepped away, behind Enso, and the sunlight threw my shadow on the ground in front of me. . . . Just a man leaning against a fence on an evening stroll.

Away in the distance on my left I could see the cars going over the railway bridge on the Norwich road, and farther still, down toward Newmarket on my right, there were glimpses of the traffic in and out of the town.

The town, the whole area, was bursting with thousands of visitors to the Guineas meeting. They might as well have been at the South Pole. From where I stood, there wasn't a soul within screaming distance.

Just Enso and Carlo and Cal.

I had watched Cal in his efforts on my right wrist, but it seemed to me shortly after they had finished that it was Carlo who had been rougher.

I turned my head and understood why I thought so. He had somehow turned my arm over the top of the rail and strapped it so that my palm was half facing backward. I could feel the strain taking shape right up through my shoulder and I thought at first he had done it by accident.

Then, with unwelcome clarity, I remembered what Dainsee had said: the easiest way to break a bone is to twist it, to put it under stress.

Oh, Christ, I thought; and my mind cringed.

14

I said, "I thought this sort of thing went out with the Middle Ages."

Enso was not in the mood for flippant comment.

Enso was stoking himself up into a proper fury.

"I hear everywhere today on the racecourse that Tommy Hoylake is going to win the Two Thousand Guineas on Archangel. Everywhere, Tommy Hoylake, Tommy Hoylake."

I said nothing.

"You will correct that. You will tell the newspapers that it is to be Alessandro. You will let Alessandro ride Archangel on Saturday."

Slowly I said, "Even if I wanted to, I could not put Alessandro on the horse. The owner will not have it."

"You must find a way," Enso said. "There is to be no more of this blocking of my orders, no more of these tactics of producing unsurmountable reasons why you are not able to do as I say. This time you will do it. This time you will work out how you *can* do it, not how you cannot."

I was silent.

Enso warmed to his subject.

"Also you will not entice my son away from me."

"I have not."

"Liar." The hatred flared up like magnesium, and his voice rose half an octave. "Everything Alessandro says is Neil Griffon this and Neil Griffon that and Neil Griffon says, and I have heard your name so much that I could *cut—your—throat!*" He was almost shouting as he bit out the last three words. His hands were shaking; and the gun barrel wavered round its target. I could feel the muscles tighten involuntarily in my stomach, and my wrists jumped uselessly against the straps.

He took a step nearer and his voice was loud and high.

"What my son wants, I will give him. *I . . . I . . .* will give him. I will give him what he wants."

"I see," I said, and reflected that comprehending the situation went no way at all toward getting me out of it.

"There is no one who does not do as I say," he shouted. "No one. When Enso Rivera tells people to do things, they do them!"

Whatever I said was as likely to enrage as to calm him, so I said nothing at all. He took another step toward me, until I could see the glint of gold-capped back teeth and smell the sweet heavy scent of his aftershave.

"You, too," he said. "You, too, will do what I say! There is no one who can boast he disobeyed Enso Rivera. There is no one alive who has disobeyed Enso Rivera!" The pistol moved in his grasp and Cal picked up his Lee Enfield, and it was quite clear what had become of the disobedient.

"You would be dead now," he said. "And I want to kill you." He thrust his head forward on his short neck, the strong nose standing out like a beak and the black eyes as dangerous as napalm. "But my son—my son says he will hate me forever if I kill you. And for that

182

I want to kill you more than I have ever wanted to kill anyone."

He took another step and rested the silencer against my thin wool sweater shirt, with my heart thumping away only a couple of inches below it. I was afraid he would risk it, afraid he would calculate that Alessandro would in time get over the loss of his racing career, afraid he would believe that things would somehow go back and be the same as on the day his son casually said, "I want to ride Archangel in the Derby."

I was afraid.

But Enso didn't pull the trigger. He said, as if the one followed inexorably from the other, as I suppose in a way it did, "So I will not kill you. . . . But I will make you do what I say. I cannot afford for you not to do what I say. I am going to make you."

I didn't ask how. Some questions are so silly they are better left unsaid. I could feel the sweat prickling out on my body, and I was sure he could read the apprehension on my face; and he had done nothing at all yet, nothing but threaten.

"Alessandro will ride Archangel," he said. "The day after tomorrow. In the Two Thousand Guineas."

His face was close enough for me to see the black-heads in the unhealthy putty skin.

I said nothing. He wasn't asking for a promise. He was telling me.

He took a pace backward and nodded his head at Carlo. Carlo picked up the holdall and produced from it a truncheon very like the one I had removed from him in Buckram's box.

Promazine first?

No promazine.

They didn't mess around making things easy, as they had for the horses. Carlo simply walked straight up to me, lifted his right arm with truncheon attached, and brought it down with as much force as he could manage. He seemed to be taking pride in his work. He concentrated on getting the direction just right. And it wasn't any of the fearsome things like my twisted elbow that he hit, but my collarbone.

Not too bad, I thought confusedly in the first two seconds of numbness, and anyway steeplechase jockeys broke their collarbones any bloody day of the week, and didn't make a fuss of it. But the difference between a racing fall and Carlo's effort lay in the torque and tension all the way up my arm. They acted like one of Archimedes' precious levers and pulled the ends of my collarbone apart. When sensation returned with ferocity, I could feel the tendons in my neck tighten into strings and stand out taut with the effort of keeping my mouth shut.

I saw on Enso's face a gray look of suffering—narrow eyes, clamped lips, anxious contracted muscles, lines showing along his forehead and round his eyes—and realized with extraordinary shock that what I saw on his face was a mirror of my own.

When his jaw relaxed a fraction, I knew it was because mine had. When his eyes opened a little and some of the over-all tension slackened, it was because the worst had passed with me.

It wasn't sympathy, though, on his part. Imagination, rather. He was putting himself in my place, to savor what he'd caused. Pity he couldn't do it more thoroughly. I'd break a bone for him any time he asked.

He nodded sharply several times, a message of satisfaction. There was still a heavy unabated anger in his manner and no guarantee that he had finished his evening's work. But he looked regretfully at the pistol, unscrewed the silencer, and handed both bits to Cal, who stowed them away under the raincoat.

Enso stepped close to me. Very close. He ran his finger down my cheek and rubbed the sweat from it against his thumb.

"Alessandro will ride Archangel in the Guineas," he said. "Because if he doesn't, I will break your other arm. Just like this."

I didn't say anything. Couldn't, really.

Carlo unfastened the strap from my right wrist and put it with the truncheon in the holdall, and they all three turned their backs on me and walked away across the field and through the wood to the waiting Mercedes.

It took a long inch-by-inch time to get my right hand round to my left, to undo the other strap. After that, I sat on the ground with my back against one of the posts to wait until things got better. They didn't seem to, much.

I looked at my watch. Eight o'clock. Time for dinner, down at the Forbury Inn. Enso probably had his fat knees under the table, tucking in with a good appetite.

In theory, it had seemed reasonable that the most conclusive way to defeat him had been to steal his son away. In practice, as I gingerly hugged to my chest my severely sore left arm, I doubted if Alessandro's soul was worth the trouble. Arrogant, treacherous, spoiled little bastard; but with guts and determination and talent. A mini battlefield, torn apart by loyalty to his father and the lure of success on his own. A pawn, pushed around in a power struggle. But this pawn was all, and whoever captured the pawn won the game.

I sighed, and slowly, wincing, got back on my feet. No one except me was going to get me home and bandaged up.

I walked. It was less than a mile. But far enough.

The elderly doctor was fortunately at home when I telephoned.

"What do you mean you fell off a horse and broke your collarbone?" he demanded. "At this hour? I thought all horses had to be off the Heath by four."

"Look," I said wearily, "I've broken my collarbone. Would you come and deal with it?"

"Mm," he grunted. "All right."

He came within half an hour, equipped with what looked like a couple of rubber quoits. Clavicle rings, he said as he proceeded to push one up each of my shoulders and tie them together behind my back.

"Bloody uncomfortable," I said.

"Well, if you will fall off horses . . ."

His heavy eyes assessed his handiwork with impassive professionalism. Tying up broken collarbones in Newmarket was as regular as dispensing cough drops.

"Take some codeine," he said. "Got any?"

"I don't know."

He clicked his tongue and produced a packet from his bag. "Two every four hours."

"Thank you. Very much."

"That's all right," he said, nodding. He shut his bag and flipped the clips.

"Have a drink?" I suggested as he helped me into my shirt.

"Thought you'd never ask," he said, smiling, and dealt with a large whiskey as familiarly as with his bandages. I kept him company, and the spirit helped the codeine along considerably.

"As a matter of interest," I said as he reached the second half of his glassful, "what illnesses cause sterility?"

"Eh?" He looked surprised, but answered straightforwardly, "Only two, really. Mumps and venereal disease. But mumps very rarely causes complete sterility. Usually affects one testicle only, if it affects any at all. Syphilis is the only sure sterility one. But with modern treatment, it doesn't progress that far."

"Would you tell me more about it?"

"Hypothetical?" he asked. "I mean, you don't think you yourself may be infected? Because if so——"

"Absolutely not," I interrupted. "Strictly hypothetical."

"Good." He drank efficiently. "Well. Sometimes people contract both syphilis and gonorrhea at once. Say they get treated and cured of gonorrhea, but the syphilis goes unsuspected. Right? Now, syphilis is a progressive disease, but it can lie quiet for years, doing its slow damage more or less unknown to its host. Sterility could occur a few years after infection. One couldn't say exactly how many years; it varies enormously. But before the sterility occurs, any number of infected children could be conceived. Mostly they are stillborn. Some live, but there's almost always something wrong with them."

Alessandro had said his father had been ill after he was born, which seemed to put him in the clear. But venereal disease would account for Enso's wife's extreme bitterness, and the violent breakup of the marriage.

"Henry the Eighth," the doctor said, as if it followed naturally on.

"What?" I said.

"Henry the Eighth," he repeated patiently. "He had syphilis. Catherine of Aragon had about a dozen stillborn children, and her one surviving child, Mary, was barren. His sickly son Edward died young. Don't know about Elizabeth, not enough data." He polished off the last drop of his glass.

I pointed to the bottle. "Would you mind helping yourself?"

He got to his feet and refilled my glass, too. "He went about blaming his poor wives for not producing sons, when it was his fault all the time. And that extreme fanaticism about having a son—and cutting off heads right and left to get one—that's typical obsessive syphilitic behavior."

"How do you mean?"

"The pepper king," he said, as if that explained all.

"What had he got to do with pepper, for heaven's sake?"

"Not Henry the Eighth," he said impatiently. "The pepper king was someone else. Look, in the medical textbooks, in the chapter on the advanced complications which can arise from syphilis, there's this bit about the pepper king. He was a chap who had megalomania in an interim stage of G.P.I., and he got this obsession about pepper. He set out to corner all the pepper in the world and make himself into a tycoon, and because of his compulsive fanaticism, he managed it."

I sorted my way through the maze. "Are you saying that at a further stage than sterility, our hypothetical syphilitic gent can convince himself that he can move mountains?"

"Not only convince himself," he agreed, nodding, "but actually do it. There is literally no one more likely to move mountains than your megalomaniac syphilitic. Not that it lasts forever, of course. Twenty years, perhaps, in that stage, once it's developed."

"And then what?"

"G.P.I." He took a hefty swallow. "General paralysis of the insane. In other words, descent to cabbage."

"Inevitable?"

"After this megalomania stage, yes. But not everyone who gets syphilis gets G.P.I., and not everyone who gets G.P.I. gets megalomania first. They're only branch lines—fairly rare complications."

"They would need to be," I said with feeling.

"Indeed, yes. If you meet a syphilitic megalomaniac, duck. Duck, quickly, because they can be dangerous. There's a theory that Hitler was one." He looked at me thoughtfully over the top of his glass, and his old damp eyes slowly widened. His gaze focused on the sling he had put round my arm, and he said as if he couldn't believe what he was thinking, "You didn't duck quick enough."

"A horse threw me," I said.

He shook his head. "It was a direct blow. I could see that—but I couldn't believe it. Thought it very puzzling, as a matter of fact."

"A horse threw me," I repeated.

He looked at me in awakening amusement. "If you say so," he said. "A horse threw you. I'll write that in my notes." He finished his drink and stood up. "Don't stand in his path any more, then. And I'm serious, young Neil. Just remember that Henry the Eighth chopped off a lot of heads."

"I'll remember," I said.

As if I could forget.

I rethought the horse-threw-me story and substituted a fall down the stairs for Etty's benefit.

"What a damn nuisance," she said in brisk sympathy, and obviously thought me clumsy. "I'll drive you along to Waterhall in the Land-Rover when we pull out."

I thanked her, and while we were waiting for the lads to lead the horses out of the boxes for the first lot, we walked round into bay one to check on Archangel. Checking on Archangel had become my most frequent occupation.

He was installed in the most secure of the high-security boxes, and since Enso's return to England I had had him guarded day and night. Etty thought my care excessive, but I had insisted.

By day, bay one was never left unattended. By night, the electric eye was positioned to trap unwanted visitors. Two specially engaged security men watched all the time, in shifts, from the owners' room, where the window looked out toward Archangel's box; and their Alsatian dog, on a long tethering chain, crouched on the ground outside the box and snarled at everyone who approached.

The lads had complained about the dog, because each time they had to see to any horse in bay one, they had to fetch the security guard to help them. All other stables, they had pointed out, had a dog on duty only at night.

Etty waved one arm to the guard in the window. He nodded, came out into the yard, and held his dog on a short leash so that we could walk by safely. Archangel came over to the door when I opened the top half, and poked his nose out into the soft Mayday morning. I rubbed his muzzle and patted his neck, admiring the gloss on his coat and thinking that he hadn't looked better in all the weeks I'd been there.

"Tomorrow," Etty said to him, with a gleam in her eyes, "we'll see what you can do, boy, tomorrow." She smiled at me in partnership, acknowledging finally that I had taken some share in getting him ready. During the past month, since the winners had begun mounting up, her air of constant worry had mostly disappeared, and the confidence I had remembered in her manner had all come back. "And we'll see how much more we'll have to do with him to win the Derby."

"My father will be back for that," I said, intending to reassure her. But the spontaneity went out of her smile, and she looked blank.

"So he will," she said. "Do you know . . . I'd forgotten."

She turned away from his box and walked out into the main yard. I thanked the large ex-policeman guard and begged him and his mate to be especially vigilant for the next thirty-four hours.

"Safe as the Bank of England, sir. Never you fear, sir." He was easy with certainty, but I thought him optimistic.

Alessandro didn't turn up to ride out, not for either lot. But when I climbed stiffly out of the Land-Rover after the second dose of Etty's jolting driving, he was standing waiting for me at the entrance to the yard. When I walked toward the door to the office, he came to meet me and stopped in my way.

I stopped also, and looked at him. He held himself rigidly, and his face was thin and white with strain.

"I am sorry," he said jerkily. "I am sorry. He told me what he had done. . . . I did not want it. I did not ask it."

"Good," I said casually. I thought about the way I was carrying my head on one side because it was less painful like that. I felt it was time to straighten up. I straightened.

"He said you would now agree to me riding Archangel tomorrow."

"And what do you think?" I asked.

He looked despairing, but he answered without doubt. "I think you will not."

"You've grown up a lot," I said.

"I have learned from you." He shut his mouth suddenly and shook his head. "I mean—I beg you to let me ride Archangel."

I said mildly, "No."

The words burst out of him, "But he will break your other arm. He said so, and he always does what he says. He'll break your arm again, and I—and I—" He swallowed and took a grip on his voice, and said with much more control, "I told him this morning that it is right that I do not ride Archangel. I told him that if he hurt you any more you would tell the Stewards about everything, and I would be warned off. I told him I do not want him to do any more. I want him to leave me here with you, and let me get on on my own."

I took a slow deep breath. "And what did he say to that?"

He seemed bewildered as well as distraught. "I think it made him even more angry."

I said in explanation, "He doesn't so much care about whether or not you ride Archangel in the Guineas. He cares only about making me let you ride. He cares about proving to you that he can give you everything you ask, just as he always has."

"But I ask him now to leave you alone. Leave me here. And he will not listen."

"You are asking him for the only thing he won't give you," I said.

"And what is that?"

"Freedom."

"I don't understand," he said.

"Because he did not want you to have freedom, he gave you everything else. Everything . . . to keep you with him. As he sees it, I have recently been holding out to you the one thing he doesn't want you to have. The power to make a success of life on your own. So his fight with me now is not really about who rides Archangel tomorrow, but about you."

He understood all right. And it was a revelation.

"I will tell him he has no fear of losing me," he said passionately. "Then he will do you no more harm."

"Don't you do that. His fear of losing you is all that's keeping me alive."

His mouth opened. He stared at me with the black eyes, a pawn lost between the rooks.

"Then what—what am I to do?"

"Tell him that Tommy Hoylake rides Archangel tomorrow."

His gaze wandered down from my face to the hump made by the clavicle rings and the outline of my arm in its sling inside my jersey.

"I cannot," he said.

I half smiled. "He will find out soon enough."

Alessandro shivered slightly. "You don't understand. I have seen. . . ." His voice trailed away and he looked back to my face with a sort of awakening on his own. "I have seen people he has hurt. Afterward, I've seen them. There was fear in their faces. And shame, too. I just thought—how clever he was—to know how to make people do what he wanted. I've seen how everyone fears him . . . and I thought he was marvelous." He took a shaky breath. "I don't want him to make you look like those others."

"He won't," I said, with more certainty than I felt.

"But he will not just let Tommy ride Archangel, and do nothing about it. I know him. . . . I know he will not. I know he means what he says. You don't know what he can be like. You must believe it. You must."

"I'll do my best," I said dryly, and Alessandro almost danced with frustration.

"Neil," he said, and it was the only time he had called me by my first name, "I am afraid for you."

"That makes two of us," I said. I looked at him with compassion. "Don't take it so hard, boy."

"But you don't—you don't understand."

"I do indeed understand," I said.

"But you don't seem to care."

"Oh, I care," I said truthfully. "I'm not mad keen on another smashing-up session with your father. But I'm even less keen on crawling along the ground to lick his boots. So Tommy rides Archangel, and we keep our fingers crossed."

He shook his head, intensely troubled. "I know him," he said. "I know him. . . ."

"Next week at Bath," I said, "you can ride Pulitzer in the apprentice race, and Clip Clop at Chester."

His expression said plainly that he doubted we would ever reach next week.

"Did you ever have any brothers or sisters?" I asked abruptly.

He looked bewildered at the unconnected question. "No. My mother had two more children after me, but they were both born dead."

15

Saturday morning, May 2nd. Two Thousand Guineas day.

The sun rose to another high golden journey over the Heath, and I inched myself uncomfortably out of bed with less fortitude than I would have admired. The thought that Enso could inflict still more damage was one I hastily shied away from; yet I myself had blocked all his tangents and left him with only one target to aim at. Having engineered the full frontal confrontation, so to speak, it was too late to wish I hadn't.

I sighed. Were eighty-five thoroughbreds, my father's livelihood, the stable's future, and perhaps Alessandro's liberation worth one broken collarbone?

Well, yes, they were.

But *two* broken collarbones?

God forbid.

Through the buzz of my electric razor I considered the pros and cons of the quick getaway. A well-organized, unfollowed retreat to the fastness of Hampstead. Simple enough to arrange. The trouble was sometime or other I would have to come back; and while I was away the stable would be too vulnerable.

Perhaps I could fill the house with guests and make sure I was never alone. But the guests would depart in a day or two, and Enso's idea of vengeance would be as strong as Napoleon brandy.

I struggled into a sweater and went down into the yard hoping that even Enso would see that revenge was useless if it lost you what you prized most on earth. If he harmed me any more, he would lose his son permanently. The only reasonable course now left to him was to retract his threats, salvage what he could of Alessandro's regard, and quietly go home.

But would he be—could he be—reasonable?

It had long been arranged that Tommy Hoylake should take the opportunity of his overnight stay in Newmarket to ride a training gallop in the morning. Accordingly, at seven o'clock he drove his Jaguar up the gravel and stopped outside the office window.

"Morning," he said, stepping out.

"Morning." I looked at him closely. "You don't look terribly well."

He made a face. "Had a stomach ache all night. Threw up my dinner, too. I get like that, sometimes. Nerves, I guess. Anyway, I'm a bit better now. And I'll be fine by this afternoon, don't worry about that."

"You're sure?" I asked with anxiety.

"Yeah." He gave a pale grin. "I'm sure. Like I told you, I get this upset now and again. Nothing to worry about. But look, would you mind if I don't ride this gallop this morning?"

"No," I said. "Of course not. I'd much rather you didn't. We don't want anything to stop you being all right for this afternoon."

"Tell you what, though. I could give Archangel his pipe-opener. Nice and quiet. How about that?"

"If you're sure you're all right?" I said doubtfully.

"Yeah. Good enough for that. Honest."

"All right, then," I said, and he took Archangel out,

accompanied by Clip Clop, and they cantered a brisk four furlongs, watched by hundreds of the thousands who would yell for him down on the racecourse that afternoon.

Etty was taking the rest of the string along to Waterhall, where several were due for a three-quarter-speed mile along the Line Gallop.

"Who shall we put on Lucky Lindsay, now we haven't got Tommy?" Etty said. And it presented a slight problem, because we were short of enough lads with good hands.

"I suppose we had better swap them around," I said, "and put Andy on Lucky Lindsay and Faddy on Irrigate, and——"

"No need," Etty interrupted, looking toward the drive. "Alex is good enough, isn't he?"

I turned round. Alessandro was walking down the yard, dressed for work. Long gone were the dandified clothes and the pale string gloves. He now appeared regularly in a camel-colored sweater with a blue shirt beneath, an outfit he had copied from Tommy Hoylake on the basis that if that was what a top jockey wore to ride out in, it was what Alessandro Rivera should wear, too.

There was no Mercedes waiting behind him in the drive. No watchful Carlo staring down the yard. Alessandro saw my involuntary search for the faithful attendant, and he said awkwardly, "I skipped out. They said not to come, but Carlo's gone off somewhere, so I thought I would. May I . . . I mean, will you let me ride out?"

"Why ever not?" said Etty, who didn't know why ever not.

"Go ahead," I agreed. "You can ride the gallop on Lucky Lindsay."

He was surprised. "But it said in all the papers that Tommy was riding that gallop this morning."

"He's got a stomach ache," I said, and, as I saw the wild hope leap in his face, added, "And don't get excited. He's better, and he will definitely be O.K. for this afternoon."

"Oh."

He smothered the shattered hope as best he could and went off to fetch Lucky Lindsay. Etty was riding Cloud Cuckoo-land, along with the string, but I had arranged to have George drive me down later in the Land-Rover in time to watch the gallops. The horses pulled out, circled in the paddock to sort out the riders, and went away out of the gate, turning left along the walking ground toward Waterhall.

With them went Lancat, but he, after his hard race two days earlier, was just to go as far as the main road crossing, and then turn back.

I watched them all go, glossy and elegant creatures on one of those hazy May mornings like the beginning of the world. I took a deep regretful breath. It was strange, but in spite of Enso and his son, I had enjoyed my spell as a race-horse trainer. I was going to be sorry when I had to leave. Sorrier than I had imagined. Odd, I thought. Very odd.

I walked back up the yard, talked for a few minutes to Archangel's security guard, who was taking the opportunity of his absence to go off to the canteen for his breakfast, went into the house, made some coffee, and took it into the office. Margaret didn't come on Saturdays. I drank some of the coffee and opened the morning mail by holding the envelopes between my knees and slitting them with a paper knife.

I heard a car on the gravel, and the slam of a door, and just missed seeing who was passing the window through misjudging the speed at which I could turn my head. Any number of people would be coming to visit the stable on Guineas morning. Any of the owners who were staying in Newmarket for the meeting. Anyone.

It was Enso who had come. Enso with his silenced leveler. He was waving it about, as usual. So early in the morning, I thought frivolously. Guns before breakfast. Damn silly.

The end of the road, I thought. The end of the damn bloody road.

If Enso had looked angry before, he now looked explosive. The short thick body moved like a tank round the desk toward where I sat, and I knew what Alessandro meant about not knowing what he could be like. Enso up in Railway Field had been an appetizer: this one was a holocaust.

He waded straight in with a fierce right jab onto the elderly doctor's best bandaging, which took away at one stroke my breath, my composure, and most of my resistance. I made a serious stab at him with the paper knife and got my wrist bashed against the edge of the filing cabinet in consequence. He was strong and energetic and frightening, and I was not being so much beaten by Enso as overwhelmed. He hit me on the side of my head with his pistol, and then swung it by the silencer and landed the butt viciously on my shoulder, and by that time I was half sick and almost past caring.

"Where is Alessandro?" he shouted, two centimeters from my right ear.

I sagged rather spinelessly against the desk. I had my eyes shut. I was doing my tiny best to deal with an amount of feeling that was practically beyond my control.

He shook me. Not nice. "Where is Alessandro?" he yelled.

"On a horse," I said weakly. Where else? "On a horse."

"You have abducted him," he yelled. "You will tell me where he is! Tell me—or I'll break your bones. All of them."

"He's out riding a horse," I said.

"He's not!" Enso shouted. "I told him not to."

"Well . . . he is."

"What horse?"

"What does it matter?"

"What horse?" He was practically screaming in my ear.

"Lucky Lindsay," I said. As if it made any difference. I pushed myself upright in the chair and got my eyes open. Enso's face was only inches away, and the look in his eyes was a death warrant.

The gun came up. I waited numbly.

"Stop him," he said. "Get him back."

"I can't."

"You must. Get him back or I'll kill you."

"He's been gone twenty minutes."

"*Get him back.*" His voice was hoarse, high-pitched, and terrified. It finally got through to me that his rage had turned into agony. The fury had become fear. The black eyes burned with some unimaginable torment.

"What have you done?" I said rigidly.

"Get him back," he repeated, as if shouting alone would achieve it. "Get him back!" He lifted the gun, but I don't think even he knew if he intended to shoot me or to hit me with it.

"I can't," I said flatly. "Whatever you do, I can't."

"He will be killed," he yelled wildly. "My son—my son will be killed!" He waved his arms wide and his whole body jerked uncontrollably. "Tommy Hoylake . . . It says in the newspapers that Tommy Hoylake is riding Lucky Lindsay this morning."

I shifted onto the front of the chair, tucked my legs underneath it, and made the cumbersome shift up onto my feet. Enso didn't try to shove me back. He was too preoccupied with the horror trotting through his mind.

"Tommy Hoylake . . . Hoylake is riding Lucky Lindsay."

"No," I said roughly. "Alessandro is."

"Tommy Hoylake. . . . Hoylake. . . . It has to be, it has to be!" His eyes were stretching wider and his voice rose higher and higher.

I lifted my hand and slapped him hard in the face.

His mouth stayed open, but the noise coming out of it stopped as suddenly as if it had been switched off.

Muscles in his cheeks twisted. His throat moved continuously. I gave him no time to get going again.

"You were planning to kill Tommy Hoylake."

No answer.

"How?" I said.

No answer. I slapped his face again, with everything I could manage. It wasn't very much.

"How?"

"Carlo . . . and Cal . . ." The words were barely distinguishable.

Horses on the Heath, I thought. Tommy Hoylake riding Lucky Lindsay. Carlo, who knew every horse in the yard, who watched all the horses every day and knew Lucky Lindsay by sight as infallibly as any tout. And Cal . . . I felt my gut contract much as Enso's must have done. Cal had the Lee Enfield .303.

"Where are they?" I said.

"I—don't—know."

"You'd better find them," I said. "Go out and find them. It's your only chance. It's Alessandro's only chance. Find them before they shoot him—you stupid, murdering sod."

He stumbled as if blind round the desk and made for the door. Still holding the pistol, he bashed into the frame and rocked on his feet. He righted himself, crashed down the short passage and out through the door into the yard, and half ran on unsure legs to his dark red Mercedes. He took three tries at starting the engine before it started. Then he swept round in a frantic arc, roared away up the drive, and turned right onto the Bury Road with a shriek of tires.

Bloody, murdering sod . . . I followed him out of the office but turned down the yard.

Couldn't run. The new hammering he'd given my shoulder made even walking a trial. Stupid, mad, murdering bastard. Twenty minutes since Alessandro rode out on Lucky Lindsay . . . twenty minutes, and the rest. They'd be pretty well along at Waterhall. Circling round at the end of the Line Gallop, forming up into groups. Setting off . . .

Damn it, I thought. Why don't I just go and sit down

and wait for whatever happens. If Enso kills his precious son, serves him right.

I went faster down the yard. Through the gates into the bottom bays. Through the far gate. Across the little paddock. Out through the gate to the Heath. Turned left.

Just let him be coming back, I thought. Let him be coming back. Lancat, coming back from his walk, saddled and bridled and ready to go. He was there, coming toward me along the fence, led by one of the least proficient riders, sent back by Etty, as he was little use in the gallops.

"Help me take this jersey off," I said urgently to the rider.

He looked surprised, but lads my father had trained never argued. He helped me take off the jersey. He was no Florence Nightingale. I told him to take the sling off as well. No one could ride decently in a sling.

"Now give me a leg up."

He did that, too.

"O.K.," I said. "Go on in. I'll bring Lancat back later."

"Yes, sir," he said. And if I'd told him to stand on his head, he would have said "Yes, sir" just the same.

I turned Lancat back the way he had come. I made him trot along the walking ground. Breaking the Heath rules. Tut-tut. Breaking my own spirit, too. Cantering couldn't be worse. I twitched him out onto the Bury Hill ground which wasn't supposed to be used for another fortnight and pointed him straight at the Bury Road crossing.

Might as well gallop. . . . I did the first five furlongs on the gallop and the next three along the walking ground without slowing down much, and frightened a couple of early-morning motorists as I crossed the main road.

Too many horses on Waterhall. I couldn't from more than half a mile away distinguish the Rowley Lodge string from others. All I could see was that it wasn't yet too late. The morning scene was peaceful and orderly. No horrified groups bending over bleeding bodies.

I kept Lancat going. He'd had a hard race two days earlier and shouldn't have been asked for the effort I was urging him into. He was fast and willing, but I was running him into the ground.

It was technically difficult riding in clavicle rings, let alone anything else. However, the ground looked very hard and too far down. I stayed in the saddle as the lesser of two evils. I did wish most fervently that I had stayed at home. I knew all about steeplechase jockeys riding races with broken collarbones. They were crazy. It was for the birds.

I could see Etty. See some of the familiar horses.

I could see Alessandro on Lucky Lindsay.

I was too far away to be heard even if I'd had any breath for shouting, and neither of them looked behind them.

Alessandro kicked Lucky Lindsay into a fast canter and, with two other horses, accelerated quickly up the Line Gallop.

A mile away, up the far end of it, there were trees and scrub and a small wood.

And Carlo. And Cal.

I had a frightful feeling of inevitable disaster, like trying to run away through treacle in a nightmare. Lancat couldn't possibly catch the fresh Lucky Lindsay up the gallop. Interception was the only possibility, yet I could misjudge it so terribly easily.

I set off straight across Waterhall, galloping across the cantering ground and then charging over the Middle Canter in the opposite direction to the horses working there. Furious yells from all sides didn't deter me. I hoped Lancat had enough sense not to run head on into another horse, but apart from that my only worry— my sole, embracing, consuming worry—was to get to Alessandro before a bullet did.

Endless furlongs over the grass . . . only a mile, give or take a little . . . but endless. Lancat was tiring, find-

ing every fresh stride a deeper effort. . . . His fluid
rhythm had broken into bumps; he wouldn't be fit to
race again for months. . . . I was asking him for the
reserves, the furthest stores of power, and he poured
them generously out.

Endless furlongs . . . and I wasn't getting the angle
right. . . . Lancat was slowing and I'd reach the Line
Gallop after Alessandro had gone past. I swerved more
to the right . . . swayed perilously in the saddle,
couldn't even hold the reins in my left hand, and I
wanted to hold on to the neck strap with my right,
wanted to hold on for dear life, and if I held on, I
couldn't steer. . . . It wasn't far, not really. No distance
at all on a fresh horse. No distance at all for Lucky
Lindsay.

All the trees and brushes up ahead. . . . Somewhere
in there lay Carlo and Cal . . . and if Enso didn't know
where, he wasn't going to find them. People didn't lie
about in full sight, not with a Lee Enfield aimed at a
galloping horse; and Cal would have to be lying down.
Have to be, to be accurate enough. A Lee Enfield was
as precise as any gun ever made, but only if one aimed
and fired while lying down. It kicked too much to be
reliable if one was standing up.

Enso wouldn't find them. He might find the car.
Alessandro's Mercedes. But he wouldn't find Carlo
and Cal until the thunderous noise gave away their
position . . . and no one but Enso would find them even
then, before they reached the car and drove away.
Everyone would be concentrating on Alessandro with
a hole torn in his chest, Alessandro in his camel jersey
and blue shirt which were just like Tommy Hoylake's.

Carlo and Cal knew Alessandro. . . . They knew him
well . . . but they thought he had obeyed his father and
stayed in the hotel . . . and one jockey looked very
like another from a distance, on a galloping horse. . . .

Alessandro, I thought. Galloping along in the golden
May morning . . . straight to his death.

I couldn't go any faster. Lancat couldn't go any

faster. Didn't know about the horse's breath, but mine was coming out in great gulps. Nearer to sobs, I daresay. I really should have stayed at home.

Shifted another notch to the right and kicked Lancat. Feeble kick. Didn't increase the speed.

We were closing. The angle came sharper suddenly as the Line Gallop began its sweep to the right. Lucky Lindsay came round the corner to the most vulnerable stretch. . . . Carlo and Cal would be there. . . . They would be ahead of him, because Cal would be sure of hitting a man coming straight toward him. There weren't the same problems as in trying to hit a crossing target.

They must be able to see me, too, I thought. But if Cal was looking down his sights, leveling the blade in the ring over Alessandro's tan sweater and bent black head, he wouldn't notice me . . . wouldn't anyway see any significance in just another horse galloping across the Heath.

Lancat swerved of his own volition toward Lucky Lindsay and took up the race, a born and bred competitor determined even in exhaustion on getting his head in front.

Ten yards, ten feet . . . and closing.

Alessandro was several lengths ahead of the two horses he had started out with. Several lengths ahead, all on his own.

Lancat reached Lucky Lindsay at an angle and threw up his head to avoid a collision, and Alessandro turned his face to me in wide astonishment; and although I had meant to tell him to jump off and lie flat on the ground until his father succeeded in finding Carlo and Cal, it didn't happen quite like that.

Lancat half rose up into the air and threw me, twisting, onto Lucky Lindsay, and I put my right arm out round Alessandro and scooped him off, and we fell like that down onto the grass. And Lancat fell, too, and lay across our feet, because brave, fast, determined Lancat wasn't going anywhere any more.

Half of Lancat's neck was torn away, and his blood and his life ran out onto the bright green turf.

Alessandro tried to twist out of my grasp and stand up.

"Lie still," I said fiercely. "Just do as I say, and lie still."

"I'm hurt," he said.

"Don't make me laugh."

"I have hurt my leg," he protested.

"You'll have a hole in your heart if you stand up."

"You are mad," he said.

"Look at Lancat. . . . What do you think is wrong with him? Do you think he is lying there for fun?" I couldn't keep the bitterness out of my voice, and I didn't try. "Cal did that. Cal and his big bloody rifle. They came out here to shoot Tommy Hoylake, and you rode Lucky Lindsay instead, and they couldn't tell the difference, which should please you. . . . And if you stand up now they'll have another go."

He lay still. Speechless. And quite, quite still.

I rolled away from him and stuffed my fist against my teeth, for if the truth were told I was hurting far more than I would have believed possible. Him and his damn bloody father. . . . The free sharp ends of collarbone were carving new and unplanned routes for themselves through several protesting sets of tissue.

A fair amount of fuss was developing around us. When the ring of shocked spectators had grown solid and thick enough, I let him get up, but he only got as far as his knees beside Lancat, and there were smears of the horse's blood on his jodhpurs and jersey.

"Lancat," he said hopelessly, with a sort of death in his voice. He looked across at me as a couple of helpful onlookers hauled me to my feet, and the despair on his face was bottomless and total.

"Why?" he said. "Why did he do it?"

I didn't answer. Didn't need to. He already knew.

"I hate him," he said.

205

The people around us began to ask questions, but neither Alessandro nor I answered them.

From somewhere away to our right, there was another loud unmistakable crack. I and half the gathering crowd involuntarily ducked, but the bullet would already have reached us if it had been coming our way.

One crack, then silence. The echoes died quickly over Waterhall, but they shivered forever through Alessandro's life.

16

Enso had found Carlo and Cal hidden in a clump of bushes near the Boy's Grave crossroads.

We found them there, too, when we walked along to the end of the Line Gallop to flag down a passing motorist to take Etty quickly into Newmarket. Etty, who had arrived frantic up the gallop, had at first, like all the other onlookers, taken it for granted that the shooting had been an accident. A stray bullet loosed off by someone being criminally careless with a gun.

I watched the doubt appear on her face when she realized that my transport had been Lancat and not the Land-Rover, but I just asked her matter-of-factly to buzz down to Newmarket and ring up the dead-horse removers, then to drive herself back. She sent Andy off with instructions to the rest of the string, and the first car that came along stopped to pick her up.

Alessandro walked off the training ground into the road with a stunned, stony face, and came toward me. He was leading Lucky Lindsay, which someone had caught, but as automatically as if he were unaware the horse was there. Three or four paces away, he stopped.

"What am I to do?" he said. He spoke without hope or anxiety. Lifeless. I didn't answer immediately, and it was then that we heard the voice.

A low distressed voice calling unintelligently.

Startled, I walked along the road a little and through a thin belt of bushes, and there I found them.

Three of them. Enso and Carlo and Cal.

It was Cal who had called out. He was the only one capable of it. Carlo lay sprawled on his back, with his eyes open to the sun and a splash of drying scarlet trickling from a hole in his forehead.

Cal had a wider, wetter, spreading stain over the front of his shirt. His breath was shallow and quick; and calling out loud enough to be found had used up most of his energy.

The Lee Enfield lay across his legs. His hand moved convulsively toward the butt, but he no longer had the strength to pick it up.

And Enso . . . Cal had shot Enso with the Lee Enfield at a range of about six feet. It wasn't so much the bullet itself, but the shock wave of its velocity; at that short distance it had dug an entrance as large as a plate.

The force of it had flung Enso backward against a tree. He sat there now at the foot of it, with the silenced pistol still in his hand and his head sunk forward on his chest. There was a soul-sickening mess where his paunch had been, and his back was inseparable from the bark.

I would have stopped Alessandro seeing, but I didn't hear him come. I heard only the moan beside me, and I turned abruptly to see the sweat spring out on his face.

For Cal, Alessandro's appearance there was macabre.

"You . . ." he said. "You . . . are dead."

Alessandro merely stared at him, too shocked to understand, too shocked to speak.

Cal's eyes opened wide, and his voice grew stronger with a burst of futile anger.

"He said . . . I had killed you. Killed his son. He was out of his senses. He said . . . I should have known it was you. . . ." He coughed, and frothy blood slid over his lower lip.

"You did shoot at Alessandro," I said. "But you hit a horse."

Cal said with visibly diminishing strength, "He shot Carlo . . . and he shot me . . . so I let him have it . . . the son of a bitch. . . . He was out . . . of his senses. . . ."

The voice stopped. There was nothing anyone could do for him, and presently, imperceptibly, he died.

He died where he had lain in wait for Tommy Hoylake. When I knelt beside him to feel his pulse, and lifted my head to look along the gallop, there in front of me was the view he had had: a clear sight of the advancing horses, through the sparse low branches of a concealing bush. The dark shape of Lancat lay like a hump on the grass three hundred yards away, and another batch of horses, uncaring, were sweeping round the far bend and turning toward me.

An easy shot, it had been, for a marksman. He hadn't bothered even with a telescopic sight. At that range, with a Lee Enfield, one didn't need one. One didn't need to be of pinpoint accuracy; anywhere on the head or trunk would do the trick. I sighed. If he had used a telescopic sight, he would probably have realized that what he was aiming at was Alessandro.

I stood up. Clumsily, painfully, wishing I hadn't got down.

Alessandro hadn't fainted. Hadn't been sick. The sweat had dried on his face, and he was looking steadfastly at his father.

When I moved toward him, he turned, but he needed two or three attempts before he could get his throat to work.

He managed it, finally. His voice was strained, different, hoarse; and what he said was as good an epitaph as any.

"He gave me everything," he said.

We went back to the road, where Alessandro had tethered Lucky Lindsay to a fence. The colt had his head down to the grass, undisturbed.

Neither of us said anything at all.

Etty clattered up in the Land-Rover, and I got her to turn it round and take me straight down to the town.

"I'll be right back," I said to Alessandro, but he stared silently at nothing with eyes that had seen too much.

When I went back, it was with the police. Etty stayed behind at Rowley Lodge to see to the stables, because it was still, and incredibly, Guineas day, and we had Archangel to look to. Also, in the town, I made a detour to the doctor, where I bypassed an outraged queue waiting in his surgery, and got him to put the ends of my collarbone back into alignment. After that, it was a bit more bearable, though nothing still to raise flags about.

I spent most of the morning up at the crossroads. Answered some questions and didn't answer others. Alessandro listened to me telling the highest up of the police who had arrived from Cambridge that Enso had appeared to me to be unbalanced.

The police surgeon was skeptical of a layman's opinion.

"In what way?" he said without deference.

I paused to consider. "You could look for spirochetes," I said, and his eyes widened abruptly before he disappeared back into the bushes.

They were considerate to Alessandro. He sat on somebody's raincoat on the grass at the side of the road, and later on the police surgeon gave him a sedative.

It was an injection, and Alessandro didn't want it. They wouldn't pay attention to his objections, and when the needle went into his arm I found him staring fixedly at my face. He knew that I, too, was thinking about other injections; about myself, and Carlo, and Moonrock and Indigo and Buckram. Too many needles. Too much death.

The drug didn't put him out, just made him look even more dazed than before. The police decided he should go back to the Forbury Inn and sleep, and steered him toward one of their cars.

He stopped in front of me before he reached it, and gazed at me in awe from hollow dark sockets in a gray gaunt face.

"Look at the flowers," he said. "On the Boy's Grave."

When he had gone, I walked over to the raincoat where he had been sitting, close to the little mound.

There were pale yellow polyanthus, and blue forget-me-nots coming into flower round the edge; and all the center was filled with pansies. Dark dark purple velvet pansies, shining black in the sun.

It was cynical of me to wonder if he could have planted them himself.

Enso was in the mortuary and Alessandro was asleep when Archangel and Tommy Hoylake won the Guineas.

Not what the father and son had planned.

A heaviness like thunder persisted with me all afternoon, even though there was by then no reason for it. The defeat of Enso no longer directed half my actions, but I found it impossible in one bound to throw off his influence. It was not until then that I understood how intense it had become.

What I should have felt was relief that the stable was safe. What I did feel was depression.

The merchant banker, Archangel's owner, was practically incandescent with happiness. He glowed in the unsaddling enclosure and joked with the press in shaky pride.

"Well done, my boy, well done indeed," he said to

me, to Tommy, and to Archangel impartially, and looked ready to embrace us all.

"And now, my boy, now for the Derby, eh?"

"Now for the Derby." I nodded, and wondered how soon my father would be back at Rowley Lodge.

I went to see him the next day.

He was looking even more forbidding than usual because he had heard all about the multiple murders on the gallops. He blamed me for letting anything like that happen. I saved him, I reflected sourly, from having to say anything nice about Archangel.

"You should never have taken on that apprentice."

"No," I said.

"The Jockey Club will be seriously displeased."

"Yes."

"The man must have been mad."

"Sort of."

"Absolutely mad to think he could get his son to ride Archangel by killing Tommy Hoylake."

I had had to tell the police something, and I had told them that. It had seemed enough.

"Obsessed," I agreed.

"Surely you must have noticed it before? Surely he gave some sign?"

"I suppose he did," I agreed neutrally.

"Then surely you should have been able to stop him."

"I did stop him—in a way."

"Not very efficiently," he complained.

"No," I said patiently, and thought that the only one who had stopped Enso efficiently and finally had been Cal.

"What's the matter with your arm?"

"Broke my collarbone," I said.

"Hard luck."

He looked down at his still-suspended leg, almost but not quite saying aloud that a collarbone was chicken feed compared with what he had endured. What was more, he was right.

"How soon will you be out?" I asked.

He answered in a smug satisfaction tinged with un-disguisable malice. "Sooner than you'd like, perhaps."

"I couldn't wish you to stay here," I protested.

He looked faintly taken aback, faintly ashamed.

"No . . . well . . . they say not long now."

"The sooner the better," I said, and tried to mean it.

"Don't do any more work with Archangel. And I see from the Calendar that you have made entries on your own. I don't want you to do that. I am perfectly capable of deciding where my horses should run."

"As you say," I said mildly, and with surprisingly little pleasure realized that I now no longer had any reason for amending his plans.

"Tell Etty that she did very well with Archangel."

"I will," I said. "In fact, I have."

The corners of his mouth turned down. "Tell her that I said so."

"Yes," I said.

Nothing much, after all, had changed between us. He was still what I had run away from at sixteen, and it would take me a lot less time to leave him again. I couldn't possibly have stayed on as his assistant, even if he had asked me to.

"He gave me everything," Alessandro had said of his father. I would have said of mine that he gave me not very much. And I felt for him something that Alessandro had never through love or hate felt for his.

I felt . . . apathy.

"Go away, now," he said. "And on your way out, find a nurse. I need a bedpan. They take half an hour, sometimes, if I ring the bell. And I want it now, at once."

The driver of the car I had hired in Newmarket was quite happy to include Hampstead in the itinerary.

"A couple of hours?" I suggested when I had hauled myself out onto the pavement outside the flat.

"Sure," he said. "Maybe there's somewhere open for tea, even on Sunday." He drove off hopefully, optimistic soul that he was.

Gillie said she had lost three pounds, she was painting the bathroom sludge green, and how did I propose to make love to her looking like a washed-out edition of a terminal consumptive.

"I don't," I said, "propose."

"Ah," she said wisely. "All men have their limits."

"And just change that description to looking like a race-horse trainer who has just won his first Classic."

She opened her mouth and obviously was not going to come across with the necessary compliment.

"O.K.," I said resignedly. "So it wasn't me. Everyone else, but not me, I do so agree. Wholeheartedly."

"Self-pity is disgusting," she said.

"Mm." I sat gingerly down in a blue armchair, put my head back, and shut my eyes. Didn't get much sympathy for that, either.

"So you collected the bruises," she observed.

"That's right."

"Silly old you."

"Yes."

"Do you want some tea?"

"No, thank you," I said politely. "No sympathy, no tea."

She laughed. "Brandy, then?"

"If you have some."

She had enough for the cares of the world to retreat apace: and she came across, in the end, with her own brand of fellow feeling.

"Don't wince when I kiss you," she said.

"Don't kiss so damned hard."

After a bit, she said, "Is this shoulder the lot? Or will there be more to come?"

"It's the lot," I said, and told her all that had happened. Edited, and flippantly; but more or less all.

"And does your own dear dad know all about this?"

"Heaven forbid," I said.

"But he will, won't he? When you get this Alessandro warned off? And then he will understand how much he owes you?"

"I don't want him to understand," I said. "He would loathe it."

"Charming fellow, your dad."

"He is what he is," I said.

"And was Enso what he was?"

I smiled lopsidedly. "Same principle, I suppose."

"You're a nut, Neil Griffon."

I couldn't dispute it.

"How long before he gets out of hospital?" she asked.

"I don't know. He hopes to be on his feet soon. Then a week or two for physiotherapy and walking practice with crutches, or whatever. He expects to be home before the Derby."

"What will you do then?"

"Don't know," I said. "But he'll be three weeks at least, and leverage no longer applies. . . . So would you still like to come to Rowley Lodge?"

"Mm," she said, considering. "There's a three-year-old Nigerian girl I'm supposed to be settling with a family in Dorset."

I felt very tired. "Never mind, then."

"I could come on Wednesday."

When I got back to Newmarket, I walked round the yard before I went indoors. It all lay peacefully in the soft light of sundown, the beginning of dusk. The bricks looked rosy and warm, the shrubs were out in flower, and behind the green-painted doors the six million quids' worth were safely chomping on their evening oats. Peace in all the bays, winners in many of the boxes, and an air of prosperity and timelessness over the whole.

I would be gone from there soon; and Enso had

gone, and Alessandro. When my father came back, it would be as if these last months had never happened. He and Etty and Margaret would go on as they had been before; and I would read about the familiar horses in the newspapers.

I didn't yet know what I would do. Certainly I had grown to like my father's job, and maybe I could start a stable of my own, somewhere else. I wouldn't go back to antiques, and I knew by then that I wasn't going to work any more for Russell Arletti.

Build a new empire, Gillie had said.

Well, maybe I would.

I looked in at Archangel, now no longer guarded by men, dogs, and electronics. The big brown colt lifted his head from his manger and turned on me an inquiring eye. I smiled at him involuntarily. He still showed the effects of his hard race the day before, but he was sturdy and sound, and there was a very good chance he would give the merchant banker his Derby.

I stifled a sigh and went indoors, and heard the telephone ringing in the office.

Owners often telephoned on Sunday evenings, but it wasn't an owner; it was the hospital.

"I'm very sorry," the voice said several times at the other end. "We've been trying to reach you for some hours now. Very sorry. Very sorry."

"But he *can't* be dead," I said stupidly. "He was all right when I left him. I was with him this afternoon, and he was all right."

"Just after you left," the voice said. "Within half an hour."

"But how?" My mind couldn't grasp it. "He only had a broken leg, and that had mended."

Would I like to talk to the doctor in charge? Yes, I would.

"He was all right when I left him," I protested. "In fact, he was yelling for a bedpan."

"Ah. Yes. Well," said a high-pitched voice loaded

with professional sympathy. "That's—er—that's a very common preliminary to a pulmonary embolus. Calling for a bedpan—very typical. But do rest assured, Mr. Griffon, your father died very quickly. Within a few seconds. Yes, indeed."

"What," I said with a feeling of complete unreality, "is a pulmonary embolus?"

"Blood clot," he said promptly. "Unfortunately not uncommon in elderly people who have been bedridden for some time. And your father's fracture—well, it's tragic, tragic, but not uncommon, I'm afraid. Death sitting up, some people say. Very quick, Mr. Griffon. Very quick. There was nothing we could do, do believe me."

"I believe you."

But it was impossible, I thought. He couldn't be dead. I had been talking to him just that afternoon.

The hospital would like instructions, they delicately said.

I would send someone from Newmarket, I said vaguely. An undertaker from Newmarket, to fetch him home.

Monday I spent in endless chat. Talked to the police. Talked to the Jockey Club. Talked to a dozen or so owners who telephoned to ask what was going to happen to their horses.

Talked and talked.

Margaret dealt with the relentless pressure as calmly as she did with Susie and her friend. And Susie's friend, she said, had incidentally reported that Alessandro had not left his room since the police took him there on Saturday morning. He hadn't eaten anything, and he wouldn't talk to anyone except to tell them to go away. Susie's chum's mum said it was all very well, but Alessandro never had any money, and his bill had only been paid up to the previous Saturday, and they were thinking of asking him to go.

"Tell Susie's chum's mum that Alessandro has

217

money here, and also that in Switzerland he will be rich."

"Will do," she said, and rang the Forbury Inn at once.

Etty took charge of both lots out at exercise, and somehow or other the right runners got dispatched to Bath. Vic Young went in charge of them and said later that the apprentice who had the ride on Pulitzer instead of Alessandro was no effing good.

To the police I told the whole of what had occurred on Saturday morning, but nothing of what had occurred before it. Enso had recently arrived in England, I said, and had developed this extraordinary fixation. There was no reason for them not to accept this abbreviated version, and nothing to be gained by telling them more.

Down at the Jockey Club, I had a lengthy session with a committee of members and a couple of Stewards left over on purpose from the Guineas meeting, and the outcome of that was equally peaceful.

After that, I told Margaret to let all inquiring owners know that I would be staying on at Rowley Lodge for the rest of the season, and they could leave or remove their horses as they wished.

"Are you really?" she said. "Are you staying?"

"Not much else to do, is there?" I said. But we were both smiling.

"Ever since you told that lie about not being able to find anyone to take over, when you had John Bredon lined up all the time, ever since then I've known you liked it here."

I didn't disillusion her.

"I'm glad you're staying," she said. "I suppose it's very disloyal to your father, as he only died yesterday, but I have much preferred working for you."

I was not so autocratic, that was all. She would have worked efficiently for anyone.

Before she left at three, she said that none of the owners who had so far telephoned were going to remove their horses; and that included Archangel's merchant banker.

When she had gone, I wrote to my solicitors in London and asked them to send back to me at Newmarket the package I had instructed them to open in case of my sudden death.

After that, I swallowed a couple of codeines and wondered how soon everything would stop aching, and from five to six-thirty I walked round at evening stables with Etty.

We passed by Lancat's empty box.

"Damn that Alex," Etty said, but with a retrospective anger. The past was past. Tomorrow's races were all that mattered. Tomorrow at Chester. She talked of plans ahead. She was contented, fulfilled, and busy. The transition from my father to me had been too gradual to need any sudden adjustment now.

I left her supervising as usual the evening feeds for the horses and walked back toward the house. Something made me look up along the drive, and there, motionless and only half visible against the tree trunks, stood Alessandro.

It was as if he had got halfway down the drive before his courage deserted him. I walked without haste out of the yard and went to meet him.

Strain had aged him so that he now looked nearer forty than eighteen. Bones stood out sharply under his skin, and there was little in the black eyes except no hope at all.

"I came," he started. "I need—I mean, you said, at the beginning, that I could have half the money I earned racing. . . . Can I still—have it?"

"You can," I said. "Of course."

He swallowed. "I am sorry to come. I had to come. To ask you about the money."

"You can have it now," I said. "Come along into the office."

I half turned away from him but he didn't move.

"No. I . . . can't."

"I'll send it along to the Forbury Inn for you," I said. He nodded. "Thank you."

"Do you have any plans?" I asked him.

The shadows in his face, if anything, deepened.

"No."

He visibly gathered every shred of resolution, clamped his teeth together, and asked me the question which was tearing him to shreds.

"When will I be warned off?"

Neil Griffon was a nut, as Gillie said.

"You won't be warned off," I told him. "I talked to the Jockey Club this morning. I told them that you shouldn't lose your license, because your father had gone mad, and they saw that point of view. You may not of course like it that I stressed your father's insanity, but it was the best I could do."

"But . . ." he said in bewilderment, and then in realization, "Didn't you tell them about Moonrock and Indigo—and about your shoulder?"

"No."

"I don't understand . . . why you didn't."

"I don't see any point in revenging myself on you for what your father did."

"But he only did it—in the beginning—because I asked."

"Alessandro," I said. "Just how many fathers would do as he did? How many fathers, if their sons said they wanted to ride Archangel in the Derby, would go as far as murder to achieve it?"

After a long pause, he said, "He was mad, then. He really was." It was clearly no comfort.

"He was ill," I said. "The illness he had after you were born. It affected his brain."

"Then I—will not—?"

"No," I said. "You can't inherit it. You're as sane as anyone. As sane as you care to be."

"As I care to be," he repeated vaguely. His thoughts were turned inward. I didn't hurry him. I waited most patiently, because what he cared to be was the final throw in the game.

"I care to be a jockey," he said faintly. "To be a good one."

I took a breath. "You are free to ride races anywhere you like," I said. "Anywhere in the world."

He stared at me with a face from which all the arrogance had gone. He didn't look the same boy as the one who had come from Switzerland three months before, and in fact he wasn't. All his values had been turned upside down, and the world as he had known it had come to an end.

To defeat the father, I had changed the son. Changed him at first only as a solution to a problem, but later also because the emerging product was worth it. It seemed a waste, somehow, to let him go.

I said abruptly, "You can stay on at Rowley Lodge, if you like."

Something shattered somewhere inside him, like glass breaking. When he turned away, I could have sworn that against all probability there were tears in his eyes.

He took four paces, and stopped.

"Well?" I said.

He turned round. The tears had drained back into the ducts, as they do in the young.

"What as?" he said apprehensively, looking for snags.

"Stable jockey," I said. "Second to Tommy."

He walked six more paces away down the drive as if his ankles were springs.

"Come back," I called. "What about tomorrow?"

He looked over his shoulder.

"I'll be here to ride out."

Three more bouncing steps.

"You won't," I shouted. "You get a good sleep and a good breakfast and be here at eleven. We're flying over to Chester."

"Chester?" He turned as he shouted in surprise, and went two more steps, backward.

"Clip Clop," I yelled. "Ever heard of him?"

"Yes," he yelled back, and the laughter took him uncontrollably, and he turned and ran away down the drive, leaping into the air as if he were six.

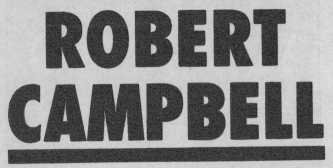